THE ALCHEMIST
OF NETLEY ABBEY

A Hildegard of Meaux

medieval mystery – book 8

CASSANDRA CLARK

ISBN 978-1521521397

www.cassandraclark.co.uk

Also in the Hildegard of Meaux series

Hangman Blind

The Velvet Turnshoe

The Law of Angels

The Parliament of Spies

The Dragon of Handale

The Butcher of Avignon

The Scandal of the Skulls

The Alchemist of Netley Abbey

and to come...

Murder at Meaux

Such is the nature of this fickle and philistine realm...

Richard II

His pale, rebellious features were reflected in the polished lens showing a brow puckered with concentration, a shock of wild black hair, a wide, sceptical mouth and eyes that had their own luminous depths.

As he inched the lens over the things on his work-bench a startling world was revealed. His fingertips, for instance, were not smooth as supposed, but fissured with crevasses, whorls and ridges like the mountains of Snowdonia. He lifted his head to check the alembic where the elixir dripped from the spout into the dish below. All was well.

Outside in the garth the bell for Vespers began to toll. He ignored it.

Two things interested him, first, to find a liquid that would restore life to the dead, and second, to get hold of the Stone that would turn base metals into gold. He was not a magician as the ignorant said. He was a herberer, an apothecary, a seeker into the true nature of things.

Owain laughed, of course, and called him his royal alchemist and claimed he was on a wild goose chase, unlikely to find anything like life in dead matter using such crude instruments as they had, but he could not deny that his lenses magnified all manner of things invisible to the naked eye. It followed that more powerful lenses would reveal even more secrets in the world that lay beneath.

There were three things the alchemist should do - observe, record and assess. Long ago he made a vow that he would dedicate his life to doing exactly that.

Now he adjusted the lens to observe the elixir dripping from the spout.

It was dead matter. A concoction made up according to the rules in the latest book to be brought in from the east.

For some time he could hear only the sound of his own breath whispering on the air while the elixir trickled through its labyrinths into the dish. His natural impatience made him want to hurry things along but he reminded himself of a saying of his old mentor: you must learn the patience of a huntsman if you want to wrest Nature's secrets from her.

After a time, his glance slowly sharpened. He held his breath. His knuckles gripped the lens holder and turned white.

His body became rigid with an unearthly fear, a feeling that turned eventually to terror. He dare not move a muscle. Then his fear revolved to show its other side and an ecstasy of joy took over and his fingers trembled. Euphoria pervaded his entire being.

It was true! There it was – life!

A minute thing was swimming in the purity of the distillation that pooled into the dish. He saw it with his own eyes!

He lifted his head, squeezed his lids shut, then re-applied one eye to the lens.

It was a thing smaller than the head of a pin. It

swirled in the liquid against the imperceptible current, too small to see in detail, it continued its aquatic dance of pure joy as he watched. It was an atom as the Ancients had described. Until now no-one had possessed the means of observing one.

He took the lens and wiped it. When he peered again the light had changed. The little atom had vanished.

Praising God for the grace of that brief vision he rested the precious lens on a cloth lying on the bench and rubbed his face. He must have been crying because the back of his hand came away wet. But they were tears of joy. We are not creatures living in a world of brute indifference after all, he exulted. There are living things beyond our sight and kenning! We are part of God's holy plan but not in human solitude as we often feel but bound, one to another, in a great chain of being that stretches throughout the entire cosmos. And this little speck of life proves it. Why? Because a dead thing cannot move of its own volition.

At once he knew what he had to do.

He would repeat his experiment. If it proved itself once again he would catch a live thing, a mouse, say, and kill it, submerge its body in the elixir and then bring it back to life again. By replicating what he had just done he would know it was a true thing because the mouse would live.

His thoughts flew on.

He would next find something bigger, some creature such as a dog or a cat or - he drew in his breath at his own daring - if that worked, what would he not do? Where was the limit in so noble a cause?

He would find some *one*, then, a person, some no good losel from off the streets like Jankin, perhaps, and kill him and - he pictured the bath into which he would plunge the corpse and he could imagine how it would twitch slowly, so slowly, into life – first a spasm of the fingers, an eyelid's flicker, or legs threshing for purchase on the sides of the bath…and then?

Would he become God himself if he restored

the fellow to life? With the secret in his grasp who could say he would not ascend to the Godhead? Total domination over life and death would be his.

I go too far into heresy, he chided, when the wheezing approach of his apprentice announced him.

The door opened to reveal the youth, all skin and bone, a lad with no kin after the return of the Plague took his entire family...a youth with little to offer apart from his tidiness and eagerness to please...one whom, it must be said, no-one would ever miss.

The friar gave a long, assessing stare at the threadbare tunic, the blue eyes, the flaxen curls to his shoulders...he was a Saxon lad to his bones.

'You needn't come in, Jankin.' He cleared his throat to stem the tremor in his voice. 'I have an errand for you. I need a mouse.' He paused. 'A live one...Go on then! Jump to it!'

The Saracens from Outremer knew a thing or two, he was thinking as Jankin, glowing with purpose, went out.

Their secret knowledge came back with the merchants' ships, and with Henry Bolingbroke's Teutonic Knights, and through Bohemia by way of Queen Anne's retinue, and sometimes it came from Castile.

Who knew how accurate it was, what proportion of lies to truth was contained in their texts? All he could do was get his facts straight, the stars in propitious alignment, the equations and formulae worked out to perfection, the ingredients purified to their essence, and himself, of course, pure, unimpeachable and living in a state of grace... and then the process, orderly and properly performed, so that he was able to make his observations in a detached and prayerful manner.

He felt moved by a sense of Divine Purpose. Now on the road to power he could not turn back. He would discover the truth at the heart of the cosmos, what made it work and what its purpose was. He felt light-headed.

There was a movement in the doorway. Time must have flown because, when he jerked a glance across his workshop he saw Jankin already framed in the doorway.

One arm was held stiffly out in front of him. From between his fingers something was dangling and dancing on a thread.

'Your little mouse, magister. Am I to feed him?'

Hywel shook his head.

'What shall I do with him?'

'Kill it, of course. Then bring its body to me.'

CHAPTER ONE

It was with a feeling of relief that they eventually left Salisbury behind with its petty civic rivalries and small town concerns. The recent parliament in London, already named by many the Merciless Parliament because of the barbaric manner in which the members of King Richard's inner council had been executed with little heed to the law, had impinged on their own activities in the town - but for most people the fate of the king was as irrelevant as if it was taking place on the moon.

'Now for the north!' called Abbot de Courcy as his big, black stallion champed at the bit and Hildegard and the two monks militant, Gregory and Egbert, followed him out of the stable yard.

'I'll be glad to see home again!' Hildegard shouted, sitting easily astride her grey mare as it cantered beside the stallion. 'How everything must have changed at Meaux in our absence!'

'Not too many changes, I hope!' Hubert called back as the wind tore at their faces and swept

Hildegard's hair from beneath her coif allowing it to stream in gleaming tendrils behind her. The abbot's reckless mouth curved in a smile of pure happiness as he exchanged a glance with her. 'Miles to ride yet, my dearest Hildegard. What joy it is on a fine, bright, summer's day like today to be riding home with you beside me!' He reached across to link hands. 'And when at least we reach our destination you have promised to give me your answer and change our lives forever.'

It was mid-afternoon when they made their first halt. It was at a farmstead belonging to some of Gregory's kinsmen on the edge of the Royal Forest. They were to spend the night there after a short day of riding to allow him to bid them farewell before traveling north.

As they sat round the fire pit later, eating nourishing country fare and with mugs of ale in their hands, Gregory smiled round at everyone. 'I thank you, my lord abbot, our dear Hildegard, and you, Brother Egbert, you old reprobate, for agreeing to make a little detour to see my dear kinsfolk. And you,' he lifted his mug to include a couple of aunts and uncles and several pretty female cousins, all as tall and notable as himself, 'I bless you for receiving us with such open hospitality. Who knows when I'll be in the south again? Blessings on you! I wish you well!' He stretched his long legs before the fire, his clever, mobile face expressing contentment at this companionable start to the long journey that lay ahead.

'We're glad of the detour,' Brother Egbert observed. 'A full day in the saddle after our soft living in Salisbury would have us groaning with aching backsides. Happily this is a gentle start to a long though pleasant journey.'

Egbert, a tough, four-square Cistercian monk looked every inch the sword-carrying militant he was, unlike Gregory who seemed all willow and vapour until he had a sword in his hand, and then there was no-one to beat him. Egbert gave one of the kinswomen a soft look. 'I confess, I shall be sorry to drag myself away from the temptations of the secular world,' he murmured with an appreciative smile.

And so it was the four Cistercians, cheered though somewhat stiff in the limbs set off next morning at dawn on a mazy pathway through the forest that led them, they were confidently informed, towards the London road no more than twenty miles distant.

Once the sun rose it turned out to be one of those hazy July days when mist settles low in the valleys and drifts between the trees, to spread a veil over the woods that, no matter how long the journey, beguiles with softness and secrets. The track was so well hidden by shifting mists that more than once Egbert was heard to affirm that the sun would soon burn it off.

They rode on in a dream-like silence, down into misty valleys and up between rows of sentinel-straight trees to the summits of small rounded hills and every time they ascended someone thought to say, 'Now we'll see the track laid out plain before us,' and every time their prophecy failed.

It was already late by the time Gregory began to hint that his stomach told him to stop and eat and the words were barely out before Egbert drew his horse into a small clearing and slid down into the untrodden grass with a sigh of relief.

'It strikes me folk round here have no taste for travelling,' he observed as he pulled down his saddle bag and unstrapped it to reveal the gift of food inside, made up in similar wise for each of them by Gregory's kin. 'See how the track's overgrown with moss? And the grass is barely trodden except by deer or some such. Stay-at-home folk round here, are they, Gregory?'

'My kin, certainly are. They have enough to do on their farms, they say, without going far from home with no good reason. I'm a source of wonder to them and they can scarcely believe I've spent seven years in the Holy Land. Go on, they say, tell us more. You saw how they kept us up late last night, demanding to know every last trifle of our exploits there.' He yawned. 'I wish they'd curbed their curiosity somewhat - I could sleep the rest of the day through.'

Taking his own pack from the saddlebag he began to eat but something seemed to be bothering him other than tiredness and he kept looking round and staring up at the sky until Hildegard was forced to ask between mouthfuls of bread and cheese, 'What is it, Gregory?'

'We've been making good time along this track and would surely now be close to the road they mentioned and yet I can see no sign of it. The ground is virtually untrodden. Doesn't it strike you as strange?'

Their abbot agreed. 'I've been thinking the same but put my trust in their better knowledge. Now you say they rarely travel any distance from their demesne I wonder how surely they know the way. Didn't you tell us none of them had even travelled as far as Southampton, let alone London?'

'I admit I'm tending to lose faith in them too,

Hubert. With no sun it's difficult to gauge our direction. What do you others think?'

Hildegard reluctantly admitted she felt they had traveled too far south. 'Look at the sky behind those trees.' She gestured towards a dip in the ground where the track wound out of sight between boles of ancient beech and the tree tops, in full and glorious summer green, parted a little to reveal levels of blue stretching to the horizon. An unbroken vista of trees with no sign of farm or homestead to break the view lay beneath. 'Is it not much lighter in that direction?' She pointed. 'To me it shows we're riding south.'

'It is lighter, granted, but maybe it's a mere thinning in the clouds?' suggested Egbert with his usual optimism.

Hubert asserted his authority as abbot. 'I share some unease. Let's go on as far as the next turning and take stock again. Everyone agreed?'

'Agreed.' Gregory drained his flask, reinserted the cork, stowed it in his saddle bag and was first to sit astride his horse again. Without waiting for the others he dug his heels into his steed's flanks and set off at a gallop with the two monks streaming after him in a race to be first to reach the next turning.

Hildegard followed at a more leisurely pace. They had been lured off the main track by the promise of a short cut their hosts had mentioned but they had clearly not found it. The journey was so pleasant despite the deceptions of summer mist that nobody wanted to suggest turning back. They had ridden on somewhat blindly down the narrow lanes that ran like the veins on the back of a hand, reveling in the dream-like silence of the woods, enjoying sudden glimpses of tree-covered hills floating magically above the mist, trusting, too readily as it now seemed, to providence when they should have paid more attention to the windings and wendings of the way.

The woodland were broken up now and then by the brilliant green levels of the deer lawns, and by ponds and rills, with sudden herds of deer, heads lifted, still as trees as the riders passed harmlessly by.

Hildegard's own idling thoughts, accompanied by the lulling of constant bird song, dwelt on Meaux, on its open skies, its bell-tower, its great grey stone-carved gatehouse, the distant bleating of sheep, the random sounds of the lay-brothers going about their business in byre and barn, and the singing of the monks and her own nuns in their grange across the abbot's canal. Her longing to be home again erased all other thoughts.

The decision Hubert expected her to make about their future scarcely troubled her in this present idyll. Time for that when they reached their destination. For now it was enough to ride by his side, to wake each morning in the certainty of seeing him going about his duties, to hear his laughter and his provoking nonsense with his brother monks. Snatched moments of felicity in a life of duty and piety should surely not be begrudged them?

Contentedly she allowed her mount to amble along the track as it would, making no attempt to catch up with the men just yet. In the distance their random shouts came belling between the trees as they raced on until the sound of their voices were folded into the silence of woodland in high summer.

It is not true silence, she was thinking, the air is full of sounds, bird song, rustling leaves, some sounds near, some far, some familiar and some unidentifiable. It was a surprise then when a slight change from lower down the track sent an unexpected tremor through her even before she identified it.

Huntsmen, she decided. It would be helpful if they would guide them onto the right track.

Jolted out of her reverie she heard a shout rend the air, an oath followed and then there was an alarming sound like steel against steel and the crashing of a frightened horse rampaging through the undergrowth. It urged her to send her horse galloping down the track and when she burst through the screening undergrowth into the next clearing she was in time to see Hubert's horse bolting in fright and a figure in white writhing on the ground in evident pain.

She took in the rest of the scene at a glance. Egbert had dismounted and drawn his sword. Two strangers, both wearing bassinets concealing their faces but not their snarls of derision, were advancing on the monk from two directions. Hubert was unable to help because he was lying on the ground, holding his right leg in both hands and muttering under his breath, while Gregory was dealing with two more attackers as they tried to grapple him off his horse.

His sword was raised and a flashing smile split his tanned face as she heard him shout, 'Monastics, think you? Helpless, you say? Come on, then, my friends, let me show you how helpless we are!'

Before either of them could drag him off his horse he brought down his sword perpendicularly in one smooth movement onto the shoulder of one of his assailants with professional fore-knowledge of what would happen.

It split the links of the man's mail neatly apart, leaving a bloody gash that sent his sword flying from his grasp. He went howling into the bushes with one hand to his shoulder. Gregory picked up his sword and turned to the second assailant.

Egbert, short and stocky and as strong as a bull, was unbothered by his two opponents, making short work of them, unswording one and holding the other to the ground with the tip of his blade pricking at his throat while he plucked his sword from his resistless hand.

Hildegard's eyes widened in fear as someone else emerged from the trees where the horses were waiting and advanced on Hubert with his sword raised. Without a thought she kicked her horse forward with the idea of running the man down but Gregory, noticing what was happening shouted, 'Hildi!' As she glanced back he threw a sword to her. She grasped it in both hands and bore down on Hubert's attacker. Before she could beat him back he caught sight of her, leaped bodily at the horse and pulled her to the ground.

The impact shook the breath out of her and she lost the sword in the grass and they struggled while she tried to get her knife from her sleeve. She managed to grip him by the neck of his mail shirt and bring the blade within inches of his throat. Cursing, he rolled away and she followed but he had had enough. His fellows were already leaving him behind and with another oath he threw himself onto the back of one of the horses and roared off into the trees.

One man remained. He gave a shocked glance at the unexpected apparition of a nun and two fighting men in monk's habits, dropped the saddle-bag he was about to purloin, and ran for the last of the horses.

In a moment, as quickly as if it had been no more than a dream, the glade emptied, bird-song resumed, and Gregory slid down from his horse and sheathed his blade with a satisfied grin.

'Where did they spring from?' he demanded of nobody in particular. 'I would follow them but feel they're unlikely to return now they've tested us. At least we're a couple of swords to the good.' He went over to where Hubert was still lying in the grass holding his leg. 'What ails, my lord abbot? No taste for a fight?'

Through white lips Hubert uncharacteristically grunted a reply. 'Give me a minute. I fell from my horse when they leaped out without warning. He reared and threw me down. My own fault. My thoughts were elsewhere.'

'What's wrong with your leg?'

'I fell awkwardly. It's nothing. Let me groan a while to relieve my feelings.'

Egbert came over. 'Let's have a look at you.'

'It's nothing.' Hubert flinched from his touch. His face was rigid with pain.

Hildegard shook out her sleeves and replaced her knife in its sheath. 'Let Brother Egbert have a look, my lord. Just to make sure nothing's broken.'

Hubert was already trying to stand but wincing and cursing under his breath. Gregory held him still. 'Has he broken it, Egbert? Have a look will you while I hold him.'

Together they forced Hubert, protesting violently, back onto the ground long enough to roll up one of his leggings and as soon as they did so they could see the bone of his right shin jutting through the skin.

'It cannot be, it cannot be,' Hubert was muttering. 'We have miles to ride yet. I will not have it. Put me back on my horse.' He pressed one hand over the bone and attempted to push it back into place. His face was contorted in a grimace of pain.

'You won't be riding anywhere with that for a while. Not unless you want to finish your life on sticks.' Egbert was adamant. 'Keep still and let me splint it for you then we'll decide what we're going to do next.'

It was by common consent that Gregory, who claimed to sense water down the deer track by which their assailants had fled, was chosen to ride on ahead to find out how the land lay and if they were anywhere near where they were supposed to be.

'They had mud on their boots, did you notice?' Gregory glanced round at them. 'Maybe it was from a wallow or a pond or maybe they've recently made a river crossing. I favour that view because their horses were mud-stained to their bellies. If there's a river, it's all to the good. I'll find it.'

Marvelling that he had been able to notice anything in the suddenness of the attack they could not help but agree.

'Bring my sword over so I have it to hand,' growled Hubert, gesturing to where it lay in the grass.

'I can see them off, don't worry, my lord.' Egbert gazed speculatively up into the tree underneath which Hubert was now propped and reached up to swing himself onto a branch. He began to climb.

'I'm not useless either.' Hildegard handed Hubert his sword and uneasily felt for the knife inside her sleeve.

'I'll be back as soon as I've had a look from the top of that next hill,' Gregory assured them.

He remounted and plunged off down the track and they heard him crashing about in the undergrowth for some time before the sound faded.

'He's keen on the idea of a river,' Hubert stated with the air of somebody trying to keep their thoughts off other matters. 'Does he imagine I'm going to swim to Meaux?'

'With respect, Hubert, it'll be easier to float you down on a log to sanctuary than haul you on a make-shift sled through this close-packed woodland.'

Hubert gave a half-smile at the look-out in the tree. 'You imagine sanctuary somewhere close by, brother? If we're well off the intended route the only sanctuary we're likely to find is in the earl of Arundel's dungeons.'

Hildegard shivered. 'Do you think those men were Arundel's?' The thought had not occurred to her before now. 'They wore no blazon that I could see.'

Egbert called down from his perch halfway up the beech tree. 'Did you notice anything about them?'

'Not I.' Hubert shook his head.

'Nor I.' Hildegard frowned. 'But I wonder, is Forest Law so slighted hereabouts that men can attack and plunder at will?'

Egbert called down. 'I believe we've strayed out of the Royal Forest and have somehow reached disputed land. This is wildwood and unenclosed. Some small-time vassal of Arundel's will have the run of it.'

'I agree. I can't imagine Arundel allowing his own men to roam unchecked, not with game here for the taking.'

'Whether they were our enemy's men or not, let's hope they can keep their mouths shut about four Cistercians roaming the woods.' Hubert closed his dark eyes, more dark than ever now as pain dilated his pupils.

Concerned to see him in this unaccustomed

state Hildegard went to her saddle bag. 'I've got a cure here.' She took it over to him. 'You'll need bone-knit later but for now a pain killer will help.' While she opened a flask of water for him, Egbert climbed higher into the tree.

'Nothing but heat haze,' he called down. 'It's like the sea in every direction. No sign of those devils. And no sign of Gregory either. All I can make out is a fold in the hills where the mist thickens. Let's hope it conceals this river he believes in.'

Hubert swallowed without demur an elixir Hildegard handed him saying, 'If we're really riding south as you believe, Hildegard, we may have looped close to one of the rivers that flow into Southampton Water. If we follow it down stream we must come to a settlement of some sort.'

Gregory burst back into the clearing not much later and confirmed his guess. 'It's a river, all right. I assume it's the Itchen and, best of all, further down-stream is a Cistercian house called Netley

Abbey. If I'm right we'll soon be back among our brothers. You might remember I was there not long ago?'

'I assume you didn't come this way?' Egbert swung down from his look-out in the tree.

'No, I took a boat from Hythe. I don't know this side of the river at all, at least, no more than you do and I fancy you wish you didn't know it even as well as this. So,' he turned to Hubert, 'all is not lost!' He glanced at the neat splint Egbert had fashioned from a straight branch of beechwood. 'We can help you a little way through the woods to the river bank. It's not far. Then we can either gather withies and make a raft or set our prayers to summon up a waterman with an eagerness to help.'

It turned out that their prayers, if they offered any, were answered in full. They came across an old fisherman with wild hair and untamed beard sheltering from the heat of the sun in the shade of a tree on the river bank. He had a line in the water.

Glumly confirming that he was in contention with the River Itchen for its fish when asked if Netley lay downstream he jerked his thumb in that direction and claimed it was no more than a short way with the tide as it was.

'I'm floating back in the direction of Hound,' he explained. 'Netley is no distance from there.'

A small but serviceable coracle was pulled up next to him on the bank. Gregory's persuasive manner, some coin and the fisherman's eagerness to keep in with a Cistercian abbot, though from a far region as they explained, soon had Hubert lying in the vessel with Hildegard beside him.

'This is way off our intended route,' Hubert remarked.

'Do you have a better suggestion, my lord?' Egbert turned to Gregory. 'They have facilities there to treat a broken leg, we assume?'

The boatman chipped in to reassure them. 'That apothecary of theirs will work his magic, do not doubt it. A clever fellow you can trust. He's mended enough broken heads in the wars than to be bested by a mere shin bone.' He gave Hubert a sharp glance. 'Beggin' your indulgence, my lord abbot. I don't doubt that it's painful enough, your leg, at present.'

'I've been pained worse many times,' Hubert answered through gritted teeth, 'but never so inconveniently.'

Gregory and Egbert led Hildegard's palfrey as well as Hubert's horse which, shame-faced, had eventually returned to seek his master. They agreed to keep to the river bank and ride on ahead. According to the boatman this was possible without, he added, getting their feet wet for no good reason.

'First we'll make sure your worthy boat is stout enough to carry its burden without sinking and once reassured we'll ride on to warn the brothers to receive an injured man. All's well,' Gregory added, for Hubert's benefit. 'This is nothing. We'll soon be on our way home again.'

Hubert gave him a black look. 'It might be all well with you, Gregory, but I'm going to have to stay trapped in some out of the way cell as an invalid until I can sit a horse.'

As Egbert had predicted, the sun quickly burned off the mist. The river slid like oil between banks of willow. It had been hot work leading Hubert, painfully astride his horse, through the woods but now, with the boat to take him the rest of the way, Gregory and Egbert would lead the other two horses along the top of the bank towards the abbey.

From the coracle Hildegard watched the men shadowing the boat and as soon as it left the shallows and was rocking safely on the ebb Gregory raised one hand to signal that he and Egbert were riding on.

The sun blazed down from a cloudless sky. Even the boatman commented. 'Been like this for three days, it has, ruining my fishing.'

'It'll end soon, no doubt. You know the weather,' Hildegard consoled him.

'Aye, and I know those weather prophets. They say we'll have another week of it till St Swithin's, then forty days more like it. If they're right we'll be done for good and proper. No crops. No dairy. Sheep dying for want of fodder. And if no sheep, no wool...then where will we be?'

He fell silent as if to let the menace of famine hover in the air until, turning his attention to the task of guiding the coracle into the fast-flowing tide, he drove them into its deep and dangerous embrace, and they were off down river to Netley.

But for her anxiety about him, Hildegard was happy to be alone at last with Hubert. She wanted, in any little way she could, to ease his pain and raise his spirits but there was something else, too, because of what had previously passed between them, some vestige of joy in being alone with him with nobody but an indifferent boatman to mar their intimacy.

With no interest further than tides and currents and the safety of his craft, the boatman paddled them all too swiftly towards their destination.

After a few moments Hubert reached for

Hildegard's hand, his thumb circling her palm, and when he pulled her closer the old fire smouldered between them.

'I would expect you to take advantage of your predicament,' she reproved, eyes sparkling and making no attempt to draw away.

'Pitiless woman,' he replied in like mood. 'Surely I deserve one small kiss to ease my agony?'

She gave him a kiss then as she had been longing to do since they left Salisbury and was conscious again of the dear, familiar scent of his skin and how easily he could ignite her resistless desires – only the vows that bound them both in an iron promise of fidelity to their Order stood between them.

Hubert's lips brushed her cheek, her fingers twined in his hair, and he murmured, 'Mea culpa, Hildegard. To bring this on you! I know how much you were looking forward to going home. Are you angry with me?'

She rested her cheek against his. 'I can imagine

no feeling less appropriate than anger. All I wish is that we can find a safe place where you can rest and have good folk heal you.'

This mingling of joy and mutual desire was curtailed soon enough. As evening began to spread its lavender veils over the land, with light draining into Southampton Water like mercury into a cup, the boatman dug his oar deep into the flood to turn the coracle towards the shore.

'Here we are,' he called over his shoulder.

A wooden jetty reared darkly from a shingle beach and beyond that one hulked shape, the wooden sides of a few fishing boats lay upended above the tide line.

Off shore, riding at anchor in the deep middle channel was a trading cog, its main sail furled, pennants drooping.

Two familiar figures were already striding down the bank to the shore and half-a-dozen hooded abbey servants followed carrying a stretcher between them. As the boatman ran his craft onto the beach, a crowd of onlookers jostled at the water's edge. With a few murmured instructions from the lay-servants Hubert was brought ashore even though he tried to fling off any help, at first determined to step onto dry land unaided and only reluctantly persuaded to recline on the stretcher so that he could more easily be conveyed up to the abbey.

Hildegard scrambled ashore last, pausing only to thank the boatman for his trouble and pay him double the coin he asked, then, in the wake of the group carrying the abbot she climbed the short slope up to a path that cut between a few trees towards a grey and imposing building on the summit.

'There it is,' announced Gregory. 'Netley Abbey at last!'

CHAPTER TWO

The conversi, those lay-brothers, the servants of the abbey who had not taken any vows but were still promised to celibacy, hefted the stretcher with its burden through the imposing gatehouse and at a brisk though careful pace crossed a corner of a great courtyard towards an open door.

Hildegard had an impression of cloisters running round three sides of a garth and opposite the gate house the massive edifice of a church with elegant, soaring columns, slender windows of glittering glass, and a porched entrance where several monks in their white Cistercian habits were coming and going. The voices of choristers floated in ethereal and solemn cadences across the roof tops.

Turning to follow the stretcher through the open door of what must be the infirmary, she was halted by a hand on her sleeve and a woman saying, 'Greetings, domina. Follow me, if you will.'

It was a wide-beamed bustling lay-sister in a

grey habit with a white coif askew on her head. 'I'm instructed by the guest master to conduct you to your quarters, domina.'

A blur of movement and colour from nearby resolved itself into several towns people in gaudy clothes standing at the near end of the cloister. On seeing a nun being shown inside there were speculative murmurs about her connection to the patient being carried in, one rumoured to be not only a distinguished guest but interestingly close to death's door.

Hoisting her saddle bag onto one hip Hildegard called after Gregory as he headed towards the stables. 'I may join you in the infirmary if that's where they're taking him?'

'We shall expect you. Find your bed first then come to us.'

The lay-sister was briskly opening a path between the on-lookers and when Hildegard caught up with her she waved a hand towards the women standing by. 'These good ladies will attest to my service, I hope, domina.'

The women nodded in agreement. One in particular, with a mass of red-hair tied up in a scarf which could not control such abundance offered Hildegard a warm smile. 'We are pilgrims, domina. You need have no fear that your meditations will be disturbed by us. We are the quietest women alive.'

An elderly old fellow at her side whom Hildegard took to be her husband, growled a good-natured contradiction that earned him a slap on the wrist. 'Don't frighten the sister right off, Simon, or she'll be sending herself out to look for more congenial lodgings.'

'I can assure you I shall be happy with anywhere warm and dry at present.' She glanced across towards the infirmary again.

Noticing this, the lay sister took her by the arm. 'Your abbot will be well cared for here. But come, you must be tired after your long ride and a cramping sail down river. Follow me.'

Again Hildegard had only a blurred impression as they hurried inside, stone steps, a wide doorway, the coolness of a shadowed hall, more steps, a communal sleeping chamber, and a swathe of satin, draped and gleaming, a bale of thick, dark wool, and something shining in the midst of it, and a hand, suddenly and incongruously, emerging to box the ear of a haloed angel, first one side, slap, then the other, and a stark, mute, pale face, shocked and blushing, and before Hildegard could take this in she saw the round blue eyes of a Saxon boy in a fustian tunic standing in another doorway with a clothes chest hefted in his arms, but she was already being hurried away underneath an arch and down a corridor of doors with the murmur of voices behind them and then, at last, breathless, was brought to a stop at a door transverse to the others, which her guide flung open.

Revealed was a small, plain chamber, one narrow truckle bed pushed against the wall, one prie-dieu of a very plain and simple construction, and one deep window loop, its shutters half open facing out towards the river with the extended wall of the gatehouse abutting it on the right.

'And this, domina, is the best I can offer but apart from the wall of the gatehouse obstructing the view to one side it is, in my estimation, the best chamber in the house.' She turned, confiding, 'We always leave it vacant to the last because some of my ladies do not like the noise of men arriving and departing below their window and they often prefer to sleep in the same long chamber as everyone else. More sociable, I suppose. But you, as a Cistercian, will not heed that.'

'I shall not,' Hildegard managed. 'This is a chamber to suit my requirements. I shall be content here insofar as I can feel content, given the reason for our sojourn at Netley.'

'Ah, that's most unfortunate. God willing, your lord abbot will soon be well enough to travel on. But let me show you, here,' she pointed to the top of a narrow staircase beside the door, 'you can go down straight into Cloister Garth where you may quickly reach your invalid. I understand that our own apothecary will attend him but you may wish to see to some of his needs yourself.'

Gregory and Egbert must have smoothed the path for her. 'I do so wish,' she agreed.

'Then you may come and go as you please by means of this little back stair.'

Such was the sister's eagerness to display the facilities offered to the abbey's many guests that it was some time before Hildegard managed to escape and make her way across the yard towards the infirmary. When she was shown in, Hubert was lying on a bed in a single cubicle surrounded by a waist-high partition sufficient to serve the dignity and privacy of an abbot.

She saw that he was being adequately attended already by a monk and a couple of practical looking laymen as well as by a friar wearing the grey habit of a Franciscan. The latter was offering medicine from a glass vial when Hildegard arrived and did not look up.

'We have cleaned and re-splinted his leg and this white poppy made up by our apothecary, Friar Hywel, will give him much needed sleep,' the monk in charge told her when introductions had been made. Gregory and Egbert had apparently been and gone already.

Hubert's broken leg was encased in a wooden frame, open along the top and held in position by leather straps. Water had been sluiced into it and a bandage soaked in honey as antiseptic had been wrapped loosely over the break in the skin. It was the wooden case that kept the broken bones firmly in position.

'Interesting,' Hildegard observed. Hubert would not be walking anywhere with his leg in that contraption.

'An old Roman system,' explained the monk. 'It keeps the leg immobile until the bone has had time to knit and we can keep the wound clean at the same time by dousing it with well water without disturbing it.'

The apothecary, a young Franciscan, gaunt and pale-faced, with a shock of thick, black hair and eyes too dark and luminous to ignore, placed the vial on a ledge and melted without a word into the shadows.

'He will sleep now, domina,' said the monk. 'I suggest you join your brothers in the refectory. There's food for you and your companions. Our cooks are always ready for the arrival of hungry travellers.'

As she left, the friar followed her out but when she turned to ask him directions to the refectory he was already striding away down the cloister.

'So do we have a plan of action?' asked Egbert while they were polishing off bowls of fish stew and great hunks of new bread.

'One thing's for sure, Hubert will not be going anywhere for some time. Not astride a horse, at any rate.'

'I shall stay with him,' Hildegard said. 'But what about you two?'

'We have no pressing business.' Gregory glanced at Egbert. 'Unless Hubert has some instructions for us?'

'He's on tenterhooks about how his abbey is

faring in his absence. He expects it to have gone to rack and ruin while he's been away.'

'It's his own fault if he's left incompetents in charge.' He chuckled. 'I can't imagine that. I'm sure things are well at Meaux.'

'No, but.....' Egbert grinned. 'You know Hubert. He doesn't trust anybody's competence but his own.'

'I'm sure he trusts you, Egbert, and you too, Gregory, on every level. And maybe that's why he might want you to stay close at hand.'

'I'm sure that's the best arrangement, all round.'

'By the way, who is this new abbot they have here?' She meant, as both monks understood, what side had he taken in the recent mass executions in London. The young king's main allies had been purged from government leaving him vulnerable to the machinations of his uncles, the dukes of Warwick and Gloucester and their ally the earl of Arundel whose domain was no further than a horse-ride away. 'The lay-sister told me that Abbot Philip has been in place for only a year and has yet to be tested by anything more taxing than providing hospitality for pilgrims.'

'Philip of - ? Where was it?'

'De Cornforth? Cornhampton? Something like that. He's unknown to me. I heard his name when we were at Beaulieu but only in passing. Who appointed him, do we know?'

'It would be through the usual channels at Citeaux on advice from St Mary Graces. At least Gloucester and Arundel haven't stolen the right to make appointments within our Order so far.'

'So far,' added Egbert heavily.

Wine was brought but it was not this that made everyone fall silent. Their thoughts, inevitably, turned towards King Richard and how he was faring in the face of his recent catastrophic defeat in parliament. Power was now definitely in the grip of the five barons calling themselves the Appellants.

Gregory's bleak, astonished, skeptical opinion was expressed when he said, 'Those self-styled

Appellants imagine they can do a better job of running the country than King Richard but I can't help feeling they're deluding themselves. We shall have to wait and see. One thing's certain. They will not be suing for peace with the French. In fact, I wouldn't be surprised if Arundel isn't already arming his militia for a new invasion.'

'Rich pickings even now,' Egbert averred. 'You'd imagine the French peasantry over there had been stripped of everything of value. Certainly much of it is said to've finished up adorning Arundel's castle.'

'We should be careful,' Gregory lowered his voice. 'We're too close to his domain to risk being picked up by his spies. I suggest we all hold our counsel while we're here, not out of fear but out of prudence.'

'Nothing new in having to watch our tongues.' Hildegard put down her beaker of wine. 'Can one imagine a country where one would be free to speak one's mind?'

'Wyclif certainly dreamed of it, poor old

fellow.'

'And his followers have such dreams but it's Arundel's brother who's making life intolerable for free-thinkers and scholars.' The brother, Richard, had been made Archbishop, now that King Richard's supporter, Alexander Neville, had fled the realm.

'I'm to my bed.' Egbert yawned. 'We'll keep silent. Watch and wait. Offer succour to the needy, as does the abbot here, and pray that we shall soon be back at Meaux.'

Hildegard did not sleep for an age. The air was stifling and her small chamber was like an oven even with the shutters thrown wide. It would be good for everybody if they had a decent harvest, and it would be so if the hot weather kept up but the sun had been like a brazen shield at high noon and now, at night, even the stones of the abbey itself seemed to be heated by a lingering inner fire.

She threw off her sheet and lay in her shift staring wide-eyed at the ceiling. Outside came the usual night sounds, an owl on the hunt, a breeze rustling through the trees surrounding the abbey enclosure and, outside in the lane leading up to the gatehouse no-one passed.

It was so silent the click of counters from the porters' lodge could be heard. Soon the bell for Matins would begin to toll. She thought of going down to join the others and began to haul herself from off the bed to prepare when the frail drumming of hoofs stayed her hand. The sound came closer. She heard it change as the riders started up the lane towards the abbey. Midnight was late for a travelers to be seeking hospitality.

People from all levels, high to low, were still fleeing London after the Merciless Parliament, fleeing for their lives whether in guilt or fear. In Salisbury they had even come across the king's personal secretary, the Head of the Signet office, after he sought anonymity as a mere canon in the cathedral but he was only one of hundreds to flee the threat of summary execution by getting out of London as fast as he could.

The merchants who had supported King Richard with loans and practical means, had been forced to accept the execution of their mayor, Sir Nick Brembre. It had taken only two days from impeachment and trial to execution for the dukes to rid themselves of this major financier of the king. His execution had sent a quake of fear throughout the City. Even now, others would be living in terror and praying that their support for the young king, offered out of loyalty, might be overlooked by those who were redefining their largesse as the capital crime of treason.

The purpose of starving the king of money was obvious. Without resources, he would not be able to finance an army to match the ones of the Appellants and thus would be forever in their power.

The riders came to a halt beneath her window. A short command brought the porter to the gate. A mumbled conversation followed and evidently he was satisfied because she heard him open the double gates into the outer garth.

The horses – she thought there were two - were stilled to a random snort, a tinkling of bridle ornaments and then, clearly, a voice emerged from out of the night. It was a full, rich sound but the words were unfamiliar. A reply in the same language echoed from underneath the archway. The porter must have had someone with him but now the door to his lodge slammed shut.

The two voices were less guarded now they were alone, but the language, she thought, as she went to stand beside her window, was not English. What was it? And who was arriving secretly in the dead of night? Was it something to do with Arundel?

She could not forget how she and the abbot with his two monks militant had been pursued all the way from Avignon back to England by Arundel's men only weeks before. As Admiral of the Southern Seas he had posted spies at all the ports along the coast to halt anyone either coming into the realm or trying to leave it without his writ. Fortune decreed that they had been able to get back in without being stopped.

Doubtful that four Cistercians were important enough to have drawn the earl's own militia all the way to Netley after their lost meanderings in the woods she strained to hear what was being said.

To her astonishment she managed to pick out a few words of Welsh. It was a while since she'd lived in the Welsh Marches. Not since she had been widowed had she set foot in the small castle near Penarlag, her home through the short, unhappy years of her marriage to Marcher lord Hugh de Ravenscroft. Frequent efforts to grasp the intricacies of the language had given her enough understanding to be able to pick a few words now – then the name Sycharth sharpened her attention.

She knew that place.

It was the fortified manor house of a man named Owain Glyn Dwr. Worse, he was in the service of Arundel.

A Welshman descended from two royal dynasties, he was famous throughout Wales and the borderlands. As a landowner and a prince he was respected by both sides, being a peacemaker in the endless disputes between the Marcher lords. After she left the border country and took the veil his name had cropped up now and then – he distinguished himself in the French wars under the command of Arundel, and against the Scots when they invaded the north of England. But for the fact that the invaders had turned back for some inexplicable reason, York itself, and certainly the Abbey of Meaux, would have been swallowed up by the Scots despite the military prowess of Arundel's army and this captain Glyn Dwr. Most recently he had been made personal body-guard to Arundel.

Now someone discussing Glyn Dwr's manor in the Berwyn Mountains was outside.

She leaned as close to the window loop as she could, her face pressed against the warm stones. The first voice, distinguished by its richness and sonority, was saying something rapidly to the man who had emerged from the gatehouse after the porter went back inside. The man replied, courteously, deferentially, indeed. Was it one of the monks or one of the lay servants?

Straining forward, she tried to peer down into the lane but the angle was wrong and all she could make out was the empty path. As well as that the voices were speaking too rapidly for her to catch their meaning but she heard a chuckle and a slap like two palms meeting that brought things to a conclusion. The night-door grated on its hinges as somebody pushed it wider, footsteps entered under the arch, then the door slammed behind them.

Despite the heat, Hildegard reached for her cloak and pulled it on. When the bell sounded she would go into Matins and see if she could find out who had arrived like an assassin in the night. It was undignified to have listened at her window but she was frighteningly aware of the danger should an ally of Arundel have gained admission to the abbey.

He must have a reason for secrecy.

Now she prayed that it was nothing to do with

Abbot de Courcy, his two monks and their activities in Avignon when they had foiled the earl's plot against King Richard.

CHAPTER THREE

The cloisters were lit at intervals by cressets set in wall-brackets fixed to the pillars. They shed just enough light to find one's way without stumbling but not enough to be able to make out the identity of the hooded figures going in to Matins.

The guests worshipped in a small chapel near the gatehouse but Hildegard did not follow them, assuming it was more likely for the mysterious rider to attend in the Church itself. The group heading for the chapel were pilgrims waiting at Netley for the ship to take them overseas, couples wishing to make sure of their after-life in heaven or widows and widowers fulfilling vows to a deceased partner, along with one or two on some private penance of their own. Among them were others with business interests connected to the busy river trade that connected Netley to the Isle of Wight, the ports of the Narrow Seas and the wider world. Whether they were men or women she was unable to discern in the darkness.

She let them go then turned off into the church. Several conversi in rough brown habits and soft-soled night boots were already crowding at the back while the monks themselves were still filing in, emerging straight from their dortoir down the night stairs that brought them directly into the Choir.

She thought she could make out Gregory's tall broad-shouldered figure as they entered but all had their hoods up, faces in shadow, looking much the same in their white habits and she couldn't be sure.

A glance round revealed no-one who might be the rider in the night. The friar who had attended Hubert as he was brought in on his stretcher was standing somewhat apart but close enough to see his devout expression as, with his hood falling back, he raised his face towards the east. Eventually he looked round, pulled his hood down and joined the others in the flowing Latin of the Office.

The discipline of having to come out in the middle of the night, take a few hours rest, and then come out again for Lauds was so familiar it no longer tired her so that when a man came in late, unabashed, forcing a space for himself with a view of the altar in the nave she gave him an alert glance from under her hood.

He was fiftyish, above average hight, broad-chested, probably with a voice as rich as his stature would suggest. But he did not look Welsh. His hair was fair revealing an almost reddish tinge in the candle glow. A fleshy face did not suggest a fighting man like Glyn Dwr either. His garments, from what she could make of them in the candle-light, were those of a merchant, a successful one with a showy capuchon on his head, an expensive deep-dyed blue cotte and a fur over one shoulder despite the summer heat. He was certainly no monastic and she wondered if he was a respected donor to the abbey's upkeep to be privileged to worship here.

His glance shifted over the bent heads and before he turned to include her in his scrutiny Hildegard quickly dropped her gaze.

It was one of the shorter Offices and as soon as it was possible to join the other guests drifting out of the chapel into Cloister Garth she followed them in the direction of the guest quarters. Egbert caught up with her.

'Domina,' he whispered, as formal as if he expected someone to be listening, 'I looked in on Hubert before coming here. Will you go and speak to him?'

'What? Now?'

Anxiety must have shown in her expression because he reassured her. 'Nothing alarming. You know where to find him?'

'Unless he's had a miraculous healing I suppose I do! Walk with me?'

'I surely will. Then maybe you can tell me why you looked so alarmed when I tugged your sleeve just now.'

Together they went into the cloisters but not before Hildegard had watched the late-comer in the vermilion capuchon cross the yard with the other guests in the direction of their sleeping quarters.

In a low voice she said, 'Someone arrived on horseback shortly before Matins. He had one retainer by the sound of it. A man from the abbey, whether one of the brothers or a conversi, spoke to him in Welsh.'

Egbert showed immediate interest.

'I couldn't catch all they said but the name Sycharth was mentioned.' She explained its significance.

'So you think Arundel's spy, this Glyn Dwr himself, may have been tipped off? About us?' He sounded shocked. 'We're nobodies.'

'He's a good revenger, is Arundel, he and his brother both. He won't like the fact that we scotched his plan to get Pope Clement on his side against King Richard. But I agree. We're not important. There's too much else going on in Westminster to waste time on us. And anyway, I don't see how they would know we were anywhere near here when we scarcely knew ourselves.'

'No-one knew - apart from those lawless devils

who waylaid us.' His glance held hers.

'It seemed a random attack.' She eyed him doubtfully.

'I know it did.' He took her by the arm. 'Not to worry. We'll keep a careful watch and I'll find out who this newcomer thinks he is.'

'How will you do that?'

'I'll ask one of the fellows at the gatehouse after a few stoups of ale.' He left her at the door of the infirmary.

Hubert was as white as the sheet that covered him. Even by the flickering light of a tallow candle his eyes were dark in the deep sockets above angular cheekbones. When he saw Hildegard enter he reached out and despite the shrouded figure in attendance pulled her close. 'Thank you for visiting my sick bed,' he greeted in a voice of exaggerated pain and then he gave his familiar roguish smile. 'I am waited on with more assiduity than ever I receive at Meaux.'

He indicated the friar who, with a tread as light

as thistledown, had followed Hildegard out of the church and across the courtyard.

He materialized beside the bed with arms folded inside his sleeves, acknowledged Hildegard with an austere nod then turned his attention to Hubert. 'How are you faring, my lord? I have something to help you sleep if you're feeling restless.'

Hubert shook his head. 'I want for nothing at present, brother. You may get to your bed as you well deserve. My gratitude for your attentions. You're setting a high standard for my own people to live up to.'

Though dismissed the friar lingered. 'I think I would like another look at your wound, my lord, if I may?'

Hubert nodded but was clearly annoyed at having someone else present now Hildegard had arrived. 'Have you settled into your accommodation?' he asked of her in a formal tone.

Hildegard said she had and with a close look at the friar asked, 'How do you think the patient is faring, brother?'

'As well as one would wish, domina. If he can be persuaded not to attempt to discard the brace too soon he should make a good recovery.'

'I fear the lord abbot is a poor patient.'

'We must do what we can to make sure he does himself no further harm.'

The pleasantries over Hubert broke in. 'Domina, I'm told by Friar Hywel that soon the tide will be right for the trading cog we noticed to come in close enough to discharge her cargo. I imagine it'll be all bustle and chaos on the quay and in the abbey when that happens?' He turned to the friar.

'I'm told the ship has brought goods from Outremer, my lord, so we should expect many exotic spices to delight our palates.' He gave a thin smile. 'And I hope, also, many antidotes for the ailments that will result from over-indulgence.'

'Prepared for all things, brother?'

'I endeavour to be so.'

'And when do you expect this mayhem to break

out?'

'I have observed the phases of the moon, my lord, and I calculate that there will be enough water the day after next to allow the vessel to anchor in the channel closer to the shore. Until then she will remain in mid-river.'

'And after that will she take off the pilgrims on the first leg of their journey?' Hildegard asked as if out of interest to know how long the guest house might be busy but in reality to hear him speak again.

'Indeed she will. Bound for France. Let's hope their billets of passage will be respected. St James will no doubt take care of his own.' The friar's lips twitched but he said nothing more.

He seemed satisfied with Hubert's wound and replaced the bandage. 'I shall bid you goodnight.' He bowed with palms together and left as silently as he had entered.

Hubert watched him leave then as soon as he was out of sight patted the bed beside him. 'Now tell me why you're looking like that.'

'Like what?'

'Like a bird about to be pounced on by a large ferocious cat.'

'Am I such an open book to you?'

'Sometimes. I would not venture to claim that your thoughts are always open to study. But, come on, quit stalling. Something seems to have disturbed you. What's the matter?'

'You mean something more than a natural worry about your state of health?'

'Hildegard – ' he warned.

'Well, if you must know, it's the friar…' She bit her lip.

'Brother Hywel?'

'Yes. He does prowl like a cat. I had no idea he'd followed me across the garth.'

'That's a small thing to arouse anxiety.'

'It's more than that. It's his voice. It's quite distinctive…and it's not the first time I've heard it.' Then she told him about the midnight rider and the hurried conversation in Welsh below her window. 'I heard the name Glyn Dwr, and

Sycharth, and we know Glyn Dwr is one of Arundel's body-guards.'

Hubert smoothed the back of her hand. 'Fear not. Arundel will have forgotten us by now. The bloody purge of the king's ministers is sending everyone fleeing from London. There are bigger fish around than us, ones who might turn on those traitorous Appellants and make them rue the day they decided on vengeance to further their ambitions.'

'Egbert thinks much the same.'

'But you're not convinced?'

'It seems odd, that's all. Even if you're right,' she said slowly, 'what's he doing here of all places?'

'Are you sure it was Glyn Dwr himself, or could it be that his name simply cropped up in conversation? Nothing strange about that when two Welshmen get to talking things over.'

'You may be right.' She frowned. 'We're too near Arundel's fief for comfort. I'll be glad when we can leave.'

'But what can Arundel do? Even if one of his spies had bothered to tell him we're here, he can't have us hauled out of the abbey. This is sacred space. We can claim sanctuary in the church. Even he, surely, would not attempt to dislodge us from so holy a place?'

'I see that we can only wait until daylight to discover the truth.'

Hubert would be helpless to defend himself should anyone try to drag him from the abbey precinct by main force.

He held onto her hand as she rose to leave. 'Are you going already?'

'I must get some sleep, Hubert. I'm dozing on my feet. It's not surprising I feel menace in the air. Ordinarily I wouldn't give a second's thought to our encounter with that gang in the woods. Now, with this latest threat, if it exists, I can't get the fear of danger out of my mind.'

She shivered and was only partially reassured when he squeezed her fingers between his own and said, 'Go then. Fear nothing. Sleep well.'

Exhausted after the previous day, it was already daylight when Hildegard woke to the sound of footsteps in the corridor outsider her chamber. She realized that it was probably guests going down to Prime. She must have slept through the summoning of the bell but been awoken by the lightest of footsteps. Throwing her summer cloak over her shift and pushing her hair back under her coif she opened the door and poked her head out. Several women were coming out of the shared chamber further along the corridor. They were yawning and discussing what fare would be on offer to break their fast.

Recognising several of them as those who had been standing near the gatehouse when Hubert was carried inside, Hildegard joined them.

'Have I missed Prime?' she asked in astonishment. She had hoped to have another chance of seeing the mysterious Welshman and discovering whether he posed a threat or not.

One of the women was the unisputed centre of

the group. With red hair piled haphazardly under a white kerchief she gave a sympathetic laugh. 'You must have slept well,' she replied. 'Prime is over. Come in to break your fast with us.'

They walked down into the garth. The sun was already beating down in an intense assault that made the red-haired woman pull her kerchief over her face. 'I burn so,' she explained, 'I must ask that herberer for some chamomile. At least we have the shade of the cloisters for protection. They say this heat-wave is going to last for another week. I dread the thought of going on board ship with so little protection from the sun.'

'And it will be unloading its cargo soon, I hear?'

'I hope so, and then we can go on board and our adventure begins!' She was a voluptuous woman of about Hildegard's own age and briefly the nun imagined herself before she was widowed and took her vows. She might have stayed as a guest accompanied by her husband exactly like this, to set out on a long pilgrimage overseas, maybe with the purpose of reaffirming their vows to each other – but then she thought, more realistically, that with Hugh it could never have happened. He was committed to war and the acquisition of material wealth and had met his death because of it.

'I saw you with your husband as I arrived,' Hildegard reminded. 'I believe he's called Simon?'

'That's right, the old owl. And I am Alicia, but Lissa to you, domina.'

She yawned behind her hand, stretched a little and said, 'Forgive me. We had a long ride from Winchester to get here and arrived only shortly before you did and what with those bells tolling through the night I've scarcely had a minute's sleep. I can't imagine how you manage it all the time. I hope it's true about the ship. We have to wait until it's ready to sail again and I'm so impatient!.'

They walked across towards the refectory, talking about the excitement of taking ship and the dangers of pilgrimage and all the other problems of travel while the situation with the French was so uncertain.

'Although, the way things are I'm somewhat pleased to be leaving,' Lissa added. 'I hope by the time we return the realm will be at peace again and our dear young king will have all his honours reinstated as is right and just.' She covered her mouth with her hand and murmured, 'I can't stand that Arundel. He takes all our young men from round here to fight in his army then sends them home without any pay. No wonder he's able to strut around in that big castle of his. Forgive me, domina,' she broke off. 'I should not talk so openly. Simon is always telling me I'll land myself in trouble one of these days with my big mouth.'

'You only express what many are thinking,' replied Hildegard.

Entering the refectory and seeing the men already seated at the table reserved for guests, Lissa invited Hildegard to join her and her husband who found a space for them both on the bench. It turned out that one or two others had arrived only the day before as well and they shared stories about the difficulties of the journey while the barefoot conversi supplied them with bread and cheese and a jug or two of watered wine.

Two young women in their twenties were sitting opposite and Hildegard's new companion, Lissa, suddenly burst out laughing. 'My! You two look like peas in a pod. I've only just opened my eyes enough to have a good look at you. Are you sisters?'

They nodded. 'They call us Mistress Sweet and Mistress Sour,' one of them said. 'We leave you to decide which is which.'

It was a challenge and Lissa gave them a shrewd glance. 'If it's not impertinent I'd say you were Mistress Sour,' she smiled kindly at the speaker. 'But I would imagine it's a somewhat inaccurate description of your nature.'

The young woman laughed. 'You've scored a bull there, mistress. It's because I think before I speak and have dark hair while my twin here speaks before she thinks, don't you, Ceci? And has fair hair,' she added with a lugubrious glance at her sister's tumbling flaxen locks. 'Men go for that Saxon colouring,' she added, 'and she makes the most of it, don't you, Ceci? Speak up.'

Ceci was staring at a woman further along the bench who had trailed after them from the guest house and now she came to with a jerk of her head. 'They do,' she replied equably, 'but I can't help that.' She gave them her full attention. 'We're not pilgrims. We're dairy women, if you want to know. We have our own dairy business which we're seeking to expand. That's why we're staying at Netley. We hope to do business with the cellarer here. We'd like to persuade him to take our cheese for the abbot's lodging for when he entertains his special guests.'

'We're also going to the Monday market at Hound,' the dark-haired sister added, 'to see what opportunities are there.'

A man had risen to his feet when the woman joined and now sat down again. He leaned over.

'So where is this dairy of yours?' he asked.

Mistress Sour answered. 'It's near Southampton. I may as well tell all before my sister spills it out. When our mother died, a very admirable dairywoman and a widow for all our childhood, she bequeathed the business to us and, like new brooms, we decided we would make a clean sweep and expand beyond our nearby weekly market. We began to take in more milk from the many little villages around who produced more than they could use. Soon we had to move to bigger premises for our cheese-making as we also inherited a secret ingredient which makes it, I say this without boasting, some of the best cheese on the market.'

Her sister picked up a lump of the thick cheese that she had cut off from the wedge that had been set out for them. 'This,' she said, 'is nothing like the cheese we make. This is coarse stuff. We're grateful to the monks for providing it for all that. But ours is for the discerning. We sell to some of the best houses in Southampton.'

The man rose to his feet again and bowed. 'You may call me Master John,' he announced in resonant tones. 'I own the ship at anchor. I buy and sell. I also transport pilgrims across the Narrow Sea.' He glanced round the table. 'You others will be my guests once you're on board my ship the St Marie, so welcome, one and all.' He smiled benignly on the two sisters who smiled back.

Hildegard had already recognised the ship-owner as the late-comer at Matins, the one she had mentally marked out as a merchant. This was no ordinary merchant though if the ship was entirely his. Most owners took out shares in a suitable vessel in order to spread the risk, sometimes as little as a ninth but usually at least a third, and then there was insurance on top of that. Trading was a risky business these days, especially with the frequent raids from the French coast and the pirates out towards the Spanish coast. Wine ships trading down as far as Guienne often had armed men on board to repel attackers. And then there was the weather. Unpredictable and in the hand of God. She wondered if the ship merchant had many wealthy backers.

A pretty though somewhat sharp-featured woman with hair as black as ebony was sitting on the opposite side of the trestle further downs and now she exclaimed in a high, tweeting voice, 'So you are our ship owner, our saviour! Now I am reassured.' She glanced round. 'May I introduce myself to everyone? I am a widow but you may call me Delith as we are going to be ship-board companions, and this silent body beside me is my maid, Lucie.' She looked at the merchant from under her lashes. 'I confess, master, I've been so frightened at the thought of putting out to sea - one hears such terrible stories about unseaworthy vessels and their unscrupulous owners who only want to take our money and then care nothing whether we live or die and preferably die so they can collect on their insurance - but now, with someone as reassuring as you, master, my fears have dissolved.'

She took a breath after this outpouring and, stalled in whatever he had been about to say to the sisters, the ship-owner turned to have a good look at whoever had put such instant faith in him and held his fellow ship merchants with such cynical disregard.

The woman's black hair was oiled and severely plaited and pinned under a white coif, tightly tied. She fluttered her eyelashes then demurely directed her gaze down to her cleavage and two ample breasts showing above an unexpectedly low-cut bodice. Invited to follow her gaze, the merchant faltered, decided to accept her invitation and gave a complicit smile. 'And are you traveling alone, mistress?'

'Oh no,' she opened her eyes wide as if in innocent misunderstanding. 'I travel with a most devout group of pilgrims. Several are still at their prayers inside the church.' She leaned far forward for the merchant's benefit and whispered, as if it were a great secret, 'We're traveling all the way to Compostela to kneel at the feet of St James. It is fitting, is it not, that his feast day will be celebrated here in this very abbey only a short while after we leave? It will be as if he is watching over us from beginning to end.'

A yellowy-looking, sparsely bearded old fellow further along the trestle glanced up from the small book open on the board beside him at the mention of St James. 'If all goes well, mistress, we should be on the point of arrival when their celebrations start here. Isn't that so, master?'

The merchant gave a quick nod, his glance scarcely leaving the dark, young widow as she fingered the lacing of her bodice and began to twirl the loose end between her fingers.

Mistress Sour butted in. 'As I was saying, we're here to do business.' She gave the ship merchant a challenging stare.

Master John dragged his glance from the winding and rewinding of the bodice string and his eyes narrowed with a calculation of shared interest when he met the steady grey gaze of the more serious of the sisters. 'Come and talk to me when you're finished here, dear ladies, if you will. I have affairs of business in this little stretch of country. It is so far from the towns it tends to be forgotten but I believe there are chances here not available elsewhere.'

'It happens to be ideally placed for overseas trade,' Mistress Sour observed with a calculating smile.

The dry, yellow man turned a page with a pair of wooden tweezers and went back to his reading.

Lissa leaned against her husband and sighed. 'It's so hot even in here, my dearest. Shall we go for a walk by the river, to cool down?'

'Whatever my little bluebird desires,' he answered, patting her hand with its cluster of rings.

She rose to her feet and lifted the mass of red hair tumbling out from underneath her coif from off her neck to cool herself and, catching sight of the ship-owner's glance, let it fall in a leisurely manner through her fingers to cloak her shoulders in its shimmering and extraordinary colours. 'The rest of the pilgrims should arrive today, master.

How many shall we be?'

'I have five or six on my tally, mistress.'

'So we wait for only one or two more?'

'There is no hurry. The friar tells me the near channel will not be right for us to discharge our cargo until the day before the full moon, then we'll take a day to scrub the St Marie from top to bottom to make it pleasant for your good selves, then a day to get everyone on board with enough victuals to satisfy the greatest gourmand, and off she goes as the tide lets us. We shall have ample time to get to know one another before then.' His glance seemed to be dragged unwillingly back towards Delith twirling the string of her bodice, an action at variance with the severity of the plaited coils of her hair and the demure expression under it.

She's pretending not to have noticed that look, thought Hildegard sitting unregarded at the end of the row. She wondered who would make the next move in the little dance of attraction and desire that had started on its first uncertain steps. Maybe nothing would come of it. It was only a short time before the moon brought a favourable tide, the ship would sail and the master would be left behind to consider his profit.

CHAPTER FOUR

The ship in question, the St Marie, was a wooden trading cog, wide-bellied, with a large square sail amidships furled over the yard arm. She lay exposed to the glare of the sun on a winking bed of mirrors with no sign of activity on deck. The crew would be lying below out of the firey heat, Hildegard surmised, from where she herself reclined with Gregory and Egbert on the bank above the beach. Even so it would be stifling down there among the bales of cargo.

She had crossed the seas in a trading cog much like the St Marie on her way to Tuscany with the minstrel, young Pierrekyn Haverel, the time he had smuggled the little pearl-studded turnshoe and its secret all the way to Florence. His wonderful playing and singing had accompanied them all through Flanders, over the Alps and beyond.

That was the one thing missing here, music, if you discounted the singing of the monks. She said as much to the other two lying on the grass beside her.

It was the dead time before the mid-day Office when usually they would have been busy at their books or about the abbey on some essential work but today the heat-wave had brought the regularity of the usual monastic day to a halt. It was simply too stifling to do more than lie about in the shade and, as Gregory said, there was a limit to the amount of time anybody could be expected to spend in church.

By common consent they had agreed that the coolest place was under the shade of some trees above the waterfront where a fragile breeze made a leaf tremble now and then.

'Are you both asleep?' she murmured when there was no response to her idle comment about music.

'Not at all,' replied Gregory, opening one eye. 'It's simply too hot to summon up the strength to turn out an answer. I do wonder, though,' he went on, 'about these guests here.'

'The invisible Welsh prince?' Egbert suggested

without opening his eyes. 'Are you sure you didn't dream his arrival, Hildegard?'

'Maybe I did,' she agreed, without the strength to argue. 'Hasn't the night porter mentioned him?'

'He was off duty when I went by the gatehouse earlier. I'll catch up with him later, see what he can tell us.'

'And what about this ship merchant,' Gregory continued. 'He's surely too big for a small place like this? What's he doing here?'

'He did remark on how out of the way it was, a good place to do business with little competition.'

Gregory appeared to fall asleep again until he said, 'Remind me, Egbert, what Abbot Philip said about the goods he's sending over-seas?'

With eyes still shut he replied, 'Apart from pilgrims? He's sending embroidered cloth, Opus Anglicanum…for some prelates in Rome…worth a king's ransom. Or…' his words trailed off, 'you know what I mean. Worth more than its weight in gold?' He chuckled at his feeble attempt at a joke.

'Philip was hinting that it was to fulfil an order

for the Pope himself.'

'It may be so. I find Abbot Philip difficult to follow. He's a nervous sort of fellow for an abbot.'

'New in the job,' Gregory drew his lips back to reveal his even white teeth in derision. 'I'm looking forward to hearing what Hubert thinks to him. Of course,' he added generously, 'this is a small place, beautiful though it is. They don't have the resources we have at Meaux. Their wool exports come mainly from others. They're middle-men without the pasturage we have in the north. They don't necessarily attract top men to the top jobs.'

Hildegard liked to hear Gregory talk of 'we' – it was many years since he had been at Meaux. He had been there in the time before she joined the order but his loyalty to the place was still intact. Now she said, 'Surely the top men are the most devout, not the best businessmen?'

'You've got a point there – ' Egbert broke off as if he had been about to name someone they all knew but careful not to impugn Hubert's piety he added, 'Nobody wants an abbot who'll run the place into the ground for want of practical sense.'

'I shall go to sleep if we sit here much longer,' Hildegard changed the subject. 'And those two sisters, they're full of what you'd call practical sense and as for their piety…'

'And the widow…' Gregory contributed.

Another drowsy silence followed.

'Well, nothing's expected of us. We're guests,' he eventually continued. 'At mid-day Egbert and I shall go in and try to make it rain with our voices. That's really all they expect of us.'

'Yes, Hildegard, make the most of it,' Egbert agreed. 'This is the beginning of a long sojourn until Hubert is fit to travel again. Once he's stumping around on crutches you'll have your time cut out trying to keep up with him.'

'I'm sure he wouldn't mind if you decided to go north without him.'

'I'm expecting him to suggest it.' Egbert picked a blade of grass and began to chew it. 'But

I'd like to make sure he's going to be safe here before any of us leave.'

'Me too,' agreed Gregory. 'I can't get the measure of this place at all.'

'Arundel's dark wings hovering over us all?'

Gregory shook his head. 'Something to do with the place itself. Despite its ethereal beauty – the masons' exquisite workmanship - the sumptuous, painted glass - its proportions - that glorious east window…everything in fact that makes it a place of visual harmony…cannot explain the sense of unease beneath the surface. The place is more than it seems.'

Before they got up to leave at the first summoning of the bell they saw the ship- owner strolling down towards the waterfront. He stood gazing out towards the St Marie as if willing its cargo unloaded, set on its way, and the profit safe in his coffers. A second figure came down and stood at a short distance from him, her face shielded from the glaring sun by a floating veil of some light stuff of pure white. As she stood there on the shingle she wound its diaphanous veils around her head like a nun's snood giving her a devout and touch-me-not appearance.

Hildegard sat up on one elbow to watch.

A voice beside her put her thoughts into words. It was Gregory, following her glance. With a humorous chuckle, he remarked, 'There goes Mistress Delith with her next mark.'

Hildegard turned with a startled glance. 'Do you know her already?'

'Which of us monks does not? She made the calculated mistake of turning into the Chapter House just as we were about to start the day's business this morning. "Oh do forgive me, my lord abbot," says she, kneeling at his feet and looking up with soulful eyes. "I was trying to find the refectory." Abbot Philip was beside himself with pleasure and dispatched one of the lay-brothers to set her on her way at once with his blessing.'

"Why do you say 'calculated'?'

'There was more than I've just related but you get the gist. Not one of the fifteen brothers who happened to be present did not succumb to the unaccustomed aura of such a vibrantly female presence. Their confessors will be over-worked today.'

'She is very pretty if you like dark-haired women,'

'And she knows it…And glories in it too. That's the sin.'

'I met her in the refectory. She's a strange one to be going on pilgrimage with her head so full of vanity.'

'There now, the ship-owner has noticed her and acknowledges her.'

Egbert sat up. 'What are you two talking about?'

'Pilgrims, Egbert, and their mixed motives in setting forth to visit the holy shrines of France and Galicia. This particular pilgrim is attempting to lure the ship-owner to his doom before she leaves.'

Egbert followed his glance. 'Is this a betting situation because if so I have no inclination to have my debt of penance augmented.'

'Nor do I. It'd be a fool's game.'

Egbert watched as Delith moved closer to the ship-owner so that her sleeve brushed his. 'She already knows he's wealthy but does she know he's married?'

'Is he?' Hildegard wondered about his omission of that fact when he introduced himself earlier.

'His wife is an invalid. She's being cared for in the infirmary until the ship leaves when she hopes to leave with it to find a saint overseas, stronger than our own, who will restore her health.'

'From what Hubert said the monk in charge gives little for her chances.' Gregory crossed himself.

The two standing by the water's edge began to pace slowly along the shoreline away from the abbey until eventually they came to a stop where a dozen or so small boats were pulled up onto the shingle nearby with a boatman mending a net beside them. Master John went to have a word with him and Mistress Delith followed in his footsteps, chatting all the while.

Heat haze draped the far bank of Southampton Water where a few trees and a huddle of fishermen's huts glimmered, a scene far enough distant to have all the enchantment of a promised land. Soon the sun would reach its zenith, forcing a further loosening of garments and, among themselves, an unusual slowness of thought. Hildegard yawned and closed her eyes.

After a time the frail sound of a bell from inside the abbey wavered into the morning again and this time could not be ignored. 'That is the bell, isn't it?' someone remarked superfluously.

Gregory rose to his feet with unaccustomed languor. 'This is like being in Outremer. I haven't felt really warm since I stepped off the ship at Marseilles.'

Together they ambled back towards the gatehouse. The day porter was still on duty and Egbert, with maybe the thought of ale on his mind, did no more than raise a hand as he stepped past the guard-room door.

As they entered Cloister Garth a lay-brother Hildegard had noticed fetching and carrying in the infirmary ran up to her. He made a graceful obeisance before speaking with unexpected formality. 'Domina, your lord abbot wishes audience with you.'

'I'll come at once. Is anything amiss?'

'Not that I know of, domina.'

The two monks went on ahead. Said Gregory over his shoulder, 'We must go in to pray in order to uphold the piety of Meaux among the mysterious denizens at Netley. Let us know if the abbot needs our services.'

She saw them enter the cool shadow inside the church as she followed the flashing, sturdy legs of the messenger.

The infirmary, too, was in a deep recess of shadow, cool as water and as silent. Hildegard went to stand over Hubert where he was lying with his leg fixed in its brace.

When he opened his eyes and saw her smiling

down at him, he remarked, 'Caught as if in a gin trap. You may do with me what you will.'

'I see you only wanted to spoil my rest on the river bank,' she observed.

He held out his hand so she could slip her own into his. 'You were coming in for the mid-day Office I hope and expect?'

'Which you have now made me forfeit.'

'Not at all. You can join them at once. I only want you to visit the magister in his den afterwards to get some more of that knit-bone concoction. I intend to be on my feet as soon as possible.'

'Why did you not send for a servant?'

'Because your face is fairer than any of the lads here and if you must know you are the only medicine I really need. I'm feeling better already, just looking at you.'

'Fair words, my lord.'

'Why do you call me lord when you know I'm your slave?'

'You'll never be anybody's slave. But it shall be done. Knit-bone. Anything else?'

'Only your presence if you can spare one moment in your day for me?'

She smiled. 'One little moment, maybe, who knows? We'll have to see.'

'Such cruelty! Go then, and offer a prayer for me if you regard me with an iota of kindness.'

As their handclasp was released she noticed a cubicle with a screen across it at the far end of the infirmary. 'Is someone in serious straits?' she asked him, indicating the screen.

'She's the wife of the ship-owner. I fear she's in need of all the prayers she can get.'

'Brother Egbert mentioned her and how seriously sick she is, poor woman.'

'You might sit with her awhile when you come back?'

'Of course, if she'd like that. Can you spare me?' she teased.

He was serious when he said, 'I believe her need is far greater than mine.'

When Hildegard reached the church the monks,

indistinguishable from each other, were still filing in. A choir of boys was singing. It was a sweet sound and while everyone was mumbling through their prayers she waited in expectation to hear their voices again.

Her hope was rewarded and Gregory, whose voice was not as bad as he made out, was audible behind the screen in its familiar resonant bass. To her joy, a tenor among the guests standing at the back began to sing. At first he merely allowed his voice to underpin those round him but then as if the effort to keep it caged was too much he allowed it to take flight and like a released bird it soared above the rest with such overwhelming beauty Hildegard turned her head to see who it was.

A stranger stood at the back, a shortish, barrel-chested man in his thirties, plainly dressed as if not wishing to draw attention to himself but thwarted, now, by the natural glory of his voice. He stood as if beatified as the music carried him along.

As the last note died he knelt swiftly and bowed

his head in a sort of apology for drawing attention to his singularity – or, maybe, as if a great sorrow was bearing down on him. Both hands clenched. He stayed like that until everyone had left and not until the last footsteps faded did he lift his head to look about. His glance collided with Hildegard's before she could avert her astonished face and with brutal speed he rose to his feet and walked out with a strong, athletic and military stride.

To fulfil her errand on Hubert's behalf she went to look for the friar in his small lean-to drying shed in the herb garden. After what seemed like a mysteriously bruising encounter in the church it was a pleasure to push open the gate into the sunlit enclosure and breathe in the heady perfume of a hundred different herbs.

She walked down a south-facing slope between well-tended beds, most in full flower. As there seemed to be no-one around she lingered until she heard voices in the distance. When she made her way towards them she realized it was the friar and his apprentice in fierce argument. She hesitated. Was it right to break in on it?

Before she could make up her mind she heard the friar shout, 'You Saxon sot-wit! Get out of my way or I'll wring your neck!'

Rounding a hedge she saw Jankin higher up the garden, in full view and close enough to see his blue eyes flash like polished stones as he glared down at someone on the other side of the hedge.

Red-faced he shouted back, 'I am Saxon! Yes! I can't help that! Nor can you help being a witless Welshman!'

Hywel came into view and she saw him throw his head back, outraged, with incipient violence in the gesture. 'You insolent young devil! I'm your master. I could have you whipped for that! Haven't your women folk told you not to speak to your masters like that?'

'Nobody tells me anything!'

'I'm aware of that! Maybe I'll have to show you how it's done!'

He took a step forward and then stopped.

Something in the boy's eyes, bright as stars and on the edge of mischief must have drawn off his anger in an instant. 'I'll say it again, Saxon sot-wit!' but his voice was softer.

'Master, my deep apology, I was unwise and will do better in future. But I cannot help who my forebears were and it seems to me we Saxons have a right of conquest in this land, despite our own conquered position by the blamed Normans. We are both conquered peoples, you and I, and should honour our shared state.'

Hywel went to him and cuffed him on the shoulder. 'I suppose now you're going to ask me a riddle just to drive home your superior conquering?'

'I'll do a trance for you if you wish?'

'I can do my own trances, thank you all the same.' He looked at his apprentice oddly. 'These trances of yours, what do you do?'

'I shut my eyes and call on my gods.'

'Easy as that?'

'Don't you find it so when you call on your

gods – or are you as godless as the Normans say?'

'You'd better be calling on your godlings soon enough if I have any more cheek from you. You'll seal your fate with that tongue of yours one of these days. Now, let's get to work. Those lenses need polishing up in the workshop but first I need to satisfy that pilgrim's whim. You know what to do.'

Jankin pulled a face but disappeared into the bushes on the other side of the hedge.

Hildegard decided that it was time to make her presence known.

CHAPTER FIVE

The friar knew all about the knit-bone she wanted, that concoction as Hubert had called it and, smiling, suggested they go up to the drying shed where he would get some for her.

It was a small, aromatic wooden hut, filled with bundles of herbs in different states of preparation hanging from the beams. He measured some of the cure into a glass vial for her at once, saying, 'He's an impatient fellow, your abbot. Nature will take her course.'

'He knows that but imagines he can encourage her to hurry along when he demands it.'

'No one can demand anything of Mother Nature. She has her own times and seasons and we poor mortals can do nought but measure, observe and acquiesce. You should remind your Abbot de Courcy that most people would relish the experience of lying at rest and being waited on.'

'He longs to get back to his own abbey and see how it's been wrecked in his absence.'

'Let's trust his prior and his cellarer were well-chosen.' He handed her the vial after stoppering it with a piece of waxed linen. 'I have an elixir of cider made from our own apples here, domina, if you would care to try some? It's just the thing on such a scorching day.'

Together they went to sit outside on a bench in the shade of a vine which someone had trained around several posts to allow for a kind of canopy against the glare of the sun. It was cooler under the green shade and enchanting with the scent of rosemary and lavender saturating the air.

'Is this sort of weather usual around here, brother?'

'It happens when the planets are in the appropriate alignment. It's a difficult calculation to serve as prophecy, however. Not many bother risk trying to predict the weather to any great extent. Tides, yes, especially here with its strange double tide due to the proximity of the island.'

'That must be a great advantage?'

'It is. It allows the merchants more time to load

and unload their cargoes than at ports further along the coast. The Cistercians at Netley have been rather slow to take advantage of it. They suspect any kind of systematic study of the natural world. They're suspicious of my use of the astrolabe too, some of them imagining it as an instrument only used by astrologers and not of honest seekers after facts.' He leaned towards her. 'Your abbot is interested in it, having traveled to the East, and he said you would be too.'

'I'm interested in all things.'

'He calls you Hildegard.'

'So do most people who like to talk outside the usual run.'

'Then we are Hywel and Hildegard?'

Aware of a sudden devouring ambiguity in his manner, she said hurriedly, 'Of course...but the ship-owner, Master John, seems keen to improve his trade overseas, or so I gather from what he told us. Surely he would never sneer at the use of an astrolabe to predict the tides?'

'Quite so. He sees himself as another Ser

Datini.' He raised his eyebrows to gauge whether she was following him or not.

'The merchant?' When he nodded she said, 'He commands most trading activities along the coast from Rome to Avignon. I heard of him when I was in Florence a few years ago.'

'Just so. Whether our south coast will ever be as profitable as Datini's along the Middle Sea is another matter as we are further from Venice and the east than those ports where he makes his fortune. And whether Master John will take full advantage of his position depends on more than a mere wish for material gain. As do most things in this life.' He frowned. 'Where's that riddling Saxon lad of mine? Jankin?'

A scuffle in the rosemary hedge made him call again. 'Is that you? I know you're there. Come out!'

Grinning, blue eyes dancing, the apprentice appeared carrying a struggling blackbird with limed feet. 'I caught her just as you shouted. You nearly scared her away with your racket.'

'Well, give it here then tell our guest the riddle you tried on me and see if she gets it.'

'I'll keep the bird for a little while as she's trembling with fright.' He crooked his arm so the bird could rest there while he stroked its head with impressive gentleness. 'My riddle, domina, is this: I have a bed but never sleep, I have a mouth but never eat, I run but never walk, what am I?' He gave her a brilliant smile that disarmed her. What an imp he was! 'You may have a little time to solve it, domina, as did the magister.'

'Don't give away my secrets, boy. Entertain us. How old are you?'

'No idea.'

'Eighty-seven?'

'Mebbe thereabouts. How would I know?'

'It's the morning dew you wash in that makes you look about fifteen, is it?'

'Could be.'

'What's the first thing you remember?'

The boy's face, recently mobile with humour, became still. Sensitive to the silence Hywel gave him a nudge with the toe of his boot. 'Cat got your tongue?'

He shook his head. Hywel turned to Hildegard. 'He won't swim with the others lads but sits on the bank like an old dame and watches them. I'm trying to winkle out the truth from him. See what he's made of.'

Turning back to the boy he asked, 'Well, how do you explain it? Are you a witch in disguise, afraid of water?'

'I wish I'd never told you.' He had turned sulky and jutted his lower lip.

'What? And have us wondering why you were frightened washing yourself last full moon?'

'A big wave sweeping all away frightens me. It came to me in a trance.'

'And you with no ark at your command?'

He shook his head and stared at the ground.

'I think some things are private, brother Hywel. This may be one of them.' Hildegard gave the boy a soft glance. He stuck his fists inside his tunic and gazed into the distance.

'How long has he been with you? I see you have probably not lost anything in the feeding of him.'

'Skin and bone, true. Yet he eats more than the abbot's stallion and the entire stable of brood mares together. I don't know where it goes. Into the soles of his feet and down into the pit of hell, maybe.'

'Magister, I am here and hearing. Am I not loyal for all your skimping of victuels?'

'Not in the matter of a mouse you're not.'

A brief and sudden air of antagonism tainted their mood again and Hildegard broke in, 'Back to your riddle, Jankin, might I hazard an answer now I've had time to think it over?'

'What, then?'

'Is it a river?'

He gave a short, sharp smile. 'Join the magister. He got it as well. I can see I'll have to improve my skill if I'm to uphold my Saxon honour.'

'Saxon honour? You mean your paltry victory

at - ?'

'It was enough to rout your useless Welsh Llewellyn and his cowards!'

'You'll pay for that remark if there's any justice in the world.'

'Which there is not as you keep telling me.'

'We'll have to pray harder then, won't we?' He ruffled Jankin's flaxen hair. 'I'm going to take the shears to this crop of wheat one of these days. See if you're so pert when you look like a Welsh lad.'

'You'll have to catch me first!'

'Here, before you go running off, rouse that blackbird snug in your arms and let's fulfil the lady's desire.'

Jankin handed over the bird. It began to struggle at the change but Hywel stroked its head to keep it calm. 'You may go, Saxon, where ere thou wilt. Return before Tierce. You can come into church and help make all right with the world by the power of your prayers.'

'Is he an orphan?' asked Hildegard after he left, charmed by the unlikely sense of equality existing between master and apprentice.

'I found him on the streets of Southampton with a gang of child pick-pockets. They had the audacity to imagine they could pick mine! I soon showed them otherwise. He was the only one to stand his ground and argue with me.' He turned to her with his penetrating dark eyes. 'Imagine that, Hildegard! In his view it was I who was the miscreant for carrying my pouch padlocked to my belt and displayed on my person! "Putting temptation in the way of hungry boys!" he claimed.' He turned to her again with his guileless smile, 'What are we coming to when thieves reckon themselves to inhabit heaven's realm above we poor, innocent, benighted victims? I decided he might as well have a chance to save his soul and work for me. He's a quick learner and not to be bested in anything except in the matter of water and then he's a babe-in-arms.'

Friar Hywel's chuckle showed that with the creation of an air of easeful amity between them she might venture a question.

'Hywel,' she began with his name as they seemed to have moved quickly onto somewhat intimate terms, 'a most wonderful tenor joined in our prayers just now. I haven't seen him before. It made me wonder if he's the rider who came in late last night?'

He gave her a sharp glance. 'What rider?'

'A Welsh-speaking one.'

His face became wooden and he made some play of holding up his cider and inspecting it with more assiduity than it appeared to warrant before observing in an even tone, 'There are many visitors to Netley Abbey…well-placed on Southampton Water as it is. Who can keep track of them all?'

'I imagine one who could keep track would be the man who greeted him in welsh,..Hywel.'

The friar replaced the mug beside them on the bench and turned to her. 'I have a task to accomplish for one of the pilgrim ladies. Would you excuse me?'

His shout brought Jankin springing out of the

bushes again, only stopping when he saw the blackbird held in Hywel's hands. 'I beg you, magister. In all your kindness will you change your mind if I crawl on my hands and knees for a week?'

Hywel ignored him.

Gripping the trembling body of the blackbird between his knees he only grunted, 'Do something useful and pass that knife.'

Jankin reluctantly went inside the hut and returned with a long narrow-bladed knife. For a moment he held it blade outwards as if to ram it into something until he seemed to remember to turn it so that Hywel could grasp the hilt without harm.

The blackbird squirmed between the friar's knees.

Hildegard stared.

Spreading one of its wings, he quickly snipped the pinion feathers then turned the bird around and snipped the corresponding one on its other wing. It took only seconds. The bird lay still. Even its black eyes did not wink, held in a suspension of terror. Hywel thrust it towards Jankin. 'Now take it to her.'

As he reached out the friar changed his mind. 'No, on second thoughts bid the dame fetch it herself. If she gets possession of it she may forget that it needs paying for, both the bird and the remedy she requested.'

The boy went out and Hywel gave Hildegard a long look. Nothing was said.

She picked up the vial of knit-bone and was about to leave when he muttered, 'It felt no pain. There are no means of feeling pain in a bird's pinions.'

'But it cannot fly. How do we know it does not feel another kind of pain at being turned into a creature of earth instead of air?'

He did not answer directly. Instead he got to his feet with the blackbird lying quietly in the crook of his arm and handed it to her. 'Stay a while. I may need your protection. It will be a kindness you may believe I do not deserve.'

She did not have long to find out what he meant. There was a commotion on the path, a trilling call, 'Magister? Magister? Your boy has found me!'

Hildegard was inside the hut pouring a drop of water into a dish to give to the bird, and Delith did not see her from outside. She had her little maid, Lucie, at her heels. Both of them followed Jankin under the canopy of vines. He stood to one side, his eyes wide-open, staring at the maid. Delith pushed her way between them.

'My dear magister, how kind of you, I am grateful beyond words.' Her high voice became more intimate. 'Perhaps there's a way I may show my gratitude?' She paused then added, 'without the gross exchange of coin between us?'

'Payment in coin for the procuring of the bird and its cure will suffice, widow.'

'Come now.' Her tone became a purr. 'We all know how friars prefer to be paid.'

'Do we, indeed?'

At that point, if she had any sense, she would

have stopped there, but she had none and therefore continued in her folly. Hildegard, in astonished immobility, glanced out of the hut in time to see her nudge him familiarly with one elbow. 'You are but a man. And when it comes to it men are all the same.'

'When it comes to it, mistress, I shall endeavour to demonstrate another point of view.' Wooden faced, he moved towards the hut.

Catching sight of Hildegard standing inside with the blackbird in her arms, Delith let out a little scream of surprise.

'Here's your blackbird.' Hildegard held out the bird to forestall any further comment.

Frowning for a moment Delith snatched the bird and then made a great show of pressing it to her cheek despite its struggles to escape, murmuring nonsense about its singing for her alone and how she would love it forever.

'That will be two pence, mistress,' said Hywel firmly, 'and then our business is concluded.'

The air seemed to be burning up when she stepped from under the canopy and walked back into the abbey. The sun continued in its state of serene brilliance. In Cloister Garth which was beginning to serve the function of a village green people were talking of rain with a fervour previously unheard. They dragged themselves from one patch of shade to another. The monks pulled up their hoods against the battering of the sun's rays and then had to push them down again because of the heat engendered by the woolen fabric. The novices droned somniferously at their lessons without reproof. A little group of guests sat in the shade of the cloisters at a distance, and when the bell sounded for Tierce no-one moved.

Lissa and Simon were propped back to back as if finding it cooler that way. Delith fanned herself with the edge of her head-scarf while trying to train the bird to sit on her shoulder and Master John, someone remarked, was wisely out on the river. The two sisters were no-one knew where and the silent yellowish fellow was still staring at the pages of his book but with a stillness that suggested that he had not the strength to trail his eyes across the page.

It seemed no cooler inside the church when Hildegard entered than it did outside. Even the incense seemed to burn like raging coals sending yet more heat into the air as the sacristan swung the censer back and forth. Sweat ran down the faces of those few who could make it as far as the church doors.

Near the altar in the nave a handful of monks, in their snow coloured robes, looked no cooler than anyone else. Egbert, hood thrown back, wiped his hand across his shining forehead and the frizz of hair round his tonsure stood up like very flames themselves. The prior was flush faced. The sacristan's burning candles seemed like a further small assault on the swooning monks. One of the more elderly corrodians dropped to his knees and gripped the side of the misericord as if to draw cold from inside the wood itself.

The prior looked round at his wilting brothers

and took pity on them. 'This will be short. Let us pray.'

The Welshman with the magical voice did not appear as Hildegard regretfully noticed. Hywel and his boy, however, were down near the front, slipping in late and appearing least overcome by the heat than anyone. When the time came to sing Hywel's voice rang out and the boy joined him. After she had seen how they contested the valour of each other it looked to Hildegard now as if they were in contention again, the boy's broken treble still high enough to skirt the top notes like a sky lark while Hywel smiled, accepted defeat, and filled in with a few bass note flourishes.

She thought of the blackbird, rendered earth-bound, and wondered why Delith had wanted the friar to perform a mutilation that would thwart its nature – and why the friar had agreed.

Above all, she wanted to know why Hywel had avoided her question about the rider in the night, the one who spoke Welsh as well as he did.

'My lord, you are in the best place possible today. Outside it's like a baker's oven. Even Gregory is moving slowly if you can believe it.' The joke was that Gregory was never still long enough to catch cold.

Hubert gave a lazy smile. He looked rumpled. His black hair was longer than it should be, the angles of his face boyishly softened by his enforced rest.

'Are you tired?' She peered down at him.

'Somewhat.' He gave a comfortable sigh and moved his dark head on the pillow. 'Whatever's in that concoction of Hywel's it certainly making me feel sleepy enough to – '

He even failed to finish what he was saying and instead gave a long yawn. Hildegard shook her head. 'If this is how you respond to visitors I'd better leave you in peace.'

Raising a hand he gestured towards the end of the chamber. The screens that had been across earlier had been taken down and the bed was occupied by a figure that scarcely made a mound under the one thin cover. 'Mistress Beata would welcome you. I gather she feels bereft by her current lack of company.' Hubert closed his eyes. 'Forgive me, Hildegard. I cannot keep my eyes open. Try as I might. I don't know what he put in that elixir of his.'

Smiling to herself at the sight of Hubert, usually so vigorous, now showing no more strength than a kitten, she went along to see this other patient.

The woman was more alert than Hubert and watched her as she approached and when she was close enough to hear she croaked, 'He said you would come.'

'Who?'

'Your Abbot de Courcy. He said, "My Hildegard will come to amuse you."' Her pale-eyed glance was swift and all-seeing. 'He's a handsome man. His abbey must be teeming with women come to see him under the pretext of piety.'

Hildegard laughed. 'Very shrewd, mistress. That's exactly it. I'm afraid he's rather short on female admiration at present.'

'He'll survive – which is more than I will. Come, sit on the edge of my bed and tell me what's happening outside. This is my lovely saviour, by the way.' She nodded to a soft-footed lay-brother who had silently appeared. 'They're complaining of the heat or so I hear, Alaric?'

He gave a gentle nod, his whole demeanour one of gentleness and forbearance. His soft brown eyes lingered on Mistress Beata's face. 'Are you up to talking, mistress?'

'Don't be dull. She's only just come in. You know I'm dying not only with my lungs but of boredom too. I've complained often enough. Now come and sit down where I can enjoy looking at you.'

'Just so, mistress.' With an indulgent smile, he sat down on a stool at the foot of the bed.

Hildegard settled beside the patient too and they began to talk.

'I'm Beata, wife to Master John of – ' a spasm of coughing shook through her emaciated body and she pointed with a shaking finger towards a beaker on the ledge next to her but Alaric was already on his feet and reaching for it. When the storm had passed she said, 'This will be the death of me. I haven't long now. Worry not, my dears, I am at peace.'

Alaric held the beaker to her lips.

'Is that something made up by the magister?' Hildegard asked.

'Tincture of white horehound. They grow it in abundance at the next vill, hence its name.'

'The place they call Hound?'

'Do you know it?'

Hildegard shook her head.

'Noted for its Monday market. Busy place. Before I took to my bed I went there several times with my man. He's managed to poke a finger into most pies round here since we - ' she broke off than added, 'as I'm sure you've realized if you're as perspicacious as your abbot claims.'

They chatted for a while, Beata asking Hildegard many personal questions which for some reason seemed reasonable and not at all intrusive. She was insatiable, the poor woman, for news of everything happening out in the living world.

Her recurrent spasms of coughing, however, weakened her, and after a short while she touched Hildegard on the arm. 'Come back again, my dear. I like you. We can talk scandal about the monks next time - and then confess our wickedness to one of them - so that it gets back to them and sends them all aflux.'

Her skin had a silken sheen but when she smiled it was covered in the creases caused by age and good-humour and she made a maze of it now at the thought of teasing the monks out of their complacency. Both cheeks were flushed, with two round red circles the size of pennies, a sign, Hildegard knew, of her illness. Her wasted body was no more substantial than a child's.

'I will come again, Beata, and you can tempt me to wickedness if you will. I shall take pleasure in that. I hope we will not shock you, Alaric?'

'I will be my pleasure, domina.' He got to his feet as she left and bowed with a soft smile.

When she passed Hubert's cubicle a few moments later he was sound asleep.

He will regard it as the plotting of women against the world of men, she thought as she went out into the furnace of Cloister Garth. To tease the monks. Hubert wasn't above doing that himself when he thought they were becoming too serious. She imagined the plotting Mistress Beata might have had to do to keep hold of her husband. He was a man who would require those about him to run to keep up.

Before she could go further she heard a flurry of voices and a man's jovial laughter from over by the gatehouse. Glancing across she saw the two sisters and the day porter in conversation. He seemed to be wearing a strange, wide-brimmed straw hat that came down over his eyes and the girls were laughing and encouraging him as he spread his arms like a blind man and blundered into them, an excuse, Hildegard assumed, to make free with them as if helpless to do otherwise.

The girls had a dozen or so hats on strings over their shoulders.

'Come on, master, try this one instead. This is the one to make your girl swoon,' called Mistress Sweet persuading him to don a smaller one. She clapped. 'That's perfect! I could swoon over you myself if you were not already spoken for.'

'It was made for you,' agreed Mistress Sour. 'A very nice fit.' She sounded not at all sour but light-hearted and well-pleased with something. It could not be the weather, surely? thought Hildegard, unless it was the extra trade the sun happened to bring them.

The rest of the guests were still lying in the shade of the nearby cloister. Now Mistress Lissa called over. 'What have you got there, my dears?'

Mistress Sour went over, content to leave her sister to finish the deal with the porter, and unhooking the hats from her shoulder as she went. 'See, Lissa, we went to the market in Hound to sell our cheese and instead we bartered it for these straw hats. We took all the vendor had and he has promised us more for next week if we wish. But I demurred because the weather will probably break and we'll be left with sun hats when what we'll probably need are waterproofs against the rain.'

'These would do nicely as either,' suggested Lissa, taking one of the hats and putting it on over her coif and her abundant hair. 'I love these broad brims. How do I look, Simon?' She nudged her husband awake. 'Shall I have it?'

'What's that, my dear?' He blinked up at his wife.

'You silly old owl, look at me! What do I have on my head?'

'Charming, my sweet. You look beautiful in everything you put on.' He began at once to delve into his pouch. 'I am so taken, I shall buy it for you as a memento of our stay at Netley Abbey.'

'My pet, what would I do without you? But I had no intention of allowing you to buy it for me -'

'I know. But it is my delight.' He addressed Mistress Sour. 'And do you have one of these for men folk or did that porter get the last one? You should know we feel the sun's hammer blows as much as women, if not more so, because of our thinner thatch.'

Mistress Sour selected one for him and he put it on. 'Double sale,' he said to her. 'Try the rest of these folk. I doubt there's not one who won't buy.'

Mistress Sweet came up. She had a secret smile. 'And we've scarcely set foot in the abbey. I am so happy. We've had a lovely day, Genista.'

Simon was right. Everybody bought one and even Hildegard, reluctant at first, allowed herself to be cajoled into being fitted out. 'There is really nothing more perfect in this weather,' she excused her vanity. 'How clever you both are to think of getting hold of so many.'

Still half-drugged by the heat and thankful for her sunhat as she stepped out into the glare she headed towards the guest house with the idea of lying down for a while in the cool of her chamber. Taking a mis-turn, however, she found herself not at the foot of the stairs leading to the upper floor but in a small corridor off the ground-floor entrance.

With the idea that the stairs might be concealed behind one of the doors that faced her she pushed at the first one she came to. When it swung open she was astonished to see a small chamber with a high window through which sunlight shone in a bright gleam onto a man sitting at a table. A goblet and a jug of ale were to hand. His shirt was unstrung and his naked feet were resting comfortably on a foot-stool.

Very much at ease he glanced up as startled as she was when the door flew open. She backed out with a mumbled apology. His hand, she noticed, had darted at once to the knife on the table in front of him. What was more unexpected was that she recognised him. It was the mysterious visitor with the rich and powerful tenor voice.

Confused and a little annoyed with herself at being put-out by the unexpectedness of the encounter, she hesitated when she reached the entrance lobby then decided to return and offer a greeting and an apology in Welsh. Better, she decided, to risk stirring up trouble than to live in a state of uneaseful ignorance.

She went back along the passage and reached the door at the exact moment that the key was swiveled in the lock against intruders.

'So that's how it is,' she told Gregory and Egbert when they met later in the guest refectory. 'But you said you would ask the porter at the gatehouse when he came back on duty, Egbert. He must know who he is and to whom he owes his allegiance. Have you spoken to him yet?'

'We'll have to wait until Vespers unless you fancy lining up the conversi and giving them an inquisition. They'll know who he is if anybody does.' He gestured towards the building where the laymen and women had separate living quarters.

'They'll be less tight-lipped than that day-porter. He wouldn't even look me in the eye when I asked him. Clearly something was bothering him.'

'Friar Hywel knows too but refused to answer when I asked him.'

'Something's up. Arundel's man planted here? For what reason?'

'At least he's not bothering us. If he'd wanted us he'd have shown his hand by now.' Egbert, as usual, looked on the side of things that would cause least concern.

'Any man of Arundel's is a threat to us,' Gregory observed. 'I'll be glad when we're out of his domain and into more friendly territory in the north.'

CHAPTER SIX

The two sisters had made sure they kept a straw hat aside for Master John because when he came into the precinct looking hot and harassed they were lying in wait for him in the cloisters nearest the gate house. Evidently they did a deal with him of some sort because he at once put a hat on his head at a rakish angle and swept Mistress Sweet into a quick hug. The three of them got into conversation at once and established themselves a little way away from the other guests as if to talk business.

Delith noticed this and took it as an excuse to stroll past with her blackbird and her little, faithful maid, as if she had not even noticed them. To give him credit, Master John scarcely looked up either.

'The example of Ser Datini must be ever uppermost in our merchant's mind,' Gregory observed after Hildegard had explained what the friar had told her. 'I'm still wondering where he hails from, this Master John. He seems to be a rather large fish for this particular sea.'

'Maybe he's extending his business down from Southampton,' Egbert suggested.

'There hardly seems any point when there's good such harbourage up at the town quay.'

'It seems to me his accent is rather further north than Hampshire,' Hildegard added. 'He sounds like a Midlander and if he is it might account for him trading outside the jurisdiction of the Southampton merchants. They won't be likely to accept him in the Guild if he's an outsider.'

'And, to his advantage, they can't dictate to him here and he doesn't have to account to them either,' added Egbert.

'Ah,' Gregory murmured, and left it at that.

'Friar, tell me if you will, when will this weather break as break it must?' It was Master John himself, dabbing at his face with a linen cloth as he spoke. The two sisters had retreated indoors. Mistress Delith was sitting in the shadow of the cloister again with her little entourage and watching Master John with a small, pious lowering of her lids whenever he glanced at her.

'My impatience,' the merchant continued, 'is because I need to get my goods unloaded from my ship as soon as we can bring her into the near channel. Better to bring a cargo off in good weather than bad, don't you think?'

'I beg your indulgence, master, but I'm no weather prophet.'

'But you are a prophet, or so I've heard?'

'I'm little more than a herberer, master, although I happen to dabble in astronomy which some fools mistake for astrology. A profound difference exists as I'm sure I don't need to tell you. The one is a proper study of the stars and planets and the other is a fanciful idea that we can see into the future by staring witlessly at the night sky. I regard astrology as the work of the devil along with numerology, necromancy, palmistry, cards of all kinds and every other kind of divination.'

'No summoning of devils for you then?"
Master John guffawed at the idea. 'But surely,
magister, by looking at the stars, measuring their
courses, you can tell when war and famine are
written there? It must be so.'

'Must?'

'Of course! Just look at the moon and its effect
on the great waters of the world. No-one these
days disputes that the one causes the other, do
they?'

Hywel shook his head. 'That is true and I
suppose from that you deduce that the other
planets affect us in ways too subtle for us to
measure?'

'It seems reasonable. The problem is that your
spy-glasses are not powerful enough. But the time
will come. I'm convinced of it.'

'Should it be my purpose to interfere with
God's design?' The friar gave an uncertain smile.
'What I can predict with my astrolabe…' he
paused for effect'

John leaned forward, 'Yes?'

'…are the tides.'

John snapped his head back in a laugh. 'You caught me there, you rogue. But it's not to denigrate your skill to ask for more. We merchants need to know where to send our goods and when. Imagine how even more useful it would be to know when markets are going to rise and fall so that we could send goods to catch the tide of buying and selling? So far we have to rely on our native wit as those two young sisters have demonstrated with their straw hats today. How much more reliable a chart of some sort would be if it could tell us when to sell our most costly items and when to keep them in the knowledge that a better price will come.'

'But if such knowledge is generally known any advantage would surely be lost?'

'But then, magister, the speed and courage of the merchant would determine the victor.'

'I beg your graceful indulgence at my foolish limitations,' Hywel said with an exaggerated lilting of his accent. 'I am not and can never be your man. The Church frowns on dabblings into divination. Scrying into the future is rightly seen as an attempt to control His Divine Purpose and subvert it to our own ends. It would attract those whose only wish is for total domination.'

Hildegard and the two monks exchanged looks. They watched Master John move off, smiling, unaware that he was being tailed again by Delith and her patient little maid. Delith, meanwhile, was making a great show of petting her blackbird with many little pouting kisses although to a close observer, judged Hildegard, she was holding it to her shoulder with what might have been regarded as sheer force.

She recalled now the slap across the face of that little angel with its halo of blonde corkscrew curls peering out from a mound of fabric in the guest chamber on the evening she had arrived. The young lad carrying the clothes chest must have been Jankin.

'Have you been into his secret chamber yet?' Gregory interrupted her reverie.

'Whose?'

'Brother Hywel's.'

'I didn't know he had one. And why should it be I to enter it?'

'Of we three you seem to have had most to do with him.'

'Only on errands for Hubert to the herb garden. He's got an insatiable desire to walk again and it's knit-bone all the time – which I doubt can fulfil all the high claims he makes for it.'

'He?'

'Hubert.'

'He'll have to learn patience as he's always advising us,' Egbert chuckled with satisfaction. 'It's a case of the biter bit!...I wouldn't mind having a look inside the friar's den though. He's got an astrolabe in there, they say.'

'Why don't we go and ask him if he'll show us how it works?' Gregory made no move to shift from his comfortable perch on the half wall of the cloister.

'If you want to scorch yourself by going out

into the desert of the Garth then do so.' Egbert didn't move.

'I've got one of Mistress Sour's sunhats and so have we all. This is nothing to Outremer. Our Saracen brothers would laugh at us. Come on, old fellow, let's go. It's a while until Vespers.'

'Who are you calling old fellow?' Egbert was off the wall with alacrity and half way across the blazing garth almost before Gregory himself got down. Hildegard watched them go and then, on an impulse, decided to follow.

They had only gone half-way across when a commotion at the gate house drew their attention and that of others about the place. What they saw was the day porter and his lad outfacing three newcomers leading horses under the archway. They wore mail but were bare-headed and suffering from the sun. Their horses were accoutred in the cloth of some lord and well-appointed. The porter had called for them to stop and they were choosing to ignore him.

Hildegard put a hand on Gregory's arm.

The porter's voice came to them clearly. 'I have my orders. No arms within the abbey precinct. It has always been so. I have no instructions to say otherwise.'

All three men were wearing swords.

Ignoring that fact the porter reached out to grasp the bridle of the first horse to bring it to a halt. Its rider came round from the other side and pushed him away.

Hildegard felt Gregory and Egbert come simultaneously to full alert. 'Don't!' she warned. 'We're on abbey land.'

'You don't need to tell us,' Egbert muttered.

Without a word he and Gregory set off towards the gatehouse.

Hildegard felt a shiver run through her. Now she had had a proper look at the colours on the horse's caparisons she recognised them. They were those of the earl of Arundel.

Hurrying after her two companions to warn them she came up just as the porter was repeating his request. His voice wavered a little. 'We cannot have armed men within the abbey precinct and if you object I shall have to seek out the abbot himself to find out if there's a new rule I know nothing about.'

'He's right,' Egbert interrupted. 'But there is no such ruling. We are men of peace here. Leave your weapons at the gatehouse like good fellows and then you will be most welcome.'

A second man called, 'and who might you be?'

'I might ask you the same question,' replied Egbert easily.

'I'm the captain. Answer my question.'

'My captain, if you want to put it that way, is the abbot of this precinct, and this man here is his deputy and it is he who decides who comes in and whether they are allowed to bear arms. Do as he says and all will be over. I can see you've had a hard ride and would prefer to be sitting in the cool of the refectory drinking cold ale.'

'Aye, we would,' the captain agreed with a sneer, 'but with our own swords by our sides.

Now move back and let us in.'

He was a raw-boned, dark-haired fellow, not old but old enough to be conscious of the sharpness of his sword, the protection afforded by his mail shirt and the power and ruthlessness of the lord who maintained him.

By contrast Egbert was approaching forty, he was unarmed, and his only protection was a Being whose general design for mankind was unknown.

Undeterred, the monk folded his arms. 'You can't come in unless you leave your swords in the gatehouse. They'll be safe there. It's a clear enough request.'

'I'm not accustomed to monks telling me what to do. Move aside.'

'I don't think I will,' replied Egbert in a disarmingly good-natured tone.

'We'll see about that, you bloody tonsured…' Words seemed to fail him. 'Now I'm telling you. Get out of my way before I cut you down!' He pushed his way in front of his companions. In the silence that followed, his sword, partly withdrawn from its sheath as a warning, made a surprisingly loud sound.

Egbert stood without moving.

By now a crowd had gathered. The porter was sweating. His boy was wide-eyed with fright.

Master John had come over and one or two others including Simon, hobbling on his stick, and Delith, clutching the blackbird, and accompanied as always by her little maid. Out of the corner of her eyes Hildegard noticed Hywel and young Jankin and one or two lay-brothers coming to see what was up. The rest formed a loose circle round the intruders but none of them could do much, unarmed, untrained and in one or two cases, too old, against three young, fit, armed men spoiling for a fight.

The first man started to lead his horse forward, deliberately brushing past the porter so that he had to step hurriedly back to avoid being trampled. Everybody froze as they came on.

Then Gregory made a move. It was a small movement of his right hand, scarcely noticed by anyone until they saw a sword glittering full-length out of its sheath with the monk pointing it without a tremor at its owner's throat.

There was a belated gasp.

Gregory's voice was pleasant and unhurried. 'Do as the porter says. You heard my brother ask you courteously to hand over your swords. Now I am asking you. With perhaps less courtesy.'

'Go on, Jack. Push past him. He won't touch you!' roared the captain of the trio.

Gregory drew a delicate line across the man's throat. 'You do keep a sharp sword, Jack,' he complimented as a thread of red, springing, and drop by drop gathering and trickling down inside the mail shirt, appeared. Jack himself was gazing fixedly at Gregory as if in a dream.

Simon had hobbled to the front of the group and was leaning on his wife's shoulder because Egbert had grasped his stick in both hands.

A long silence ensued when nobody moved.

Gregory was the first to lose patience. 'Let's take them,' he said out of the corner of his mouth to Egbert.

Afterwards nobody could say exactly in what order events took place. The end of it was clear, however. Jack was lying on the ground underneath his horse's hoofs, groaning, two swords were somehow transferred from their owners to the porter and his lad who then hurried inside the gatehouse and slammed the door, and the three surprised intruders were staring at two monks, one armed with a hazel stick and one with a purloined sword, both smiling in a most unwarlike manner.

'Now you may enter the holy precinct of Netley,' announced Gregory with a sweep of an arm towards the abbey.

A burst of applause arose from the onlookers and the blackbird gave its first melodious trill.

CHAPTER SEVEN

When the three new-comers had been conducted to the guest-master's office by a large and sturdy-looking bunch of abbey servants the crowd was reluctant to break up. It was shortly before Vespers anyway and there was no point in leaving the garth with so much to talk about.

'Who would imagine two unarmed monks could best a trio of armed men?'

'Three against two,' someone else emphasized.

'That they should even contemplate entering abbey grounds fully armed like that,' said someone else. 'It's beyond belief.'

The yellowish man with the book came up belatedly and they turned to explain everything to him but he seemed to know what had happened. 'I was over in the cloister,' he explained. 'I saw it all. Most impressive. Like Ajax and Achilles.'

Hywel fell into step beside the two monks as they began to head towards the church. 'That was neat,' he remarked. 'Did you acquire such skills before making your vows, or afterwards?'

'Whatever we learned was acquired in boyhood and how we honed our skills has come from long years on the road to Jerusalem.' Egbert looked back at the sunlit garth. 'This hot weather brings it all back. We might be outside the sacred walls at this very moment.' He wore a look of regret, then, somewhat bemused, turned abruptly to enter the dark portal of the church.

'That porter and his lad were quick to take advantage of events,' Hildegard observed as she and the two Cistercians from Meaux stood together in the shade of the porch afterwards. The sun was still burning down. Few guests had attended the mid-day Office. They were not obliged to do more than show up at Prime and attend the short mass that followed, although the more devout pilgrims went to the other canonical offices as they felt the need.

'I see they've got reinforcements over there,'

Gregory observed with a glance towards the gatehouse. 'Let's stroll over and see what they make of it. Then I must go inside out of this molten heat and do some reading.'

So saying they went over to be greeted with great good-heart by the day porter. 'And here they are, the heroes of the hour,' he exclaimed to the night porter and his boy who had joined him in the shade under the arch.

'We were saying how quick off the mark you were,' Egbert grinned. 'Where are their weapons now?'

'Under lock and key.' He added with a lugubrious expression, 'I expect the abbot will be having something to say about it tomorrow morning at Chapter.'

'Nothing much he can say but to condemn such presumption,' Gregory suggested.

He shrugged and frowned in reply and his colleague gave a mocking laugh. 'We shall see, brother, we shall see.'

'I'm not counting on anything,' the day porter

admitted. 'I only hope somebody will speak on my behalf.' He looked worried.

'Is there any doubt?' exclaimed Egbert. 'We all saw what happened with our own eyes.'

'You might escape censure, brother, being from foreign parts, and with your abbot here to defend you, but it might well be different for me.'

'Count on us,' replied Gregory, looking puzzled. 'We're not to be trifled with. You did what you could.'

'Speaking of that,' Egbert interrupted. 'Are they the only mercenaries in the abbey at present?'

'You asked me that before…'

The night porter stepped forward. 'Leave this to me, Osric. Brother,' he lowered his voice and took Egbert by the arm. 'We owe it to you to let the identity of the man who arrived in the night be known to you. We owe it to you especially after what happened just now. He's one of the Welsh militia leaders who rode with Arundel in the north a while back and he's been part of the earl's personal body-guard ever since.'

'I feared as much,' Egbert replied. He shot a glance at Gregory who was listening to this with a wooden face.

Hildegard moved closer as the night porter whispered a name into Egbert's ear. It was loud enough for her worst fears to be confirmed. 'It's Glyn Dwr. Prince Owain as his men call him.'

'Riding with no men of his own?' Egbert looked puzzled.

'Aye, we've discussed that among ourselves already but we've come up with no good answer. He obviously doesn't want to draw attention to himself. Is it to have a secret look at the lie of the land, do you reckon?'

'Or the sea and its safe havens?' suggested the day-porter.

'Or, indeed, both?' Egbert concluded. He turned to Gregory. 'We were right to be concerned.'

Hildegard had heard mixed reports about Owain Glyn Dwr. True, he marched with Arundel but then the earl held land in Wales close to Glyn

Dwr's manor at Sycharth and it was common-sense to maintain good relations with so powerful a neighbour. On the other hand Arundel was a known enemy of King Richard – he had amply demonstrated his allegiance at the recent Merciless Parliament – and that was surely a fact that told them all they needed to know about Glyn Dwr's allegiance as well.

'Is Arundel planning a move against the French again?' Hildegard asked. 'If Glyn Dwr is here to look over the river ports it could mean Arundel is planning to assemble his invasion fleet here.'

'It could very well be, domina, and if that's the case Netley Abbey will be on the front line.'

An air of gloom hung over the three of them as they departed. 'No more than two hours ago we were wondering what to do with ourselves and planning a visit to view the astrolabe,' Egbert broke the silence. 'Now we have to think of our lord abbot's safety. If there is going to be a bit of a fight he's in no position to defend himself. We shall have to have him moved.'

'That'll be an uphill struggle unless it's straight back to Yorkshire.'

'He can't even walk on crutches yet,' Hildegard pointed out.

'We'd better leave off thoughts about astronomy at present and go and inform him of this latest turn.' Gregory led the way when the others nodded.

'Keep him calm, Hildegard. You know what he's like,' murmured Egbert as they crossed the garth.

When they reached the infirmary it was a pool of welcome shade but with no time to waste they made straight for Hubert's cubicle only to find their host, the abbot of Netley himself, already ensconced in a wooden chair that had been dragged from elsewhere.

He treated the monks to a lordly smile, greeted Hildegard in a flustered manner, then bade them all be seated. Hubert, eyes like two black pits, face as wan as ever, was lying back with what Hildegard could only describe to herself as a skeptical attitude.

Thinking it was something to do with their sudden appearance in a group she was surprised when he said, 'Honoured though I am for your attention, Abbot Philip and I were discussing a serious matter to do with the security of the abbey.'

'You mean that fracas at the gate earlier on?' asked Egbert, straight to the point. But he was wrong.

'My porter over-stepped the mark there. I'm at pains to comply with every wish and command of earl Arundel's vassal as the porter well knows. He should have let them in.'

'But with respect, my lord, they were fully armed and had no intention of handing over their weapons.'

'I shall hear your version of events at Chapter.' Philip inclined his head. 'I'd like to hear your version, brother.'

'And so should I,' Hubert interrupted, regaining control over the conversation. 'But this is something deeper of which that is but a symptom. With your permission, abbot?'

'Oh, please do, yes, please go ahead, Hubert. By all means. I fear there will be no other solution than the one we've discussed.'

Intrigued, Hildegard sat down next to Hubert, being careful not to allow her sleeve to touch his and Egbert and Gregory arrayed themselves about the cubicle as best they could.

'It is this,' Hubert began. He lay back for a moment with his head on the pillow and Hildegard thought how handsome he looked even with his pupils dilated by Hywel's poppy tincture and his face as white as parchment. Hair too long, she noted, as he began to speak, but how black it is, how softly rumpled it looks and she longed to reach out.

'Abbot Philip has brought a dilemma to my notice which, sadly in these unfortunate times, is not unique,' he was saying when she brought her attention back. 'He has told me in confidence, of course,' Hubert opened both eyes and pierced each of them in turn with a look that would allow no loose talk, 'that he is being forced to pay a tribute of considerable and regular sums for a detachment of militia to defend him from attack. The abbey is vulnerable. It is not a castle. It was not built to be so. Its founders believed that the sanctity of its inhabitants was protection enough.'

Gregory made a small impatient movement but said nothing.

Hubert continued. 'Abbot Philip fears that there are people posing as pilgrims within the abbey precincts, allies of those who threaten him. Three armed men, as we know, arrived this very day, sent by their overlord to escort the wagon carrying the earl's imported goods from off the St Marie. But what else might they demand? He does not know. All he knows is that should he fail to keep up his payments he will have no protection. He is not sure what to do about it.'

Before either Gregory or Egbert could interrupt

Hubert gave a faint smile. 'I can read the minds of my two brothers, knowing well their characters. They will say as I do that you should throw these people out.' His glance fell full on Abbot Philip who seemed to shrink in his chair.

He gnawed his lip and eventually managed to say, 'Then the knight whom I cannot name would attack us in the knowledge that the earl himself would turn a blind eye.'

Hubert did not sigh audibly but the suggestion of one hung in the air. 'After I'd got rid of the enemies within,' he continued, 'I'd hire a handful of mercenaries, a couple of good archers, swordsmen, such like, make sure the abbey's defences were in good repair, ensure enough food in my cellars for a short siege, then make my stand. I would also send messengers to our headquarters at St Mary Graces in London and to our French one at Citeaux, giving them the full story and demanding that they bring their influence to bear on the Pope, on Parliament, and the King. As it's a question of a local lord I would find out his enemies and enlist their help with the promise of a manor or two for their pains.'

'I agree,' Gregory said at once.

'And so do I,' Egbert growled.

'I see.' The abbot pulled at his vestments and looked thoughtful. 'All that will be quite an undertaking.'

'Your alternative is to pay up and pay and pay again until the abbey's resources are so depleted your work here will be impossible.'

Abbot Philip said slowly as if working out an alternative, 'When thieves break in it's as well to hide one's treasure.'

'The thing to do, if I may have permission to speak,' broke in Hildegard, not waiting for an answer, 'is not to allow them to break in in the first place.'

Hubert nodded and closed his eyes. If it came to an attack on the abbey he knew he would be useless in a fight at present.

'I see you are in accord, my lord abbot, brothers - domina,' he added belatedly as if not wishing to admit her presence now she had seen him weak in front of others. 'Quite in accord and remarkably so, quite in agreement, yes, all concurring. However, I fear my prior and the rest will not sing with one voice.'

'Maybe it's something you will discuss in Chapter?' suggested Hubert.

'I could never do that. We cannot discuss hiring paid killers. We are monks. We are vowed not to raise arms against our fellow man.'

'Even though they make free use of your abbey and are draining its resources to nothing?' Hubert's disdain was barely concealed. 'Do you not have a duty to protect those who have given you their trust? What do you imagine will happen to them if the abbey is attacked?'

'Nobody would dare to harm us.' Despite his words he looked uncertain. 'If we pay – if we pay the knight who has promised us protection we shall be safe. He has given his word.'

'Meanwhile he asks more and more from you.' Hubert closed his eyes.

Abbot Philip saw it as a sign to withdraw. 'My prayers are with you, my dear Hubert. I trust my people will continue to give you the best care they can.'

When he left in a rustle of crisp linen Hildegard realized that the friar had entered on gossamer footsteps in the silent manner she had noticed before. She wondered how long he had been standing there and if he was one of the enemies within.

When he saw that Hildegard had noticed him he moved off just as silently to the far end of the long chamber.

Gregory waited until they were alone then told Hubert about the presence of Glyn Dwr in the abbey and the suspicion that Arundel was planning to use it as a base for an invasion of France. 'It makes Netley a place under the menace of the war lords, not the haven we imagined,' he finished. 'I suspecte4d all was not as it seems.'

Hubert glared down at the contraption fitted round his broken leg. 'Knit, curse you,' he muttered, then corrected himself. 'Please God and all the angels in heaven, allow my wound to heal so that I may more perfectly fulfil your divine will, amen.'

'What do you make of that, then?' Egbert asked as they eventually left Hubert to take his medicine and sleep.

'I praise the lord that Hubert is our abbot,' Gregory replied. 'I also suggest that we keep an eye on those three cut-throats who forced their way in here as if they had permission from someone with power.'

'Whether Abbot Philip likes it or not, by capitulating to this vassal of Arundel's he lays himself open to the abbey being taken over. Unless he fights back there'll be nothing to stop it being used as a military base.'

'Can he really accept a situation like that?' Hildegard looked askance.

Gregory gave a dry smile. 'Does your chamber

door have a lock, Hildegard? I suggest you use it.'

'He'll keep on paying. There will be no attack.' Egbert was adamant.

'We can't leave Hubert to defend himself, if it does come to it. What are we going to do about that?' Hildegard glanced back towards the infirmary with an anxious frown.

Shadows were lengthening across the garth and filling in the spaces between the arches of the cloisters. Despite the lingering heat she shivered. 'I wish we could get out of here. It's beautiful but it's full of subterfuge.'

'Fear not. No-one will attack because Abbot Philip will go on paying until he has nothing left,' Egbert repeated. 'It's really not our concern. As for Arundel and his plans, it's better to keep the place intact so he can use it. All the monks need to do is keep on praying.' He frowned. 'I do hate to see the militia make fools of our Order, though. They think we're sitting ducks.'

'We can only wait and see what their plan is. It may be no more than tribute they're after,' said

Gregory. 'What I don't like is the idea of Glyn Dwr spying out the land. His presence puts our suspicions on a different footing. Far more serious is the menace of war.'

'Southampton won't allow any but the king's ships there.'

'And an invasion of France is expressly against the king's wishes.'

'And don't forget Lord Berners was executed on the orders of Gloucester for starting secret peace talks with Charles of France. King Richard is betrayed on all sides by Gloucester and the other two war-mongers.'

'One of whom seems to have Netley Abbey in his pocket,' finished Hildegard.

The friar came up behind them. 'A scene of beauty and tranquility,' he observed, falling into step beside them. 'Who would imagine that under the surface all is not at peace?'

Hildegard gave him a close look. His face, angular and intelligent, with those burning eyes that gave no clue as to the purpose of his remark was turned to her. She greeted him in Welsh. He offered a complicit smile in return. What did he want to find out? She wondered. Did he suspect that they knew Glyn Dwr was secretly within the precinct?

'Earlier today,' he began, 'before we were invaded,' he gave an ironic smile, 'I heard some comment about my astrolabe.' His spoke in English to include them all. 'Would you care to have a look at it?'

Gregory gave him a side-long glance. 'Where is it?'

'This way. Follow, if you will.'

It was a small, close chamber built onto the end of the house where the conversi, the lay-brothers lived as if it had once been a store for their goods but had somehow been taken over. With a long window down one side giving an even light onto a work bench, it was sheltered from the glare of the sun by its northerly aspect. Despite this the shutters were flung wide to draw in a slight breeze and the first thing Hywel did was close the top section, casting a gloom over the cell.

'Jankin!' he called. The apprentice shuffled from out of a pile of blankets in the corner.

'Been sleeping?'

'I deemed it too hot to run errands, magister, even for you.'

'Don't give me any of your cheek. Show deference to your betters. Here, who are these visitors?'

'The three monastics from a far-away abbey in the North of England,' the boy replied.

'And what do you know about them?'

'What should I know?'

'I asked first.'

'Nothing, magister.'

'Diplomatic, good. And what do they know about us?'

'Everything, I shouldn't wonder.'

'Is that so?' Hywel turned suddenly to scrutinize Brother Gregory for an answer.

Unperturbed Gregory exclaimed, 'I doubt

whether anyone can know everything about anyone else. Heaven forfend! We would never have our swords out of our grasp.' He was standing near Hywel's work bench and glanced casually along it. 'Is this it?'

He pointed a long finger at a brass dish-shaped object with numerals incised round its edges.

'Pick it up. See if you can work it out,' offered Hywel. Turning to Jankin he said, 'Get us something to drink, there's a good lad.'

When Jankin had gone out Hywel said, 'It has a thousand uses. My use is to predict the tides around the coast here. I can tell you when there will be a high tide three months hence.'

'Will that be important – three months hence?' Gregory asked, as guileless as could be.

'Who can tell? A more subtle instrument may be needed to forecast something of that order.'

'Three months? Noihing more definite than that?' Gregory gave him a level stare.

'I am not a necromancer.'

'We've heard otherwise,' riposted Egbert.

'As you would from the ignorant. They know no better.'

Just then one of the young lay-brothers carrying a jug of wine and three wooden beakers followed Jankin inside. 'Where shall I set them down?'

'Anywhere you like,' Hywel instructed off-handedly. He did not address him by name but turned back to the astrolabe which he took from Gregory as if retrieving his most precious possession, which, indeed, it may have been.

The servant placed the jug on the bench along with the three beakers and paused as if unsure whether to pour or not.

'Alaric, are you waiting to see it burst into flames or something? Fill them, will you?' Hywel turned back to what interested him more.

Alaric flushed slightly, filled the beakers then searched quickly for his master's goblet, filling it to the brim. He glanced at Jankin and raised his eyebrows. Jankin gave a quick glance at Hywel then nodded towards a small cup on a shelf. Afterwards, job done, he melted back against the wall but did not leave. Hywel was too busy explaining the instrument to notice.

It was the same lay-brother who attended Mistress Beata. Despite the fact that they often looked similar in their short fustian tunics and bare feet Alaric was noticeable for his fine, slender features and his gentle manner. He had been treated kindly by Mistress Beata and been welcomed by her.

It was a fact that lads from the poor farming families who were too many to keep were sent to the abbeys as servants. In lieu of cash they were given board and lodging and a life of order in an unpredictable world. Only the rich and well-connected filled the ranks of the brotherhoods. She thought it unfair that money rather than native wit, temperament or ability should determine the status of these children. Without servants the great abbeys could not survive because they did all the hard labour both on the granges and within the precincts and there was never a monk or nun who did not have several servants always on hand.

What was worse, in Hildegard's opinion, was that they were not allowed to learn to read or write so their prospects were limited within the Orders.

Alaric was a delicate-looking youth of about eighteen, sturdy calves browned by the sun, clipped fair hair, Saxon colouring with eyes in that shade of blue that always seems to be looking into the distance. He moved neatly, like a dancer, yet his apparent pleasure in being useful seemed to hide an air of melancholy.

The men were still discussing the workings of the astrolabe and when Hywel handed it back to Gregory she asked about the thousand uses.

'The measurements of the stars and the motion of the planets, time-keeping therefore, making the timing of the canonical hours more constant and not reliant on the sun, navigation, surveying.' He smiled. 'It was invented, so we're told, by one of your kind, domina, by Hypatia, a woman mathematician in Ancient Greece.'

'I've heard so. May I have a closer look at it when Gregory has sated his curiosity? It was explained to me how to work it long ago and I wonder if I can remember what I was told.'

'Do so, by all means.'

The two youths, Jankin, the apprentice, and the less-privileged Alaric were crowding as close as they dare to watch Brother Gregory, with the disc resting on one shoulder, try to align the rete with the symbols. While their attention was fixed Hywel took the opportunity to tap Jankin on the shoulder.

'Now we have the presence of a jury let's go through your theft again.'

Jankin went white. 'My theft, magister?'

Hywel nodded. 'I entrusted you with the capture of a mouse. You brought me one and then, lo! You claimed my mouse had run off. I suspect you were lying to me. What do you think, brother?' He appealed to Egbert who was fingering through a book lying open on the bench.

'I?' He glanced at Jankin. 'Did it run off?'

Jankin nodded.

'With encouragement or is that another lie?'

asked Hywel. After a long and delicate pause, he asked, 'Why did you let it go?'

Jankin was silent for too long because Hywel repeated the question and then asked, 'You must have had a reason or are you truly a sot wit and do things without purpose?'

'If I let him go I did it because it's a living thing and I love all things that live.'

Alaric made a movement in the shadows quickly stifled.

'I see,' said Hywel. 'So having established the fact that you disobeyed me - *if* you let it go, as you prevaricate – then comes the question of punishment.'

'It's punishment enough to know I've fallen into your trap and admitted to being the agent of its escape and been bested by a Welshman into the bargain.'

'Enough punishment for so heinous a sin as lying to me? Tell me, if it had been a crocodile with snapping jaws would you have let it go?'

'I doubt it because in the heat of the moment as

its jaws came down I would have weighed my own life with the good I may do in the world compared it to the good a crocodile might do then weighted the matter in my own favour.'

'A process which demonstrates that you regard your own worth, though more than that of a crocodile, as less, in fact than that of a mouse?' Hywel opened his eyes in mock astonishment.

Jankin shifted, angry with himself for a moment, but found nothing to say in his own defence.

'So where is my mouse now? C'mon, don't compound your insolence.'

'He's here.' He stepped back as he brushed his pouch with something in it. His fists clenched.

'Show me,' Hywel demanded.

Jankin couched one hand inside and held the other cupped as, between his fingers, a mouse peered out.

Hywel nodded. 'I see it. The creature touched your heart, did it? There's no accounting for what moves us. Well, don't just stand there. Are you going to feed the little monster?'

'I give him my crumbs, magister,' Jankin muttered in a sullen tone.

'I have some spare cheese here so why don't you give it that? Alaric, fetch the cheese.'

'Are you intending to fatten him up the better to complete your work?' Jankin asked with a wary expression.

Hywel laughed. 'Do you think so darkly of me? I'm quite disarmed by your argument for the value of life even though you did not take it to its conclusion. Are you disarmed too, Alaric?' Without waiting for a reply he took a crumb of the proferred cheese and held it out. 'Feed it. Let's see how tame we can make it.'

'It's a he, magister, with a wife and a little family.'

'Is he really doing experiments on mice?' Hildegard asked as she left the dark little cell with Gregory and Egbert and stepped out into the heated afternoon.

'It seems so. He's curious about everything, their substance, their habits, what they are capable of doing. Did you see the books on that shelf?' Egbert was impressed.

'I expect he's dabbling in the dark arts,' Gregory looked scathing. 'Despite his denial we saw many would-be necromancers when we were overseas, men like him, whose curiosity leads them down many a dark and evil path to the gates of hell itself. A necromancer to his finger-tips.'

'I see no reason to accuse him of communicating with the dead,' Hildegard chided.

'Magus, alchemist then,' Gregory replied, amused. 'How does he see himself, I wonder?'

'He must have those books brought in.' Egbert suggested.

'I wonder how he pays for them?' Gregory narrowed his glance.

'Maybe he really can turn base metals into gold?' Egbert chuckled. 'Surely by now somebody has managed to do it and has thought to sell the secret to the world?'

Both men laughed.

'He teases that lad of his but I suppose it helps keep him on his toes.' Gregory gave a sideways look. 'The sorceror's apprentice?'

'He ignores the abbey servant,' Hildegard broke in, 'although I can see no reason for doing so.'

'You always have soft feelings for the underdog,' remarked Gregory. 'It's a good quality. I'm not criticising.'

'I noticed Alaric standing half-hidden behind a pillar in the cloister when the novices were having their lessons this morning,' Egbert told her. 'You would have wept, Hildegard, he had such longing on his face as they went through their Latin. It seems a shame when a lad has a natural interest not to foster it.' He looked thoughtful. 'More than a shame, a cruelty.'

'That's as well,' Gregory butted in, 'but what was it Hywel mentioned about the tide three month's hence? What was he trying to tell us?'

They walked on in silence for a few moment until Hildegard remarked, 'Three months from now puts us at the Equinox.' She looked at the other two. 'Extra high tides. Helpful to anybody wanting to launch an invasion across to France.'

CHAPTER EIGHT

By the time they went inside the heat still lingered in the garth even though the sun had dropped below the bank on the other side of Hampton Water. The echoing guest hall was full of newcomers, petty traders waiting for the cog to unload or waiting to go onboard themselves to whatever business awaited them on the Isle of Wight or on the other side of the Narrow Sea.

The abbey servants hurried between the trestles with bread cakes shared between two, with heavy jugs of red wine from Aquitaine, with whole fish from the ponds, with fried eels, with eggs, with good, plain food, lavish and freely given.

Egbert nudged Gregory and whispered to Hildegard, 'Don't look now but those three militia are sitting in a huddle at the far end. I see they have knives with them.'

Gregory said, 'So have we all, the better to slice our cheese.'

Hildegard warned, 'Don't stare at them.

They'll take any opportunity to continue their fight once they recognize you. They were thoroughly humiliated by you.'

'They humiliated themselves by regarding us so lightly,' Gregory corrected. 'They shouldn't assume they can march in anywhere they like. A holy writ runs here.'

'Why has Arundel sent them?' Egbert asked again. 'Is it only to fetch cargo off the ship? Or are they here to wrest tribute money from the poor old Netley brothers? I think I'll go and find out.'

Hildegard put a hand on his arm. 'Let me. I can speak to someone who's bound to know without you having to provoke them.' She had noticed Mistress Lissa and her husband sitting at the next table and went over.

After a greeting and one or two pleasantries she asked Lissa if she knew what the men were doing here.

'I do happen to know,' replied Lissa with a toss of her red hair. 'They're waiting for the St Marie to unload. It's rumoured that there's something special on board being brought in for the earl. It must be special,' she added scornfully, 'if it takes three armed men to convey it back to his treasure house.'

'Now then, Lissa, my sweeting, it's not for us to know. It may be the crown and all the king's jewels. It may be a troupe of Nubian slaves. It may be...' he waved a hand to include the entire world, 'but we should mind our own business and not seek to pry into that of others.'

'You're too easy-going, Simon, my owl. It would certainly be the crown if only Arundel had managed to get his hands on it but that's one thing he couldn't fix at Gloucester's parliament of hate.'

Simon shook his head at his wife and turned to Hildegard. 'Ignore her, domina. She doesn't mean three-quarters of what she says. She's as loyal to whoever as need be – '

'Don't you tell me about myself, master. I know what I think and I say what I think – '

'Then you will get into serious trouble one of these days, my angel, and I will have to be the one to get you out.'

'You are a fond old fool, Simon, no wonder I love you, but you must not seek to restrain me from what I feel is right. I do not and cannot like who-know-who and that's an end of it.' She shot Hildegard a bright smile. 'I don't know what the royal court is coming to. I'm sure the domina feels the same, don't you?' Her eyes shone with a questioning and complicit gleam as she tapped Hildegard on the back of the hand and leaned forward. 'We women know what's right and wrong. We're not so easily fooled by these powerful lords who tell us only sweet nothings while all the while they're stealing the very bread from between our fingers.' She looked across the table. 'Isn't that so, Mistress Delith?'

Caught listening the widow jerked up her head and bestowed a nervous glance round the table before saying hurriedly, 'Of course, mistress, we women know full well what rogues men are,' she gave a tittering laugh to show she meant nothing more serious than the usual claims against them.

Out of the corners of her eyes she glanced down the hall towards the three militia. 'I suppose they're hired to do the bidding of a vassal of the lord Arundel,' she remarked. 'They look so young, scarcely torn from their nurse's leading strings. I wonder they choose such a life. So unpleasant and horribly, horribly dangerous.'

'May hap they have no other skills to trade,' remarked Simon, scarcely giving them a glance. 'It's not given to every man to become an apprentice. I can't see any one of them being taken into a guild. They are fixed, mistress,' he smiled contentedly at Delith, 'as are we all in the destiny the lord God has allotted us.'

Lissa gave a snort. 'I can't see God alotting to anyone the instruction to break fully armed into an abbey precinct.' Her fiery hair sparked as if to emphasise her scorn. She gave her husband a withering glance and he tried to pacify her by saying, 'To accuse them of breaking in is surely too strong, my pigeon?'

After Hildegard excused herself she returned to

the two monks and told them the gist of Lissa's comments.

'At least it can't be arms, not with all this attention, Surely even he wouldn't dare bring in arms openly as if to display his willingness to rebel.' Egbert rejoined.

'We'll see what they bring in when they come ashore with it. At present everybody's waiting for the tide,' Gregory said. 'Did our magician tell us when it might be?'

Egbert shook his head. 'Let them wait. The tide means nothing to us at present,' he sighed with impatience. 'We're only waiting for our lord abbot to be fit enough to get back on his horse.'

Despite their own indifference to the growing moon and its effect on the tides and the resulting release of business activities when goods could be brought ashore a hubbub of growing excitement filled the refectory after Compline. It was crowded, it was over-heated, it was a confusion of newly arrived travelers and traders, wearied and expectant, and the sound rose to the rafters with no sign that it would abate until well into the night when everyone had exhausted themselves.

Hildegard made her excuses to the men by telling them she would look in on Hubert on her way to her sleeping chamber. It was still hot and the star-filled sky seemed to hang close above the towers and walls of Netley when she stepped outside.

She stood in the dappled shadows of the garth to breathe in the scented air for a momnet. A shrouded figure was leaning against the wall of the building further along and did not look up until the three mercenaries came tumbling out behind her with drinking vessels in their hands. They were praising the wine which their lord, they claimed, had brought in to sell on to the Cistercians and they, as deserved, were enjoying the benefit of his foresight.

The figure against the wall shifted at the sound then melted out of sight before Hildegard could see who it was but, without noticing anything, the militiamen continued to talk in the loud voices of people who have had too much to drink.

She crossed the garth to the infirmary as they rolled on their way into the cloisters, voices echoing and distorted by the stone vault. Wondering how long it would be before the guest master begged them to consider the sleeping monks in the nearby dortor she reached the infirmary and entered its sweet-smelling gloom.

Closing the doors behind her as quietly as she could she was surprised to see no sign of the usual half-dozen lay-brothers on duty. Except for the slight mound of Mistress Beata lying in her bed at the far end in the shadows and Hubert in his usual place near the doors, the rest of the cubicles were empty. It was no hotter here than anywhere else but she suspected the conversi of trying to find respite from the lingering heat elsewhere.

It was a fact that it seemed almost hotter now than during the day-time. The air was ominous with the threat of thunder and stifling enough to bring on headaches. Hildegard pressed her fingers to her temples and ran a finger inside her belt to release the stickiness of her linen shift against her skin.

Hubert was propped up in his bed with a book in his hands and a candle by his side. He looked as cool as ice and as handsome as ever and when he heard the door he put the book down.

'I've missed you. Where have you been?'

'Nowhere special. We had a look at Hywel's astrolabe. Did they bring you something to eat?'

Unexpectedly he pulled her down beside him. 'Kiss me, Hildegard. For once there's no-one to see us.'

'Oh Hubert, no,' she tried to pull away from his embrace but his heated skin, seductive with the scent of pine oil, his feverish mouth, the touch of his lips on hers overcame her resistance and with a half-hearted attempt at escape she melted into his arms. 'You told me you would wait for my answer when we reached Meaux,' she whispered when she could tear her lips from his for a moment.

'What if I can't wait?' he demanded in a voice hoarse with desire. 'What difference does it make now or later? Are you going to reject me? I want you. I can only speak the truth. It's no sin to speak the truth, Hildegard, my dear heart. Where's the sin in this?'

'You are cozening and you know it.'

'Are we so sure that what we're told about sin is right? What about praising God for the gift of human love? Surely it must mean that it's right to do as our deepest feelings urge?'

'Hubert, you can't expect me to throw everything away with no thought of the consequences. I only came in to say goodnight because I couldn't bear not to see you before I went to sleep - and now you're asking me to make a decision that will change everything... '

'Come into my bed, come here now. We're as private as we can ever be.'

'But look, Mistress Beata is only down the hall,' she faltered.

'Hywel gave her a strong dose of his sleeping draft. He would have given a draft to me if I hadn't resisted. Come to me, here, now,

Hildegard.   I'm longing for you.   You're my heart's desire and my body yearns to be one with yours.'   He covered her mouth with firm kisses again and again until she was beginning to lose all resistance.

'Let me touch you, Hildegard, let me feel your skin next to mine.   This is no sin.   I've seen no sentence that tells us it's so.   No-one has ever read such a sentence.   No such words exist.   We make prisons for ourselves with imaginary laws which have no binding in reality. It's against nature to deny ourselves the love and desire we feel for each other.   This no passing desire and you know it. We cannot live a life of denial. That would be the sin, the sin against our true natures, against life itself.'

'It will put our immortal souls in jeopardy. You know that.'   Her fingers seemed to move of their own volition through his thick, dark hair as, even now, she was incapable of tearing herself away.   'It'll mean we'll have leave the Order.   We cannot live double-lives.   We know the Rule.'

'Will you do that for me?'

'Leave the Order?' She was trembling not only with desire but with the enormity of what he was asking her to do. 'You cannot ask me yet. You promised to wait at least until we returned to Meaux. I've found solace in my widowhood within the priory at Swyne. I've found fulfillment of some kind in my duties. You're asking me to give it up...' She put her fingers to his lips to stave off another kiss. 'I don't know whether I have the courage or the strength to - '

'Not even for me?'

'It could only ever be for you.'

'Then let's do it. Let's leave. Let courage be our guide.'

'And live together like...' she cast around in her mind for names. 'It could not be like Abelard and Heloise... they were separated in the flesh by what his abbot did to him. Castration? Hubert, no!'

'They made an example of him to deter others...but it failed, Hildegard. You saw the cardinals in Avignon with their mistresses, their concubines…I don't want that for us. I want us to live freely and openly in the world, not in the midst of lies and the corruption of the flesh…'

'Then how do you mean? Like…' A smile twitched her lips. 'Like Simon and Lissa? Like a merchant and his wife?'

He laughed out loud. 'We can live however we choose once we're free.'

'Once we are free…?'

He took her face between his palms and raised her mouth to his. 'Let's seek the Blessed Isles, to love, to pray, to live, and never lie.'

'If only, Hubert, my dear lord, if only…'

'I see I've shocked you. Lying here with nothing on my mind but you I've considered it most deeply and have come to the conclusion that it is a terrible thing to be separated from love at the behest of a few old churchmen whose blood has lost its fervour. Life is finite. We serve God by taking hold of it and living to the full.' He held her in a close embrace for a long, delicious, heated moment, his desire unassuaged, his will unmoving, yet his spirit undespairing. 'It shall be so, my heart. I vow it.'

A sudden sound at the great doors brought her trembling in alarm from his embrace. 'Who's that?' she whispered, swivelling to look.

The doors swung wider to reveal a figure standing in the entrance.

A man's gruff voice made a muffled apology from under his hood and the figure withdrew.

'Who was it?' she whispered still held in the circle of Hubert's arms. 'Were we seen? Hubert! We must have been seen! What will happen? Was it Abbot Philip? One of his men?'

'I care not.' He held her in a grip of steel. 'He's gone now, whoever it was, skulking about, forget him.'

She glanced fearfully towards the door. 'If we were seen…'

'Excommunication. Only the pit of hell to receive us.' He paused to look tenderly into her face as if he had never seen it before, gently touching and exploring it with the tips of his fingers, all the while murmuring, 'I dare risk the pit of hell for one night with you.'

'Let me go and find out who came in,' she whispered. 'I fear for you, not for myself. They would destroy you and wreak their revenge on someone they have honoured as abbot and advisor at Citeaux, someone they have trusted, someone who holds the authority of the Order in his hands and can destroy it for a reason they will not understand. Let me go, beloved. I'll come straight back.'

Wresting herself from his embrace and still shaking she went to the door, turned her head once to look at him to find his dark eyes, deep with desire, fixed on her, and then she opened the door and slipped outside.

The moon was nearly full. It seemed to sail through its sea of stars on a bed of cloud. Her heart sang with love for Hubert, her abbot, her lord, her desire.

Before she could step into the garth a hard hand

came at her out of the darkness, gripping her by the arm with savage strength, jolting her into the moment, and a voice, growling with menace said, 'So this is where the ladies of the night ply their trade? I thought it would be down on the quay, such is the tradition of sea-farers.'

'What did you say?' She struggled against him and in the darkness of the porch she could not make out who it was who spoke with such threatening intensity. His anonymity made her fight back more wildly. 'Take your hands off me!'

He used his strength to force her deeper into the shadowed recess.

'Was that Abbot de Courcy buying his nightly pleasure?' came the voice against her ear. 'I believe it must have been. There's only the old woman left in there, such is the wild good health of these pale monks. Do you service others?'

She managed to free one hand and bring it up to where she thought the voice came from and a bestow a loud smack across the stranger's face. His hood fell back. By the glimmering of the moon she recognised him at once.

'You?' Her mouth hung open.

'Have we met? Never in like circumstances, I'll wager. Have a wife at home whom I love.'

He released her and she raised one hand again.

'No,' he growled, 'Not again or I shall have to be avenged.'

'Prince Owain.'

He gave a start and glanced hurriedly across the garth. 'You really know me?'

'I opened the door into your chamber by mistake today. When I returned to beg forgiveness the door was locked. I also know of you. I understand you are in the personal body-guard of the earl of Arundel.'

'You understand, do you?' He surveyed her in the half-light with a sardonic expression.

There seemed no answer so she did not waste her breath.

He lowered his voice. 'Tell me what four Cistercians from a distant northern abbey are doing here at Netley?'

'If you know that much you probably know the answer already,' she retorted.

She would never admit what had happened to them in the woods. He must already know if the men who attacked them on the way here owed fealty to the same lord as himself and she would not give him the satisfaction of telling him about Hubert's injury at their hands.

By the light of the moon she could read the confusion on his face. 'I'm not in the habit of asking questions to which I know the answer.' He said something under his breath in Welsh and glowered at her.

It prompted her to pose the same question to him. 'What business do you have with the abbey?' Then, incautiously, she answered it herself. 'Armaments, I suppose. Arms for your lord? They can be brought in more discreetly to Netley than to the town quay at Hampton. No-one here will guess what he's planning.'

His response surprised her. 'Do you have evidence for that?'

She shook her head. 'What more evidence would I need than that of plain logic? Given what has been happening in London, what else would someone bring secretly into the country at a time like this in order to strengthen his hand?'

'Hah!' He threw his head back. 'Rumour! Just like a woman!'

When she raised her hand again he stepped back. 'My apologies, domina. That was unfair. It's only that we have come to the same conclusion ourselves. With what we, too, call logic. Masculine logic.'

'We?' She ignored his ridiculous claim to an objective system of rational thought as it was too commonplace to counter.

Instead of replying he asked, 'That really is Hubert de Courcy lying in there with a broken leg?'

She offered a wary nod at this change of tack. Clearly he did not know everything.

'He's one of Abbot Philip's men?' Half to himself he said, 'This place is as full of strangers as Westminster.'

He bestowed on her a glinting, moonlit, humourous, bitter smile and for a moment his dark-eyed charm disarmed her but then she began to move away with a dismissive goodbye in Welsh. He was dangerous. If his lord Arundel wanted he could have them arrested, without the need for any legal charge. Look at the slaughter at Westminster during Lent.

He called after her, 'Prince, you called me. Are you going to stand by that and give me your fealty?'

She kept on walking.

When there was a sufficient distance between them she turned to see if he was going to go into the infirmary but he was standing in the shadow of the porch, scarcely visible, head cocked on one side as if listening to something. As she watched she realized he had been the shrouded figure leaning against the wall when she left the refectory, and now, here he was again, and again he melted into the darkness so that she had to blink to make sure he had really vanished.

Before she could think of returning to Hubert the three mercenaries came marching round the corner of the infirmary from the direction of the stables. He must have picked up on the sound. But why leave? They were allies.

'I tell you,' one of them was saying, 'that's his horse and it's saddled and bridled ready to go.'

'Then we have to make sure we get to him before he gets to it.' The dark-haired, raw-boned captain of the three who had hoped to outface Gregory that afternoon was marching a pace or two in front of his men as if to emphasise his leadership.

'But where the hell is he? Saw him earlier. I know I did. Then he vanished into thin air like a wraith. They say the Welsh are magicians.'

'Yes, well, we'll just have to make sure he doesn't get chance to use any of his spells, won't we?'

'If we plant ourselves here we'll see him when he emerges from his hole,' said the leader. 'Settle down now and keep your eyes skinned. He's got to come out some time.'

'Aye, and he's as trapped as a rat – '

'Hold on! Who's that?'

One of them had noticed Hildegard coming onto Cloister Garth.

'It's a nun.'

The three came over. She knew who they were looking for before he even spoke. 'We're seeking a man of ours, sister. You ain't seen any man lurking about by hisself, have you?'

'Several, captain. The pilgrims are gathering to take ship as soon as the tide is right. Is he anyone in particular?'

'He certainly is.' The captain made a brief though belated obeisance. 'He's a turn-coat. An intruder in the abbey precinct. Shouldn't wonder if he isn't planning to murder everybody in their beds. But don't be alarmed. We aim to apprehend him before he does so, following our orders.'

'And then?'

'And then, if it's of any concern of yours, we'll

take him back to Arundel Castle where he'll receive his just desserts.'

'Of what crime is this miscreant guilty?'

'Treason, sister. A most heinous crime.'

'I shall certainly let you know if I see a traitor wandering about.' With that she walked on leaving them to ponder the nature of irony.

Unwilling to change direction now the militiamen were on the watch she headed towards the refectory but there was no sign of Gregory or Egbert within. Deciding she would warn them about Glyn Dwr when they came down for Matins she went back into the cloister.

It was empty.

Pools of shadow lay in the intervals between the flickering lights of the cressets but nothing moved within the pools. From where she was standing she could see the three mercenaries at the far end within sight of the infirmary, the other buildings, and the stable block on the opposite side. Between them the door of the refectory stood open spilling forth a wedge of light and making visible anyone who crossed it. From inside continued the hum and buzz of conversation.

Apart from the mercenaries on look-out the garth remained empty. From their corner the men had a clear view of anyone attempting to cross it.

She wondered what to do. It made no sense to imagine they were searching for Glyn Dwr as if he were an enemy. Yet what else was she supposed to think? She decided that the best thing was to return to Hubert on the pretext, if challenged, that she was returning to see if there was anything he needed for the night – and with that in mind she retraced her steps. The three on watch were sharing a flagon of ale or wine, and talking in bored, desultory tones while throwing dice on the flagstone at their feet. This time they ignored her.

As soon as she stepped into the shadow of the porch at the infirmary doors she discovered she was not alone. He was still there and to confirm it she heard him whisper, 'Hush, now. It's Owain.'

'What is it?' she matched her whisper to his own.

Close to her ear he asked, 'Are those three fellows still lurking about out there?'

'Yes. Why?'

'They're after drawing and quartering me - my head on London Bridge and limbs parceled out to frighten the king's friends in four different towns. Are you going to shout and warn them I'm here?'

'And if I do?'

'I doubt whether you'd manage more than a squeak.' He showed the blade of a knife.

'I don't know your quarrel with them but any enemy of Arundel is a friend of ours. If you want to keep your head on your body for a little longer there's another door inside the infirmary which comes out round the back of the building. From there you can probably reach your horse where it's waiting for you in the stable yard, or so they said.'

'I saw you talking to them.' He looked as if he was working out whether he could trust her or not. Then he came to a decision. 'I shall put my life in your hands, domina. I have no choice. You see, I am unarmed. Can you show me the door you mention?'

'Walk ahead of me so they see only one shape should they chance to look this way. Quick, slip inside. Go now.'

Hubert was reading his book again. He looked up in surprise when he saw Hildegard hurry in with a stranger striding with firm military steps in front of her.

'This is Prince Owain Glyn Dwr,' she announced, before he could say anything. Anxious to get Glyn Dwr outside in case the men should follow, she whispered, 'Hubert, don't ask me why but I'm going to save his head from those ruffians of Arundel's who are sitting in wait for him in the garth.'

Hubert understood at once. 'Owain. Prince. There's a door half-way down the hall - '

'I've already told him about it.'

'Then go with him,' Hubert suggested. 'Hywel uses it all the time to reach his workshop. From there it's a short step to the stables.'

When Owain gripped the abbot's hand, he said,

'For King Richard – '

Hubert replied, 'And the true Commons,' adding, 'Godspeed, my friend.'

They had already reached the door when there was a bang behind them and the double doors at the entrance slammed back against the wall as the three men stormed in.

Pushing Owain out of sight, Hildegard managed to cruck her head under the lintel and close the door noiselessly behind them. They were just in time.

'Hurry!' she urged the prince.

Running on ahead she led the way round the side of the building, passing the wall of the frater and crossing a short open space into the lee of the lay-servants' quarters. A lighted candle in the window of Hywel's workshop made her grab Owain by the arm and pull him in through the door. Hywel was at his work bench. He jerked to his feet in alarm.

At that moment he was holding a lighted spill to

a heap of charcoal in a brass dish underneath a retort. Now it fizzled out. His face was stark with fear until he recognised the intruders.

His expression changed. He dropped to one knee, murmuring, 'My lord Owain!'

'Up, no time for that. I need my sword. I'll finish them, the blackguards, all three.'

'I beg you not to think of it. You'd bring the hounds in full cry after you.'

'I have no choice! Where is it?'

'You must leave at once.' In Welsh he added something Hildegard was slow to catch but then Glyn Dwr objected. Trying to follow what was said she had the impression that he was telling Hywel that he must have 'it' – but what? His sword? They were talking too rapidly and Glyn Dwr seemed at last to persuade Hywel of something.

'I give you my word,' she heard Hywel say. He added, 'Your sword is here.' Going to the workbench he pulled aside a cloth under it and drew forth a heavy, business-like weapon. When he handed it over he knelt and touched his forehead to his lord's hand.

Owain pulled him to his feet and clapped him on the back. 'This will be remembered, brother. I'll get out of here and not disturb the peace of the abbey. They'll not be dragging me back to Arundel without a fight.'

Hywel called for Jankin. The boy emerged at once from his blankets, rubbing sleep from his eyes, alert to the urgency in his master's voice.

'Go out and find those three militiamen wherever they are. If they start to come over here create a diversion. Get them to help find your lost mouse, anything, but keep them away from the stables until Prince Owain rides, understood?'

Jankin yawned and nodded then ran out.

'Come with me,' Hywel instructed, adding, 'if you will, my lord,' and with only a cursory bow swept from the workshop whose door, fortunately, gave onto a side of the building out of sight of the garth and separated from the stables by only a short stretch of grass.

There, waiting in the yard when they arrived, was an already saddled horse with one of the lay-brothers impatiently holding him by the reins. It was so dark, with only one sconce in the wall further down, that it took a moment for Hildegard to discover that it was Alaric.

Hywel was terse. 'If anyone comes in wanting horses you're to delay them as much as possible. Understand?'

'How am I to do that, magister?'

'I leave that to your own ingenuity.'

While he'd been speaking Owain had pulled himself onto the horse's back and was heading towards the gate. He raised one hand when he reached the archway before disappearing out into the night.

'Back into my workshop, domina. We are busy with an experiment to beat the common ague and know nothing about anything else.'

'Yes, but, where was the night porter just now?'

'Paid.'

'Here, is it that nun again?' The one called Jack who had finished up underneath his own horse's belly without his sword was the first to speak as the three men, empty scabbards swinging mockingly by their sides, and after knocking loudly on the door of Hywel's workshop, marched in uninvited.

Hildegard bent her head over the work bench, thankful that she had put up her hood so that she looked much like any other nun in white.

Hywel faced them in immediate, high and invincible rage. 'Do you fellows have permission from your superior officer for breaking into my workshop in this violent manner when I'm engaged on difficult and important work?' he demanded. 'If so, lead me to him. This is an outrage!'

Stalled, the men milled near the door. Their manner betrayed their suspicion that the man who faced them was a magician with malign powers, someone who could probably put a curse on them as soon as look at them.

Holding up a vial of some milky liquid, the use of which Hildegard had no definite opinion, she busied herself among some other bottles and retorts on the work bench while watching the men out of the corners of her eyes.

The raw-boned captain gave a wary glance round the cluttered cell. Its mystery was manifest in the chart on the wall, the symbols for the sun and moon, signs for the planets that everyone knew, and the malevolent glow of a big brass disc with arcane symbols round the rim. It was obvious that there was no possibility of a man hiding anywhere here. 'Did you hear that noise out in the garth?' he demanded.

'Noise? I'm too busy to heed the ribaldry of outsiders,' Hywel replied in a cutting tone. 'Answer my question if you will, captain.'

'That noise was us. We seek a traitor, magister. We have carte blanche from our commander to seek him out wherever we suspect he might be hiding. I beg your gracious pardon for disturbing your experimenta.' He glanced at Hildegard again

and Jack piped up, 'Weren't she – just now, I mean
– '

'The sister, my help-meet, is engaged on
meticulous work, please do not disturb her. This is
a long and costly experiment – Now, if you'll
leave us in peace…?' He edged them towards the
door.

Thwarted, but unsure how or why, the three
sloped away, the last one to leave giving the door a
good bang behind him to show that he knew
Hywel was a treacherous, deceiving devil who had
not heard the last from them.

CHAPTER NINE

'My gratitude, domina.' Hywel gave her a long and steady look when they were alone as if trying to unpick the very warp and weft of her thoughts. 'I wonder how they knew lord Owain was staying in the abbey?'

'They must have tracked him from wherever it was he came from.'

'So it would seem.'

'If I was able to discover the fact by chance I'm sure that anyone else, especially if they were looking out for him, could do so.'

'Are you suggesting we have informers at Netley?'

'On whose behalf would they pass information?'

'I don't need to answer that, do I?' He gave his faint, derisory smile and regarded her with a meaningful glance that came from the depths of his sharp, unillusioned and skeptical intelligence.

To counter it and draw from it what she could she asked, 'Why should Prince Owain come here? Is that also something you will not tell me?'

'Which answer do you want? The first one would be that he approves of Cistercians and fosters their activities. His forebears founded the famous abbey of Valle Crucis in Wales over two hundred years ago. He has always protected it from threat. I suppose he feels the same way about all Cistercian foundations... and the monks and nuns who inhabit them.'

'And other answers? You implied more than one.'

'Those you will have to discover for yourself.' He frowned. 'Forgive me. Many lives hang in the balance.'

Her first thought that it might be something to do with Abbot Philip's concerns about the protection he said he was having to pay, her second was that it might be to do with the smuggling into the country of armaments.

He who is strongest, wins. That was the lie by

which these men of power lived. They blindly forsook the teachings of the monastics, the values of humility, compassion and right living. Little wonder they were disregarded, she thought, when the actions of the monastics so often ran counter to their teaching. Accusations of hypocrisy were often well-founded. She was only too well aware of that. Made miserable by the dilemma Hubert had presented to her she could not condemn anyone if they fell short of their vows. She was on the brink of doing so herself.

Hywel was staring at her as if he could read her mind. His shock of dark hair gleamed in the overhead light from the candles standing on the low roof-beam, placed in that position the better, she supposed, to allow him to work at night. In the silence she pondered the nature of his work, the rumours it attracted, but thought it pointless to ask. He had made it clear he would only tell her what he wanted her to know.

She glanced towards the door with the intention of leaving but Hywel read her mind almost at once and moved forward to prevent her.

'No, not yet. Wait until Jankin returns and I can send him into the stables to see if the other one has prevented the men riding in pursuit.'

'Alaric, you mean.'

'Him.'

'And you doubt his ingenuity.'

Hywel gave a start followed by a light laugh. 'That, yes.' He cocked his head. 'I've heard no horses leaving since Prince Owain rode out, have you?'

She shook her head.

From over by Cloister Garth came a racket as of men searching and not finding.

Not long afterwards the door opened and Jankin came tumbling inside. 'I failed you there, magister. When I let the mouse loose they just sneered and tried to stab him with their eating knives saying what a piffling roast he would make. Then they swarmed off to the kitchens to turn everything awry. After that they began working their way down towards here. They've gone to search elsewhere now. Did they catch their traitor?'

'No thanks to you if they did. Was that the best you could do?'

'Mea culpa,' he muttered, head bent, one hand, however, caressing the peeking little head protruding from his pouch.

'Where did they go? Did you at least notice that?'

'They disappeared into the night.'

'And you didn't follow because not only are you afraid of water you're also afraid of the dark?'

'I couldn't see which way to go. They went quiet. Like stalking an animal. The moon gave no light. She's hiding now behind the clouds.'

At least the prince Owain had managed to get away. But what if the mercenaries went out after him? He would not be difficult to follow through the woods.

Hywel must have had the same idea.

'Your chores are not over yet. Go into the stables, find Alaric and see what he's up to. Watch without being seen. I don't like this silence. There's something wrong.'

'Watch what?'

'Watch and learn or watch and tremble. It depends on what happens.'

After he left Hildegard remarked on Hywel's attitude towards Alaric.

He frowned. 'He's an illiterate. The country swarms with them.'

'He's kept illiterate by the Rule.'

'If it offends you take it up with the abbot or with the Pope or whoever decides these things. It is not in my remit. I treat him for what he is.'

'Then there will be consequences as we saw seven years ago when the people rose up against the intolerable laws imposed on them by those who've always taken power for themselves.'

'There is only so much one man can do, or one woman, against an unjust world.'

'But they are Arundel's men?'

'So we assume.'

'So why pursue Glyn Dwr?'

Hywel didn't bother to answer.

Hildegard went to the door and pushed it ajar to see if she could tell what was happening over in the stable block but as Hywel had remarked silence hung over the building.

Outside it seemed hotter than ever. The air was like a warm cloth covering the face, a blind-fold rather, as it was a night without light. The stars she had admired earlier were veiled by clouds. A bronze aura where the moon floated invisible and full of menace - no longer the light, silvery disc as before but a malevolent and baleful red – emerged from behind the clouds for a moment. Even then it was soon extinguished by bruise-coloured storm vapour sweeping up from the West and darkening even the one frail bronze light that had briefly shown itself. The wind blew in a sudden hot gust from the direction of the river bringing a swirl of debris, followed by a crack of thunder.

Hywel was beside her. Instead of looking at the changing sky he was staring towards the stable yard. 'What the devil is going on over there?' he muttered. 'Why is it so quiet? Stay here. I'm going over.'

'So am I.'

Seeing that it was useless to argue he plunged off into the darkness with Hildegard following the slight sound of his steps through the clammy darkness. Rain began to fall in large, single drops. By the time they reached the pale, looming, stone pillars at the entrance they were drenched.

Instead of going on Hywel stopped so abruptly that Hildegard bumped into him. His face was a pale blur when he turned to her.

In a voice tinged with horror, he whispered, 'What the hell is that? Do you see it?'

Peering over his shoulder into the darkness Hildegard became aware that something was hanging in the air above their heads. As she watched, it floated and turned and hovered. Then it rose up, blurry and indistinct, and floated evanescently before moving on.

It was uncanny.

She could not understand what it was and could

not help but grip Hywel by the arm. 'What is it?' she whispered.

'It's like a spirit, or an angel, or – I don't know what…' his voice tailed off when he noticed the mercenaries huddled in the yard in a silent group just in front of them.

Jankin, too, was a pace away, transfixed.

Unnerved by the weird apparition as it hovered in the air everyone continued to stand in a terrified silence.

The spirit hesitated. Then it began to float across the yard with a faint, slow, unearthly sound, and they could see that it was headless, and apart from the strange whistle of breath that accompanied it, it moved in an uncanny silence that was more unnerving than if it had spoken aloud. It was so far beyond human movement that they could make no sense of what they were seeing.

As they watched it rise up and begin to float towards them a crack of thunder rent the heavens.

One of the mercenaries lost his nerve and let

out a howl, a sound submerged in the dying, rumbling echo and gabbling and snatching at his companions he tried to drag them between the ghostly thing and himself.

'It's a haunting!' he shouted. 'The dead have risen! Run for your lives!'

Hildegard felt a blast of air as the three panicked men hurtled past within a hair's breadth without even noticing her. She caught at Jankin as he followed them. 'Wait! Let's see what it is.'

Hywel stretched out a hand as if to touch the weird apparition but found nothing in his grasp.

'It's too far away,' Hildegard breathed. 'The darkness gives the illusion that it's closer than it is. It's floating somehow…Treading the air…'

As they watched the spirit simply vanished.

'Gone,' Jankin whispered in awe.

It had dissolved like mist.

'The horses are quiet. Where are they?' Hywel asked, speaking in hallowed tones.

A feeling of dread settled over Hildegard. The horses? 'The stable doors are shut.' For some reason she felt more fear for the horses then at the sight of the ghost. She began to grope her way forward into the darkness towards the stables.

Everyone had forgotten about the rain. It was falling like a thousand knives now, vindictive, relentless, kicking up the mud in the yard, blinding them, turning everything to blur and shadow, and setting up a constant hiss. Thunder rolled from one side of the abbey precinct to the other. Lightning flashed across the sky.

In the distance she heard shouts.

Forcing herself forward one step at a time she reached the first of the stable doors. The others started to follow. Jankin caught up and slipped his hand in hers.

When she found the bolt, she hesitated before drawing it back. Then, dreading what she might find, she kicked opened the door.

A choking, foetid heat emanated from the horses within. They were caught munching hay, shuffling in their sleep, and heads lifted as soon as the draught from the door alerted them to human presence. She stepped forward into the darkness. The animals seemed unperturbed by the apparition outside.

Hywel and Jankin followed.

She heard Hywel's boots scrape on the threshold. He began groping along a ledge for something and the eventual rasp of a flint was loud in the silence. His disembodied fingers were lit by the small, bright flame pressed to the wick floating in the dish and a gold light slid rapidly through the stables to glint off the eye-balls of the horses and shine their coats and make shadows leap more strangely up the walls.

Nothing seemed out of place. A rake stood by the wall. A bucket was on its hook. The horses, having sensed nothing to frighten them, carried on eating.

A footstep in the hay-loft above made Hywel utter a warning. Then a shape emerged. It paused at the top of the ladder before climbing down towards them. It was not headless. When it came closer, emerging from the shadows, a fair, fine, and very human face shone in the flame-light. Blue eyes glinted. Lips moved. And it spoke.

'I see they've gone without their horses? Is that what you wanted?'

It was Alaric.

Moving with the precision of a dancer – or, decided Hildegard, with sudden dawning, of an acrobat – he walked up to them and stood in the pool of light.

He addressed Hywel directly. 'I trust that was ingenious enough for you, magister?'

Back in Hywel's workshop, shaking the rain off their clothes, hair plastered to their skulls, puddles of water forming at their feet, no-one ventured to ask anything until warm flasks of wine were in their hands. Hywel was sitting on a high stool, and they were ranged round on whatever they could find to lean against.

Hildegard waited for Hywel to begin.

He didn't hesitate.

With a level glance he demanded, 'So tell us how.'

'Simple.' Alaric glanced round. 'Didn't you see it? The rope? I tied one end to the tree that overhangs the wall and the other to a hook inside the hay-loft. A shortish distance but I judged it might be enough.'

'And?' Hywel's dark face probed for more.

'I was lucky the moon went behind the clouds before I started. It added to it, don't you think?'

'You know you had everybody scared shitless?'

'I hoped it would be so. Having heard those fools with their lucky rabbits' feet and all the nonsense they perform when dicing, I thought they might be disposed to believe in ghosts as well.'

'A pale, headless thing walking in mid-air. Oh, I see it all now. It certainly looked like the very devil.' His eyes narrowed. 'You've learned to walk on air?'

'I may live on air, magister but I don't yet have the ability to walk on it. It was the rope.'

'Yes, yes, I know it was the rope. I'm not some

village sot wit. But how did you manage to walk on it?'

'A skill I learned when I was a child.'

'You're a child now,' he snapped.

'I'm seventeen. Or thereabouts.'

'How'd you make yourself headless?' asked Jankin with a quick, fearful glance at Hywel as if he feared being snapped at himself for venturing a question.

'I thought you might like that. I pulled my tunic over my head and covered myself with a horse blanket. Look!' Dragging his tunic by the shoulders so it covered his head he stuck out his arms like a grotesque, headless man.

Hywel drummed his fingers on the bench. 'What else can you do?'

'All kinds of things.'

'Go on, then, tell us how.'

'I was made an orphan by the Death about the time some mummers came to the vill where I lived and I decided to run away with them. Better than ploughing fields. They were pleased enough to take me with them. A child always brings attention when it can perform tricks. '

'And you performed tricks?'

'After I'd been drilled, yes. It's not easy. These are no light accomplishments. I had many a tumble, bruises without score, a cracked head, raw fingers from juggling, whipping when I failed, as I did, often, at first. Aches and pains you wouldn't believe. Look!' He suddenly sprang forward onto his hands and walked a few steps round the cramped chamber then righted himself with a flourish.

'Very good.' After three slow hand claps Hywel gave the ironic smile that hid a multiplicity of thoughts. 'Should I ever need an acrobat, heaven forfend, I know to whom I shall turn. Why did you leave that life?' he suddenly rapped. 'Are you on the run from the law?'

'No, I am not!' Alaric looked offended. 'If you want the truth, and why shouldn't you, they were too ribald, too drunk, too feckless, too thieving, too whoring, too violent, too – too homeless,' he added his mouth tightening. 'Sleeping in ditches one night and in palaces the next. Then back, like as not, to the ditch. The life of a monk seems to be as close to heaven as anyone deserves in this life...and I wanted...I thought...'

'So you thought you'd become a monk? Just like putting on a mummer's garb?' Hywel threw his head back with a vigorous laugh. 'What a dreamer! They take only the sons of the wealthy, my lad. You don't have a chance. Anyway, you can't read.'

All the life suddenly went out of Alaric and he stared rigidly at the floor.

'I am sure,' Hildegard stepped forward, 'that if Alaric was given the chance he could learn to read and then become a novice. After that he could decide it it's the life for him. Other boys from similar backgrounds have done as much.'

'Are you going to teach him, domina? You might drum a few letters into his thick skull but you'll be moving on before your job's done. Then we'll have a half-lettered man who believes honest labour is beneath him and you won't give him a second's thought.'

He stood up. 'Enough of this. I'm to my bed for an hour or so. Your ingenuity is as surprising as it was useful, Alaric, but you'd better get back to the dortoir and put all thoughts of joining the brotherhood out of your mind.'

He began to douse the candles along the beam then without a word or backward glance went to the door.

Jankin looked as if he had been about to say something but then apparently thought better of it and instead climbed into his pile of blankets and pulled them over his head. Alaric slipped outside and vanished into the rain.

Wondering where Hywel slept, as she crossed Cloister Garth she heard him utter a clipped goodnight before he turned off towards the men's guest house and trudged off.

He's well placed to hear the gossip of the pilgrims and the other passing guests in that dormitory, she thought, and also to find out what's going on among the monks by virtue of his grey habit, too. She could well see that. With the times being so uncertain, many people felt that their only security lay in not being caught unawares. Information could mean the difference between life and death. And allegiances could change. A man might even serve two masters and receive pay from both. It was known to occur. Often.

As she climbed the back stair that led straight up to the door of her chamber her thoughts sifted through what she knew and what she could only surmise.

For instance, what would have happened if Alaric had been unable to stop the mercenaries from riding out after Glyn Dwr? One unarmed youth against three? The odds were not in his favour.

And one man, no matter how illustrious his lineage, what chance against three armed ruffians? A body could lie in the woods for months - or forever - without being discovered. Delivered up to the huntsmen. An enemy done for.

Then again, her thoughts revolved, sometimes it's as foolish to underestimate a person's capabilities as it is to over-estimate them. She wondered if Hywel had learned anything useful along those lines tonight.

Apart from Hywel and herself, Cloister Garth had been empty. No sign of the mercenaries. Scared witless by a fair-ground trick?

The rain still fell. Soon Matins would come round again.

It was little wonder that she tossed and turned on her bed with so many questions clamouring to be answered. She had thrown off all her clothes as soon as she came in and locked the door.

Lying naked on the coverlet she had been staring up at the ceiling for hours. Sleep would not come. The rain was still pounding down with a malign insistence and the distant thunder that had earlier helped to put the men into a panic now rolled around the heavens from one side to the other as flashes of lightning skittered over the ceiling.

It was hotter than ever. She wondered if hell would be hotter. Maybe she would find out if she didn't watch her step. Hubert surely could not be serious about leaving the Order? It was his whole life just as it had become hers. Outside, what would they do? How would they live? The thought of where they would set up home could have no answer. She did not see herself as chatelaine of a large household once again with all the droningly familiar duties that entailed. Maybe they would travel? But to what purpose? As scholars? Wandering the world? She could not envisage a life without the people and places she knew or to live unprotected in a barbarous world of strife and danger.

Suddenly a searing white light filled the chamber, brighter than all the others. It flickered three or four times and was followed by a massive crash like a tower falling to the ground. In a moment she was out of bed and at the window.

Through its narrow slit she could see nothing but the dark silhouettes of the trees above the shore until suddenly a sheet of flame leaped into the air from the direction of the river illuminating everything around it. The light became more intense and seemed to set the waters themselves aflame.

Moments later the thump of running feet along the corridor, slammed doors, voices, a high-pitched scream and below her window the hoarse shouts of the night porter as he tried to restore order above a clamour of counter instructions filled the night.

CHAPTER TEN

Without thinking she snatched up her shift, pulled it over her head, scrambled into her wet boots again, searched for her saddlebag and pulled from it her waterproof riding cloak and was already pulling it on as she unlocked her door and flew down the narrow stairs.

Stuffing her unloosed hair inside her hood she ran towards the gatehouse where a rabble from all parts of the abbey in similar disarray were converging. Head and shoulders above them all Master John waded through them as if they were of no consequence.

'My ship!' he was shouting. 'My ship!'

The St Marie was on fire.

'Wool out, wine in!' an incautious voice observed. 'At least the wine'll be mulled!'

'No wine on this one, fellow,' snarled the ship-owner, pushing the man out of the way. 'There's cargo onboard worth more than gold itself.'

A crowd of lay-brothers, belting their tunics as

they ran barefoot down the muddy lane to the shingle beach, were already turning over the boats pulled above the tide.

Hildegard saw Hywel hurl himself down the bank after Master John with a stream of helpers in their wake.

Flares appeared but were hardly needed. Their guttering light paled in front of the massive light emitted by the burning ship. At some point it had been moved to an anchorage in the inner channel. It made it easier to reach and figures swarmed among the boats and began to drag them into the water. Master John ran straight in until it was up to his thighs as if he would walk out to his ship but someone shouted and another held him back, bellowing, 'No master, get in the boat! We'll row you out!'

'We have to get the crew off!' shouted one of the lay-brothers as he followed.

Out on the lurid flood one lone boat left the burning vessel. It had two huddled passengers and someone at the oars. Behind it, glaring like the opened gates of hell itself the cog's wooden planks buckled in the blaze with a hissing, snapping sound, her mast turned to a pole of fire while on deck a few shapes moved about as if blown by the flames to no purpose.

'Why don't they jump?' one of the pilgrims shouted above the roar of the flames.

'They can't swim, that's why,' another voice grunted. 'Poor devils, they'll fry!'

All the boats were quickly put in the water and half a dozen or so bobbed about on a sea of reflected fire.

Master John was in one of the first and could be heard shouting at the oarsman to put his back into it. 'My cargo!' he roared. 'I've lost my ship! Save my cargo or I'm a dead man!'

His oarsman dug the sweeps deep into the running tide with all his strength.

The moon was full and Southampton Water was swollen, bank to bank, and running powerfully in its deep channels with the surge of the incoming tide. In places, dancing in the light of the torches, shallower waters ran over the sand-banks that lay in drifts under the surface. Only a local man could find a way through such labyrinths. Hildegard could still hear Master John weeping and praying and cursing in turn as the boat with what must have seemed like agonizing slowness picked its way through them towards the St Marie.

'He cannot think of going on board?' someone said beside her. It was Gregory.

Hildegard looked round. 'Where are your brothers?' she asked, expecting to see a crowd of monks coming out to help get the crew off. Only the lay-brothers were down on the beach along with pilgrims and guests and others with interests on board the stricken vessel.

'Didn't you hear the Matins bell? They've gone in to pray.' He made no other comment but his tone made her glance sharpen. 'And Egbert?'

'He's here, of course.' He glanced down the beach to where a figure in a white habit, knee-deep in the water, had just pushed off the last of the boats. 'How many on board, do you know?'

'Not many. Maybe half-a-dozen or so.'

Egbert came up just then and Gregory said, 'We need more boats. We can do more to pluck survivors from the water by rowing out than standing here.'

'They say there's more in that shed along the beach. Come on!'

The two men sprinted over the shingle towards some trees.

Hildegard watched them go, and, undecided, called after them, 'I'll only take up space if I come with you. I'll find another boat.'

Of the half-dozen or so already leaving the beach a one-man coracle remained and she started to run for it only to find herself in contention with someone else. When she saw it was Hywel she gasped, 'Do you want it?'

'I do. I have goods on board.'

'Do you need help?'

He barely shook his head as he began to haul the vessel over the shingle.

Hildegard conceded the point and helped him

push it right into the water. He scrambled for the paddle. In the lurid light from the stricken cog his face looked stark with fear.

By now the St Marie was surrounded by a flotilla of rescue boats but they were small, barely able to take more than one or two passengers at a time. She watched them circle and struggle to keep steady in the inrushing tide. The lightning had hit the mast and a smell of burning tar and pinewood filled the air as it blazed like a gigantic candle.

The ship's bows faced upriver and the anchor chain in the stern was pulled taut by the tide. A figure too distant to make out was hanging from it by both hands but instead of climbing down into the boat below swung up and began to climb towards the deck. A rope ladder had been let down amidships and lines thrown over the side so the crew could escape. Instead of swarming down to safety, they jostled to a halt above the surface. Shouts broke out. After a moment, fearing fire more than water, one of them jumped and vanished in the reflected fires. He surfaced and began to flounder in a mirror of flame.

A rescue boat reached him just as he was being swept under the ship and somehow they hooked him from the water and dragged him on board. Others began to jump then and more confusion followed as the men were picked up one by one and brought into the smaller boats.

Master John was visible, standing in the bows, as his oarsman neared the ship while John bellowed something, too far off to be intelligible.

Clearly seen in the lurid light, a couple of sailors grasped the sides of his boat, tipping it in their panic and as it began to go over she saw the master grab an oar from his boatman and bring it down again and again onto the fingers of the men hanging on. The boatman flung his other paddle into the bottom of the boat and, unaided, dragged the two men onboard.

The ship-owner took it as an opportunity to stride across onto another boat nearby and from there was able to reach out for the ladder and begin to climb onboard.

Despite the blazing deck he didn't pause when he reached the top but, instead, climbed over the gunnels and disappeared. His desperation was understandable. The ship and her cargo represented his entire life. And it was about to be destroyed by the fiery hand of God.

'That you, domina?' Jankin came up beside her. 'I only knew you by your voice when you spoke to the magister,' he said. 'You sound quite calm.'

'No point in hysterics even though it's a catastrophe. Let's hope nobody's lost.'

'Nor their precious goods.'

He gave her a quick glance but she didn't reprove him, merely saying, 'One obviously more valuable than the other.' They both turned to stare out towards the bobbing rescue boats. 'I think they've got everyone off now, praise be,' she added.

While the cog blazed the light it cast over the surface was enough to show the boats, laden low in the water, winding through the sandbanks back towards the beach. There was no sign of anyone trying and failing to swim nor grappling to be allowed into a boat. Hildegard felt a sense of relief sweep over her. 'I think they've got them all,' she repeated.

'I was asleep, dreaming of ghosts, when I heard shouting,' Jankin added in a chastened tone. 'I'd hate to be out there in that black water.' He shivered.

'Where's Alaric?' She glanced round at the by-standers. A group of nearby lay-brothers, standing waist-deep, were guiding the first boat to shore. The white habits of the two Cistercians stood out in the darkness. She saw them run down to the water's edge with a coracle between them.

'Row this one back to the ship and make sure everybody is off,' Gregory instructed. 'We'll go back for another.' A few shapes leaped into action almost as soon as he finished speaking. It was all confusion.

'What are they going back for?' she called.

'The ship man is still onboard!' the oarsman of the first boat shouted back. 'He refuses to leave the ship.'

'We'll persuade him!' called Egbert, turning to follow Gregory as he ran back towards the store. Jankin followed.

Hildegard went down to grab the bows of the first boat as it beached. Three people were on board but while the oarsman and one of his passengers climbed straight out into the water as soon as the shingle grated under the stem, the third figure, hood up, refused to release their hold.

'Get out, I'm going back!' urged the oarsman. 'Come on!' he roared when they didn't move. 'You heard what they said. The ship man is still onboard.'

Putting out a hand he tried to push the passenger out of the boat. 'Move, will you! They've got to get him off!'

In the struggle the two of them fell in a heap and the hooded figure scrambled away, crawling blindly up the beach and collapsing above the tide-line among a drift of weed and shells.

Hildegard went over.

Nobody was close by now. All hands were pushing the boat back into the water with the oarsman at once pulling away from the shore as soon as a couple of conversi were aboard. By now the other boats were crowding into the shallower water near the shore with the crewmen they had rescued and in the clamour of the hero's welcome each was given the scene became a blur of bodies lit by the torches and by the more brilliant though distant illumination of the fire.

The ship was burning more fiercely than ever. It was made of wood. The sails had flared and been torn apart by the flames and small pieces of sail-cloth sparkled in the sky like dancing angels and were carried on the up-draft caused by the fire until they vanished into the darkness. The great pole of the main mast was a flaming brand of monstrous proportions.

Hildegard hoped Master John was not about to risk his life for his cargo however precious he thought it.

The figure at her feet was an undistinguishable bundle of dark fabric but was beginning to realise that the danger of drowning was over. Hildegard bent down and twitched the hood.

A frightened face stared up at her.

It was Delith.

With no explanation necessary Hildegard stooped to offer her hand. 'You're on dry land. Give praise for your deliverance. Come, stand up if you can.'

Without speaking the widow rose to her feet. She tried to straighten her clothing, brushing the sand off it, smoothing its creases, but her hands were shaking. She did not look at Hildegard again. She took a step but would have stumbled if Hildegard had not reached out.

'Hold onto me. When you're ready maybe you'll want to go back to the abbey? I'm sure the kitcheners will be preparing something for the survivors of such a calamity.'

Delith linked her arm in Hildegard's and

together they headed back up the bank. When they reached the wooded track leading to the gatehouse Delith muttered, 'I can manage now, domina. My gratitude for your help.'

Hildegard watched the slight figure, hood already concealing her identity again, make her way towards the abbey gate. 'Well,' she thought, 'so that's how it goes.'

CHAPTER ELEVEN

Standing at the top of the bank she watched the scene below. Boats were still plying back and forth. Some were laden with goods, others with reluctant crew. Cries of relief rose as yet another sailor stumbled ashore. Lissa and Simon appeared belatedly on the scene from between the trees and Lissa came over to where Hildegard was standing on the bank.

'I couldn't get Simon out of bed and didn't want to leave him behind. It looks as if we've missed it all, domina.'

'Not quite. They haven't brought the ship man off yet. He's refusing to leave her. And then there's the cargo. They seem to be bringing some of it off already - although I would imagine that's the last thing to worry about when lives are at stake.'

'Is John out there?' asked Lissa.

'He went on board to see what he could rescue,' Hildegard told her.

'It'll be his ruin.'

'He may yet save something,' Simon said in a consoling tone. 'Never lose hope. That's what I always say.'

'Yes, you do, Simon, my wise old owl. You always say that.' Lissa was staring out towards the ship with an unexpected look of dismay on her face. Before she averted her head Hildegard was sure she had caught sight of a glistening tear rolling down her cheek.

In one of those sudden reversals of weather which, to the superstitious appear to confirm the value of prayer if that's what they've been asking for, a cloud burst overhead. Rain began to course down in torrents. It was an all-embracing douche as if funnelled from the spout of a giant acquifer.

At once the hiss of steam from blackened timbers was heard and the sickening smell of things burning floated across the water to those onshore. One by one the boats with their drenched occupants returned.

Still the ship man refused to leave. He could be

seen on deck arguing with those in the two or three rescue boats that remained, and apparently refusing to desert the now steaming and blackened wreck. Hildegard could see the two Cistercians urging him to come off but now the rain was beginning to quench the flames he looked even more inclined to stay. It was only with some shoving from what looked like the ship's boy and the combined shouts of those circling in the boats that at last – at last – he was persuaded to leave.

The final boat was carried rapidly on the flood as the tide raced under it and the rain hissed like a million serpents all around. Even those well-wishers who wanted to cheer the ship man ashore went running for shelter under the trees although, when at last he staggered up the beach, a triumphant mob braved the torrent to hoist him onto their shoulders and carry him every step of the way back into the abbey.

Hildegard was glad of her waxed cloak. Still wearing it she went to join everyone in the warming house. There was a sense of triumph in the air now that everyone had got off safely but an imminent sense of wonder at the cost to be borne by Master John was palpable.

He was white-faced. He could not speak. His eyes seemed to calculate loss beyond anything anyone could imagine.

Only because of his wet clothes was he persuaded to remain in the warming room with everyone else. Then, with a beaker of warm wine in his hand, he gradually came to himself. Even so, it was plain to see his spirits were like lead under his bluff exterior.

'Gone,' he muttered in everyone's hearing. 'All gone. Finished.'

She wondered about the wealthy backer they had imagined when they first heard him talking about his activities and hoped it might be true. Poor man, she thought, ignoring the memory of him smashing the paddle down onto the hands of the men trying to climb aboard his rescue boat. If he was imprudent not to insure his cargo he had no room for complaint, but why would he not do that? Was his confidence in this possible backer such that insurance was unnecessary?

A sympathetic crowd gathered round him and tried to cheer him up. His drinking vessel was filled and refilled. It was the newcomers, Hildegard noticed, the ones whose names she had not yet learned, who were most concerned. The two sisters made comforting noises but had not seen the fire as they regretfully admitted so were unaware of the sheer scale of his loss. Simon made a contribution, urging him to seek comfort in prayer, but the others, the core group who had sat out the heat-wave together the previous day were mainly silent.

The ship man himself was in tears. For someone who had day-to-day courage above the ordinary he was in a state of incredible collapse. Nothing would console him.

'I loved her!' he sobbed. 'My heart is broken. I loved that ship. I shall never love another as much as I love her.'

Lissa turned to Delith who was warming both hands round her cup of wine. 'Fancy, a man can feel love after all. Who'd believe it?' She glanced at Simon. 'Apart from you, of course, my darling owl. But would even you wail for me as much as the ship man wails over his wooden boat?'

'My little lark,' murmured Simon with his gentle smile. 'I would set up such a wailing if you left me that heaven would weep with me. But I fear you do not understand a sea-farer's mind. They love their ships because she saves them from harm and is their mother, their Virgin saint and all the angels of heaven combined. Of course he mourns her. She is a being above and outside the world and human love cannot encompass that feeling of grief the poor man feels.'

Lissa gave a sort of flounce but the derision in her eyes was enough to end this, for them, quite sharp exchange. She only added, 'That is an answer and no answer, my old owl.'

Delith was standing mutely by. Unusually she had no opinion to offer.

Before anyone ventured to suggest returning to their sleeping chambers the door edged open and with a gust of rain sweeping him inside a stranger entered. As everyone turned to stare he began to shake the rain from off his cloak and slick back his pale, sparse hair.

Delith, standing next to Hildegard, must have decided she had had enough and pulled up her hood, crossed her arms over her chest as if cold, and headed for the small door leading into the undercroft of the dortoir. It gave a small snick as she closed it.

Everyone's attention was on the new-comer as he eventually threw off the cloak to reveal a bright velvet cotte the colour of dandelions.

He glanced round the group. 'Good people, I've come to find my wife. She's absconded with my life savings. I'm told she's here, intending to take ship to France in the guise of a pilgrim.'

The previous night's storm did not clear the air. Even as early as Prime, the heat bore down on Netley with renewed ferocity. The air was swamp-like, liable to spread a miasma of plague throughout the precincts. People sweated and pulled at the necks of their clothes to allow in a draft of air. Already two or three guests and a monk or two waited outside Hywel's workshop to ask for a preventative dose of whatever he could prescribe.

In the middle of Southampton Water, the St. Marie still rode at anchor. She was a black shell, like a death ship, but miraculously afloat. Now the tide had turned she seemed to strain towards the open sea.

Prime was well attended given the late night and the excitement that had preceded it. The monks looked content in the sufficiency of their support. The merchant, Master John, wore the mantle of a ruined ship-owner, his grieving ship man, the pilgrims thwarted of their adventures overseas and hoped-for absolution at the foreign shrines, and even the man searching for his absconding wife, prayed more fervently, it seemed to Hildegard, with even greater belief in the power of prayer than before.

Afterwards she made her first visit of the day to her lord abbot. He was wide awake this time, looking stern, with a frowning monk sitting beside him. Both turned as she approached. The monk found her a stool.

'I have heard all,' Hubert told her. 'Or maybe not quite all?'

'None of us know the whole story,' the monk interrupted. 'The work of the devil is apparent in every aspect.' He gave a nod in Hubert's direction. 'I will not encroach on your visitor's time. Send one of the lay-brothers along if you need anything more, my lord. I will keep you informed, as instructed.'

Bestowing a curt obeisance to acknowledge the abbot's superior status, he left.

'What a night!' she exclaimed, leaning over to kiss Hubert on the mouth when no-one was looking. 'You would not want to have been there in so furious a time, my dearest. The flames were terrifying. Luckily everyone was brought off safely although it's a major tragedy for the ship-owner.' She sat down. 'You're looking serious, Hubert.'

'You haven't heard. I know you can't have heard because Philip wants it kept a secret for the time being.'

'Heard what?'

His expression did not alter. 'You know the monks are saying it was God's punishment for the evil of our ways?'

'They always say that whenever the weather runs to extremes – '

'But this is about more than the storm.'

'You mean the loss of Master John's ship and his cargo? What evil has he done?

'Nothing to do with him.'

'What, then?'

'Not everyone was saved.'

'What?...You mean - ?'

He looked somber. 'No doubt you were told that everyone was brought off safely but it's not so. Before the ship man left he found a body below deck.'

'A body?' She half-rose in astonishment.

'Just so.'

After a pause she asked, 'Was it one of the crew?'

Hubert did not answer straightaway. He was frowning. At last he admitted, 'He does not know.'

'How could he not know?' The answer dawned. 'Poor fellow. Disfigured in the flames?...It was truly terrible, Hubert,' she continued rapidly, 'I'm amazed more of the crew weren't lost, especially given their reluctance to trust themselves to the water. Those lay-brothers are to be admired for their speed and organization in getting them off safely.' She squeezed his hand. 'Our two brothers also pulled their weight as we would expect. But how could anyone be over-looked? I don't understand.'

'He found him in his own private alcove below deck where he keeps his charts and personal belongings as ship master...He believes it was a death caused, not by fire, but by other means.'

'What other means?'

'It appears that the man died horribly if his remains are anything to go by. The ship man is scarcely sane, by all accounts. He's babbling about devils.'

'Devils?' She gave Hubert a skeptical glance. 'He was grieving about the loss of his ship when he came ashore,' she told him. 'There was no mention of a body let alone devils.'

'Maybe that was his way of dealing with the shock,' Hubert replied.

'Surely everyone else will know what he's saying by now? I haven't spoken to anyone since I left the warming house last night.' She cast her mind back to what was said. 'And all that time the ship man knew he had lost one of his crew?' She frowned. 'Is Master John aware of this?'

Hubert looked uncertain. 'My Netley Abbey brother did not mention anyone else, merely saying that Abbot Philip had been informed and wished it to be kept secret until he had taken time to meditate on the matter and pray for guidance.'

'Am I supposed to know?' she asked him.

He kissed the back of her hand. 'I keep no secrets from you, dear heart.'

'The ship man was the last to leave…?'

'He insisted on speaking to Philip shortly before Prime, to urge the abbot to send an exorcist. He was in quite a state, I'm told. "Free my ship of devils," he was pleading. Why he should imagine devils on board is anybody's guess.'

'Is the body not a matter for the Sheriff?'

'There's some confusion about how far the jurisdiction of the abbey extends. Some say above the high-water mark, while others say below it and half-way across Southampton Water. Meanwhile the poor man is afraid the devil will run free to harvest the souls of others while the law clerks dispute the matter.'

Hildegard told him what she had seen last night after the lightning bolt struck the St Marie. 'It was such confusion. At first people were running everywhere. They had to find enough boats - those little fishing boats on the beach are hardly big enough to take more than a couple of passengers - most are no more than single coracles - you remember the one we came down river in? It's an amazement that those conversi managed to get the rest of the crew off safely in such craft – it was fortunate the ship had been brought into the near channel ready to unload her cargo today - they must be distraught now to find they overlooked someone. If they know, that is.'

Hubert was silent for a moment before saying, 'I have received such kind treatment since arriving here,' he gnawed his bottom lip. 'I would like to offer help. It's clearly a case of murder, don't you think? Abbot Philip must suspect as much. The man had no burn marks on him, or so the ship man says. If I could get out of this thing,' he scowled at the wooden contraption in which his broken leg was encased. Even before he spoke again Hildegard knew what he was going to say. 'Well,' he confirmed her suspicions. 'Will you?'

'Stand in for you in this matter?'

'Is it too much to ask?'

Slowly she shook her head. 'They have shown you much courtesy and care, as you say. For that reason alone I will do my utmost. Now, where shall we begin?'

'First I suggest you call Gregory and Egbert. You know you can rely on them. Bring them here. Let's thrash this matter out and then cast our net.'

So it was, with little to go on, even after thrashing

it out as Hubert suggested, the three Cistercians found themselves a few hours later in a pitching wooden boat sculled by one of the local fisherman, in the company of Master John, the grieving ship man, and a monk from the abbey, destination the St Marie.

Sunlight flashed from off the water in dazzling contrast to the gaunt, smoke blackened shape of the ruined trading cog now at anchor in the inner-channel. The closer they approached the stronger was the assault of the acrid stench of smoke as it floated across the water. Maybe it was the great pine pole of the main mast which still stood, though lightning blasted, that made Hildegard see it as the finger of doom pointing heavenwards.

As if trying to lighten the dark mood that had settled over the occupants of the boat Master John exclaimed, 'It's a miracle she's still afloat! We've that to thank God for.'

They came up close.

The ship man asserted that it was no miracle. 'She's the best little cog afloat. I told you she would never let us down. Even through the Bay of Biscay she was as stout-hearted as any man could desire.' There were tears in his eyes again. 'Let me on board first, I beg you. Give me a minute alone with her.'

There was silence on the matter of devils and exorcism.

Gregory bent his head to his two companions. 'I'll follow to keep him in sight. This whole business is odd.'

The bows of St Marie loomed like a black cliff above them as they came in under her side. Their own small boat banging against her oak boards with a dismal clacking sound emphasized their own puny nature in face of the greater desolation.

The oarsman sculled vigorously to a place amidships where it would be easier to climb up and reaching for a dangling line above their heads held the boat steady. 'You folk get aboard. I'll go round starboard to see if I can find a longer line to fasten to. I'll wait for you round there. Tide's beginning to run again.'

The ship man could scarcely wait to scramble up the rope and pitch himself over the side onto the deck. Gregory, long-legged and athletic, kirtled his habit and followed with ease.

He called down to the others, 'You'll have to tread carefully. Some of the planks are burned through.' His head disappeared and Hildegard guessed he was following close behind the ship man.

With some difficulty she was hoisted on board by Egbert pulling from above. He had had no difficulty in swarming up a trailing line. The monk needed even more help than Hildegard but Master John, waiting for them both to find their feet on board, courteously climbed up last. He was almost as tall as Gregory and fit for a man who was a merchant and presumably unused to much physical activity.

The monk, finding it difficult to keep his balance on the heat-buckled planks, was rubbing soot off his hands and shaking out the white skirts of his habit with a mouth pursed in distaste. 'Are we expected to go below deck?' he asked.

'I expect so,' Hildegard replied. 'If that's where they found the body.' She turned to Master John. 'Had you already left the ship when he was found?'

He turned to look at her. 'Yes,' he replied after a moment's consideration. 'I was not the last to leave by any means.' He trod with caution over the blackened planks then held out his hand to Hildegard. 'They're still warm. Let me guide you.'

The shipman had not long to commune alone with his beloved. When they found him he was standing in the bows. In his hand he held a charred piece of wood but let it drop before wiping the back of his hand over his face when he heard them crunching about, then he turned, brisk and now suddenly in command of both himself and his ship.

'I suggest we go below at once. I reckon she's sound enough to be saved. We'll have to get to work, shan't we, Master John? As soon as the devils are got out of her we can make her good for another thirty years. Come, follow me, I know where to tread.'

The merchant's face was impassive and he made no false promises about refurbishing the ruined ship but he followed in the steps of his ship man with Gregory next while the monk, a Brother Heribert, and Hildegard herself picked their way after. She was impatient to get below but the monk was still fussing about the grime on his habit so by the time she climbed down the three short steps it was already crowded by those who had gone first. Gregory and the merchant were standing with crucked necks under the low timbers. Stooping, she joined them.

Bales of goods concealed under waterproof covers were stacked along the walls. Hildegard prodded one but it gave to her touch, proving that what the merchant had said last night about not bringing in wine was true. It was fabric of some kind.

There was only a narrow space between the bales and the men filled it but they had also made a small deferential space round a pile of what looked like rags heaped on the floor, then she saw that what they partly obscured was a body in a foetal position. Something was grasped in one talon-like hand and the other dragged at his throat. The face was bloated and almost unrecognisable as human.

At first Hildegard thought it must be one of the crew as had been suggested all along but then she gazed at him in shock.

Brother Heribert, still fussing with the soot on his robes, came belatedly down the steps, to where they were all standing then he himself gave an audible gasp. Master John and the shipman turned to him with expressions that bordered on the accusatory.

Gregory and Egbert were crouching down beside these remains of a human being.

When Egbert stood up he said, 'This is unexpected. He's one of ours.'

CHAPTER TWO

A babble of voices were released by his
acknowledgement that the body was one of his
own Order. The Cistercian habit of unbleached
stamyn surely proved it.

The ship man was heard above the others. 'I
guessed that at once when I saw him but what I'd
like to know is what was he doing on board my
ship?'

Gregory was crouched next to the body and
looked up at Brother Heribert. 'Do you know
him? Is he from Netley?'

The monk came a little closer and replied in
slow horror, 'I think I do indeed know him,
brother. He may be one of our choir monks.
Without a closer look I will only guess that it is
Brother Martin. See his ring?'

The little finger of the claw-like hand wore a
wide plain band with the letter 'M' scrolled on it.

His name meant nothing to the visiting
Cistercians. Heribert filled in a few details. 'He's

been at Netley for six years. A trustworthy, disciplined sort of fellow. Well-liked,' he added, 'although clearly not without his secrets - for why else would he be on board.'

'Was he helping get the crew off?' asked Hildegard.

'I thought the brotherhood was instructed to help by praying for the ship and all on board,' remarked Egbert with his usual bluntness. 'So what exactly do you mean when you say disciplined, brother? He can't have been all that disciplined to be here, unless...' he tailed off as an idea struck him.

Heribert began to stutter. 'I've always found him a strict upholder of the Rule. That's what I mean.' He glanced down at the body then turned away and rushed up on deck. They could hear him throwing up over the side.

'He's not a pretty sight,' Master John said in a low voice. 'Why is his face puffed up like that? Is it poison?'

'He has something in his hand,' Hildegard

pointed out. 'Can you see what it is, Gregory? It looks like a key.'

'It is a key,' he replied after a closer scrutiny. 'When the rigor leaves him we shall endeavour to find out which lock it fits.'

When Heribert, shame-faced, returned, Gregory suggested he say a short prayer for his brother and in the silence following, as the ship rocked on the changing tide, with the clanking of the anchor chain setting up a doleful chime, under obvious thoughts about death and eternity and the fate about which we can know nothing, Hildegard wondered how she had not noticed the unfortunate victim on the beach last night.

The question troubled her while the men discussed what to do next but she was no nearer an explanation when she heard them agree to leave Brother Heribert on board to keep vigil beside the body while they themselves returned to the abbey to make arrangements to bring the body back to its resting place within the precinct.

As they made their way up on deck Hildegard

wondered aloud if Abbot Philip had been expecting anything specific in the cargo and had sent the unfortunate brother to fetch it off.

Heribert knew nothing about that. His nose quivered in distress. 'We expected a few books, that's true. Nothing out of the ordinary that I know of.' He frowned. 'I'm sorry I cannot help. You must speak to the sacristan about that. Meanwhile I shall pray for our brother's soul.'

The ship man hailed the boat that was waiting for them below then told them that now he was on board his own ship he was staying put. 'If you want me you know where to find me.' He gave Master John a long look. 'Send a couple of my lads out. We might need help to keep what's left of your cargo safe. Did you manage to take much off?'

'Some.' He swung one leg over the side. 'Any preferences?'

'My bo'sun will draw lots.' As the merchant grasped the ropes the ship man muttered, 'Get a promise out of you-know-who.' He indicated what he meant by rubbing his thumb over his palm. 'I can try to get her up river to a boat builder there.'

With the promise to return with more help in order to take the body back to the abbey and deal with what could be retrieved of the cargo, John slid down the rope into the boat after the others and, lighter now with fewer passengers, and helped by the tide, the craft made a swift crossing back to the beach.

Egbert agreed to go and sort things out with the prior before joining the other two at what he called HQ.

They were sitting beside Hubert's bed when he returned. 'I've told him,' he announced. 'I couldn't speak to the abbot. He was in meditation in his lodging. Apparently he'll welcome us should we so honour him by a visit after Chapter.'

'Did you find out anything from the prior?' Hubert asked.

'He's a cold, dead fish. He expressed no surprise nor grief at the death of Martin. Maybe they didn't get on. I asked him about the goods they were expecting. He said they were importing nothing out of the ordinary.'

'But what, exactly, did he say?'

'I asked him. He seemed affronted. He said I could get a list from the sacristan if I thought it important. They get books twice a year, he says. Some to copy. Some to read. That's why it's a bit of an event. I managed to get a better idea from the sacristan – but all he knew about were the spices, some ivory, ox-horns, paper, nothing else other than some plate for their altar and a couple of bales of silk and velvet.'

'Do they always use Master John and the same ship man?' Hildegard asked.

'John came on the scene a year ago. They've never had any problems. The St Marie is well-founded. He claimed everything has been satisfactory – which I imagine is high praise coming from the prior.'

'Any ideas why Brother Martin went out there?'

'And,' Hildegard butted in, 'was it under instructions or in defiance of them?

Egbert ran a hand over his tonsure making his grizzled fringe stand up-right. 'I believe they may have a lunar view of the truth.'

'By which you mean - ?' Gregory raised his eyebrows.

'It rises in visibility and splendour then wanes to nothing. They claimed to know nothing about Brother Martin's reason for going out to the ship. Which in itself suggests that someone is obscuring the truth about Martin's presence on board.'

'And, more specifically, how and why he was poisoned?'

'Exactly, Hildegard, exactly.' Egbert shot her a dark look in agreement.

Gregory stretched his long limbs into the space under Hubert's crib. They were still sitting round his bed but appeared to be getting nowhere with their discussion.

'Let's go back to last night. We seem to agree

that, pending the coroner's assessment, Martin was poisoned. At the time we were too busy trying to get the boats down to the water to take much notice of anything, but what about you, Hildegard, you were on the beach from the beginning. Did you see anything that might be relevant?'

She began to describe everything she had seen but stopped abruptly in mid-sentence. 'You know, I did see something. This is probably nothing but before the first boat reached the shore when the fire was at its brightest, I saw a boat arrive at the ship. It must have been the first to get there. Someone climbed out of it and went hand over hand up the anchor chain to get on board. At that point the crew were leaning over the side making up their minds whether to drown or be consumed by fire.'

'Was it someone in a hurry to get on board?'

'Everyone was in a hurry once they understood what was happening. You can't blame anyone for being quick to get out to her.'

'What happened to the boat this fellow was in?'

'I don't know.   I was distracted by everything else and when I looked back he must have been already on board and the boat – I don't think it had anyone else in it. I don't remember.'

'So we can't go questioning the boatmen about it.'

'Was it Brother Martin, do you think?'

'Climbing an anchor chain?'

Egbert nodded.   'He was a youngish fellow, we're told.'

'He was too far away to see if he wore a habit or not. It could have been Martin.'

'If it was he'd have tucked up his habit – it would've looked like a lay-brother's tunic at that distance.'

'We'd better follow it up somehow.   The first man on board?   Eager to help or after something valuable in the cargo?'

'Find out if the crew hanging over the side saw him. They might know who he was.'

'It's not likely unless they regularly put into the haven here and even so, they rarely come ashore.'

'True but I'll do it and at once, before they fulfil their master's request and join him on the St Marie.' Egbert hurried out.

'We need this list of books. I'll go and get it. Maybe there was something more valuable than anybody's letting on? Why else would anybody be fingering through the cargo?' Gregory got up. 'Are you coming with us to face the abbot in his den, Hildegard?'

'If you want me to?'

Gregory rolled his eyes in answer and he, too, left in haste.

'And what about you?' Hubert reached for her hand.

'I have an idea,' she replied. Rising, she went to the door. 'Are they still looking after you?'

Hubert gave a wan smile full of fake self-pity. Then he blew her a kiss. 'Don't forget to report back.'

The workshop door stood open. When Hildegard appeared Hywel was measuring a coloured liquid into one of the retorts. He glanced up. 'Just making some of that bone-set your abbot likes so much.'

'I'm not sure he likes it so much as the promise of it making him better the sooner.'

Hywel, smiling, set the vessel on the work bench and pushed a stool forward. 'And what can I do for you, domina?'

After telling him that she had a question for him, she asked him point-blank what had so worried him the previous night. 'You were as desperate as everyone else to get out to the ship but for you I believe it was a little more than the thought of the help you could give to save the crew. Forgive me,' she added, 'I mean no slur on your character. Some things are valuable beyond any price, perhaps?'

He frowned and his lips tightened. 'I am deficient in charity. I know I am. It has often been said. It is my greatest failing.' He looked pensive then caught her eye. 'If pushed I would say I deemed the crew and the conversi well able to sort things out between themselves. They are all practical fellows.'

He got up and went over to his shelf of books. For a friar he had a surprising number but before she could say as much he pre-empted her, 'The abbey is generous in its lending. The new abbot regards my attempts to predict tides and measure the stars and motions of the planets as practical work and useful to him in his overseas trade. However, prediction based on number can sometimes merge into prophecy… ' He frowned. 'To be honest, I was waiting for a particular volume on another subject. As I'm sure you've deduced from even a cursory glance at my work bench my main interest is to discover the true nature of metals.'

She waited for him to explain.

'Since al-Razi discovered that *aqua regia* could dissolve gold the study of metals has gained momentum. Robert of Chester wrote the first translation from the Arabic of a book called The Composition of Alchemy and since Adelard of

Bath and many others, including Peter Abelard, Anselm and Roger Bacon, have made their contributions.' He turned his luminous gaze on her to see if she understood. Seeing that she was interested, he continued. 'Since their day the search for the reverse process has fuelled the imagination of us all. And here,' he handed her a small volume, 'is the first part of a book copied from an earlier text. I was waiting for the second volume. It should have been on board the St Marie.'

'And it wasn't?'

He shook his head. 'The casket it was carried in was there. I have it.' He pointed. 'See, this book fits in neatly.' He showed her by dropping the book into the wooden box and taking it out again. 'The one that should be inside, however, has been removed by someone.'

'Who knew you were expecting it?'

'Everyone. I make no secret of my researches. Apart from Abbot Philip they don't take them seriously anyway.'

'But someone must have decided to get there first.'

His face was devoid of warmth. 'So it would seem.'

She held back from mentioning the body they had been to inspect earlier that morning. Maybe he knew. Maybe he didn't. She shivered. He gave so little away. 'This casket – did it have a key?'

'No doubt. Why do you ask?'

'Who would have the key in their possession?'

'The ship man, probably. I don't know. I've never thought about it. I leave the transportation of cargo to those directly involved. I trust them to know the importance of security.'

'So someone would have had to get hold of the key – unless it had been left in the lock?' He made no answer. 'And you say that the casket was already open when you found it? I assume you found it on board?'

It was a leading question but he did not fall for it. Instead he replied with an irritated shrug, 'You saw me leave in one of the coracles, didn't you?

You know I was there.'

'And the casket was where?' she persisted.

'It was thrown down on deck. Someone had decided it was worthless. But they must have known the worth of what it contained.'

'And recognizing the casket you brought it with you?' Again he didn't answer so she held out her hand. 'May I see?'

He handed over the casket so she could have a closer look. It was gilded but of plain workmanship of oak with beveled edges. It appeared to have been dropped in the sea and was water-stained inside and as she turned it between her hands a few drops of water dripped out. Enough, she decided, to wash away any sign of poison.

When she asked how it had come to be so wet he said, 'It would have been the rain. If you recall it was lashing down after the ship caught fire. I simply hope the book is being kept somewhere dry at least. I worry for so precious an object. Precious to scholars, that is.'

'Was it something any of the brothers would have wanted?'

'I doubt it – unless they intended to destroy it as a work of the devil! He gave a humourless smile.

'Is that what you fear? That someone might have thrown it overboard?'

'It's probably lying at the bottom of Southampton Water at this very moment.'

Handing the casket back she glanced round. The main purpose of her visit was not with the friar. 'No apprentice today?'

He replaced the casket on the bench. 'He'll be about.'

'And Alaric?' That was the point of her visit, but she hid her interest under an air of nonchalance.

'I would imagine he's attending to his chores.' He smiled faintly. 'Or entertaining the rest of the conversi with his juggling tricks.'

Hildegard got up to go. 'I do hope you find the contents of the casket safe and sound.'

'It's devastating.' His voice shook. 'More than

that - I'm in the middle of an experiment and cannot proceed until I have the rest of the formula from the book.'

While the men were in Chapter Hildegard looked for Alaric but finding him busy with chores in the kitchens and unlikely to be able to talk in confidence for some time yet, she eventually sought peace inside the church.

The founders had dedicated it to the glory of St Edward the Confessor and, against Cistercian teaching, it was richly decorated, the walls painted in white and maroon geometric patterns and the glass in the lancets vividly coloured showing familiar scenes from the Bible. Only the tiled floor reminded her of Meaux because they were the same patterns that came from their own workshops, with heraldic beasts, and the coats of arms of many illustrious dynasties.

A familiar feeling of transcendent joy swept over her as she sat with her back against one of the pillars in the North transept.

Hubert wanted her to give up her participation in the celebration of the spiritual that formed such a deep part of her life nowadays. Perhaps lightly at first she had taken her vows as the best route out of a difficult situation but her faith, skeptical it was true, and constantly questioning, had deepened into something unexpected over the years. She felt more and more convinced that someone should embody and cherish a feeling for the ineffable mystery of life. Someone had to bear witness to it lest it be destroyed by the blood lust, ambition and brutality of the times.

So much mindless violence ran through all corners of the world. A heedless disregard for the virtues of kindness, compassion and love now contaminated every aspect of daily life. Men gloried in violence, the more brutal the more admired, and women and children were expected to acquiesce in the coarseness of ambition such men fostered. Every difference led to disagreement ending in violence and the hand of peace was disregarded. Only the brutal seemed to thrive.

Thus it ever was, she told herself. Even so, she could not turn her back on the one chance she had been given to make a change for the better. What could she do outside the Order as a mere wife? She could not even own her own property or go to law. At least, as *a femme sole*, she would be free to do those things on an equal footing with any free man - but that wasn't what Hubert was asking of her.

Always the image of Hubert before her, her light, her love. She could not turn from him either. Whatever he desired, she desired too.

While she tried to form the words that would clarify her dilemma and lead more clearly to an answer the West door opened and someone came inside. Heated whispering followed, then, as if assuming they were alone two voices became raised in argument. It was a man and a woman and the latter she recognised at once.

It was Mistress Delith. She was in a fury. 'I'm not coming back! Never! Never! So don't waste your breath. I don't know how you found me! How did you find me, you snake?'

'I have my contacts, I told you.'

'I'm not going back to all that!'

'You'll do as I tell you.'

'I will not!' There was the sound of a scuffle. Then Delith again. 'Do they know who you are?'

'Who?'

'That lot in the guest house?'

'Nah, not them. How would they?'

'What did you tell them?'

'My wife's run off. I'm a merchant from Winchester way.'

'That's a laugh. Did they believe you?'

'Why wouldn't they?'

'Then keep it like that.'

'I won't have to, will I? I've told them I'm looking for my thieving, runaway wife. And you're coming back with me… today!'

'No, I am not! Don't you get it, you thick-wit? I've had it with you! You're a complete stranger. I've never set eyes on you in my life. I shall deny all knowledge of you. I'll have you done for abduction. I'm a respectable widow. My husband's dead. I'm going on pilgrimage. You say otherwise and you're a dead man!'

'You? On pilgrimage! That's a laugh! When were you planning to leave?'

'As soon as I can, once they get hold of this buggering ship the master says he'll lay on for us in place of the one that got burned.'

'I've heard so much about last night my head's done in. What happened?'

'It was struck, wasn't it?'

'What? By a fiery thunderbolt? No wonder it was struck if you were on board!'

There was a pause. He asked, 'You were, weren't you?'

'What if I was?'

'There's your proof! It was a sign!'

'Aye, it was! A sign we can't set sail when we want to!'

'Ha! I guessed as much. So much for wanting a different life! Still turning tricks.'

'I was not!'

'I hope it was worth your while.'

'Don't you bother about me!'

'How much did you get out of it?'

'It's got nothing to do with you!'

'Oh yes, it has! As far as I'm concerned you're still whoring for me. Why else do you think I dragged myself into this dump? You don't get away from me that easy. What you earn is mine!'

'Don't you threaten *me*!'

There was a crack followed by a scuffle.

Hildegard looked up in alarm.

The woman's voice croaked, 'Take your hands off me, Lionel.'

'Fair's fair. You're my best little whore. I'm not letting you go so easy! How much did you make out of 'em?'

'I got nothing, you sot wit. I admit I went over for that, who wouldn't? But then I had a better idea.'

Delith's voice came from further away. 'I'll let you into a secret if you promise to lay off. Pretend you don't know me for a bit. I've got a plan. It'll be worth your while in the end.'

'What secret?'

'Something that'll give you more than you've ever dreamed of… but you'll have to trust me and do as I say.'

The man must have followed because Hildegard, already half-rising from her position behind the pillar, heard him say something about not wanting to be double-crossed. Then his words were cut off as the great oak doors slammed behind him.

The monks were filing out of Chapter when Hildegard crossed Cloister Garth to join Gregory and Egbert. Alaric was as elusive as before and she still hadn't managed to have a word with him.

'He didn't make a murmur about the ship other than to say that our prayers – their prayers,' Egbert corrected, as she joined them, 'were answered and the Lord spared them with little loss of life.'

'Who's this? Abbot Philip?'

He nodded. 'He said nothing about Brother Martin either. Now he wants to talk to us in private. Come on. He's already gone over to his lodging.'

As they left the main buildings and crossed the grassy expanse to the secluded corner where the abbot's large, stone-built house stood, Hildegard told them about the conversation she had overheard in the church. 'I didn't have time to let them know I was there. It was a man and a woman. They launched straight into an argument - '

'Who's the swain and the damosel in this story?' asked Egbert before she could go on. 'I'm imagining a lovers' tiff here.'

'Not that at all. The swain as you call him is a fellow who arrived last night during the storm – he wears a bright yellow cotte – you can't miss him – and he's claiming to be a merchant from Winchester. In fact,' she paused, 'it seems he's Delith's pimp. Can you believe it?'

'I have a strong ability to believe everything I

hear,' Egbert answered. 'It's easier that way. So the damosel was Mistress Delith? What were they arguing about?'

'He wants her to return to her old life but she refuses because she has a secret that will give him more than he's ever dreamed of, or so she says.'

'Some scandalous fact about someone or some *thing* she's managed to get hold of?' hazarded Egbert.

'This missing book of Hywel's?' Gregory suggested, dismissing blackmail for the moment.

'She could sell it for a decent sum – if she could find a buyer.' Egbert judged.

'I'm sure her man could find a buyer even for something like that if what he says is true about his contacts. But no,' Hildegard shook her head. 'I don't see how she can have it. I saw her as soon as she got out of the boat. She was sick with terror and almost fell at my feet. I would have noticed something like a book. Those narrow sleeves she wears. Nowhere to conceal anything as bulky as a book.'

'It must be some bit of cargo she's stolen,' Egbert suggested. 'A cup, a spoon. That sort of thing would appeal to her from what little I know of her, God forgive me for such a thought.'

Gregory had been unusually silent. Now he indicated the sub-prior standing under the porch as they approached. 'We're expected.'

'Over here!' the sub-prior greeted. 'The lord abbot is within.'

The sub-prior was a portly, busy little man, quite unlike the cold fish prior, and quickly ushered them into the abbot's solar and asked them to wait while he announced them.

Unlike the church this was a plain enough chamber, in the Cistercian style, but one or two objects immediately caught Hildegard's attention. A wonderful tapestry hung on one wall. It was a hunting scene and looked like the very fine work for which Normandy was well-known. The silk thread had a sheen that gave a suggestion of real life as if living creatures were hiding among the leaves with real fruit hanging from the branches.

On the abbot's lectern was a bible, reasonably enough, but from it hung a page marker in the exquisite and expensive embroidery called Opus Anglicanum.

Before she could comment the swish of Abbot Philip's robes announced his arrival from the adjoining chamber. He was attired with no less magnificent discretion as she had already noticed. His cope was embroidered along the hem with small figures in a narrative involving saints, lions, the sun and moon, and mermaids. Making much of this garment he went to sit in his carved wooden chair, an object no less noticeable for its handsome carvings.

Orders from Citeaux to be plain in dress and habitation could clearly be interpreted in several ways.

The group from Meaux stood as they were in their plain, white, somewhat grubby robes, unadorned, sandaled, and not invited to sit.

Philip twisted his abbot's ring round and round on his finger before he spoke. 'I am figuratively kneeling at your feet,' he began. 'Dear people, I beg your utmost discretion in what I am about to say. Do I have it?'

There were murmurs of acquiescence.

'You already know of our predicament here at Netley, the sums we have to pay in order to continue in our service to God. And now – ' the ring twisted and its balas ruby was like a drop of blood in a shaft of sunlight winkling through a chink in the half-closed shutters and the abbot looked eaten with anxiety as if he could scarcely continue. 'My brothers, sister, friends, we have lost…because of the storm last night…a most valuable import. It would have saved us from the current depredations of our protector…but now it is lost, doubtless never to be seen again.' He gave a groan and reached for the edge of the lectern to steady himself as he rose to his feet. 'That is unimportant, dear people. It is nothing, it is negligible, of course, when compared to the death of our dearly beloved Brother Martin.'

Gregory, perhaps imagining the abbot on his

actual knees before them and wishing to ease his joints, broke in, 'And how may we assist you, my lord?'

The abbot gave him a piercing glance. 'I see you here in our midst as strangers from another part of the world. Your minds will be unsullied by prejudice or pre-conceived ideas. You will therefore be the more open to the truth of what happened that dreadful night. No presuppositions will cloud your minds. Your own abbot suggested the idea. I want you to find out how Martin died - and who caused his death.'

'Is that all?' muttered Egbert under his breath.

'My lord,' Gregory humbly bent his head, 'may I beg you to reconsider your request? We cannot assume anyone caused his death until the coroner has seen him. Then, if such is the case, I beg you to tell us where to start. We will gladly do as you ask in the matter of discretion.' He turned to his two companions. 'I'm sure we are agreed that such a heinous crime…if there is one… must be punished and the criminal brought to justice?'

They were outside standing in the middle of Cloister Garth where no-one could overhear them. As they left the abbot's lodging the prior had replaced his subordinate and was loitering inside the porch. He had given them a supercilious smile as if he knew full well the task given them and was equally convinced of their imminent failure.

Now Egbert kicked a stone. 'Why us? Doesn't he trust his own monks?'

'There's something behind it,' Gregory agreed.

'Have they decided under whose jurisdiction the body was found?' asked Hildegard. 'Maybe it's something to do with that.'

'If he pre-empts the authority of the Sheriff and the Coroner they may back off. It would be a way of keeping the whole business under the control of Abbot Philip himself.'

Hildegard nodded. 'But why the secrecy?'

'He won't want it to be known to this protector of his that they've lost the means to pay up.' Egbert ran his fingers through his grizzled tonsure.

'When is the coroner expected? He'll no doubt confirm what we all suspect. Brother Martin wasn't known to have an ague was he?'

Gregory frowned. 'It would be some coincidence for sickness to take him in the situation in which he was found.'

'So what now? Wait it out until the authorities arrive?' Egbert, ready for action of any kind, looked thwarted.

Hildegard shook out her sleeves. It was still unbearably hot. 'We can't do much more than act on a supposition – that the poor monk was murdered, as it seems. Perhaps we need to find out when he went on board. Was someone already there who could have given him poison?' For Alaric's sake, she hoped he had not been the figure climbing on board via the anchor chain.

Egbert made a scoffing sound. 'That puts the crew under suspicion. I can't imagine a rough and ready sailor having a dose of poison at the ready to give to any stray monk who happened to board his ship. He'd be more likely to use a gutting knife, if murder was his inclination. Poison?...Never.'

'They carry all kinds of cargo on these trading vessels,' Gregory pointed out.

'True.' Egbert frowned. 'Even so…'

'We need to know who was on board.'

'And how are we going to do that? Confusion reigned. Dozens of people went out there, nobody able to say for sure who was or who wasn't.' Egbert threw up his hands. 'What I'd really like to know is why Abbot Philip has put the burden onto us? We have Hubert to blame for this.'

'We can't rule the crew out yet.' Gregory continued a more direct line of thought.

'They were all off the ship before the body was discovered. It was the last man, the ship man himself, who found him when he was making his final check. They were all certainly on board at the time it happened.'

'I'll go and talk to him. Find out what he has to say about devils at the same time.'

They were standing by the fountain in the middle of the garth by now and Gregory sluiced fresh water over his face.

'Why would anyone in the crew want rid of a harmless monk?' Hildegard puzzled, following suit. 'More to the point, why was Martin there? See if the shipman has any idea about that.'

Egbert splashed water over his head then rubbed the hair dry round his tonsure. He glanced round at the sun-baked garth. 'Let's get out of this sun. I'm beginning to fry.'

Hildegard hesitated. 'I've got to see someone. I'll meet you in the cloisters later, shall I?'

'Come with me, Egbert. A flagon of ale should sort it out.' Turning to Hildegard, Gregory put his fingers to his lips. 'Remember, sealed as the tomb wherein forever we shall lie.

The whole thing was beginning to turn into one of those puzzles best left alone. But they could not do that because their host, on whose goodwill the health of their own abbot rested, had asked their help. Hubert, proud of the honour of Meaux, would be disappointed, too, if they failed.

CHAPTER THREE

To begin with she strolled over to join the pilgrims huddled in a sweltering group in their favourite haunt in the shade of the cloister nearest the gate house.

'It looks as if you pilgrims have to stay here for a few days more, lacking a ship,' she greeted as they made space for her on cushions someone had brought out. 'Is there any news of an alternative?'

Delith was fanning herself with the edge of her kerchief as usual and did not look up. For some reason she did not mention the rumour of an alternative ship that the merchant was trying to put on. Ignoring everyone, she was playing with her blackbird while her little maid with her little halo of blonde curls, sat with knees drawn up on a separate cushion apart. Master John, himself, did not mention an alternative vessel either.

The two sisters and the avid reader and one or two others who had lately arrived at the abbey in the expectation of a voyage to France were also present. The so-called merchant from Winchester, Lionel, wearing his yellow cotte was sitting nearby, not in the group and not out of it, his sturdy bare legs swinging idly where he sat on the wall. That he was aware of the three mercenaries and their endless dicing further along the cloister was clear and Hildegard wondered how long it would be before he joined them and let down his pretence of respectability.

Lissa was the first to acknowledge her arrival. 'I worry that my dear old husband will be too ill to go on board if we have to wait long, domina. This was to be his last journey abroad.'

Hildegard glanced round, 'Where is he just now'

'Lying on his bed. The heat is too much for him, poor old fellow.' She made a playful pull on Master John's sleeve. 'You seem unbothered by the heat, John, if I may say so.'

'London gets much hotter than this. All those houses jam-packed together with not a breath of air able to get in from the river.' He was preoccupied and did not respond to her teasing manner.

'You look tired, friend,' remarked the yellowish man lifting his head from his book for a moment.

'I'm not surprised.' Lissa turned to him. 'You'd be tired if you'd had to worry about getting the cargo off this morning. I believe you were out before Prime, John?'

'You would not see me in church at Prime…that is so. I was organizing the removal of the goods that could be saved. So much smoke damage. I'm ruined but at present have no idea how to compute the extent of my fall.'

'Poor Mistress Beata,' Lissa murmured.

Delith lifted her head.

'Come now, master, someone will have you insured.' Mistress Sour, playing with a string of wooden beads threaded round her neck, leaned over to console him. 'Isn't that so?' She turned to her sister.

But Ceci was threading a green ribbon through one of the straw hats and when Genista nudged her she glanced up. 'I'm sure the master has considered that. Even so it must be saddening to find that the beautiful things one has bought are damaged or destroyed. Things brought in with much trial and tribulation from afar. Have you managed to save much, John?'

'Some things,' he replied in deepest gloom. 'Who can say until we've compared the inventory with what's lost?'

'Where are the goods you've taken off?' persisted Mistress Sour.

'Safe in the abbot's store. He has everything under lock and key with a guard on duty. For what good that will do me now. We checked the amount of bales going in this morning while you were all at your prayers but could not do much else. '

'Cheer up,' replied Mistress Sweet. 'Never say all is lost. There's always a way out. Forget not, there is always something to sell and always someone willing to buy.'

Master John gave a sceptical grimace then softened as he looked into her upturned face.

'Your advice is welcome, mistress. Never admit defeat. No, we must never do that.'

Did any of the others know a body had been found, Hildegard wondered. It seemed not to be the case because the next moment Lissa gave a sigh and said, 'At least no-one was drowned. It's quite remarkable. What are mere material goods compared to the saving of lives?' Murmurs of agreement followed. Master John inspected his fingernails and admitted nothing.

Hildegard was glad when one of the lay-brothers approached bearing a pitcher and some beakers. 'The kitchener has taken pity on you all,' he announced. 'He sends his best ale and begs you to make the most of your enforced sojourn here.'

While everyone was helping themselves to beakers and holding them up to be filled Hildegard took the opportunity to ask, 'Is Alaric still helping you in the kitchen just now?'

'Not him! He's swimming as he does whenever he has a spare moment and after that he'll attend Friar Hywel and help in the Great

Work.'

She smiled as if it was of no more than passing interest. While John was fretting about going back on board the St Marie to make sure they hadn't missed anything, Delith was playing with her bird in a queenly manner and ignoring everyone. The others were lying listlessly in the heat and for a time no-one moved until at last Lissa rose with the words, 'I'd better see how that husband of mine is faring, poor old fellow.' She glanced at John as she spoke. 'Would you like me to call in on Beata, John?'

'That would be a kindness, Alicia. Please inform her I shall be along as soon as conditions permit.'

Lissa. John. Beata.

And then there was Delith.

'I think I'll take a stroll by the river,' Hildegard announced. 'It's so hot in the shade it doesn't seem to make any difference where we are. Look, there's not a breath of air.'

She pointed to the trees on the other side of the

abbey wall. Their branches were motionless, like the woven trees in Abbot Philip's tapestry.

Leaving Lissa at the door to the guest house she took her time to go outside the precinct. As she wended her way along the path to the river bank no-one came out to check their cargo on the St Marie.

The little lay-brother with the welcome flagon of ale was accurately informed. A group of lads were splashing about in the shallows. Southampton Water lay before her like a sheet of blue fallen from the sky

She went down onto the strand to find somewhere to sit so she could watch. One of them made a perfect cartwheel off the side into the sparkling depths.

Alaric.

When he surfaced he gave a shout and began to egg the other boys on to do the same but none of them had his grace and training. One or two jumped in with a lot of ungainly splashing and, jeering, Alaric swam under the jetty and tried to pull the others in by their ankles. They retaliated by splash-bombing him and the whole gang disappeared under a surge of spray, shouting and yelling with delight when they surfaced. To Hildegard it looked blissful. They had chosen the only cool place on such a day.

Patiently she sat on the shingle and watched. She felt uncomfortable in the heat, her summer robe sticky and hot, and eventually, unable to stop herself, she closed her eyes against the sun when the aquatic stunts began to tire her. He could not stay in the water forever.

Later, she had no idea how much later, the resonant toll of a bell drifted from the direction of the abbey calling the boys back to their duties and with evident reluctance they ran to claim their tunics where they were piled on the beach close to where she sat. They were beginning to drag them on over their wet skin as Alaric sprinted up last, shaking brilliants from his hair and grinning when he saw Hildegard. Comical in his wet breaks, he gave a bow as perfect as any seen at court.

'Are you not allowed in the water, domina?'

'Not with all these people around.' She indicated a few fishermen mending nets further along the beach.

'I can show you a more secluded pool down at the other end if you wish?' He held out a hand. 'Would you like to see?'

'Don't you have to go to your chores?'

'Only to face Master Hywel and his perpetual disdain.' He pulled a face. 'I welcome an excuse to be late for that trial.'

She got up as he began to pull on his tunic.

'I'd be delighted - if you're sure you won't get into trouble?'

'Of course I'll be in trouble. But I'd be in trouble anyway, whatever I did, you know what he thinks of me...' he broke off. 'Forgive me, I did not mean to denigrate...'

She laughed. 'I know. He doesn't choose to hide his opinions. I'm sure he would be the first to agree with what you say of him. I believe he is not ignorant of his faults.'

'You're right. It's quite painful. He's so intent on perfecting himself in order to engage in his Magnum Opus nothing less than perfection inn those around him will do. The Great Work is all he thinks about. But he's stewing now because he imagines God sent a lightning-bolt to express his displeasure at the book he asked to be sent from Outremer. Can you believe such reason and folly exist in the mind of one man?'

Surprised at Alaric's opinion of Hywel she allowed him to escort her along the beach. The other boys ran off up the bank towards the gatehouse as the bell continued to toll.

'Why do you have such an opinion of him?' she asked as they began to walk along the bank.

Alaric looked at her sideways. 'I would expect a man of learning which he undoubtedly is to have a surer grasp of his small place in the world. The truth of Scripture as it is taught us and the absence of power we have to determine the actions of God - if he exists in the form we are told - should make him both more humble and less critical of his own sense of powerlessness.'

'That's a complicated thought, Alaric. Do you mind my asking how old you are?'

'I reckon I'm about eighteen or nineteen. I met a priest once who talked to me about belief and how there are other ways of thinking about it than the one we're taught. It made sense to me. That's why…' he bit his lip. 'Am I saying too much?'

'I doubt whether any of us can say too much. Saying too little is worse. Hiding resentment and confusion in our hearts seems to me to be a sin against ourselves as well as against truth.'

'Truth? Where does that come in when we're told what it is instead of being free to work it out ourselves?'

'Why are we given the power to reason if not to use it?' Thinking it best to mention the name that hovered over this exchange – an omission that might lead to confusion - she said, 'Magister Wyclif would have agreed with you. He thought we could come to understand ideas ourselves, without being coerced into belief by those who've assumed authority over us.'

His expression did not show surprise so she continued, 'He was attacked by those churchmen who believe we're best left in ignorance…not just bishops and alal the rest,' she hastened to add, 'but women monastics too. Some of those prioresses, not my own, I'm pleased to say, but others I've met daren't take so much as a drink of water without first checking whether it's allowed or not.'

He threw his head back, his fine, fair face lifted to the sun. 'Praise the cherubim and all the saints! It's a joy to hear you say that. I dare not speak my mind here. That's why I want to learn to read. Armed with direct knowledge of what the Bible says I'll be able to counter the arguments of all-comers.'

'I hope you'll always bear in mind your own safety. The times we live in are not kind to free-thinkers.'

They came out from a stand of willows and Hywel turned his blazing, open, youthful smile on her. 'Are some things worth the risk of dying for, do you think?'

'That's for each of us to decide for ourselves.'

'Some say the flame of truth must be protected at all costs in case darker forces put it out forever.'

'So they say.'

He pointed down the slope. 'Look! There's the pool I promised. See how secluded it is? I often swim here when I'm sick of my dear lay-brothers and their constant talk of sheep.'

'It looks deep, with a swift current further out.'

'It is. Treacherous. Stay near the bank and only venture in if you can swim. It's worth the challenge for the pure joy of swimming in such peace and beauty. You can swim, can't you?'

'Of course. We used to swim in the Derwent when I was a child. Long ago!' she added with a laugh. 'It's a placid river winding through thick woodland close to where I lived as a child. We could swim to the opposite bank in moments. It's not like this.'

For a moment they both stared across the wide

stretch of water towards the fishermen's huts on the opposite bank. Too far off to observe in detail they lay shimmering in the heat haze as before, levels of blue dwindling into the darker mass of the distant Royal Forest.

'Where those huts are is a place called Deep Dale Purlieu,' he told her, following her glance. 'It's outside the King's writ, separate from his royal forest and the law of the verderers.'

'Disputed land?'

'It depends on who you are. Outlaws are unlikely to be in dispute as it's their only safe place round here – that is, if you find living rough safe enough for you.' He turned abruptly. 'So there it is, domina. Your own private pool. I hope you'll enjoy it if your Rule allows.'

He began to walk quickly away for some reason. 'Alaric!' she called. 'Wait! I want to ask you something.'

He swivelled at the top of the bank and gazed down at her.

'Last night during the storm I saw you climbing

onto the St Marie…' She paused to allow him time to deny it. When he merely stared at her she added, 'I expect that anchor chain was child's play to you.'

He gave a strange smile and turned his head. 'Indeed. Nothing to it.'

'Can you tell me who was on board when you arrived?'

'Oh I see. Is it Master John?'

'What do you mean?'

'I expect he's been claiming that his cargo has been broken open and certain precious items stolen?' He began to laugh in a sarcastic way.

'Why do you think that?'

'Because he keeps on saying so in a most pointed manner in front of any of those he would like to accuse more openly - especially we lay-brothers. He agrees with Brother Hywel on that topic. We're all thieves, didn't you know?'

'I think he's merely worried that he can't fulfil his promise to bring in certain items for the man who underwrites his ship. At least, that's what we deduce from his current anxiety.'

'And do you know who the master of this master is?' He gave her a cold glance. 'I know and I expect you do too…I'd feel anxious in his shoes.' He drew his fingers across his neck then began to stride off into the break of trees and in a moment she saw him reach the path and start out on it.

Bundling her skirts in one hand so she could climb more quickly up the bank she hurried after him. 'Alaric, tell me what you mean.'

'I'm sworn to secrecy,' he muttered when she caught up with him. 'You had no need to warn me about speaking out. I'm well aware of the danger.' His grey eyes glinted with a resigned humour, making him look older and too disenchanted with the world for his years.

'Does your discretion prevent you from answering my question about who was on board last night?' she persisted.

'You know I don't want to tell you that.'

'No hint?' She gazed at him, eye to eye,

refusing her challenge to name names before he admitted them himself. 'I don't want to put words into your mouth. I thought you might tell me of your own volition.'

'Think the worst of me.' He shrugged and began to walk off at a brisk pace so that she decided to let him go.

If anyone in the abbey apart from the abbot and those who had gone over that morning to view the body knew that Brother Martin was dead it would be the lay-brothers. They had a knack of picking up information as they went about the abbey and were not stone-deaf as some people imagined. Alaric's refusal to answer meant nothing. Soon everyone else would know what had happened whether Abbot Philip announced it or not.

On impulse she ran after him and he gave a start as he had evidently not heard her approach.

'I'm sorry, I didn't mean to startle you. If I mention Brother Martin will his presence on board be a surprise to you? Shake your head if his name means nothing.'

He closed his eyes. When he opened them he said, 'I saw him. You know I must have. He was dead before I arrived. I hope you believe that.'

He moved off and this time she let him go.

Gregory and Egbert were waiting for her in the porch at the south door when she entered Cloister Garth. She went over to them.

'Have you had a useful time?' She told them about Alaric being one of the first to go on board the St Marie. 'All the lay-brothers will know Brother Martin is dead. You know how things are here. It won't be long before the whole abbey knows, no matter whether Abbot Philip makes an announcement or not.'

'Why did you need to speak to this particular lay-brother?' asked Gregory with interest.

She explained how she had seen him go on board. 'I needed to ask him more but he's as unpredictable as a wild animal.' He reminded her of a fawn, slight and graceful but shivering with nerves at the slightest scent of danger. It frightened her to feel so protective of him when everything pointed to his involvement in the monk's death.

'We put in an appearance in church for Philip's benefit but we're off to have that jug of ale with the shipman now,' Egbert told her.

'I notice your investigations always seem to involve ale,' she said as, smiling, she left them.

CHAPTER FOUR

After she had looked in on Hubert and found him asleep again, she returned to the garth. The members of the little group of pilgrims and other guests in the cloister had changed since she had seen them earlier. Lissa had returned with Simon. The two sisters had gone over to the fountain, both wearing straw hats sporting coloured ribbons and looking self-consciously picturesque as they scooped water into their ale mugs and Delith had her back to Lionel, the Winchester merchant who was still swinging his legs nonchalantly on the wall and looking longingly at the dicemen. They were still playing but in a listless way that showed they couldn't care less who won.

The little maid, Lucie, was absent as was Master John.

It was too hot to think. Hildegard wiped a hand over her face.

'Has John gone over to the ship?' she asked. She had not seen him if he had.

Lissa shook her head. 'He went to the sacristy instead. He wanted to find out when they can start on the inventory.'

'But have they removed all the cargo yet?' She wondered how they had dealt with the fact of a dead body in the hold if so.

'That's what's making him so anxious. He thinks anybody could go over and take what they wanted with only the shipman and a couple of crew to guard it.'

'He should rest easy.' Lionel, hitching an imagined crease out of his yellow cotte, spoke up. 'Pirates won't risk coming up this far nowadays. They know they'd get a bloody nose.'

'I can't see why you say that, with respect, Lionel. We have nobody to defend us here except for the presence of the French houses at Beaulieu and a few other places – and I can't see the monks coming out with cross-bows to fight them off.'

Lionel chuckled. 'Maybe you're right, mistress, although pirates don't always come from France.' He went back to watching the dice-men.

'I do hope you're wrong, Lionel, with respect.' Lissa showed she was going to have the last word. 'I'd hate to think of our own people thieving from us.' She turned to Hildegard, 'It's so remote here. The monks glory in their isolation. It doesn't do for me, I can tell you.'

Resisting the impulse to point out that that was precisely why the monks chose to build their monasteries in the wilds, far from the little hates and quarrels of the towns, Hildegard reached for the ale jug and, after offering it round, poured herself a beaker full to quench her thirst.

They seemed stuck in a globe of heat, an airless glass globe such as the Venetians make, with an abbey constructed out of painted wood and tiny figures with no escape, destined to be trapped in mindless immobility forever. She envied the boys their freedom to swim naked and for a moment imagined returning to the pool Alaric had shown her to have a swim in private – but the effort of walking all the way back in the stifling heat was too much to contemplate.

Delith rose languidly to her feet and gave an exaggerated sigh. 'I shall go in to pray for us all and that this purgatory will soon be ended.'

With the blackbird, now resigned to its perch on her shoulder, she trailed across the garth without a backward glance and disappeared inside the dark entrance to the church. Hildegard waited for Lionel in his itchy yellow cotte to follow. But he went on swinging his legs, saying nothing, not moving except for the soft thump-thump of his heels on the stone-work as he hummed a song to himself.

Sooner than expected she noticed Gregory and Egbert pacing into the cloister on the far side and she rose to her feet. They met as if by chance at the farthest corner where the novices had their lessons.

'Anything new?'

'He says there's going to be another storm,' Egbert greeted.

'And?'

'He's worried about his beloved's ability to

weather it.'

'Come somewhere quiet and we'll tell you the rest of it.'

'His story is,' Egbert began as soon as they were out of hearing of others, 'they were all lying out on deck because of the heat.' He took a long drink from his flask. 'Two of them were playing dice. It seems to be the passion round here. Another was perfecting a wooden whistle he'd made earlier, the bo'sun was telling some yarn about sailing down Biscay way, and a fifth was cutting into the last keg the ship man had brought up for them as fast as he could. Then,' he gave a quick, sideways glance at Hildegard, full of meaning, 'someone arrived by boat.'

'Can I guess who that was?'

There was a pause then Gregory nodded. 'It was Mistress Delith.'

'She was not alone,' Egbert added.

'Someone as well as the oarsman?'

'There was no oarsman, according to the ship

man. "I reckon it was that monk who sculled the boat over," he said to us, "shrouded as he was and I only got a glimpse before he went below and I can't be sure, but I let him aboard because I thought he'd been sent by the Abbot and would come up on deck and tell me the reason why he was here when he'd done what he came to do." Not happy about that, apparently. Taking liberties, says the ship man, and he the master and all.'

'And he never did find out what the monk came for, if what he's telling us is true, because next time he saw him he was dead.'

'Well, have you asked Mistress Delith if it was Brother Martin who was with her?'

'We were on our way to do just that when we bumped into you.'

'She's in church, praying for us all at present,' Hildegard replied.

'As well she needs to, for herself most of all.' Gregory shrugged.

'Did you ask what Delith did when she arrived?'

'Of course we did.   He told us she sang a couple of songs for his boys, did a little dance, told a joke or two, and then, of course, he clammed up.'

'Gregory became impatient at that point, didn't you, brother?'

'Fakery always annoys me. If you transgress at least own up to it.'

'Greg said, "Come on man, we've not been monks all our lives. Celibacy only applies after our vows. What happened next? Who went below with her?" Give us names.'

'And what did he say?'

'That it was too hot to go below so they went behind an awning on the after deck.'

'How many of them?'

'Just one, bored with his whistling, and the bo'sun.'

'That's not just one, it's two. Can't he add up?' said Hildegard. 'What about the others?'

'They went on playing dice, apparently, and the one with the opened keg went on drinking.'

'It was then the weather broke. They crowded

under the for'ard hatch for shelter.'

'Where was the monk all this time?'

'Still below deck.'

'And Mistress Delith?'

'Tom had had his fill so she sheltered with the rest of them out of the rain. Then, of course, the mast was struck by lightning.'

'God striking them down for their sins.'

'Shame-faced, sceptical, ready to risk it all again when they've got over the shock, I shouldn't wonder,' Gregory added.

'Give him his due, the ship man treated her well, "like a lady," he told us. "I got a couple of the crew to take her safely ashore." We asked him who was still on the ship and he tallied them off on his fingers. He reckoned they could swim for it or wait for a boat to row back to fetch 'em off. He said, "Them lay-brothers had things organized, right quick they were." It was his duty as ship man to stay to the end. That's when he found the body.'

'We asked him who he'd noticed coming on

board   He said, "Lots of them. Do you think I was keeping a tally by that time?   You were there yourselves, in a boat, shouting up, in among them."   I said, "That's true, master, but we didn't go on board and murder a poor old monk."'

'He went a bit quiet after that.'

Gregory stretched his legs. 'There you have it, Hildegard. What do you make of it?'

'But was Delith ever alone after she went onboard? It doesn't sound like it.' So how had she obtained the secret she had taunted Lionel with? Or was that simply a lie to make a fool of him – holding out a false promise of gain? 'We need to talk to Delith.'

'How do we get her to tell the truth to us, of all people? Everybody lies through their teeth when they speak to us. I'll never understand why. We're the only ones who can absolve them of their sins. We're not here to judge. That'll come later.'

'Remind her of that,' Hildegard suggested. 'Why don't one of you go to her alone and get into conversation with her? Now would be a good time while she's on her knees in there.'

Gregory uncoiled his long length and stretched. 'I'll go. This little sinner intrigues me. I don't understand how anybody falls into such straits as to sell their body when they clearly hold it at greater worth than their soul.' Smiling, he loped off in the direction of the church.

A large comfortable-looking boat was pulled up on the beach. Jankin brought the news to everyone, calling down the cloister in an echoing voice that everyone could hear. 'And it's brought the coroner from Southampton!' Plainly excited he ran down to where Hildegard and Egbert were sitting. 'Did you hear that, domina?'

'About the coroner? I should think even the abbot over in his lodgings heard you.' She smiled. 'Have you told your master?'

'It was he who sent me to announce his arrival.'

Turning to Egbert she said, 'This will settle any doubt we have about Brother Martin's death.'

Jankin was accompanied by Delith's little maid,

Lucie. Her clipped blonde hair was as usual sticking out in tiny spikes like a halo and she flattened it with her hand and asked, 'What's he here for, domina? Is there trouble?'

'No doubt he'll make an announcement all in good time,' she replied. To Jankin she asked, 'Where's your master now?'

'He's on his way up with him.' Jankin turned, 'Look, here they come.'

Friar Hywel, grim-faced, was stalking alongside a brisk, well set-up man of forty or thereabouts wearing a light summer houpeland, latch shoes and a straw hat.

'No sales there for the sisters,' murmured Egbert tilting his own newly purchased sun hat to shield his eyes from the glare. 'Let's go on over to make ourselves known.' Gregory was just coming out of the church by himself and Egbert waved him over.

Already the coroner was surrounded by several monks, the sub-prior among them, and it looked as if the news had spread to a chosen few. The sub-prior bustled over to them.

'I trust you two brothers and our sister in God are willing to go back onto the St Marie with the coroner? Abbot Philip wishes it,' he added as if they might refuse.

The friar, presumably unaware of their instructions from Abbot Philip until that moment, looked irritated when Egbert stepped up and introduced themselves to the coroner and then suggested a drink before setting out for the ship. As a friar Hywel had no power in the monastery and, with a dark look at Egbert, he ceded his position. He stepped beside Hildegard and muttered, 'Did you know about this?'

The coroner drew their attention before she could think of an honest reply. He was saying, 'The lord sheriff informed me there was an unexplained death and as I was already taking a look at a poor wretch struck by lightning on the other shore it offered me the opportunity of doing two jobs in one day. Where's the body? Still on the ship, I'm told.'

'Yes, you passed it when you crossed the Water,' Gregory replied. 'We left him as he was found, until you arrived. Blessings on you, my lord, for your celerity. The question of putrefaction will shortly become a problem in this heat.'

'Let's go at once,' the coroner replied. 'We'll forgo that drink. I want to get back to the other side before dusk.'

So saying the group turned back under the gatehouse. As they passed the porter's lodge the man on duty called over to Egbert. 'A word, brother?'

Egbert went over. 'What is it? The coroner's a hurried man.'

'You remember what you asked me yesterday?' The porter gave a narrow glance after the group walking ahead and when Hildegard turned to look back he was whispering something to Egbert before going back inside the lodge.

When Egbert caught up he gave Hildegard a secret glance and opened his palm to show her a key. 'In case of need,' he said out of the corner of his mouth. It was the lodge key. Swords, she supposed. Was the man expecting trouble?

The boat had two rowing and was large enough to take everyone in comfort. The ship man was waiting on the deck of the St Marie to keep a look-out and watched them aboard.

'Down here, my lord.' He led the way to the hatch. 'Not room for us all at once. Some cargo is still on board. I'll be glad to get it off but they tell me we can't move anything more until you've had a good look round.'

When the coroner went below he had the friar at his heels. The rest followed and crowded inside as best they could.

Hildegard hung back. She took the opportunity to question the ship man. 'I understood Master John has taken some of his cargo into safe storage within the abbey precincts?'

'He's only taken off some valuables kept in there where I could keep an eye on them myself.

Most of his imports are in the hold or on deck. He lost much of the latter. The rest might be salvaged. The big stuff,' he explained. 'His bales of precious silks. His velvets. His plate.' After assessing her with a glance he lowered his voice, 'You know this has put a curse on my ship, domina? I hope they understand that? She'll need an exorcist before we can move her up river. I can't risk moving her until she's pure again.' The lines between his brows deepened. 'I can't fathom out what killed him. No sign of blood. Who can have done it? Or what?'

He gave her a long, frightened stare and lowered his voice. 'Was it the devil? How would the devil get onto my St Marie? We're a good ship. No worse than any other. Can you understand it?'

'Not at present.' She bit her lip. 'In confidence, master, they believe it to be some kind of poison and in that case it would have to be administered by human hand.'

'But how could that happen without the devil

being involved? Who would think of giving poison to a monk? None of my lads were down there. They couldn't have done it even if they'd been possessed enough to do something so evil. I've already told your brothers what they were up to. They never went down below, I can vouch for that. And he never even spoke to them when he came on board, that monk. He went straight below. And,' he added meaningfully, 'what was he doing with a woman like that?' His lip curled. 'That's another question that needs answering, to my mind.'

Hildegard nodded. 'I quite agree with you, master. You've hit the nail on the head.'

He gave her a complicit though subdued grimace and went to reassert his dominion over the land-lubbers making free on his ship.

'Well, my lords,' she heard him say as he poked his head down inside the hatch. 'Have you now confirmed that he's a dead man?'

The coroner was the first to climb out into the fresh air with an answer. 'We have indeed, master.'

'And your verdict as to the cause of his sad demise?'

'Poison. No doubt of that. Tell me, my good fellow, do you carry anything on board of such a pernicious nature? Herbs from foreign lands, spices whose qualities are in doubt?'

'Only the usual, my lord.'

The coroner stroked his beard while he considered all possibilities. 'These fiendish poisons from Venice are the work of the devil. Do you know…' he glanced round to astonish them, 'they've concocted a poison that they can put on the saddle of a man's horse that'll kill him instantly? Or at least, that's what they say. Never come across it myself but there's always a first time.' He became brisk again. 'I've decided to leave the matter in abbey hands.'

Gregory was just emerging from below and caught these words. 'The abbot will welcome your decision, my lord, and he'll want to have Brother Martin taken to the mortuary as soon as possible, given this heat, so may we now move him?'

'You may. I shall inform the Sheriff that although the law clerks are still in discussion I have authorized the matter to be placed in your capable hands. I will inform your Abbot before I take my leave.'

Hildegard thought there was something odd about Gregory's expression even though all he did was address the ship man. 'How soon can you have him taken ashore, master?'

'Leave it with me.' He went for'ard where his two crew men were sitting and he could be heard telling them to put the body into the ship's boat and row it over. When he came back he asked, 'Will the lay-brothers fetch him from the beach? My fellas are not keen to set foot on land.'

'We'll stay with him until a messenger can be sent to have him taken to the mortuary.' Egbert glanced at Gregory who nodded.

'We must talk to Delith and find out how she came to be in a boat sculled by a monk. Knowing what some of them think about women anyway, it seems extraordinary that he should have agreed to go with her unaccompanied. They left before the lightning struck so it was not a question of Brother Martin trying to save lives and Delith begging a lift to do likewise.'

Hildegard paced about on the shingle foreshore after the coroner had been conducted up to Abbot Philip's lodgings by the friar. Only Gregory and Egbert remained.

'I can't imagine where she went earlier,' said Gregory. 'She must have changed her mind about going into pray. She wasn't in the church at all when I went looking. Nobody was.'

The death boat, as Egbert referred to the ship's small lighter with the body aboard, had already set off from the St Marie and they were watching for it to reach the shore. Friar Hywel, still visible through the trees, was accompanying the coroner as far as the gate-house from where he would be able to send for some conversi to carry the body back for laying-out in the mortuary.

'As soon as we can I'll go and find her,' Gregory continued, 'but surely she can't have anything to do with a poison as rare as the one the coroner was hinting at?'

'Henbane would be about the level of her knowledge of poisons, I would expect,' Hildegard agreed, 'the unhappy and unscrupulous wife's stand-by.   But that's out unless somebody persuaded the monk to take a good long drink of it as soon as he arrived.'

'I often wonder about these unexpected deaths and what appear to be false tears afterwards,' Egbert admitted with a grimace.   'There are too many malign plants growing around our woods and commons.   They should be dug up wherever they're found.   They put temptation in people's way.'

'That may be their purpose.   If they didn't fulfil the role of temptation, it'd be something else,' Hildegard asserted.

Their solemnity deepened as the boat scraped onto the shingle.   The two crewmen sprang out at once as if they couldn't bear to be in the same vessel as a corpse while a contingent of purposeful lay-brothers were already hurrying down the bank towards them.

'I'll go and find her,' Gregory muttered tersely. 'Everything all right with you two?"

They nodded.

'Then I'll see you later with the answer to the next piece of the puzzle.' He strode off.

Hildegard went off with the cortege straightaway and left Egbert staring after them. They took the body along the shaded cool of the path through the woods and in through the gatehouse and then the full glare of the sun scorching down on Cloister Garth and turning it to a desert broke over their heads. She dragged out her straw hat which she had taken off while on the boat and crammed it back on her head.

Idling guests looked up from the cloisters as they passed. No sign of Delith among them. She accompanied the cortege into the mortuary.

As soon as they entered its cold musty

atmosphere the chill of death seeped into her bones. No-one had said much about Brother Martin, what he was like, how they thought of him. With the poison still in his body his features were distorted horribly and there was no way of knowing whether he was young or old. The lay-sisters used to laying out bodies were already prepared.

'You may stay if you wish, domina but this will not be pleasant.'

'I feel I should know who he is,' she replied to the sister who had greeted her. 'Is there no-one to honour him from Chapter?'

'At prayers again, domina, but one or two will be along straight afterwards I wouldn't doubt.'

'He must have been a familiar figure to you all?' she suggested, helping to loosen the monk's sandals and handing them to one of the helpers. She felt an overwhelming poignancy when she looked at his feet. There was something intimate in seeing the feet of a dead man more closely than perhaps anyone had ever done in real life. They were slim with long toes, carefully clipped nails, a little grimy from walking in the dusty garth and with roughened soles from going barefoot. It suddenly struck her that he was probably quite a young man.

'How old would he have been?' she asked the lay-sister pulling aside the white habit. Pale thighs no darker than his linen breaks were revealed.

'Thirty or so I would guess. A bookish type. Never saw much of him. He tended to his own needs. He didn't have much time for us.' She pulled the habit over the corpse's head to reveal a narrow chest, lightly covered in dark hair but the distortions caused by the poison had inflamed his neck and shoulders and it was this that made him look grotesque.

His face was bloated as if pumped with air like the pigs' bladders the boys used in their games making his eyes disappear into the folds of flesh.

Hildegard bent her head at the sight of such disfigurement then straightened. 'What else may I do to help?'

'Come with me,' said the lay-sister. Hildegard recognised her as the one who looked after the guests. When they were on one side she said, 'For all his shyness he was a nice young fellow. Take no notice if anyone tells you otherwise. We must get to the bottom of this, domina. It's only right.'

'There's no way he could have taken something deliberately? I know that's a terrible thing to suggest – ' she added hurriedly when she saw the look of horror on her face, 'but sometimes we never know what straits people are undergoing until it's too late.'

'He would never go against the Church's teachings,' she replied. Her cold look made Hildegard apologise again for imputing sin to an apparently good man.

'But do you have any idea why he went out to the St Marie? I understood the monks were instructed to pray for survivors in the church. Was he perhaps looking for something?'

'All I know about him for sure, apart from his goodness and concern for others, was that Abbot

Philip regarded him as likely for promotion in the abbey hierarchy. He thought most highly of him.'

Wondering how the lay-sister knew such a thing she was wondering how to frame the question without offending her again when she supplied the answer herself. 'He already entrusted him with the keys to the sacristy. The lord abbot would never do that lightly unless he was absolutely sure of him, would he?'

With nothing much else in the way of practical help to offer Hildegard went to the trestle on which the body was lying and offered up a prayer for his soul. Before she left a monk came in from the last Office to sit in vigil beside him.

She stepped outside into a blaze of heat and light. It was only mid-day. She rubbed her eyes. It seemed an age since she'd given a thought to Hubert.

'So now you're brought up to date,' she told him after she had refilled his flask with wine and listened to his complaints about being so useless.

'We do need you, that's true,' she told him, 'but we'll try to solve the mystery of Martin's death without you. At least, not without your untangling of whatever threads we can bring to you. The solution may lie with Delith and Gregory is already questioning her. She should be able to throw some light on the mystery as she was there on board when he died.'

'Gregory hadn't spoken to her when he called in here a few minutes ago,' Hubert told her.'

'What was he doing here?'

'Looking for her. Nobody seems to know where she is.'

'I noticed her little maid when I left the mortuary,' she told him.

'With her mistress?'

'Actually no, she wasn't now I come to think of it.'

'Go and ask her where she is, Hildegard. She's bound to know. It'll save Gregory getting into a fret.'

CHAPTER FIVE

Hat tilted over her eyes she went outside again. Lucie's halo of bright hair was clearly visible. She was sitting by herself in the cloisters with the blackbird in her lap. When Hildegard went up she had the wariness of a maid who expected to be beaten. 'If you're going to ask me the same question that funny Brother Gregory did, I can't tell you,' she began.

Hildegard laughed. 'Can't or won't?'

The girl's face broke into a shy smile. 'You're just like Jankin. He always picks through words. Can't. I would if I could. I haven't seen her since she got up from over there...' she indicated the pilgrims' corner, 'and went into the church.'

'May I sit down?'

'Here, share my cushion.' She girl moved over a bit.

'Does she often go off like this?' Hildegard sat down and tucked up her legs.

'She doesn't go anywhere without telling me

where she's going and who with, for safety.'

'Safety?'

The girl blushed. 'You know…'

'I don't suppose she saw that as a consideration, here in the abbey. She surely wasn't thinking of…I mean, the men here have a holy purpose, by and large.'

'That wouldn't stop her if she had her eye on someone.'

'I meant the monks, I suppose…' she glanced across the garth towards the three mercenaries fooling around near the fountain, adding. 'Even those lads in their mail shirts will surely respect the place they're in whatever their true purpose in being here…'

'They're only waiting for the cargo to be unloaded so they can drive it back under guard to their lord Arundel,' Lucie said. 'They don't care that it's an abbey. It's free food and ale as far as they're concerned.'

Interesting, Hildegard thought, storing away the information about Arundel with an unspoken question about a cargo that needed three armed guards.

'I'm sure you needn't worry about your mistress's safety,' she reassured the girl. 'This is one of the safest place on earth.' She stopped. The St Marie hadn't proved safe. On the other hand it was not exactly within the holy abbey precincts if you wanted to run a fine tooth-comb through the argument. She bit her lip. It was foolish, even so, to talk about safety, even though Delith presumably knew what she was doing.

'I wonder if your mistress mentioned anything about going out to the St Marie last night just before the storm broke?' she asked.

The girl looked down, somewhat shamed. 'I suppose everybody knows she went out there by now and what for,' she mumbled. 'Jankin guessed at once and that monk you're friendly with knew for sure.' She lifted her pert and pretty face. 'Because I'm her maid it doesn't mean I think what she does is right. I would never do a thing like that...' A tear began to slide down her cheek.

'I'll never get away and I don't know what to do. She feeds me. She gives me clothes and shoes to wear. I was like Jankin when my mother died. I used to run errands for the merchants. Then she found me... She's...'

'She's...?'

'She's not kind to me - but at least I don't have to sleep on the streets anymore and she makes sure her...her customers,' she mumbled, 'she keeps her customers away from me.'

Or you from them, thought Hildegard, assessing with compassion the youthful, innocent and pretty face. Delith would never again have what Lucie had and some men would pay a higher price for innocence than for all the tricks of the trade. She took her by the hand. 'Are you worried about what's going to happen to you if she's abandoned you?'

'I suppose I am.' She blushed again, to a shade like the pink of a freshly opened anemone and it made Hildegard want to put a cloak of protection over her and tell her that all would be well but instead she said, 'We'll no doubt find her sitting in the cool shade somewhere happily playing with her pet blackbird. And even,' she laughed as at something unthinkable, 'even if she actually abandoned you I can guarantee you'd always find someone here to look after you. I promise you that.'

Lucie blushed even more. 'He can hardly look after himself, let alone anyone else.'

Hildegard guessed the meaning of Lucie's blushes. 'Jankin's a clever lad. He'll never go hungry, nor will anyone he cares for.'

'Thank you, domina.' The blue eyes shone for a moment. 'I shall stay here until he comes back.'

'Where is he?'

'Helping Master John and Brother Hywel count things off in the sacristy. They're going to fetch everything else off the cog before night-fall.'

As Hildegard got up to go she blurted, 'I hadn't thought of this till now but you might also find my mistress there. Hovering about Master John.'

'She has designs on him?'

'A wealthy merchant? Of course she does. He could be her means to salvation. At least, that's what she told me.'

'Lucie, maybe you can tell me why she wanted Friar Hywel to do that horrible thing to the blackbird?'

'It's going to be part of her act. She's hoping to set herself up as a seer when we get to France…if she fails to find a rich man before then.'

Hildegard saw her glance move away and then, like a sudden burst of sunshine, her eyes lit up. She rose onto her knees on the cushion and when Hildegard turned it was to see Jankin dancing towards them.

He gave a neat bow to Hildegard but his attention was fixed on Lucie and without being invited he threw himself down beside her onto the cushion and gave her a hug. Hildegard decided it was tactful to leave but Jankin stopped her. 'What do you think to this, domina?'

When she looked closer she saw he was holding out a mouse.

'Oh let me see!' cried Lucie.

'Aren't you afraid of him?' he asked her.

'What? Of a furry little creature like this? May I hold him? What's he called?'

'You can choose a name for him if you like.' He looked up at Hildegard, 'Friar Hywel instructed me to kill him for one of his experiments but I couldn't bring myself to do so. The little fellow has a wife and six tiny babies still with their eyes shut. I'll show you their nest,' he said, turning to Lucie, 'if your mistress will let you come with me.'

'Her. I've just said, she's probably making eyes at Merchant John and I'm supposed to be making friends with his wife who's ill to find out his secrets to take back so mistress can work better on him.'

Jankin frowned. 'Are you going to?'

'Would I dare not?'

'She'd never know whether what you said was true or not.'

'I hadn't thought of that.'

'Is a lie sometimes not such a sin, domina?'

'It depends. If the person being lied to is also lying it makes it a confusing point, certainly.'

'There you are then, she's lying to you so you can lie to her.' Jankin beamed.

Hildegard was just about to dispute the point when he swerved back to the topic of mice, 'I'm keeping this little fellow. I told brother friar I lost him. I think it's a good lie because it saves the life of a living creature. I'll say I can't get another one for him either because they've all swarmed to the river because of the cat one of the guests brought in. Can you believe that?' He laughed. 'Somebody coming on pilgrimage with a cat!'

'If it's a pet it can be presented to the saint,' Lucie replied.

'Or maybe the owner's a witch,' Jankin added in a dark voice, 'what about that, hey, Lucie?'

She pretended to shiver…although in view of what she had told Hildegard about Delith's intentions, maybe it was not pretence. Deciding it was time to move off Hildegard asked Jankin whether Mistress Delith was in fact in the sacristy making eyes at Master John.

He shook his head. 'Not while I was there she wasn't but her name was mentioned.'

Egbert was playing dice and he seemed to be winning. After what he had said earlier about the passion for the game she was astonished. The three mercenaries were lost in wonder at his apparently endless streak of good luck.

'He's got an unfair advantage over us - with God on his side,' one of them scoffed, defeated. He got up and headed for the kitchens saying, 'I'll go and beg more ale.'

Egbert threw down the dice and made to leave as well. 'I shall have to do a penance for this so I'd better stop now or I'll be on my knees till Christmas. Better luck, lads.' He threw down a few coins. 'Take my winnings. See what they'll do for you. I can't put them to any use.'

He joined Hildegard. 'Well, well,' he said under his breath.

'What?'

'I never expected to be playing dice with Arundel's cut-throats.'

'Arundel?'

'They can't help the fate that's been thrust upon them,' he added with a glint of compassion, 'but I wish they'd open their eyes to the light. Maybe my apparent preferment in the sight of the lord will bring them to it?''

She caught his eye. 'Egbert! You would never do that, would you?' She lowered her voice. 'Sleight of hand?' When he chuckled she said, 'You devil in monk's garb!'

'Ways and means. Worth it to save a soul? You saw how impressed they were?'

'On that same subject of souls, can you tell me if Gregory is still searching for Mistress Delith?'

'He was last time I saw him. Why?'

'Has he tried the sacristy?'

Egbert bestowed one of his special smiles on her. 'Let's go. Who did you get this from?'

The sacristy was a good-sized, vaulted chamber between the Chapter House and the misericord with a door half-way along one wall and a larger one facing Cloister Garth. It had a small ante-chamber with a locked aumbry full of books and with only a couple of narrow window slits had little natural light. A series of cressets in metal wall-brackets were placed at intervals between the storage stacks bestowing colour on a multitude of objects.

Master John's booming voice, magnified by the stone roof vault, came to them distinctly as they banged on the studded oak doors and a lay-brother inspected them through a crack. When he saw a monk and a nun he let them in. At his hip was a useful-looking sword.

'No insult, brother, domina. Just following orders. We've got some valuable stuff in here.'

'Quite right, brother,' Egbert agreed. 'Any thief would be glad to get his hands on this lot, no doubt about that.'

Grinning, the lay-brother led the way to an

inner door and pointed to the chamber beyond. 'If it's Master John and Brother Hywel you want they're in there as you can hear.'

'No-one else with them?' Egbert asked above the sound of raised voices.

'Only Brother Heribert to keep an eye on things.

Egbert indicated for Hildegard to go first.

Such was the fierceness of their argument the two men did not hear anyone enter. Hildegard stopped on the threshold and stayed Egbert with one hand.

Master John was shouting about something not being his fault and that he ran a tight outfit. 'Are you telling me my ship man is a liar? And if he isn't, I am? You scoundrel. You interfering, feckless friar, dragging me into your necromancies. I shan't take this sitting down. You're finished – '

'On the contrary, master.' Hywel sounded ice cold. 'It is not I who am finished but you yourself. When it gets out what has been stolen, and why, you'll be hounded from the county. Then what will you do? Return to London? I doubt you'll be able to. Is your ban still standing?'

'Don't you dare jibe me with that! It was a fix! Everybody with half a brain knows Nick Brembre fixed me good and proper. And now he's fixed and so is his head – on a spike on Tower Hill! I'll be back in favour before you can shake a stick. You don't think I spent two years in Tintagel Castle for nothing do you? Day after day looking at the wall of my prison cell? I know what happened and I know how they rigged the vote – '

'So why did your lord the duke of Lancaster not set you free before he sailed off to Castile? Does he count you so cheap he can do without you?'

Hywel laughed with such open scorn it was enough to send the merchant flying across the chamber towards him as if to grasp him round the throat but Hywel merely gave him a look of such hatred he was stopped in his tracks,

'I would not treat my powers so lightly, merchant, or you might find yourself on the wrong side of one of my spells.'

'I'll have you burned, you heretic – '

'Fortunately England does not burn seers and prophets - although, given the rabid incitements to do so coming from the mouths of lord Arundel and his brother it won't be long before we sink into the same barbarous practices as France and Spain – then everybody will have to watch their tongues, including you.'

'I'll get you for treason then – '

'My crime? Trying to import a book which you and your ship man have allowed to be purloined?' He laughed again. 'I do not think you will do that, master. Not if you know what's good for you.'

'Don't you threaten me, you cur!'

Egbert was gripping Hildegard by the arm until it hurt. She turned her head. 'Shall we go or stay?'

'Stay?' Egbert nodded his head faintly and stepped past her. 'My dear friends, are we interrupting something?'

Both men stared open-mouthed.

'We were, it seems, unreliably informed that Mistress Delith was here?'

Hywel gave a sneering laugh.

Heribert, flattened against the bales of goods shrank back even further.

Genial as ever Egbert said, 'A search party is out looking for the good widow. This was our last resort.' He pretended to peer round as if she might be hiding among the bales.

'Of course she's not here! Why should she be? And I told that man on the door not to let anyone in. I'll skin him alive – '

'My fault entirely, master,' Egbert broke in. 'I pulled rank on the poor fellow. Forgive him. He was coerced by me most shamefully and could not do otherwise than obey me,' and to drive home the point about rank he added, 'brother friar, master,' and inclined his head in a most abbatial manner towards each of them.

John gave a sideways glance at Hywel and they both fell back a pace. 'Can we help you?' he asked grudgingly.

'Not if she's not here. We'll let you get on with your business. Bless you both.'

He and Hildegard withdrew but slowly enough to hear John mutter, 'Did they hear anything? What are they slinking about here for?'

'You heard them. They're after one of your followers - ' but the rest of Hywel's words were inaudible.

At the door on their way out Egbert spoke to the lay-brother. 'If they give you any trouble, let me know. I couldn't help putting the fear of God in you to force our way in, could I!'

Grinning, the guard unlocked the door and let them out.

'So that's our Master John showing his true colours,' remarked Egbert as they walked away. 'I suspected he was a wrong 'un.'

'If I'm not mistaken he was known in the City of London as John of Nottingham. It must be the same man. He was accused, judged and sentenced to an indeterminate stay in Tintagel Castle. You won't have heard about all that, being abroad. Back when Mayor Brembre was elected this Nottingham was Nick Brembre's bitterest rival. Both of them played havoc with the voting system when it came to electing the City mayor - '

'By intimidation, no doubt?'

'Paying armed men to oversee the voting in the wards, throwing opposition voters out of the Guildhall at sword point, yes, that sort of thing – and worse, if rumours are to be believed. Nottingham tried to get the popular vote by breaking the victualling guilds' monopoly. It sounds fair until you understand that he was doing it to catch votes.' She sighed. 'I heard all about it when I was down there at the Parliament two years ago with Archbishop Neville. In fact it seemed to come down to the price of fish.'

'As trivial as that?'

'Not when you understand that fish is the staple diet. Pushing up the price of fish by fixing it high and using false weights brought many to the point of starvation. For the poor it became a matter of life and death. It made Nottingham popular when he was seen to challenge it.'

'Merchants think only of profit. But this Nottingham, if it is him, seems to have good in him?'

'Except that once in power he went on to establish a monopoly of his own. He thought nothing of infringing the freemen's right to elect their own leaders. Things will never change in favour of ordinary folk while that goes on. They'll always suffer by having the baron's favourites thrust upon them to serve their own interests – '

'And his master is…?'

'Arundel, of course.'

'It was no different when I left England seven years ago, factions, secret allegiances. Will it ever change? The way parliament is set up fosters the greed of already rich men.'

'Is it the same the world over?'

'There's always somebody trying to justify greed and ambition on the grounds that they know best.'

Nobody needs more than one or two gold rings, or more than a few silk gowns – and maybe a plot of land where they can grow their own crops.'

'We might debate this and a few other ideas forever.' He turned to her. 'So…we can't take the news to Gregory that we've found her. Where on earth can she be?'

They parted then as the bell was calling them into the next Office and, with no sign of Delith in church, and no sign of Gregory either, Hildegard decided it was time she paid some attention to her abbot.

'Dearest Hubert,' she began as soon as she was sitting beside him in the privacy of his cubicle. 'Are you feeling neglected?'

He opened his eyes. 'What I feel, Hildegard, is indescribable in mere words, English, French, Latin, or otherwise.'

'Try, if you like. I'm here now.'

His eyes gleamed. 'I would probably shock you rigid with the wildness of my thoughts.'

Her lip curled in mock-derision. 'I doubt that, my lord, but do try me if you wish. I can withstand any shock.'

He reached for her hand. 'Now I feel only joy to be remembered in this one small corner of your day.'

'Have you had many other visitors?'

'Apart from Gregory. Did he eventually find the widow?'

She shook her head. 'Not as far as I know. Neither of them were in church just now.'

Hubert looked puzzled. 'What was she doing on the ship, apart from the obvious? Surely she couldn't have anything to do with Brother Martin's death? It makes no sense.'

'Now we know he was poisoned everybody who was on board is open to suspicion. Delith was certainly on board when he died even though, as far as the ship man admits, she was busy most of the time.'

'It might have taken only a moment to thrust something into Martin's hand to kill him, a poisoned cup of some sort? One of these lethal concoctions from Venice?'

'But where would she get hold of any such thing? And are you also suggesting she carried it over in the coracle? And if he rowed it over why did she not offer it before they left? Why go out to the St Marie to kill him?'

'To confuse the issue of her involvement, perhaps?' He looked doubtful. 'I agree, it doesn't make sense. Not when so many of the crew can attest to her presence on board. Nor does it suggest a motive. Why Martin for heaven's sake? By all accounts he was a harmless young fellow, and, as far as I understand it, she had only just arrived at Netley – as one of the pilgrims bound for France.'

'Would you like me to get you a cordial from Friar Hywel?' she asked, changing the subject. 'You look as if you need cheering up.'

'I definitely can't spend the next few weeks like this. Although…' he sighed heavily, 'it's giving me plenty of time to contemplate of my faults.'

He squeezed her hand, 'It would be a kindness, Hildi, to fetch me something special to calm my mind.'

When she went through the little gate that led onto the path winding round the building into Hywel's herb garden she could hear the murmur of voices coming from the direction of his drying hut. It sounded like a catechism, question and answer and proceeded quickly, ending in a sudden burst of laughter. Neither voice was that of Hywel.

Pushing aside the hanging vines she ducked her head underneath and called out. Jankin jerked up as if stung and behind him Alaric pushed something out of sight. When they saw it was Hildegard they relaxed and Alaric brought out what he had so suddenly thrust aside. It was a book, one of the small chap books used by the novices in the cloister school.

'Friar Hywel not here?' she asked, pretending not to have noticed this flurry of activity.

'No, domina, but we can be your hosts in his

place. May I offer you some of his cider?'

'Is that what you two are drinking?'

'Only in enough quantity to ease our thirst, my lady.' Alaric got up straight away and demonstrated that his courtly bow had not lost any of its perfection.

When beakers of cider were filled, and in two cases, she noticed, refilled, she asked, 'So is this where you have your reading lessonst, Alaric?'

His expression tightened and she said quickly, 'I think it's a good idea if Jankin is willing to help you.'

'Alaric is teaching me to juggle in return,' Jankin told her.

'He wants to impress his girl,' mocked Alaric, for which he got a clout on the head.

'Boys,' Hildegard broke in, 'may I ask something?'

Two pairs of blue eyes stared guilelessly into her own. 'This book Friar Hywel says has been stolen from the cargo of the St Marie seems to be causing him much disappointment. Was it especially valuable, do you know?'

'It was written by a learned Saracen,' Jankin told her at once. 'I was looking forward to seeing it. They produce rare craftsmanship, apart from the nature of its contents.' He turned to Alaric, 'You could have started on that next as you're doing so well with your letters.'

'If it gets out that I'm learning to read the monks will throw me out… '

Jankin punched him lightly on the chest. 'It won't get out, you sot wit. I won't tell and I know domina Hildegard won't. You won't, will you, domina?' He turned to her.

'I think I've done what I can to encourage you,' she replied to Alaric, 'so I would be equally to blame if anyone wants to challenge us. But back to my question. Why is such a book causing the friar so much distress? The expense will be borne by the abbey here as I assume it's under their direction that he sent for it – '

'He told me it held the rest of the instructions for his great experiment.'

'And what is that?'

Jankin looked uncomfortable. 'I can tell you, it's nothing to do with measuring stars or predicting the tides. It's something darker – '

'What?' demanded Alaric. 'You didn't mention this before.'

Jankin rubbed his nose. 'I don't really know. I thought it was something to do with this little creature,' he brought out his mouse from inside the pouch on his belt. 'I don't like to think what he was planning to do to him.'

Alaric stared at the ground. 'It's a good thing it's lost then.' Gloom seemed to settle over him. 'I haven't got long,' he muttered when the silence lengthened. 'Can we get on with my lesson? I've got to attend Mistress Beata soon and she's insisting I read to her to see how far I've got.'

Mid-day came and went. The sun was a searing flame over the parched land. No birds flew. The lay-brothers straggled in from the granges complaining that the cows were refusing to give milk and the sheep were having to grub up weeds now the grass had turned sere.

The fishermen were sitting under their upturned boats for shade, complaining about the absence of fish. The kitcheners sat outside on a bench in the garth with their sleeves rolled up, sweating and complaining about the heat of the ovens.

All the doors and windows of the abbey stood open. Not a breath of air stirred the smallest leaf on any of the trees.

Out on the burning surface of the water the St Marie, blackened by the fire, wallowed on her mooring and now and then a figure moved slowly about the deck, as the skeleton crew shifted position under the shadow of the half-raised sail. It hung in shreds, propped against the burned pole of the main mast.

Even the boys who had previously found refuge in cold water swimming seemed too listless to do more than stand waist deep in the sluggish tide with tunics wound on their heads like capuchons to ward off the sun.

Hildegard sat beside Hubert in the cool of the infirmary while at the far end of the hall the only movement came from Alaric as he demonstrated his skill in juggling. The faint, frail, hoarse laughter of Mistress Beata came to them now and then. 'You are a boy,' they heard her exclaim when he suggested she try.

Eventually even Alaric was exhausted and flopped down on a stool beside her bed and when they both quickly glanced over towards Hubert and Hildegard as Beata reached for a book they, without speaking, pretended not to have seen.

Hubert murmured, 'She's breaking the rules. He's getting on at a fast rate though, more strength to him.'

'Reading?' Hildegard nodded. 'I caught him having a lesson from Jankin earlier.' She stretched and yawned. 'I think I'll have to go and lie down, Hubert. Catch up on some sleep. And still no sight of Delith.'

'Gregory says he's searched everywhere. She must have left.'

'Left the abbey?'

'And changed her mind about a pilgrimage.'

'I wonder if she's abandoned Lucie then? Oh dear. I feared this might happen. We must do something for that girl.'

'Do you think Delith's gone back to continue her trade in Hampton?'

'She didn't sound as if she wanted to do that. And why would she leave her maid behind?'

Hubert shuffled into a more comfortable position. 'I wish you could lie next to me, Hildi.'

She bent to kiss him on the cheek. 'I'm sorry Hywel wasn't there to supply a calming elixir for you. I'll try him again later.'

Hubert held onto her hand and then onto her fingers as she slowly withdrew until only their fingertips were touching. Then they parted.

It was disturbing to hear Hubert call her 'Hildi.' It was the favourite shortening of her name that Rivera, of cherished memory, had given her. *Hildi,* he would murmur, *Hildi*…while for such a short time all vows except to each other had been set aside.

Rivera had been one of the duke of Lancaster's spies when they first met, the duke's network in London and elsewhere a pervasive and dangerous presence. The duke, John of Gaunt, had even had a man who was seeking sanctuary in France assassinated and no doubt he was not the only one. It was a Welshman, Owain Lawgoch, last in the royal line of Gwynedd, and no-one would ever have known that the duke, John of Gaunt, was at the back of it if it hadn't turned out to be a botched job. The assassin had failed to hide his involvement and his name, John Lamb, had quickly gone down in the French chronicles at the scandal of an English duke, paying for the murder of a man seeking refuge in their sovereign territory.

Her thoughts were led on inevitably to Gaunt's disappointment that he had not been made regent on the ten-year old King Richard's accession to the throne. It had happened ten years ago now and was acquiring the aura of an ancient tale told round a winter fireside, except for the fact that King Richard, now a handsome twenty-year-old and humiliated by the successors to Gaunt's ambition, still reigned under the constant threat of deposition.

Such times, she thought as she lay on her bed and felt her eyes close. These days the beleaguered king was threatened by another of his ambitious uncles who imagined he had a divine right to the throne: Woodstock, the duke of Gloucester. He had strong allies in the Arundel brothers, one a commander of a powerful personal army and Admiral of the Southern Fleet, and the other, his brother, a highly-placed churchman with ambitions of his own to become Archbishop of Canterbury.

It is as Egbert suggested, her thoughts drifted: greed and ambition direct all.

She must have slept.

The next thing she knew was that someone was banging loudly on her door. Sliding naked off the bed she went towards it and pressed her lips against the crack. 'Who's there?'

'Open up, domina!' It was the voice of a stranger.

CHAPTER SIX

'What is it?' she demanded, reaching for her shift.

'A missive for Friar Hywel. Them at the gatehouse said you might take it.'

'Leave it then. Outside the door. They have paid you?'

'They have.'

'Then your job is done.'

She heard a grunt followed by the sound of heavy footsteps retreating down the length of the corridor. Evidently he had not been informed of the little back stair close by.

When she was sure he had left she opened the door a crack. A rolled parchment lay upon the threshold. Muddled by her dreams her heart was still thumping. Reaching out she snatched it up and retreated into her chamber and locked the door again.

It was addressed to Friar Hywel. It was sealed. She could not break a seal. Letting it drop onto the bed she decided she would take it to him at Nones, if he bothered to attend, or after that, to his workshop.

Few guests attended the mid-afternoon Office. Simon, leaning on his stick and Lissa in a flimsy light-green gown, were present with a few new faces all now waiting for a replacement ship to take them to France. The yellowish, bookish, elderly fellow was there of course. He never missed a single service and always sat in the same place at the back near the door where there was a stone ledge for him to sit on.

No sign of Hywel.

No sign of Delith.

Afterwards Hildegard sought the friar in his workshop. He was busy over some distilling when she entered. Liquid bubbled in a retort over a small flame and she made some remark about his dedication, to risk over-heating himself on such a day.

He looked startled. 'Is it hotter than usual, do you think?'

'Everyone seems to think so, not only me.' She still felt bleer-eyed after her sleep. 'I have something for you, brother.' She held out the roll. 'The messenger was directed to bring it to me as he could not find you.'

Hywel sighed. 'I was over on board the devil ship. Exorcising.' He took the parchment. 'This is kind.' He nodded his thanks and there and then broke the seal. Obviously he was not expecting anything private. Skimming the lines he glanced up. 'This is news that may please you. Our mutual friend has reached Winchester unharmed.'

'I'm glad to hear it.'

He handed it to her. 'Read it. He thanks you as well. I wonder what he'll say when he hears how those three superstitious fools were routed?' He chuckled. 'He knows as well as we do that superstition is no stop to the ability to wield a sword.'

As he seemed to have had his good humour restored after his argument with Master John she risked a question. 'And your loss, Hywel. Was it a mistake? Has your book been found?'

He gave a resigned shrug.

'If it was on board – in a wooden casket…' she began.

'Which was locked -' he cut in. 'So where is the key?'

'Wasn't it found when they cleared the ship?' she asked.

'No sign of it. I suspect that whoever has it murdered Brother Martin. They were opening the casket to steal the contents when he burst in upon them – No, poison doesn't fit this tale.' His glance was sharp. 'You and your brother monks seem to have taken an interest in the matter…have they come up with any ideas?'

'They have one suspect in view,' she admitted.

'Who? Master John? I don't think so. I could ruin him if it gets out that he allows thieves to ransack his ship.'

'I wasn't thinking of him…'

'Who then? That woman? The one with only one reason for being on board?' He dismissed the idea. 'A plain wooden casket isn't likely to have interested her…'

'Unless she imagined it contained jewels?'

Her suggestion hit home because Hywel gave a startled glance then tried to cover it up by moving things about on the work bench. Hildegard watched him, wondering what that shocked glance meant. Was he smuggling something else into the port?

'Of course,' he was saying, having quickly regained his composure, 'she would not know it was a mere book. She might have taken it, the key in the lock perhaps, and seeing what it was decided to take it anyway…'

'She did not have anything like a book in her possession when I saw her after coming ashore. She was too frightened by the fire and everything else to think of concealing anything.'

'But the boat, she could have hidden something in that?'

'Then someone would quickly have found it'

'Who brought her ashore?'

'The bo'sun and another crewmember.'

'Were they in on it, the three of them?'

'But why a book? Would they know how to dispose of it to turn a profi?'

Hywel's face was wood. 'Where is that woman? I'll drag the truth from her. And the others. They'll all have their price.'

'The two crew members volunteered to go back on board to keep their master company,' she told him.

'First the woman, then a trip out to the St Marie. Come with me?'

Unsure what she was letting herself in for Hildegard agreed. Anything was better than lying around, drugged by the heat, with her thoughts flying wildly around memories better left alone.

It took only minutes for Hywel to set everything to the necessary levels until he returned then he called for Jankin and told him not to let anything disturb the equipment nor let the flame go out in its saucer of oil and then they left.

'I should tell you, Hywel, Gregory has been looking for Delith all day and cannot find her. You saw Egbert and I come into the sacristy on the same trail.'

'That's what you were doing? You had Master John worried.'

As they passed the row of lounging kitcheners one of them called, 'We cannot work inside at present. Don't blame us!'

'What's the problem?' Hywel asked.

'If you can rid us of a hobgoblin, brother, we promise you extra dole at compline.'

Irritated Hywel said, 'What are you talking about? Hobgoblins? What are you bleating about, man?'

Used to his shortness of temper the kitcheners jeered and explained, 'The ovens are too hot but worse, the sluice is blocked. We cannot shift it, whatever it is. We're going to have to borrow a very small lad and push him down to sort it out if they can't fix it further up-stream.'

'That's your concern, not mine. Just make sure

we've got something to eat tonight.' Hywel made to walk on but threw back over his shoulder, 'Or find a hobgoblin and feed him on a toad by the light of the full moon!' Chuckling grimly to himself, he accompanied Hildegard to the gatehouse, saying, 'They probably will do too. They believe everything they're told.'

When they reached the strand it was difficult to persuade any of the fishermen to stir themselves. Eventually one of them said, 'you can take my boat on condition you make good any damage or loss.'

'Done,' agreed Hywel. 'We're quite capable of rowing across there ourselves without wrecking it.'

He handed Hildegard inside and each took an oar. The sun was blazing down and away from the shore the water reflected it back more powerfully than ever. Half-blinded by the dazzle they were glad when they could soon drift in under the shadow of the ship. A call from Hywel brought a head peering over the side.

'What? You again?'

'Just making sure the devil has taken himself off for good.' Hywel banged on the side. 'Let us up, there's a good fellow. We have to talk to you and your master.'

Without replying the man sent a rope ladder snaking down and they climbed aboard.

In the shadow cast by the burned and blackened sail the men had rigged up a sort of shelter and were sitting underneath, drinking, of course, and playing a game involving cards decorated with arcane symbols. A smell of burning hung in the air.

'Get those in the Middle Sea?' asked Hywel.

'We did. You yourself play?' one of them asked not taking his eyes from the cards in his big paws.

'I do but today my thoughts are on other matters.'

'This book you've lost?'

'Lost is not the word I would use. It was stolen. It was stolen from this very ship and I want to know who stole it and why.'

'The latter might be the easiest part of your quest, friar. If it was a costly item, it was no doubt worth selling on.'

'Not all that costly,' Hywel told him. 'That's what's so puzzling. True, it was in its own special box and true it was locked, but I'm told the key was in the lock which surely demonstrates that the contents were not worth much.'

The ship man came up. 'But worth you worrying about, eh? Well, I've got a clearer idea of who was where on the night, brother, and I can tell you nobody else went below deck after the monk came on board. We were all up here, me amidships, the rest in the bows – '

'Except for the woman and her marks, two of 'em you told us.'

'I was one,' a card-player announced. 'We never went below. It was stifling. Why should we?'

'And the other?'

'That's me. I can vouch for what he says. We

hadn't got the cargo on our minds at that point.'

'And afterwards?'

They glanced at each other. 'Then the lightning struck?'

'That's about it. And it was all hands to the ship.'

'I can vouch for that as well,' the ship man interrupted. 'Screaming and shouting like a lot of girls they were. Scared sh – ' he glanced at Hildegard, corrected himself and said, 'scared witless and not happy with the situation, not happy at all.'

'Meanwhile,' Hildegard said, as she had been obliquely invited into the conversation, 'the monk was down below, by himself and… '

'Going through our cargo,' finished the ship man.

It seemed to Hildegard that they were all being very slow.

Thrusting aside any suspicions about Alaric's involvement, if no-one had gone down with the monk- and they all seemed certain of that, then it must have been something in the cargo that had poisoned Brother Martin. Nobody was guilty. It was a result of his own activity in opening the casket.

Hywel must have come to the same conclusion. 'You've been helpful. This is the first time I've heard the three of you together with a story that makes sense. We must grope our way further into the labyrinth in order to find the thief, it seems.' He got up to go, turning to Hildegard, 'Shall we?'

On the way back, pulling equally on an oar apiece as before, they were mostly silent. Voices carry over water. She was sure Hywel was aware of that too because as the boat scraped back onto the shingle he said, 'Come to my workshop?'

He pushed a stool towards her before stretching out in his own wooden chair. 'They looked to me like men telling the truth.'

'Given that they might well be under suspicion of murder, I too thought they looked as if they had nothing to hide.'

Something so heinous came to mind that she was reluctant to put it into words but Hywel suggested it first, with a narrowing of his mouth.

'Poison in the casket containing the book? We should have thought of that straightaway. The coroner accidentally hinted as much.' He looked puzzled. 'Was I the intended victim, or was it a mere safeguard in case anyone tried to break into it without authority?'

'Only you know the nature of the person who sent it to you.'

'Not that then. A safeguard.'

'How would you have opened the casket if you had received it in the normal way?'

'I would have brought it ashore and taken it to the scriptorium where one of the monks would have…yes, he would have probably used his page turners on it…even so he would have had to open the lid first.'

'Were there no instructions with it? No warning?'

'There may have been. The fire sent everything

into chaos. Maybe there is such a document but if so it hasn't turned up.'

'So Delith had nothing to do with it after all.'

A sharp glance from under his finely arched brows made her exclaim, 'What, you think she has?'

'This is my understanding so far, Hildegard. Brother Martin, for reasons probably known only to Abbot Philip, hurried out to the ship before the storm broke in order to take the book off – or maybe, even, anything else he could get his hands on?'

'But more likely under instruction as you suggest…?' She was thinking about the abbot's trust in Martin and the dire need for funds to pay off his protectors. Books fetch a good price when they find the right buyer. Maybe Philip had such a buyer in mind and was desperate to get his hands on the book without delay. Impatient, she decided.

'When Martin saw the box with the key,' Hywel continued, 'he opened it and pouf! Out came the poison and he died for his pains. A little later, perhaps while her clients were dealing with the fire, Delith, quite coolly, went below, saw Martin lying dead, then noticed the opened casket and the book either inside or beside it, stole the item and made her escape.'

'But she did not have it with her when she reached the beach.'

'That is a stumbling block,' he admitted. 'What then?'

'Someone else stole it.'

'One of the crew?'

'A little later the cog was swarming with helpers trying to put out the fire, helping to get men off to safety. And –' she stopped herself in time. She could not mention Alaric. There was simply no reason to drag him into it. Hywel did not notice here hesitation because he was swearing to tear the thief limb from limb when he found him.

'Shall we leave it there for now?' she soothed. 'I don't see how Delith could avoid suffering the same fate as Brother Martin if what you say is true.'

'There are subtle devices,' he muttered. 'And don't forget it was pouring with rain. Once released any poison would have been washed away in that deluge.'

'Sometimes a problem resolves itself in our minds without our effort. Let's leave it awhile.'

He nodded. Turning he said to Jankin still attending the distillation of herbs, 'How's it going, Saxon? Have you ruined my elixir with your clumsy Saxon hands?'

'I wouldn't imagine so, friar, my revered master. Look!' he wafted both of his hands in the air, 'As delicate and dexterous as any belonging to a maiden.'

'If that's the case I'll get you sewing for me. You can stitch me a new habit with some Opus Anglicanum all over it.'

'That would be my pleasure, dread magister, as it is a Saxon skill and will no doubt come easily to me. I will do so if you will guarantee to wear it afterwards?'

'And be a laughing stock everywhere I went with your nonsense spells all over it? I might practice my Welsh wizard's skill in having you whipped for insolence if you don't get on and fetch the domina and me something to eat.'

'Can't.'

'What do you mean, can't?'

'They're still running around trying to unblock their sluice. No victuals until after vespers. Earliest.'

'This is Netley Abbey. One of the foremost Cistercian houses on the south coast. Second only to its motherhouse at Beaulieu. I should have gone there,' he added. 'They would know how to treat their alchemists.'

The antiphon sounded weak without the added richness of Glyn Dwr's voice. Hildegard gave silent praise, nevertheless, that he had reached the safe staging post of Winchester and not been picked up by any of Arundel's mercenaries on the way. The three who remained here were jostling at the back of the church looking self-conscious to be attending Vespers. They had clearly not yet managed to obtain the goods - and tribute? - they had been sent to collect and looked as if they were getting bored with having to fill in time.

Master John was standing close to the altar in an attitude of solemn piety. The monks behind the screen sang out and the pilgrims, a more respectable number in this, the cool of the evening, responded in their way.

Afterwards it was to be hoped she could get a chance to talk to Egbert and find out if Gregory had managed to question Delith. She glanced round again. Still no sign of her.

She lowered her eye lids while she thought things over. One image would not leave her. Back again it came. It was of Alaric, climbing hand over hand up the anchor chain to be first on board after the lightning struck. He would well imagine that a book would be a useful thing to obtain.

His honest, fair features swam before her. Honest? Was he? It was easy to be taken in by someone's looks. She was always in danger of doing that. The merchant, for instance, John of Nottingham, if that was who he really was, made her hackles rise, simply because he was inclined to bluster and was red-faced, over-confident, never visited his ailing wife and had thoughts, it seemed, almost entirely focused on profit.

She thought differently about Alaric, simply because he was a youth full of fun and vitality with a beguiling and innocent hope for the future, and looked fair and fine, and seemed innocent of all wrong - appearance versus reality, and yet another matter that might be discussed through the endless days and nights of eternity.

She noticed that everyone had risen from their knees and she hurriedly followed suit, and after the prior's blessing, drifted outside, still deep in thought.

A group had gathered in the porch at the west door and were talking of nothing but the lateness of their supper. 'It's most unusual,' one of the newcomers was saying. 'I often stay here when I'm traveling in the region. Can't fault the hospitality at Netley. But now?'

Murmurs followed from those who had experienced similar occasions and were non-plussed by this sudden departure from custom. A move was made to enter the refectory and wait there until someone should bring them something to eat.

They were not the only ones to be confused by a change of routine.

'Now my best skillet's gone!' one of the kitcheners was ranting in the kitchen doorway as the guests drifted past. 'What's going on round here? Are we plagued by Hob and his goblins? Who's at the bottom of it? Out with them! Let's get back to normal!'

He stopped when he noticed the guests looking in with astonished faces and eyed them back with suspicion writ large over his features. 'And a wadge of pig fat's gone but that's nothing to the skillet,' he added. Scratching his head after failing to pick out the thief from among the suspiciously innocent-looking guests, he went back into his kitchen and a few shouts and a crash followed. A defiant-looking little lad of no more than ten appeared.

'It's not fair,' he was shouting to someone inside. 'Why me? It's not my fault!'

'Nothing's every your fault, Edwin, and this time you're right. But, you see, it's not a punishment to make you our saviour, is it?'

The boy scowled and allowed an older youth to take him by the scruff of the neck and drag him back inside.

Hildegard poked her head round the kitchen door. 'Is it anything we can help you with? We're not helpless out here, you know.'

'Would you do me a favour, domina?' The head kitchener came bustling forward. 'Can you take these platters out to put in front of that lot before they tear the place apart? My lads are having a go at this blockage so I'm a bit short-handed. We're sending little Edwin down as he's the only one small enough to be able to wriggle his way through.' Then he paused. 'But I can't ask you to do a menial task like this. What am I thinking? I beg forgiveness, domina. We're at sixes and sevens here.' He began to bow and scrape.

'Don't be foolish, master. It's no problem.' She took some of the bowls from his bench before he could whisk them away, piled them up one on top of the other and took them out to the waiting guests when they were soon being passed swiftly down the length of the trestles. Deciding to go back to fetch the jugs of wine and water she returned to the kitchens.

'They're happier now but will be happier still with some of your good ale and wine in front of them,' she told him.

She glanced over towards the sluice that ran down one side of the kitchens. Usually water flowed in a stream that passed underneath the abbey walls and on into the kitchen and from there out again towards the privies where it washed out lower down the slope on which the abbey was built, finishing in the waters of the estuary. It was an ingenious arrangement and made good use of the natural lie of the land. Now, though, the sluice into the kitchen was dry because of a blockage.

'Is that poor little lad being forced down into the pipe to clear it?' she asked.

'We others've tried. Alaric was down there not long ago but skinny though he is, he's too wide in the shoulder to get into the pipe.'

Alaric, indeed, was standing nearby looking exceedingly white-faced.

'I said you were starting in the wrong place,' an older kitchener complained.

Hildegard went over to him. 'Alaric, are you all right?'

He was wet through and his tunic was bunched up making him look mis-shapen. 'Nobody knows what's down there,' he said abruptly. He swiveled on his heel and walked off into the garth as soon as the kitchener's back was turned.

Deeming it none of her concern, she picked up

a couple of full jugs and took them through. The guests looked happier now, scooping up a mash of beans from slabs of freshly-baked flat bread, sharing two by two, just as in any lord's hall. Conversation was beginning to start up again and Hildegard went to sit near Egbert and Gregory who had just come in and found places among the usual guests.

'Did you find Delith?' she asked Gregory as she climbed onto the bench beside him.

He shook his head. 'Not sight nor sign. She must have left.'

Lissa leaned across. 'I took the opportunity to have a look for her things where she keeps them under her bed. They were still there. If she has left she hasn't taken a stitch with her. Poor Lucie,' she added, 'she doesn't know what to do.' She turned to Master John who was sitting at her side, either by chance or design. 'What do you make of it, John? Simon thinks she's found someone she knows and has gone off walking, forgetting the time.'

'I know you women once you get to talking,' her husband, on her other side, broke in. 'You're fretting for nothing, wife.'

'You don't think it's for nothing, do you, John?'

'I'm sure I haven't given it any thought until now, mistress Alicia.' He bowed his head in a meaningful manner that made Lissa flutter. 'To tell you the truth, I'm rather relieved she's taken herself off,' he continued more intimately. 'I found her attention somewhat unwelcome.' He floated his fingers over the back of her hand and a look passed between them. Simon, meanwhile, was chewing on his bread and moving lumps of food around his mouth with a complaint about his teeth.

Gregory poured more wine then passed the jug along. Lowering his head he murmured quietly enough for only Hildegard and Egbert to hear, 'We have three people searching for a book for which a man has died.' His voice was pitched so low that Hildegard had to lean in closer. 'First,' he continued, 'is the abbot. May we assume his purchase of the book was made in the expectation that at some time he might exchange it at sufficient profit to pay off his protectors? He will not want to lose it.'

'Assuming he has a keen purchaser in mind,.' Egbert echoed what Hildegard had been thinking. She recalled Mistress Sweet's opinion that every object has a buyer.

'Quite so,' agreed Gregory. 'Second, the merchant, our friend John, is likely to lose whatever reputation he has if a thief is known to have been making free on one of his ships. He will also have to make good the loss from his own coffers. So he will not want to lose it either. And third, we have our brother the friar at whose request, presumably, the book was brought in. He will want it for who knows what magical and forbidden purposes of his own.'

'And someone must have known its value to them all and decided to get in first.' Egbert folded his arms. 'He's our man.'

'And that would include?'

Gregory answered Hildegard's question with one of his own. 'The prior, the friar's apprentice, and whoever Master John takes into his confidence?'

'Certainly few other people would be interested in a book,' Egbert observed with a shrug, 'should they even be able to read one if they happened to find one in their hands. But why do you include the prior?'

'No real reason beyond the fact that he's jealous about being passed over as abbot and Philip has been put in over his head. I admit it's no evidence whatever.'

'Hywel's apprentice wasn't near the cog that night,' Hildegard reminded. 'We can forget him. He's frightened of water. He stayed firmly on the beach. I know because I kept bumping into him.'

'Thus leaving the prior, unlikely, and the merchant's intimate, if he has one.'

'And what if Brother Martin wasn't working alone? He may himself have had an ally,' Egbert suggested, frowning at the untold complexities that suddenly appeared.

'But why would an ally take it?' Hildegard objected.

'Maybe he wished to keep all the profit when it was sold on? Or,' he added, 'maybe he had no wish to share the knowledge it contained, if that was the purpose for which he stole it?'

'They would need the first book as well, Hywel says. He can't get any further on with his so-called Magnum Opus, whatever that is, until he has both books. That would go for anybody else.'

'Unless, instead of using the knowledge they contained, they wished to destroy it?'

'A fanatic. Plenty of those about these days'

'Is the first book still within Hywel's keeping?'

Hildegard widened her eyes. 'Do you know, I don't think he's mentioned it.' She got up and then sat down again. 'I can't ask him now. He's sitting at the trestle over there with half-a-dozen pilgrims. Let's wait until he's finished.'

'No fish pie, tonight! Sluice is bust.' A burly lay-brother staggered in with a board piled high with pastries. 'The kitchener sends his deepest apologies and begs you receive these for your delight instead.'

'I told you they always see you well at Netley,' one of the newer guests affirmed. Several hands reached out and, evidently finding the pastries as delightful as the head kitchener hoped recommended them to their more cautious neighbours. A discussion of the fish sluice opened up. It was a device, someone explained, that shut off the stream that ran along the kitchen to trap the fish so that all the cooks had to do was reach down and pull them out, place on a griddle and serve. 'Fresh fish is always one of the delights at Netley,' the same guest announced.

Hildegard got up. 'If I may take one for later?' She stuffed a pastry into her sleeve and whispered to her two companions that she would be back and quickly left the refectory.

The reason for her sudden exit was Hywel.

Before the lay-brother came in with his largesse the friar was already on his way out. She followed him across the garth. It was still unfeasibly hot and clammy and now, late in the evening, long shadows filled the crevices between the buildings. She caught up with him just before he disappeared into his workshop.

'Hywel,' she called, making him stop. 'I saw you leave just now and need to ask you something.'

His face was a pale wedge in the twilight but just then the moon came sailing out from behind a cloud and revealed it with great clarity leaving only his eyes in shadow. He bowed his head, plunging his face briefly into darkness.

'Domina...Hildegard...what is it?' He lifted his head and the moon shone full on his face again.

'Do you still have the first book for which the lost one is the second volume?'

'I do.'

'Will the second one make sense to anyone who does not have the first?'

'I see…' he smiled, narrow-faced, shrewd. 'I can assure you no-one in England will be able to make use of it.'

'So why do you think it was stolen?'

'An opportunistic theft? Someone in a hurry, in all the panic of the burning ship, snatched the book as the first thing they saw that could be sold for profit. Such are men and women, driven by greed for no other reason than its own sake. Why? Do you have news likely to refute my theory?'

She shook her head and he made as if to take his leave and she did not stop him.

Not for one minute did she believe him. His attitude of calm did not convince. Moonlight revealed every nuance in his expression.

He was a man in a rage. It must be about more than a book. He felt outwitted by someone he despised. He was bent on revenge. But he would stay his hand only after he had retrieved the object of his desire. And for that reason he was treading with great care and a show of indifference.

When she returned to the refectory she simply told the monks that Hywel still had the first volume in his possession.

'He said the second one would make no sense -' she corrected herself, 'He said it would be no use to anyone in England.'

'Does that lead us to the prior then? He would scarcely be expected to want the book for its alleged magical uses but Abbot Philip would certainly confide in him on the value of it in raising funds to pay off their protectors Out of malice the prior might have thought to use it against the usurper of his coveted honour?'

'Are you suggesting that he sent Brother Martin to get it before it could go through the process of being unloaded and marked off on the inventory?' Egbert asked.

They looked at each other but nobody had anything useful to add.

'And Master John?' Hildegard glanced across

to where he was now sitting slightly aslant on the bench to be face to face with Lissa. Simon, on her other side, was slumped, apparently asleep after his repast.

A few phrases in John's penetrating voice floated over to them through the hubbub of satisfied diners, '…not long now…I can promise you…' and other remarks, lost under the noise.

Lissa's response could be seen but her replies were inaudible. A darting glance at her husband made her put a warning hand on John's sleeve. She rose to her feet and announced to the diners at large, 'I must see my dear old owl to his bed.'

Shaking Simon by the shoulder she caused him to splutter into wakefulness. 'Wha…? Oh my dear one, was I asleep? Did I snore?' He laughed in a jovial, unselfconscious way and struggled to his feet. 'Are we leaving, my little bird?' His glance took in the faces turned to him. 'Such pleasant company, so kind, so welcome. Goodnight, my dear friends, all's well and all be well with you.'

Leaning on Lissa and with the aid of his stick, he allowed his wife to usher him away.

Mistress Sour took the opportunity to tweak John's sleeve, distracting him from the sight of the lissome shape of his supper partner as Lissa turned, one hand lifting her weight of flame-coloured hair, the other giving him a little wave. Her frown when she saw Mistress Sour vying for his attention was not pleasant to behold. Clearly she did not like rivals.

Hildegard felt only gladness that she was beyond the distractions of desire and its jealousies.

Gregory had noticed this scene enacted between Master John and Mistress Lissa. He shook his head.

As it was time to look in on Abbot de Courcy to say their goodnights the three of them strolled across the garth together. The two monks went up the steps into the infirmary and just as Hildegard was about to follow she heard someone panting up behind her, calling her name. When she turned she saw Mistress Sweet. She was alone.

'Forgive me, domina, but I understand you're interested in the strange death of the monk on the St Marie?'

'Who could not be,' Hildegard replied.

'I have something to tell you.'

'Oh?'

'For sixpence.' Mistress Sweet's pert smile had no expectation of a negative answer and she held out her palm.

'How do I know it's anything I care to hear?'

The young woman frowned. 'You will, I assure you. But sixpence is what it costs.'

'A penny.'

'Threepence,' the retort came back quick as a shot.

'Very well.' Hildegard dug a hand into her scrip and handed over a coin.

Inviting her a little to one side Mistress Sweet said. 'I knew I'd seen Delith before and then I placed her. She's no more a widow than Abbot Philip. She's known in Hampton though. I've seen her plying her trade. She was set up in a house on the quayside by a pimp called Lionel. You've seen him. He's the fellow who arrived here on the night of the storm. They pretend not to know each other but don't be taken in. They're up to something.'

'I might ask for the return of my threepenny bit. I know all this.'

'But you may not know all. She is trying to sell something.'

'I thought you said that was her trade?'

'Something else. Something she has stolen from the ship. She offered it to Lionel but would not tell him anything about it but only stated her price. Then she offered it to my sister who of course is too astute to pay good money without seeing what she's getting for it.'

'Is this the book that's gone missing?'

Mistress Sweet shook her head. 'Nothing to do with books. She says it's something all kings will desire. More than that she will not say.'

'Why doesn't she try it with kings then?'

Mistress Sweet laughed this to scorn. 'She's as much chance of getting near a king or even a shire knight as flying to the moon. She's trying us first with the promise that we'll be able to make back our money one hundred times over.'

'I am still in my rights to ask for the return of my threepence. All you've told me is that some unfortunate woman is trying to make a living without going back onto the streets of Hampton. Any fool could see she is trying to escape that life.'

The girl at once flew into a rage. 'Take it like that then! Poor woman? The greatest harlot in Hampton? You're carrying compassion too far, domina, if indeed you are a nun. Huh!'

She gave a flounce and was about to go off when Hildegard said, 'If you can find out what she's offering for sale I'll give you a shilling. I need facts though, not a tall story or aspersions about someone's virtue.'

She turned off into the infirmary and left Mistress Sweet gaping after her.

'So Lionel has refused to buy, the sisters are circumspect… '

'And none of them have any idea what it is?'

'I'm merely sorry I didn't learn more for my threepence. I knew all this before she told me – but at least she'll dig for us in the hope of a shilling.'

Hubert looked smug. 'While you folk have been scratching around I've had the upper hand for once. I've been lying here royally entertained. That young lay-brother, the one who tends Mistress Beata so assiduously has been showing her how to juggle. He would have had me doing it if I hadn't resisted.'

'When was this?'

'Between nones and vespers. He returned just before Compline, wet through, as if he'd been for a swim, and dripping water all along the tiles. Beata scolded him as if she were his own mother so he scurried round with a cloth to wipe it up.'

'It's not the mystery you seem to think it,

Hubert.' Hildegard explained. 'He's been into the upper sluice to try to unblock it. They had to choose a smaller lad who could crawl inside the pipe. I don't think he's been any more successful though.' She remembered her pastry and took it from her sleeve. 'Would you like it?' She offered it round and it was split three ways, Hildegard herself declining a piece with her mind on other things.

As Egbert and Gregory got up to go in order to give Hildegard and Hubert some time alone to discuss matters of mutual interest they agreed that their curiosity about Brother Martin's death had been satisfied. There was no crime. He had opened a poisoned casket from Outremer and suffered the accidental and fatal consequences of so doing. If there had also been a theft then it was of a book of doubtful value that, for all they knew, now lay at the bottom of Southampton Water. Anything of any greater worth only existed in the mind of Delith wherever she now was.

'All this,' Hildegard agreed, 'and yet...' She

could not mention Hywel's face in the moonlight. It was too glancing, too vague and personal, too fanciful, and probably came down to nothing more significant than a trick of the light.

They talked things over for a while. It had been a strangely exhausting day, what with the endless heat, the sun beating down without let, and the coming and going of new people about the place, and then that argument between John, usually so sanguine, but acting like a raging monster against the cold hatred of Hywel as they fought a verbal battle in the sacristy. What had it been about? Nothing much, as far as she could see. A missing book that nobody but Hywel really wanted for itself.

Hubert looked thoughtful after this but it might have been tiredness. He said it was more tiring lying on the bed with his leg encased in the Roman contraption than if he'd had a day's hawking or ridden his horse at full gallop across the Dales.

'When shall we see the sweet green hills of home, Hildegard?'

'Soon, I hope.' She kissed him goodnight and went out into the moonlit garth.

It was almost too hot to think of going up to her stifling chamber. It was late now but the air bore down like heat from a blast furnace. The moon rode rapidly through the sky with nothing to obscure its brilliance. Spread across the heavens was an endless field of stars. They seemed so close she could imagine reaching up to pull one down.

In the steady and uncanny light she made her way across the garth towards the guest house and as she did so she had to pass the kitchens. Sounds of activity within made her put her head inside to say goodnight but then she stopped.

The little kitchen lad was standing on a table, wet from head to foot, his face made wetter by his tears. He was sobbing and a group of them were trying to console him.

'It was dark, my chick, it only looked like something horrible. It will be some weed caught on a rock and you'll laugh at this in the morning.'

'We use this sluice every day to trap our fish for table,' the kitchener's assistant broke in. 'They swim freely and happily, without restraint, all the way from a deep and beautiful lake far inland simply to reach us here.'

'It was horrible!' the lad cried on a rising note. 'I tell you! I'm not going down there again!'

'Listen, we'll wait until morning. It was a dull-witted idea to light torches and send you down. Those shadows,' the assistant kitchener faked a shiver, 'leaping and leering, they make me think of monsters even now, standing here with you lot.'

'That don't take much imagination, Ced. Have you looked in a mirror lately?'

The small lad stamped his feet. 'Set me down. I'm not going in there again. No matter how bright the day.'

Exasperated glances passed around the group. 'All right,' agreed the kitchener, 'We'll find somebody as small as you but with a braver heart who would like a penny for his courage.'

'I never said I wouldn't like a penny,' the small

boy said in a startled tone.

'Let's see how you feel after Prime, hey?'

The assistant lifted him down and swung him round. 'Off out! Go on! To bed, you little mongrel!'

As he raced outside before they changed their minds Hildegard continued on her way to bed to snatch a few hours sleep before Matins.

About to open the door at the bottom of the back stairs leading up to her chamber Hildegard caught sight of a movement in the shadows near the corner of the building. The cresset, guttering in its iron sconce on the wall, dazzled her for a moment and she stepped away from the light so she could look into the darkness.

The cloisters were deserted. The windows of the guest quarters were shuttered. Only in the kitchens on the far side of the garth would there be any aid.

'Who's there?' she demanded in a firm voice.

A shift of movement drew her attention but in a

second the knife from her sleeve was in her hand. She asked again, 'Who is it? Show yourself!'

A figure loomed from the shadows as she brought up the blade.

A muffled shout protested, 'No! No, domina! It's me!'

'Who?' She peered into the shadows. 'Who is it?'

Something shifted in the borrowed light and, detecting something familiar in the voice, she asked, 'Is that you, Alaric?'

'I must speak to you, domina. I'm in a fix.'

'What?'

'I've committed a sin and must speak to you.'

He emerged from the shadows, taller than she was, but slight and trembling, with the aspect of someone ready for rejection.

He dropped to one knee. 'I beg your indulgence.'

'Get up, Alaric,' she spoke with gentleness, 'Shouldn't you go to your confessor?'

'I can't. I need to speak to you first.' He rose

to his feet. 'It is something he will not wish to hear.'

Alarmed, she said, 'We can't stand outside in the open to talk. Come inside where it's private.' She remembered the small chamber on the ground floor where Glyn Dwr had been staying and guessed it might be vacant now.

Hurrying Alaric along the corridor she pushed open the door into the pitch black chamber. Not a sound came from within. Remembering Glyn Dwr's hand moving slowly towards his knife when she had barged in on him she felt rapidly along the ledge beside the door for the tinder, found it, struck a spark, held it to the wick of the candle and lifted it high. Light ran like liquid into the corners of the chamber.

It was empty.

She turned to Alaric. 'Well?'

He closed the door. In the candle glow his eyes looked enormous but expressed a certain abject fear. 'I've committed a sin,' he began, 'I've told a most grievous lie.' His lips trembled as he glanced towards the door. Lowering his voice, he said, 'I've stolen something. But I did it without knowledge of what I was doing - ' He broke off. 'I had no idea what I was doing, domina.'

'It can be no sin if it was done without the will to sin. Tell me what you stole.' She felt she already knew.

He found it difficult to continue. With a struggle he admitted, 'I'm living in fear for my soul. You saw how frightened Jankin was when Hywel accused him of the theft of a mouse?'

'Is it something stolen from the friar?'

'It's the book he sent for,' he confirmed her suspicion. 'The loss of it is turning him into a monster.'

'Come now - '

'He said he would put a curse forever on anyone who stole from him. I thought he meant petty thefts of his cures and instruments and especially he feared to lose his astrolabe, it's irreplaceable. But so is what I stole. Now I can't stop thinking about what he might do if he finds out who took it.'

Hildegard remembered the demonic expression on Hywel's face in the moonlight and felt some fear on Alaric's behalf. She took him by the arm. 'Tell me about it.'

'And will you help me, domina, if I tell you the truth?'

'I will help however I am able.'

Taking that as enough reassurance Alaric stood in the glow of the candle light and braced himself to confess. She could see every nuance of the changing emotions that flickered across his face and his eyes wide with fear.

'I have been taken under the wing of Mistress Beata,' he began. 'I will say nothing against her. I am pleased to serve her and she has my loyalty.' He gave a heavy sigh. 'Her husband treats her with cruel disregard in the full knowledge that she has little time left on earth. When she was younger and more active she took a full part in what she calls his 'dealings' - this was when he was a figure in the City of London. You may not know that?' he broke off to give Hildegard a searching glance.

'We did suspect as much.'

'Then you may know he's John of Nottingham, one of the city merchants in fealty to Prince Thomas of Woodstock, the new duke of Gloucester. When Master John was banished from the City it was decreed that he could not go within eighty miles of it on pain of death. And he is here!'

'Go on.'

'He owns the ship for which the pilgrims wait. Mistress Beata says she knows his mind and his business better than the back of her own hands.' His lips lifted in an involuntary smile. 'She may be at death's door but her spirit is as robust as any.'

'Did she ask you to do something for her?'

'She asked me to get hold of a special book her husband was bringing in for the abbot. She said it had been her idea to get it and that if her husband wanted it to complete his deal with the abbot he would have to pay her the market price once she had it in her possession as it was hers by right.'

'But the brothers look after her well, what would she want with money at this stage of her life?'

He shook his head. 'She's a merchant's wife, domina, she knows the price of things. She said he would pay a good price for it if he had any sense – which she was beginning to doubt.' A vestige of his old carefree smile returned but quickly faded.

'So in effect she wants –' she corrected herself, 'she wanted to get hold of the book to keep it as a hostage to fortune?'

He gave Hildegard a beseeching look. 'I failed to ask her more. It seemed unkind to probe into her motives. She did say she had stood by her husband through thick and thin and was now being denied her reward for her fidelity.' He shrugged as if he didn't understand such things. 'I have myself seen how ill-used she is and it seemed just to help her right the balance against him. Maybe,' he added, 'that was my first mistake, the one that set me on the road to hell.'

'I saw you climbing aboard the St Marie,'

Hildegard told him with a certain sharpness in her tone. 'Is that when you stole it?' There was no point in beating about the bush.

'She urged me to go on board before anyone else thought of it. I knew what to look for. She described the little wooden casket it was in and told me that on no account was I to open it. At that point I had little idea what was inside. She said it was a book but I suppose I believed that it also held jewels, something of that nature. The sort of thing people like to possess.' He gave her a quick glance to make sure she was following.

'Go on.'

'Imagine my horror when I finally got on board and managed to find the hold without being seen only to discover Brother Martin lying in that grotesque manner with the casket open and its contents gone! It was a nightmare scene, the storm raging, the fire, flames billowing in fury over the deck, the crew screaming to be saved, not daring to jump overboard out of fear at being swept away on the tide, and the body of poor Brother Martin distorted with pain - ' Tears filled his eyes. 'Afterwards, when I knew what was in the casket, I realised that Abbot Philip must have been anxious to get his hands on the book and, having lost patience while the ship lay at anchor, sent Brother Martin to fetch it. He failed and met his death. But then, in all this horror, with the little casket empty, where was this precious object?'

'What did you do?'

'Like an angel answering me, the rains started to fall in torrents and as I was crawling back over the deck to climb down into my boat again I found a book, just thrown aside, and you know how desperately I want to read and how precious books are to me, so without any more thought I picked it up and jumped into the boat with it.'

'What did you do when you came ashore?'

'I took it straight to Mistress Beata. I said, "I don't suppose this is what you want?" You should have seen her face when she saw it. "My dear boy!" she exclaimed, "You are an angel from heaven!" Then she asked me to hide it somewhere.'

'And then what?'

'I did as she asked, naturally. I realized that it was probably dangerous to have it in my possession. How dangerous was confirmed by what happened next.'

He started to shiver and his face was stark with horror.

'Alaric, you're safe now. You can unburden yourself without fear. Look,' she went over to the door and turned the key.

'I fear locks are not enough to keep me from danger.' He wilted and seemed to be on the point of collapse but then, seeing her expression, forced himself to straighten and say, 'When Friar Hywel found out that the book had gone, all hell broke loose. After the heavens had opened to rescue me they opened again with his rage and I fear there's no rescue this time.'

Hildegard put a hand on his arm. 'Alaric, why do you say that?'

He gnawed his lips then muttered, 'He was

raging and ranting about the world being lost, about the end days, cursing and crying out in a strange language and muttering blasphemies that were somehow worse than the raging but all in some demonic tongue I know nothing of and throwing things,' he added, rubbing one shoulder.

'Did you catch anything of what he was saying?'

'Only that he must have the book in order to continue his work. Then he said what was worse for me. "Whoever has stolen it will die in agony!" You can imagine how I feel after seeing Brother Martin contorted in death, knowing that's the very book I stole. If I'd known I'd have left well alone, Mistress Beata or not.'

'And now you need to give it back to Friar Hywel?' She took him by the arm. 'Have you thought of leaving it on the work bench where he'll imagine his guardian angel has left it?...Why don't you do that?'

'Because of Mistress Beata.'

'Yes?'

'She set such store by getting it, as if her life depended on it, and I cannot let her down. I gave her my word...' his lips paled. 'I confess, I'm also afraid of Hywel. I believe he knows I have it and is waiting for me to reveal the fact so that he can – so he can – '

'Do you think he'll punish you?'

'I know he will. He'll put a curse on me as he said he would.' He began to shiver violently all the while trying to pretend is was simply the cold.

Hildegard moved further into the empty chamber and went to sit on the edge of the table. It wasn't cold at present, in fact it was still stifling hot, airless and heavy, but she pretended not to notice his frenzied shaking.

'So the problem is this, putting aside his curse for the moment, you want Mistress Beata to keep the book and do with it as she wishes but at the same time you want Brother Hywel to regain possession of what belongs rightfully to his abbot?'

'And thus absolve myself of sin.'

'I see.'

'I'm in a fix, domina, as I told you. There is no way out.'

'Won't any other book do for Mistress Beata?'

He shook his head. Evidently he had already thought of that and rejected it. 'She says it's something precious that will lead to more gold than King Croesus ever dreamed of…And Brother Hywel also needs it to conclude his work.'

'What is this work of his?'

Alaric frowned. 'He will not say. It's something so secret he dare not tell anyone. Jankin has no idea and has done all he can to find out. At first he thought it was to do with the mouse but then the friar seemed to become quite attached to the little fellow – although he still insists in talking about him as 'it' and refuses to visit the nest where his tiny family live.' He added lamely, 'We have no real idea what he's engaged in but I fear the powers he may be able to summon up.'

'I don't belief in unearthly powers.'

'I didn't think I did until now…but you should have seen him rage…he was possessed…he seemed to summon devils in the air.'

'Another copy may be available,' Hildegard interrupted in a brisk manner. 'Surely he's thought of that? Might he ask the monks at Beaulieu if they have one in their collection?'

'I dare not suggest it because then he would guess that I know more than I should. He is scrying out the name of the thief even as we speak.'

'What? Now?' Hildegard exclaimed getting to her feet. 'Where is he?'

'In his workshop.'

'Then I must interrupt this nonsense. Come – '

'I'd rather not –' He hung back then, in a sudden change of mood, he went to the door and barred her way. 'I cannot allow you to face him alone, domina. I fear what he'll do to me when he discovers that I was the one who purloined his book but I fear even more what he'll do to you if he knows you're my helper.'

'But in that case, unless he's especially skilled at scrying or you or Mistress Beata tell him my name, he'll not know, will he?'

Alaric gaped at her in alarm and then a tentative smile crossed his face. 'If it's a case of choosing between two magi's I'll choose you, domina, the mage of common-sense.'

Together they went across the moonlit garth towards the corner of the cloister where Hywel had his workshop. A candle was burning to show he was inside.

'Keep out of sight. In fact, go to your bed and get some rest.' She waited until he entered the porch of the lay-brothers' house.

The door to Hywel's workshop was ajar on such a hot night, enough to let in some cooler air from outside.

'At work, brother?' Hildegard greeted after a perfunctory knock. 'I've come to find out if your book from off the St Marie has turned up?'

Hywel jerked to his feet letting a chart fall at

his feet. As he bent to pick it up she saw that it was covered in a multitude of figures criss-crossed by a geometry of triangles and squares. Hastily putting it on the work bench behind him and covering it with a cloth he came forward with his wolfish smile. 'You made me start. I imagined I was quite alone. Everyone asleep. No sound of footsteps…Well?' his eyes inched over her face. 'You look anxious.'

'I am, of course, anxious about my lord abbot for one. He frets at his confinement.'

'But he must know that it is for the perfection of his soul that it was given to him to endure this misfortune.'

'Perfection is ever our goal, quite so.'

They eyed each other for a moment.

'Now we have established that to our satisfaction,' he said smoothly, 'do you want to get down to business?'

'Business?' She covered her confusion as best she could.

'The business,' he smiled, 'that brought you

here in the middle of the night.'

Feeling wrong-footed Hildegard put her head on one side. 'This book stolen from you – '

'Is that really why you're here?'

'I was wondering it if was available at Beaulieu? Is it worth sending someone over there to find out?'

He smiled. 'I feel grateful for your concern, but no, they will not have it.'

'How can you be sure?'

'Domina – Hildegard,' he corrected. 'It is more than a book. It is unique. It cannot be repeated. That's enough!' His eyes narrowed. 'Did anyone send you to sound me out?'

There was no sign that he had been scrying, no bowl of pure water, no cards or any other sign of the instruments of prophecy apart from his hastily concealed chart with its strange symbols and diagrams.

When she looked up he was staring deeply into her eyes with a look of intense concentration. She felt he was smiling at her with a deep and compelling warmth that enveloped her entire being and she could not look away because her attention was fixed on his eyes, drawn to the deep world that lay within them. He began to speak in a slow and gentle voice about the night, how long it was, how tiring to keep the midnight Office, how she might sit down for a moment in a comfortable chair and sleep awhile…

She had no idea what else he was saying because something, a bright dart of energy from within made her fortify herself against him as she felt his power surge towards her and threaten to overwhelm her in a wave of heat and light. She resisted and put up a shield against it, against him, and it was like a battle between them, his strength against hers until the force threatening her waned, and he retreated.

Slightly dazed she watched him go to sit on a stool at the work bench. He was smiling to himself.

When he spoke it was in the friendly tones of the previous day and he begged forgiveness if he had been abrupt when she asked about the stolen book. 'If you know where it is and who stole it, Hildegard, it would be a most kind gesture to get them to return it to me. I will pay. Remember to tell them that. Forget what Abbot Philip might offer. I myself will find the means to buy it. I will pay whatever it costs.'

When he glanced up his eyes had lost the compelling power that had tried to impose his will over hers. He was a supplicant now, desperation visible in every gesture of his clenched hands and haunted look.

'Will you believe me, Hywel, if I say I don't know where it is? I will do what I can to find it if you wish.' And solve this mystery, she added silently.

'If anyone can find it I'm sure it will be you,' he returned in a guarded tone.

As there was little point in staying any longer and, in fact, still feeling weakened by the powerful grip he had exerted over her will, even if momentarily, she bade him goodnight, seeking nothing now but the safety of her chamber and the blessed solace of sleep. But as soon as she turned a corner of the building Alaric emerged from the shadows.

'I told you to go to bed.' Her words must have shocked him with their coldness because he fell back a pace.

'I wanted to make sure you were unharmed,' he muttered.

'Of course I am. I beg forgiveness, Alaric. I didn't mean to bark at you.' She shook off the feeling of ice that must have been a remnant of Hywel's power over her and took him by the arm. 'Come, walk a little way with me. Hywel has made it clear to me that he wants nothing more than to find his book. He does not know you have taken it. You have no need to fear him. But tell me, please, if you will, where did you hide it?'

'It was the quickest and most obvious place,' he began as they stood outside the guest quarters. 'When I came back off the ship and Mistress Beata told me to hide it everybody was rushing down to the waterside to help the sailors. The kitchens were empty. I grabbed a skillet from a hook as a weight and protection, placed the book inside, then wrapped the whole lot in some of that waterproof cloth the baker uses for his loaves. I slapped more pig fat round it to make sure it was well protected and then I hid it behind the fish trap. You know where that is? It's a little door in the stream running by the side of the kitchen. It's easily reached. I thought it would be undetected there. Then of course there came this terrible calamity – '

'The blockage? But was that not caused by yourself?'

He shook his head. 'It's further upstream where the water enters under the abbey buildings. It's blocking the stream that flows into the trap and I was afraid that after it ran dry they might push the little door and find the package so I went to where the water should flow in but there's something lodged inside the culvert. It's wide at the start so I went to the other end and tried ducking my head underneath and feeling along it but it narrows towards the outlet into the kitchen. Even holding my breath and diving under I could not reach whatever was blocking it.'

'I heard you visited Mistress Beata dripping wet and she scolded you for it.'

'She was like a mother, I expect. That's what they do, I'm told.' He half-smiled as if he longed for some maternal scolding. Hildegard remembered that he was an orphan, like so many children after the recent return of the Plague.

'So where is the book now? You haven't left it behind the fish door, have you?'

'Of course not. I took it to Mistress Beata and she said she would deal with it.'

'She's found a hiding place for it?' Hildegard did not keep the surprise out of her voice.

'She's a very willful and resourceful old lady.'

'So do you yourself know where it is now?'

'No. So I'm afraid I cannot tell you, domina. Nor can I tell Brother Hywel.'

'Will you find out and then return it to him?'

'I can never return it, not without Mistress

Beata's consent. I know how much it means to her to have some power over her husband.'

'Brother Hywel has offered money to match any that anyone else may offer her.'

'He has?' Alaric looked astonished. 'But he's as impoverished as I am. Surely, his Order forbids personal wealth?'

'That was his promise.'

'Am I to believe him then? Words are cheap.'

'Does he lie?'

Alaric gave a sigh. 'He appears not to – but then,' he added slyly, 'isn't that the mark of a good liar?'

'I only know what he said to me, Alaric. Go to Mistress Beata. Ask her how much she wants for it and then come back to me with her answer.'

'I'll go now.'

'And wake her?'

'She never sleeps at night. That's how we became friends. I got into the habit of sitting with her through the night to help her through her coughing fits.'

'Go then. Let's get this matter resolved. But Alaric - '

'Yes, domina?'

'Do not wake her on my account. I shall be in the refectory.'

He made a small obeisance and in the moonlight she could see him smile. It revealed the beginning of hope that all could be put right.

CHAPTER EIGHT

A sleepy lay-brother was sitting with his head in his hands at one of the trestles and when she went inside he wearily lifted his head to see who it was. 'Domina, you're sleepless too, I see.'

'You look as if you're ready for your bed. You must have had a long day.'

When he brought the aquifer over with a clean beaker he could scarcely keep his eyes open. 'It's this blockage effecting the sluice. It means I've scarcely had a minute. Without water the fish can't swim down to the trap in the kitchens so we can't take fish out when we need to. Somebody's going to have to go in the water upstream above the blockage to catch them before they get flooded all over the upper meadow and we have to pick them like daisies out of the grass.'

He wiped his hands on his apron. 'In this weather the poor little devils won't last long. They'll be half-cooked by the time we gather them in, out of the sun.'

She wondered if he thought they were poor little devils when they died in the fish trap as well. Apparently not because he went on to bewail the unnaturalness of the weather and how it was causing all kinds of strange things to happen, like a shower of frogs over Southampton way, and the sheep that gave birth to a calf, and other unlikely stories, and how it was due to a curse put out by somebody, if only they could find them and have them exorcised, but it was not to be because the sins of those at present staying in the abbey were not yet expiated. As soon as a ship could take them away on their pilgrimages the curse would be lifted.

Hildegard let his ramblings wash over her and took the opportunity to send her thoughts drifting to Hubert and why she had not gone with Alaric to the infirmary where at least she might have had a chance of a word with Hubert if he was still awake. He would be fine-tuned to the hours and with Matins coming up very soon he would probably be awake in preparation even if he could not physically attend the service.

She imagined Abbot Philip and found it hard to see him getting out in the middle of the night to officiate when he had that cold-eyed prior to attend to matters for him. Or the bustling sub-prior.

It led her to wonder what Abbot Philip felt about the death of one of his monks and how guilty he might feel at sending the poor man out to the ship for what amounted to mere profit. He was worried, of course, by the threat from his protectors.

And then she began to wonder who the man behind all this was, bleeding the abbey dry for his own gain, because surely he must know that the monks could not afford to keep on paying. And if he continued with his exactions, then what? Would he be happy to see them living in utter poverty?

How far would he bleed them before he understood that he was ruining his own chance of profit?

And how could anyone think like this anyway?

What would their thoughts be when they reached the point of death?

How would they face the Day of Judgement? Would they feel it was a life well spent, to have lived only to fill their coffers with gold?

Then she thought of Meaux. How different it was. How peaceful, how contented everyone was under the benign rule of Abbot de Courcy.

And then she wished she had gone with Alaric just to set eyes on the abbot as he slept. If he did sleep. And then she was back again at the problem of the book.

And she thought of Hywel and his strange power and how uncomfortable she felt when he looked at her as if he knew everything about her and how something like fire had stood between them, a column of flame, a clash of wills visible on some other plane, and how nearly she had succumbed.

Then she wondered what if Beata refused to barter for the book. Was it really money she wanted or was it more to do with besting her unloving husband? No good would ever come of any of this.

Still Alaric did not return.

Yawning and noticing that the lay-brother was resting his head on his arms on the trestle and was snoring lightly, she rose to her feet and trod softly to the door.

Alaric appeared just then as if summoned. 'She will sell to him if his price is right!' he told her in excitement.

With another yawn Hildegard replied, 'I shall have to go and tell Hywel then. Maybe it can wait until morning?'

Alaric looked disappointed. 'Can't we can go by and see if his light is still on?'

Taking him by the arm she led him to the door. 'I can't imagine what took you so long. I'm sure he'll have been asleep this last hour.'

So convinced was she that after making his wishes known Hywel would have turned in - at least until Matins – that she was already telling him that she would see him there when she noticed the light still burning in his window.

'Keep out of this, Alaric. As yet he does not know who has his blessed book.'

As soon as he was out of sight she knocked on the door and this time waited for Hywel to answer it.

'I knew you'd come.' He pulled her inside. 'How much do they want?'

'They want you to name your price.'

He smiled. 'High or low? How keen are they to get rid of it?'

'Not at all, I shouldn't think. I haven't spoken to them.'

He looked thoughtful.

'I'm tired, Hywel. It's the middle of the night. I'm going in to Matins and then I shall try to get a few hours' sleep before Prime.'

'When will you speak to them?'

'I'm not a go-between. I may not speak to them.'

'Them? Are there more than one or is this just a manner of speaking to allow no clue to their identity? How interesting that is, in itself. It suggests that he – or she – ' he broke off. 'She?' He was staring at her intently. 'How curious. What vistas are opened up by that one word. We know only one 'she' who went on board the ship that night.' He gave an odd grimace. 'And she has disappeared.' He got up and rearranged a few things on his work bench then looked up quickly as if to catch the truth on her face. 'It cannot be her then, can it? Unless you're – no, I don't think you'd lie. Anyway, you'll have to produce the book on payment, won't you?'

Wondering how on earth she had allowed herself to get embroiled in all this Hildegard rubbed a hand over her eyes. 'I won't have to produce anything. It's nothing to do with me…I'm really sleepy now, Hywel…I'll say goodnight.'

'I don't want to let you out of my sight,' he said in a darkly urgent voice.

'I must go.' She went to the door and opened it.

'Stay with me.' He followed her to the threshold.

'I can tell you nothing more.'

'I don't mean for any reason to do with the book. I mean – stay with me.'

His haunted looks made him handsome. The dark eyes were shadowed and his wide, sensitive mouth seemed alluringly close. She put up a hand as if to ward him off but he clasped it fervently in his own and brought it to those very lips and pressed them over and over again on the back of her hand and then, turning it, kissed the inside of her wrist.

'Stay,' he repeated. 'I beg you to stay with me if only for a little while. You are the only one who understands me, the only one who could ever be my equal in the great work. Stay, Hildegard…stay with me…You know we can do great things together. The sun, the moon. Mars and Venus. We two…in this swamp of iniquity…together we can bring redress to an unjust world.'

'How would we do that, Hywel?'

She carefully removed her hand from his and covered it inside one of her sleeves.

'I can tell you more if you'll stay with me and let me explain…It could be the saving of King Richard…not to mention Prince Owain.'

'What on earth do you mean?'

'Come - ' He stepped back and held the door wide.

After a moment's hesitation she stepped over the threshold into his cell.

CHAPTER NINE

Jankin was asleep in his blanket under the work-bench and Hywel went over to poke him with the toe of his boot. 'Wake up! Come on!'

When Jankin snuffled out of his covers he was too bleered with sleep to say anything.

Hywel poked him again. 'Get up. Go and sleep under the vines outside the drying hut. It's too hot to lie within.' As the boy rose shakily to his feet Hywel added, 'I don't want to see you before Prime.'

Without saying anything the apprentice groped his way to the door and disappeared into the night.

'Now then, let me get you a comfortable chair – '

'I'm not staying long, Hywel – '

'Only until Matins, of course.'

Determined not to let him take the initiative she asked, 'So what did you mean, the saving of King Richard. Is it to do with this book - ?'

He gave her that intent stare again and said

quickly, 'This is nothing to do with that, as such. I told you, I need…for the work to…' For once he seemed unable to find the appropriate word.

'What is this work?' she interrupted.

'I need help with it. You know about the attempt to turn base metals into gold and silver?'

'I have heard that some men believe they can do that successfully, yes. But I have heard of no instances of it having been achieved.'

'Not here, no, not in England, not in France either, but in the east, yes, maybe also in Castile - why else would Gaunt desire the - yes, there, almost surely it has been done.'

'How do you know this, have you been there and seen it for yourself?'

'No, but I believe it but only after reading the manuscripts that show how it can be done. It is well known that gold can be melted and turned into base metal so why can't the process be reversed? Think what it would mean for King Richard in his battle for survival. He would be able to afford to raise an army against those of

Lancaster, Gloucester and Arundel. It would mean the end to this constant threat of civil war. His crown would be secure. As it is, every time the barons attack him he has to give way. Look at what happened recently at Westminster. What a fool he was made to look, a weak and defenceless fool with only weak men as allies - and all because he has no army under his command.'

'And I suppose that, as well as the king, Prince Owain would welcome such a process,' she smiled slyly. 'Isn't this what you really want?'

He was handsome when he laughed as he did now. His finely chiseled features, with their slightly haggard, wasted lines, the fire that was lit deep in the darkness of his eyes, his intensity, made him touching and desirable. When his eyes met Hildegard's he read her mind at once and stopped, about to say something, then turned away, then looked back again and was about to say something again, and then stopped again.

All he managed was her name, spoken with a husky almost strangled intonation as if his very soul fought against it.

For a long moment they sat and looked at each other without speaking.

Hildegard had the sensation that she was allowing destiny to decide her fate. The reins were slipping from her hands.

Berating herself for that unguarded appraisal she fiddled with the edge of her sleeve while she gathered her wits then, lifting her head with a show of impatience she brushed temptation aside saying, 'We know it would be the saving of the king – and also of Owain and your fellow Welsh – but it will not be. There is no such process. And,' remembering the opinion of Master John, 'don't you see, if there were, anyone could obtain the secret, the price of gold would fall, we would be back where we started.'

He leaned forward, eyes glittering. 'But no-one need discover it but ourselves.'

Hildegard dismissed this idea with a scornful jerk of her head. 'How would you prevent it?'

'By involving only those I could trust with the

secret.'

'And you trust me?'

'Why would I not trust you, Hildegard?' His eyes held an animal gleam. 'You would never lie to me, would you?'

She did not reply.

He got up and came towards her, soft-footed, smiling again, and confident. For reassurance she pressed the hard oblong of the knife hidden in her sleeve. 'Who,' he asked, still smiling, 'is the go-between – the one who stands between you and the thief?'

'I cannot tell you.'

'Cannot, will not,' he muttered to himself with a sardonic twist of the lips. 'You have a strong will. Why else would I want you as an ally? But there must be a way of making you answer. I must be the stronger in this partnership.'

'There is no such thing, Hywel. I have agreed to nothing.'

'Oh but you have. You agreed when we met earlier this evening and - you know what happened then as well as I do. It was there between us, the power, the gold, the silver, the sun and the moon…the promise of an alchemical marriage.'

'I will not tell you the name of the go-between. Give me a price for the book and I shall pass it on. If it is accepted you will have your book. As for a marr…' she faltered, 'a partnership between us…that can never be.'

His face turned to wood and the light left his eyes. 'Very well. I shall pay whatever this thief asks. Tell them, him or her, whoever, tell them they will have their thief's gold, much good may it do them. But *we* shall have something else. Believe me, we two shall have an alchemical marriage.'

'I may go?'

'Am I keeping you?' He spread his arms.

When she got up, however, he came swiftly to her and took both of her hands between his own. 'Whatever you say, there is a bond of power between us and you will come to know it and to celebrate.'

Shakily she stepped outside into the calm, clear moonlight and never had the open air seemed so welcoming, so fresh, so pure. The aura in Hywel's shadowy, aromatic cell with its charts and distillations and its innocent-seeming instrument for measuring the stars clung to her like the summoning of a madman's malign obsession.

She strode out swiftly the quicker to put a distance between herself and Hywel when two figures appeared from out of the shadows near the building opposite.

She stepped back to avoid them then stalled when she heard the voice of Jankin whispering her name.

'Is that Alaric with you?' she asked, peering through the darkness.

'It is.' He stepped into the moonlight. 'We were curious to know what transpired.'

'Do we need to fear being turned into toads?' Jankin asked with a jocular air that sat ill with his worried frown.

'I gave you my word, Alaric, that I would not tell Hywel the identity of the go-between. And you, Jankin, I had no idea you were in on this marvelous secret too.'

'Impossible not to be, living in that cell of his with all the books around. I read better than he thinks. He sounds quite mad and I admit I'm afraid of him sometimes but then other times he's the sweetest man alive. It's this obsession with the philosopher's stone that's turning him into a monster.' Jankin gave her a beseeching look. 'He must have explained all that to you?'

'What? About a stone? Is this what that what it's all about?...I don't understand.'

'It's not just any old stone. It's The Stone, the one the philosophers have been searching for since time immemorial. The Stone. The Stone of Power. The one that can turn base metal into gold.'

'I think he expected to have it delivered to him but something has gone very wrong.'

'And the book?'

'It's something to do with that.'

Alaric said, 'I've asked Mistress Beata to explain but she denies all knowledge of it. "Men's nonsense," she calls it.'

Jankin said stoutly, 'Well, she can count me out of that range of men because I don't believe in it either. I'd like to see it turn a bit of old tin-plate armor into gold. That'd be a thing, wouldn't it?' He laughed. 'Friar Hywel says he's seen documents that attest to it.' He turned to Alaric. 'Be careful, brother, the dangers of learning to read are never properly explained. It can turn your head if you don't watch out.'

'You wouldn't go back to unlearning your letters, would you?' Alaric looked shocked to the core.

'I only said be careful. Don't be led astray by unlikely promises in what you read.'

'Listen, fellows,' Hildegard interrupted. 'Forget this stone. Hywel says he'll pay any price to get hold of the book. Tell Mistress Beata that and my involvement is done.'

The bell for Matins started to toll. Hildegard gazed in despair at the door leading up to her sleeping chamber and then turned towards the church. If she found a suitable corner she might snatch some sleep yet.

CHAPTER TEN

Next morning she was woken up by a shaft of sunlight shining onto her eyelids. Her sheet had been kicked to the floor and she was lying naked again in another day of stifling heat.

With a groan she rolled over and buried her head in the feather pillow but it was too late now, she was awake and after a moment or two she raised herself onto one elbow then sat up. The events of the preceding night came rushing back.

Was she mad to get involved in all this? It had started when Hubert had asked, as a favour to his hosts, to find out what had happened to Brother Martin. Then it had turned into a hunt for a stolen book. Now it seemed she was involved in a plot with a magician to save the crown of England. And possibly to assist in the overthrow of the Norman lords in Wales.

Treasonable stuff, she said to herself. It's overblown. We should never discuss these things in the middle of the night. People take leave of their senses, especially when there's a full moon as there was last night.

At first she had seen Hywel as a simple herberer, then as a cool if not cold investigator into the phenomena of natural life, asking what things were made of, when and why the stars changed their positions, what caused the world we see around ourselves and what is its purpose. Now he was engaged, if he were to be believed, in experiments that would alter the course of nature and give inexhaustible power to the man who discovered the hermetic law that could change the essence of a thing into something entirely different.

She wondered if he had given a thought to the charge of heresy that might be directed against him.

Yawning she drew on her shift, pulled a kirtle over it, the lightest she could find, brushed her hair and stuffed it inside a fresh coif, put her mantle on over the whole lot and, feet inside her sandals, unlocked her door and went out.

The first person she met along the corridor was the lay-woman who had first conducted her to her chamber. Now, catching sight of Hildegard, she exclaimed, 'Oh, my dear lady, you gave me such a shock. I thought everyone had gone outside in the excitement.'

'What excitement?' asked Hildegard with less enthusiasm than seemed to be expected.

'Why, the picking up of fish from the upper meadow, of course!' She explained. 'The stream is still blocked and has flooded out over its banks taking the fish with it. The poor things are flapping about in the grass. The cook is throwing a fit because he can't keep them all unless they're salted and he's saying who wants salted fish in mid-summer? I thought you'd be down there with everyone else.'

'They want help? All right. It must be later than I think.'

'Just before Prime, domina. It's not all that late.'

'So they haven't managed to unblock the fish

trap yet?' she asked as she went step by step down the narrow stairs to the outside door.

'They resolve to get it done this morning even if, as master kitchener says, they have to put saltpetre down there – and blow up half the abbey, if you ask me.' With her arms full of freshly laundered sheets she bustled away.

Hildegard found her way to the infirmary first. Hubert was sitting up already looking spry. His hair was neatly combed. He had on a clean shirt. His leg had a fresh bandage. There was a cup and an empty plate beside him.

'You seem to want for nothing, my lord,' she greeted, taking all this in at a glance.

'As you see.'

'Who did all this?'

'Our friend Friar Hywel.' He nodded towards the end of the row of empty beds to where Hywel was bending over Mistress Beata with a beaker of something in his hand.

Hildegard gave a sharp intake of breath. Had

he found out that his 'thief' was the wife of Master John?

Hywel turned at that moment and gazed down the long ward that separated them and as if drawn by a chain came slowly towards her. His face wore a familiar expression, as blank as a wooden mask. She could not tell whether he knew the truth, whether he had guessed it or whether he had scried it by some magical means of his own. She could only stare.

He came to within a few feet of where she stood. Still he had not uttered a word. She held out her hand. 'Is this something for Mistress Beata?'

He looked confused as if she had started speaking in tongues.

'The beaker. Is it for Beata?'

Coming to himself he muttered, 'Oh, this. Yes. Here…take it if you wish.' As he handed it to her his fingers grazed her own and he jerked back as if stung. The contents spilled to the floor and spread in a pool between their feet. One of the lay-brothers, having seen what had happened, came over.

'No matter, brother. Let me deal with this. Will you need more? I can run over to your cell to fetch it?'

Hywel stared at him for a moment as if trying to place him then shook his head. 'That'll do for her.'

Hildegard walked self-consciously down the ward, aware of his glance following her until she reached Beata lying propped in her bed. She held the beaker but did not hand it to her. *This will do for her.*

Beata pretended to take it then whispered, 'I shall not drink this at present, Hildegard. No need to tell Brother Hywel.' She gave her a meaningful look. 'Give him this.' Crunching something she had extracted from her gown she pressed it into Hildegard's palm. It was a small piece of parchment. 'It is the price. Dear Alaric has told me everything.'

When Hildegard went back to Hubert, to her relief Hywel had left. Hubert gave her a piercing glance.

'So? What was all that about?'

'You may as well know at once, I had the most extraordinary night last night,' she told him.

'It has been busy here as well,' he replied.

'Alaric?'

He smiled. 'I lost count of Beata's visitors. I don't know why people imagine that just because one is lying down one becomes deaf, but there it is.'

'What shall we do?'

'It is hardly our concern. We've fulfilled our promise to Abbot Philip. There is no murderer to apprehend. It's for him to deal with this loss of his in his own way. I would not welcome visitors to my abbey interfering in our affairs. I suggest you go and help the fisher folk in the meadow,' he gave her the smile that always threatened to break her heart. 'You look exhausted, sweeting. Go and get some fresh air then come back and tell me we can have fresh fish again.'

'More than that, I'll bring you some to eat.'

'Then my cup of happiness will overflow.'

'Maybe I should explain – '

'You need never explain to me, my dear Hildegard.'

His smile stayed with her all the way across the garth, past the Chapter House and beyond that into the upper meadow.

It was a sad and disheartening business, picking the stranded fish from out of the grass. Their rapid gasps to take in air had all the desperation of any living creature that finds it cannot breathe. The kindest thing was to kill them at once by rapping their heads against the sides of the wooden buckets that had been collected from all round the abbey.

Hildegard was about to wade forth to help when Brother Heribert who had been standing by came over to her. 'We do not need to take part, domina. Enough that the lay-brothers do our work for us while we pray. But do fish have souls, I wonder? Is it our duty to pray for their salvation?'

'The teaching is somewhat vague,' she replied, her mind on the flashes of silver starring the meadow grass as the fish floundered in the shallow overflow from the stream. 'Do they yet know how the sluice became blocked?'

He look uninterested. 'It is not our job to sort it out. I'm off to inform the prior of the latest development and to inform him that the situation is in hand. We shall soon be to rights again, I pray

He wandered off, splashing knee deep now and then as he made his way round the perimeter of the meadow towards the Chapter House.

Prime had already begun when Hildegard edged her way inside. Because the weather was as hot as ever the cool of the church was a welcome refuge and it was crowded with impatient pilgrims who wanted only to get away by the next available ship. Looking round she silently counted them off.

There was Simon on his stick beside his wife, his head devoutly bent throughout, and Lissa, her glance discretely roving and settling and roving again, but always returning to the commanding figure of Master John.

For his part he glanced out of the corners of his eyes now and then, half-smiled when their glances met, and somehow seemed to take in those nearest him as well.

One or two newcomers, innocent and eager to be on their way, exchanged smiles.

The two sisters, straw hats trailing coloured ribbons and freshly picked daisies, their eyes piously lowered, were there, and the bookish man who kept to himself, and Lucie, looking lost, her mistress nowhere to be seen.

Hildegard glanced round again. Delith was missing.

Even the three mercenaries were once again standing at the back looking useless as usual without their swords.

But no Delith.

Managing to cross from the west door into the garth as the monks, the service ended, began to file out from the other door to go into Chapter, she greeted Gregory and Egbert and, reading the signal Gregory gave her she paced over towards the cloisters. They joined her there a moment later.

'Has Hubert told you anything about last night?' Gregory asked at once. 'What is all this about the theft from the St Marie?'

She said, 'I don't know what I can add but I can tell you that Brother Hywel is offering more than he can possibly possess to get hold of it and apprehend the thief.'

'That's news to us. We heard from Hubert that there was an offer for it but not from him. But what about Mistress Delith? Is she still missing?'

'It seems so.'

'And then there's the problem of the sluice,' added Egbert. He looked troubled.

'I saw them collecting fish from the overflow before prime. What are they doing about the blockage?'

'Sending a small boy down again. Are you going over there while we're in Chapter?'

'I will do. Hubert is fretting about not being

able to eat fish!'

They parted their separate ways and when Hildegard entered the kitchens she found quite a crowd ahead of her. They were grouped alongside the half-wall next to the fish trap where the water usually flowed in. A small boy, the one she recognized from last night, was standing on the wall like a little king.

She said to lay-brother nearby, 'So they've persuaded him to go back?'

'Not without the promise of this penny he's been on about.' The man chuckled. 'We all had to swear on our saints' names we'd ensure he was properly paid for his courage.'

Hildegard gave a half-smile. 'Let's hope he earns it then. What's he doing now?'

'Making some sort of speech in case he doesn't return.' The man grinned. 'Lads? Can you credit them!'

To cheers of encouragement the boy finished his speech and was let down into the dry bed of the stream. Everyone pressed forward to watch. When he came to the entrance to the pipe he hesitated and encouraged by a few jeers from his friends he ducked his head under the entrance and dropped onto all-fours to crawl inside. They could see his feet for a moment or two before he wriggled out of sight.

An anticipatory hush fell.

'He's stuck!' somebody remarked when he failed to reappear.

Anxious mutterings arose. Some bantering remark about sending somebody else down to prise him out was received in silence.

Eventually, when it seemed this suggestion might have to be taken seriously the backs of two small boots appeared. Everyone leaned further forward. Squirming and wriggling the boy reappeared bit by bit, bare legs, rumpled tunic, a tousled head. When he was fully out he stood up, red-faced, and with a dramatic shriek flung out his arms.

'I told you all! But you didn't believe me! I touched it, I tell you! And it was like a cow's hide! And it's a devil so now will you believe me?'

Speech over he tried to scramble back up the wall as frantically as if the hounds of hell were after him and many willing hands reached down to hoist him bodily, still yelling, to safety.

Several by-standers crossed themselves. His friends, however, were still in a jocular mood.

'It'll be a piece of rubbish thrown in further upstream,' one of them insisted.

'Feared of your own shadow, you!' said another.

'You go down then if you're so sure!' retorted the boy. He seemed determined to wring everything he could from his minute of fame. 'I tell you, it was a devil lying there, not moving, dripping water where it seeps in and covered with a rough skin like – like…'

'Like a cow's hide, you said. Some devil!' And they all roared with laughter.

'Could you not push it or pull it?' asked the master kitchener, scowling at his unruly staff.

'What happened when you prodded it?'

'Nothing, master. It's jammed tight.'

'Then we'll have to send somebody in from the other end.'

'In under the water?' the assistant Kitchener asked. 'Nobody's going to do that.'

'I'll go.'

The master turned. 'You, Alaric? Are you sure?'

'I reckon I'm the only one of you lot who could hold their breath long enough to reach it.'

Eager not to put a volunteer off, the master kitchener and his retinue marched out with Alaric at their head and took the path along the stream behind the buildings to the place where it should have been freely flowing into the wide mouth of a culvert instead of flooding the meadow with fish.

Hildegard noticed a dozen or so lay-brothers already hefting the laden buckets back towards the kitchens as they approached. Most of the fish had been picked up. A cat was playing with one as it struggled for life in the grass, dabbing at it but reluctant to enter the water to snatch it up and kill it. A lay-brother scooped up the fish as he passed, dropped it onto the heap in his bucket, and scared off the cat with a kick.

Alaric had already jumped down into the stream by the time the last of the procession arrived. He had taken off his tunic and stood bare-chested in the sunlight.

Breathing deeply a few times he filled his lungs with air then ducked his head under the surface of the water and, such was its clarity, he was visible to them all like a silvery, sinuous, silvery aquatic creature as he swam into the opening.

'It narrows when it gets near the kitchens,' somebody explained as they all watched. 'That'll be where it's blocked.' One or two people were holding their own breath to match Alaric but long before he reappeared they were gasping for air.

Eventually they saw him emerge from the culvert. Dripping shards of silver droplets, he rose from the waters like a Triton.

The Master Kitchener leaned forward. 'Well?

See anything?'

Breathing deeply to refill his lungs Alaric shook his head. When he recovered he said, 'It's too dark down there to see anything, master. But I touched something. Cloth. And something soft and flowing.'

He made no attempt to climb out of the water. 'I must go back. I believe there is someone down there.'

'Some one?'

People were beginning to draw back.

'I fear what I touched felt like human hair.'

With a few deep breaths he again submerged himself and swam into the culvert. Nobody wanted to leave now even though it was time to retire to the refectory to break their fast. Besides, no-one would be present to serve them. It seemed as if the entire abbey laity was present. In Chapter the monks were missing everything.

It took Alaric two more dives into the culvert for him to say he was certain that it was a body but that it was jammed into the section of the pipe that narrowed where it was diverted into the kitchens and he was unable to move it.

'We'll have to get something to push it from the narrow end of the pipe while somebody pulls it from the water end,' declared the Master. 'If you wouldn't mind going down there yet again, Alaric, my son, after you've had something to eat and drink, of course?' He spoke with unusual deference.

Offering his hand he pulled Alaric out of the water. The sun was blazing down now, at mid-morning, and Alaric, dripping wet, his hair plastered to his skull, his eyelashes, even, glistening with water drops, was the coolest one present.

Several of the younger conversi were already throwing off their tunics and splashing down into the stream amid warnings that if they went into the culvert and got stuck, there they would stay until they too were corpses.

Somewhat subdued, everyone began to make a move towards the refectory.

Hildegard expected that as soon as food and drink was brought and an air of the familiar took over the conversation would start to buzz with speculation about who was down there. Alaric's opinion was to be trusted. The consensus was that he was a steady type, not given to wild flights, a brave lad, worthy of reward, and what he said was likely to be true.

She saw Jankin go up to him and slap him on the back. 'I would never have dared,' she heard him say. 'Good lad, and to offer to go down again!' She saw him shake his head in wonder at his friend's folly.

They are friends now, she thought as she turned away towards the infirmary. Both from similar backgrounds, one fortunate to have found an apprenticeship, the other destined to stay as a servant for the rest of his life. Alaric seemed to feel no bitterness about their differing fates.

CHAPTER ELEVEN

Hubert's eyes lit up when he saw her. 'I gather they're all down trying to solve the mystery of the blocked culvert?' he began.

'It's partially solve. They're going to get on with it as soon as they find some suitable implements with which to push and pull the blockage out.' She gave a grimace. 'It's very sad. Alaric is convinced it's a body.'

Hubert looked startled. 'Does that mean Gregory's search is over?'

Hildegard's mouth opened as his meaning dawned on her. 'Could it be?' she found herself whispering. 'Oh, no, Hubert! That would be such a dreadful thing. But how could she…how would she fall into the stream and be swept along? It's shallow enough where it disappears into the culvert.'

Hubert was frowning. 'Didn't you say she had an argument with that fellow from Southampton?'

Hildegard put her hand to her mouth. 'You

mean to say he might have – ' She shook her head. 'No, surely not! It was little more than a tiff. They spoke in anger, that's true, but only in the manner of people like that, neither willing to listen to the other.' She thought about it for a moment. 'Delith told him she had a secret that would change his life forever. It would make no sense to harm her, would it?'

She recalled how the young woman had protested against some violence done to her by…Lionel, was it?...and had told him not to touch her. She mentioned it to Hubert who merely replied, 'This is speculation. Let's wait until we see who they've found.,,Where is he, by the way?'

'I haven't seen him since…' she frowned. 'I haven't seen him since yesterday.'

'Is he still within the precincts?'

'You mean he might have…and then absconded?'

Recoiling from the horror of their supposition she told him what Alaric had said, about it being too dark to see anything. 'Maybe it's just as the conversi are saying. It's rubbish thrown in from further upstream.'

'That's the most likely explanation,' agreed Hubert.

Hildegard sat on the edge of his bed. 'I haven't asked you about your leg today.'

'It's well. Friar Hywel seems to know his business. He believes it'll heal straight and true and that I'll not be left with a limp.'

'I would still love you, even if you were confined to a chair for the rest of your life with two bent legs.' She kissed him.

There the matter was left because Gregory and Egbert emerged from Chapter, yawning and looking as if they needed some action to clear their heads. What was uppermost in Hildegard's mind was what she had heard earlier. 'Is it true Mistress Beata has had another offer for this damnable book?'

Hubert looked pained. 'Such a fuss. That's what I meant about her visitors…She was honoured by a visit from Master John - and he wasn't the only one. Sit down, brothers, and I'll tell you everything I know.'

With a glance round the infirmary to see if anyone was close by he said, 'Mistress Beata sent her husband a message by one of the young lads here to ask him to visit. He came along with an ill grace, telling her that he was a busy man, beset by the difficulties of getting the pilgrims off on another ship so he could justifiably collect their fees. He went on in this strain for a while and she bore it with great patience, I thought, and then she butted in. "A moment, my dear, I have knowledge of something that was stolen from our ship – note that, "our ship" – on the night of the fire and as you are so keen for it I thought you would be willing to pay me for it."'

'That's bare-faced! To her own husband!'

'Quite so. But ordinary behaviour to them I should imagine where all their exchanges come with a price.'

'So what did he say?'

'He grunted, '"What's this 'something' you're

talking about? – clearly not quite believing it was anything important. And then she gave him the title of the book and you should've seen him! He reared off his stool like a man shot by a bolt from a cross-bow then bent over her and hissed, "Perfidious mistress, how did you get hold of it?" "I'm not saying I have," she replied, "but I can get it for you – for a price." Then she added, "after all, dear heart, what's mine is yours and vice versa. Possession is everything as you have so often said yourself."'

'What on earth did he say to that?' Hildegard's eyes widened.

'He said he would decide on a fair price then let her know. He was only persuaded to say that after a lot of arguing. His voice is truly penetrating even when he imagines he's speaking softly.'

'Meanwhile I suppose he's losing no time trying to find her contact and the hiding place of the thing?' Gregory suggested. Hildegard blew out her cheeks and Hubert nodded.

'Just so.'

Egbert slapped his knee.

With a glance round to make sure no-one could overhear her she said, 'Hywel is after it too. It was at his instigation that Abbot Philip had the thing imported. His reason for wanting it – '

'To finish this magnum opus we keep hearing about?'

'More than that – it's connected somehow to the Philosopher's Stone.'

'That old story!' The men laughed outright and Hubert said, 'Don't they realize yet that it doesn't exist?

With their common-sense putting everything in its proper place it was a relief to hear it after the over-heated meeting with Hywel in the night. Hildegard had almost begun to believe in his talk of the sun and moon and an alchemical marriage, and other such stuff that in the light of day could be seen for nothing more than the ravings of a man who spent too much time alone.

Reluctantly she had to leave but only after she had promised Hubert to return as soon as she could.

'I have an errand as yet unfulfilled.' She brought the note Beata had given her from where it was hidden inside her sleeve so he could catch a glimpse of it. 'It's her price. To be delivered to Hywel.'

Everyone was leaving the refectory now and the usual little group were taking up their positions at the end of the cloister, near enough to the gatehouse to be first to notice if any message came through about their delayed departure.

Master John, it seemed, was already down on the waterside talking to his ship man and was said to have sent couriers to nearby harbours to find another ship. How he was going to do this was one of those mysteries that people not in the guild would never understand.

'Please God let it be soon,' Lissa was heard to say, a point of view echoed by the other pilgrims.

Alaric was back running errands as usual but now he was escorted by an admiring throng of younger conversi who followed him with dog-like devotion wherever he went.

Not wishing to let it be known that she sought Jankin she merely waved at the master of this little cavalcade as she passed on her way towards the stables. Hywel's drying hut where he prepared his herbs was close by and if she looked in there first she might find Jankin and if not she would have a ready excuse to look in on the work shop where he would undoubtedly be at work again. Her excuse was the usual stand-by, the need for cures for Hubert.

Before she reached the corner the three mercenaries came in under the gatehouse arch. They were arguing.

Such was the heat of their exchanges it was impossible to tell what the problem was until eventually the captain held up his hands.

'Hold your tongues! We have orders. We stay until we have it. The wagon should be here later today. We load it with the bales and then we're off. You won't be afeared driving through the night, will you?'

'While all the masterless men are abed?' The men, so recently angry, broke into derisive laughter.

'Then that's settled.' They walked on with the captain grumbling, 'you don't think I want to stay here a minute longer than necessary, do you? With a lot of mumbling pilgrims and them monks looking down their noses at us?'

'They'll be blaming us for this body, given half a chance.'

'If it exists.'

'Aye, it's probably a giant rat got stuck.'

'Or a fat monk.'

'Same thing.'

They marched on out of earshot and Hildegard continued on down to the herb garden.

Everything looked brittle in the strong sunlight but the heat brought out the full perfume from the leaves and for a moment she thought how lovely it must be to have a job like Hywel, working with herbs, discovering the secret healing powers of each one, recording treatments, finding cures for the sick and elderly. Hubert said Hywel knew his business. Last night had been a misunderstanding. The moon cast a ghastly aura over things which in the light of day were seen to be harmless.

Without finding Jankin she was forced to go up to the work shop. Wondering how she would lure him outside to give him the message without Hywel noticing, she was surprised to find the place deserted.

She was just standing inside, wondering if she could simply leave the little piece of parchment on the bench and, in fact, was on the point of reaching inside her sleeve for it when she happened to glance behind her. She recoiled.

Hywel himself was standing silently in the doorway watching her. He looked as if he might have been there for some time. With a shiver she met his gaze.

He waited without speaking, testing her nerve, it seemed, until, remembering her excuse, she mentioned Hubert's cure.

His response was to give her a searching glance. 'But I left him some when I was there earlier.'

'Did you?' Her voice rose of its own accord, sounding shaky and deceitful. 'I must have misunderstood.'

'It's not like you, Hildegard - to misunderstand.' He came rapidly on into the workshop.

After a sweeping glance over the bench he turned to face her. 'In fact you're surprisingly quick at understanding.' He paused. 'Aren't you?'

'Am I?' she replied inanely.

Adopting an over-casual manner he asked, 'Did you find anyone here when you walked in?'

'No. Should I have?'

'No message lying on the bench?'

'How would I know that?'

He gave a sigh. 'Would you like a beaker of my apple elixir now you're here?'

'I need to go to...'

Before she could think of a reason he

murmured, '…to avoid me. Well, then.'

Mentally kicking herself she went out without another word. Jankin was just coming across the garth with Lucie.

She went up to him. 'Remember what we were talking about? I have a reply but he's standing there – I couldn't leave it. Can you make sure he finds it?'

Jankin guessed at once what she meant and looked pleased to be given the task. 'You can trust me, domina.'

Glancing back at the workshop she saw that the door was still open. Jankin understood and moved so that Hildegard would block him from Hywel's view. He stuffed the note inside his belt then taking Lucie by the hand they strolled on.

Why did I do that? She asked herself when she reached the privacy of her own chamber. 'Why did I not hand Beata's note to him? What difference would it make whether he thought the thief had given it to me or to a go-between?

It's because I don't trust him, she answered herself. Or is it that I don't trust myself?

The compelling dark eyes filled her imagination with the promise of an unending descent into other worlds.

She did not trust him.

She did not trust the power in his inscrutable, dark, intense contemplation whenever he looked at her.

Lying on her bed with the shutters at the one window opened as wide as they would go she tried to sleep. Only sleep would make his power dissolve until it faded away without harm but as soon as she began to breathe more easily she remembered Delith and gave a shudder of fear.

Strangely, the scene in the herb garden came back. 'Stay with me,' Hywel had asked her and then Delith had appeared and made that suggestion to him and it was as if he already knew what she was going to offer and his revulsion was palpable. His face had turned to stone. If the silly young thing had understood she would not have gone on to make things worse – but she had and now, in restrospect, Hildegard remembered that she had believed he was about to strike her - something profound in him had been wounded by her expectations of him – but his icy control had taken over. Her own presence, maybe, had held him in check.

Now there was the girl's body, if the rumours turned out to be true, and whoever did it had not been held in check by anything.

Several events took place in quick succession on that stifling hot morning when Cloister Garth was beginning to acquire the appearance of a brown-baked desert.

First, a courier from Southampton came riding in before Tierce with a message for Master John. Everybody about the place saw him take it, wrench it open, read, glance round with a smug smile, then hand over some coins to the sweating rider.

Next, the thing blocking the drain started on its slow journey into the outside world of air and light. Alaric became the hero of the moment again with his many dives under water. He came up panting after the fourth or fifth time in the culvert and gave a nod to the Master Kitchener.

The bystanders thrilled with a strange fear to hear him say, 'I've attached the rope to what I believe are its shoulders, master.'

'Is the knot secure?'

'Trust me, I know about knots.'

Hildegard went back into the kitchen to fill a jug to take through into the refectory and went over to the kitchen sluice.

A couple of men were standing down there in a trickle of water. The boy was also presumably there too because one of them bent his head and called into the pipe to ask him if it was having any luck. A muffled echo came back. The man straightened. 'He says it won't budge.'

His companion scratched his head. 'It's going to take a while to shift it.'

'Aye. We'll be here all morning.'

The Master came bustling back into his kitchen.

'Can't he do anything?'

They shook their heads.

Hildegard went on into the refectory and placed the jug on the trestle within reach of the others. The two sisters were talking in low voices in that way they had that set them apart from everyone else. Now Mistress Sweet, Ceci, got up from the trestle with her wastel half-eaten but her sister, Genista, pulled her down again. 'Not yet!'

Chastened, Mistress Sweet sat down with her head lowered and a secret smile on her face. She began to nibble at her bread crust with small, feral teeth.

Lissa and Simon watched as the merchant entered with a great deal of bustle and noise. 'Greetings, John. Is that the one you were waiting for?' Lissa indicated the parchment piece in his hand.

'Good news!' He sat down beside them. 'A trading cog is being sent down from Hampton at this very moment. She'll be here soon. Then it'll simply be a question of getting you all on board.'

The pilgrims further down the trestle gave a cheer when they heard this.

Simon smiled and patted his wife's hands. 'There, my dear little skylark, didn't I tell you everything would turn out for the best?'

'Best for us, maybe, but hardly best for that poor young woman in the culvert. Will they get her out before we leave?'

'Unshriven, poor woman, but we must trust in God's divine grace.'

'I, for one, will be glad to be out of this accursed place. I scarce dare sleep at night,' one of the pilgrims admitted. There were murmurs of agreement.

'Master,' Simon stemmed the ghoulish turn in the conversation to ask, 'What are you to do about the St Marie?

'Good news there as well. She's being towed up to the docks for refitting. That seasoned oak takes a while to burn. It was her saving grace that she was so well-built. The crew of the replacement ship will take her upriver and my good and trusted ship man will command the new vessel. And then to France! Very satisfactory, if I may say so…'

'You say it's satisfactory,' Simon began with a kind smile, 'but what's this I hear about a theft? Some book gone missing?'

'That,' replied John loftily, 'is also going well. I'm in the process of buying it from someone who has come into possession of it.'

'The thief, you mean?'

'By no means. In fact, I doubt whether it was stolen at all. Someone found it, fair and square, no doubt it having been dropped in the general confusion during the storm and, it's worth not being understood, it was merely cast aside where it was found and on the basis of 'finders, keepers' it is now to be sold to the highest bidder…to myself, I may suggest, as I am the only one with a right to it and sufficient wherewithal to make a serious offer.'

Wondering if Hywel knew he had a rival, when she went to make her morning visit to Hubert,

Hildegard told him of John's expectations.

'It's not at all certain that his wife will sell it to him. She's quite amused by the number of offers she's receiving. It seems one or two others would like to purchase such a book too.'

'Do they know what it is?'

'A rather dry and esoteric account of current thinking about the stars? I doubt it. But if enough people talk as if it's something wonderful the more money will be offered for it. Beata is delighted and is doing her best to make it seem more important than it is.'

'Value, like beauty, is entirely in the eyes of the beholder,' she commented.

'What fools they are. Paying over the odds for some worthless piece of ephemera.' He chuckled. 'It makes the world go round, I suppose.'

'But who else wants to buy it?' Before he could answer she said, 'I must say, Hubert, you seem to be at the centre of events today.'

'I'm finding my stay here in the infirmary to be a source of great interest. But the other would-be purchasers you will see shortly. I gather there are two sisters here to sell their produce to the abbey, for the abbot's high table?'

'They are the ones I mentioned. The pilgrims call them Mistress Sour and Mistress Sweet... but frankly I see little difference between them other than the colour of their hair. Surely they don't imagine they can match Master John?'

'We shall see. Maybe in the end Beata will choose by paying heed to the promptings of her heart?'

Hildegard gave him a look that showed her view of this opinion. 'If you really think so,' she remarked in guarded tones.

The next thing that happened was the arrival of a covered wagon. It came creaking in underneath the gatehouse with scarcely an inch to spare on either side. The stable-hands hurried out and paid the horses much attention, suggesting that the wagon belonged to someone of importance and that they had been fore-warned.

The mercenaries swaggered up. 'Are you

staying?' the captain demanded of the waggoner.

'I am.'

'Get something to drink then. We're going to get these abbey servants to start loading when you're ready. You'll have to drive it to the sacristy yonder.' He gestured in the general direction of Cloister Garth. The waggoner nodded and he and his lad jumped down and headed for the refectory as quick as they could.

Hywel came to the door of his workshop and stood there, looking thoughtful.

Avoiding him and, and with Gregory and Egbert nowhere to be seen, Hildegard made her way alone under the gatehouse to the beach path and began to wend her way through the trees. When she came out on the bank she could see the sailors on board the St Marie moving about the deck with a show of purpose. It must be a wrench for the ship man to have to abandon his beloved to others, she was thinking but at least he had agreed to do so which must mean he trusted his employer, Master John, to see to her refit with care.

A sound behind her made her turn. It was Hywel. He came to stand beside her without saying anything.

They looked across Southampton Water, at the dancing lights as sunlight struck the waves, at the distant shore with its scattering of fishermen's huts, at the sky, an upturned bowl of heavenly blue.

After a while he muttered, 'Do you know about this?' He held out the piece of parchment Beata had given her. Jankin had done his errand.

'What does it say?' she asked, avoiding his question.

He noted that and played along. 'It says that my price may be accepted but that others have yet to place their offers.'

'Do they know what they are offering to buy?' she asked.

'Of course not. It's nothing but a commodity to them. What's this thief going to do? Will 'they' sell it to anybody purely on the basis of the money they're offered? I'm the only man in England who'll understand what's written there.' He grimaced and more modestly added, 'one of the only men, I should say.' He caught her eye and suddenly smiled. 'You think I'm mad. At least I expect you do.'

'You said you would pay anything?'

'I should have said I will give everything I have. Even so, it wouldn't amount to much. I take my vow of poverty seriously. My choice. My destiny. I'm not complaining.' He gave her a searching look. 'Master John is willing to top every other offer, I understand? That means I have no chance. I wonder, is that the only way he can regain possession of it?'

'So it seems.'

'Having to buy back something stolen from him?'

'It does happen.'

'I've never heard the like. Can't he find it? It must still be in the abbey precincts. Surely he's got enough sense to put out a search for it?'

'I think his thoughts have been engaged with

the problem of getting the pilgrims another ship so they can leave. No doubt Abbot Philip is keen for him to get them on their way as well. I heard one of the kitcheners saying they're eating the abbey bare.'

'Who's got it?' he asked abruptly, swiveling at the same moment to scrutinize her expression. 'Come on, Hildegard, you must know.'

'Hywel, I can't be involved in this – '

He grabbed her by the arm above the elbow and held it in a savage grip. 'You are involved. Up to your beautiful neck.' His face came close to hers as he stared into her eyes. 'Who are you protecting? Is it that abbot of yours? Is he involved? He seems to know a lot about what's going on. Tell me!'

'I'm sure one minute of conversation with Hubert would reveal that he's amused by it all. He can't imagine why anyone would want a treatise on astronomy in this one particular copy when another one might be obtained.'

He released her. Realizing what he had done he

took her wrist and rubbed her arm where he had held it, saying, 'I hope you don't need a salve for that.'

'Hywel, he knows about the Stone. I told him. I heard about it from – elsewhere. Does John know about it? Is that what this is about?'

Hywel became very still.

Eventually he said, 'That apprentice of mine talks too much.'

More from a wish to protect Jankin than from any other motive she said, 'Don't assume it was he.'

'Who else would know it?' He turned away. 'I cannot count on you. You feel not an iota of good will towards me. But remember something, Hildegard, this is not ended.'

He stalked off through the trees.

CHAPTER TWELVE

Shortly before tierce began the final notable event took place that morning. It was not the long-awaited pulling of the body from the sluice, however.

When Hildegard went back into the garth the wagon was still standing where it had been left with its cover rolled back. A few ropes were coiled inside ready to bind the cargo when it was brought on board.

One or two people were going about their business as usual when one of them noticed something underneath a pile of sacking begin to move.

It was a lay-brother who first noticed it. 'Hey! There's something under there!' He grabbed his nearest companion by the arm and began to back off, pointing towards the waggon. Their shouts brought others running.

A few pilgrims roused themselves from their cloistered gossip about Delith's murder and ambled over. Soon a group of spectators hung about in a wary group, eyeing the wagon.

One of the kitcheners came to his door. 'What's up, lads?'

'There's something on this wagon.'

'We saw it move.'

'What's it doing now?' He came over, beefy arms swinging, a look of skepticism on his face.

'Just lying there under them sacks. Still.'

'Dead,' somebody added.

'Lift the sainted cover off then!' Climbing onto the tail-board he reached out and gave the corner of the sacks a tug. When it slipped aside everybody gasped.

One or two stepped back in horror as at the sight of a ghost.

Indeed, to some, it was a ghost.

'I thought she was dead!' a voice exclaimed in horror, putting everyone's thoughts into words.

It was no wild animal. With a confused look on her face Delith pushed the sacking aside and rose to her feet. She stared back at her audience.

'Am I in dear Netley Abbey already?' she asked in a dazed and astonished voice.

She smiled prettily and stood for a moment, her black hair tumbling about her shoulders, a newish though crumpled russet gown adding to her usual allure while she ran both hands from under her bust and over her hips, ostensibly to smooth its creases but making such a practiced gesture that no-one could have been in doubt what it meant.

Master John, standing in the shadow of the cloisters, stepped forward.

'And then,' Hildegard explained later to Hubert, 'she was helped down by a hundred willing hands and conveyed like a queen into the refectory where the conversi, who had been thinking ill of her and assuming she had got her just desserts, could not do enough to serve her. Likewise some of the pilgrims,' she added.

'So she was not murdered by her paramour after all. Good for that, but who then, is still trapped in the sluice?'

'That we will not know until they pull out the body.'

'They need to make a list of anyone missing. People are coming and going in such profusion at present maybe that's too difficult, although the guest-master, if he's up to the job, should be able to sort it out in a moment.'

'It won't be easy. 've noticed that the pilgrims are already beginning to take their things down to the shore ready to go on board the ship when it arrives.'

Just then the double-doors leading into the infirmary opened and a figure slipped inside.

It was Mistress Sweet, her fair hair loosely braided and a smile on her face that would have melted ice. 'My lord abbot,' she made an obeisance as she passed, 'and my lady Hildegard, together, discussing church matters?'

She went quickly on down the hall to where Mistress Beata, sitting up in bed in the attitude of someone expecting visitors, greeted her and offered her a stool to sit on.

'Well, my dear. And what have you to say?'

'First, I have brought you some flowers I picked for you, mistress, and pray tell me, I beg, how are you feeling today?'

'As well as I felt yesterday. Thank you for your concern.' The amused edge to Beata's words was audible to both Hubert and Hildegard. They exchanged glances.

Ceci leaned forward to say confidentially, 'I have heard that you have a precious book for sale and as you know both I and my sister deal in precious objects.'

'No, I did not know that, my dear. And I must correct you on one thing. I do not have in my possession anything of value, although I do know where such an object is being kept.'

'That aside, my dear Beata, if I may call you so, I understand that the owner is willing to sell? And I am willing to make my offer.' She pulled a little trinket from her sleeve. 'Here is a promise of my serious wish to buy.'

Beata didn't take the gift and Ceci placed it

carefully on the bed covering. Instead Beata smiled benignly and said, 'I note your interest, my dear. If you tell me how much you can offer will you let me convey your interest to the owner?'

Ceci leaned forward and whispered into Beata's ear. The old lady's expression did not alter.

'Perhaps you will come back to me after vespers to find out whether it has been accepted?'

'Willingly, mistress.' Rising gracefully Mistress Sweet-as-ever bowed her head and floated back up the hall between the empty cubicles and out into the still shining sunlight.

Beata called down to Hubert. 'Hear that, my lord abbot? I have never been so popular in my life. To think, all it takes to bring them flocking like bees round a honey pot is a promise of something that may not even exist!'

Chuckling she lay back on the pillows. Her cough, noticed Hildegard, seemed much less troublesome of late.

To Hubert she whispered, 'Does she have it after all?'

'It is her game. She's amusing herself and will draw them on like hounds after a scent.'

'And will the quarry be caught or disappear into the forest like a chimera?'

He took her hand. 'Patience.'

Beata had three offers for the as yet unseen book, one forced from her husband, who believed he was the rightful owner until Abbot Philip settled his account, the friar, who seemed to have given up hope of ever obtaining what he himself had encouraged the abbey to purchase, and a dealer in cheese and domestic artefacts, who liked a profit when she saw one. Before Hildegard could find out if Abbot Philip was going to join this throng his sacristan was seen going into the infirmary. When he came out again he was smiling and made straight for the abbot's lodging.

Then the three mercenaries employed by the earl of Arundel to conduct into his treasury his imports from overseas were seen to enter the infirmary. This time they made less noise than when they had been in their night-time pursuit of Prince Owain Glyn Dwr. Affable, swordless, jockeying not to be in the lead, they headed for Mistress Beata's cubicle. Hildegard followed them in out of no more than native curiosity.

The captain spoke for them. 'My lord offers a sum suitable for its worth,' he told her after mentioning the existence of a book the earl had hoped to purchase from the abbot before its unfortunate disappearance. 'You can be sure his gratitude will be most generously expressed.'

Smiling with contentment Beata replied, 'Tell him this is a great honour for the one who possesses the book. I will convey your message when I can. Come to me after vespers if you will.' Still smiling, she closed her eyes.

As the men marched out again Hildegard heard one of them ask, 'Why don't we just ransack the place?'

'And have the abbot on us like a ton of lead?'

'He ain't got room to argue – when it comes down to it he'll have to pay his - ' he sniggered and the other two shushed him but when they got outside, as Hildegard observed from the doorway, they were laughing and punching each other on the arms and were clearly planning something with that air of invincibility well-armed or physically strong folk sometimes have and she turned back to Hubert to see what he made of it but his eyes were closed and he looked so peaceful that she decided to let him be.

Delith had apparently retired to her shared sleeping quarters where her bags remained. After a long walk to Hound and back to purchase various oddments for her pilgrimage she needed to rest. 'It was my only chance,' she had announced, 'and my guardian angel came along to offer me a lift part of the way back, in the earl's empty wagon.'

When the waggoner and his lad emerged from the refectory to drive it round to the abbot's stores they confirmed what she said, to some extent. They had picked her up half way between Hound and Netley. She had been half-dead with fatigue and they had taken pity on her, she being so pretty and a lady in distress, as they said.

Everybody floated back towards the kitchen sluice but although the men were now standing ankle deep in water to show that something was being dislodged inside the culvert there was still no firm news about it so, as one, they began to amble outside to the place where the stream entered.

Alaric was sitting in the sun, his tunic coiled on his head to keep the sun off, while a gang of lay-brothers set about temporarily blocking off the flow of water in order to give others time to climb inside the culvert and add their strength to the rope that was knotted round the shoulders of the corpse.

'Soon have him out now,' somebody remarked and nobody corrected him. If it wasn't Mistress Delith it could be anybody.

While she watched them Brother Heribert went over to Alaric. 'You've done well. Mistress Beata would like your attendance now, however. I fear she is sinking fast.'

In alarm Alaric scrambled to his feet, pulling

off his make-shift capuchon and slipping it on as he hurried back inside the garth in the steps of Heribert.

Hildregard went to join the pilgrims remaining in the cloister but tiring of their company changed her mind and went over to the fountain where she scooped up some water in her cupped hands to wet her face and took a long drink of sweet well-water. The sun was beating down as furiously as ever.

Before long, as she knew he would, Alaric reappeared. He came straight across to her.

Quiet-voiced, he told her, 'She is not sinking. She's as well as before. But I have it. She wants me to show it to Friar Hywel then take it straight back again. I'd like someone to come with me.'

'Shall I?'

He nodded with relief. 'Jankin seems to have disappeared. I haven't seen him all morning.'

'He'll be in the drying shed no doubt. Shall I fetch him?'

'I'll come too.'

Realising he felt the need for reinforcements

she led the way. As quickly as they were able in the intense heat they made their way over ground that only days ago had been covered in grass but was now as hard as baked clay. They slipped through the side door into the herb garden.

The sun was nearing its zenith.

Jankin, with Lucie beside him, was sitting in the shade of the vines desultorily picking the heads off a pile of lavender stalks that lay across their laps. A heady scent filled the air.

Noticing Alaric's expression Jankin dumped his share of lavender into Lucie's lap and slowly rose to his feet. 'What is it? Have you dragged her from the sluice already?'

'She's back, large as life. Didn't you hear the commotion? She claims she's been in Hound all this time, buying stuff for her journey.'

'That's a relief. Hear that, Lucie? She's back and you've got a mistress after all.'

Lucie did not look especially pleased. 'Is she asking for me?'

Hildegard told her she might have an hour or so

before she was needed as Delith had gone to lie down. 'It's something else.' She indicated Alaric and he pulled a small package part of the way from his sleeve.

'You've got it? She trusts you with it?'

'Why shouldn't she trust me? Will you come with us? It's best to have a couple of witnesses. I have to take it back to her when he's had a look.'

Solemn-faced, not knowing what their reception would be they moved off up the garden towards Hywel's workshop with Lucie calling, 'Wait for me!'

CHAPTER THIRTEEN

He was lying back in the wooden chair with his grey robe loosened at the neck to reveal a scruff of black chest hair. His eyes were shut. His face looked washed out, his breathing shallow, and when they entered he did not move.

An empty beaker that might once have contained his special apple elixir was lying on the floor beside him.

'Hywel?' Hildegard's voice was low but it acted like a whip.

His eyes snapped open, his mouth sagged, he bent forward to get up then jerked to a stop when he saw the other three, one of them a girl he had only seen in the distance, filing into his workshop.

Noticing his embarrassment Hildegard went over. 'I didn't mean to alarm you. Alaric has something to show you.'

Rubbing a hand over his face Hywel tried to pull himself together. 'Wha…?' he slurred.

'It's the thing you want to buy,' Alaric said at

once. 'I've been allowed to bring it to show you as a special privilege because it was thought best that you should know what you are offering all your wealth for.'

'Best, is it?' He knuckled both his eye sockets. 'And you're the go-between? I should have guessed.' He shook his head, becoming more alert but not fully in control. 'Best for whom? This thief, to taunt me with it?' He darted a glance at Hildegard. 'You said you didn't want to be involved.'

Alaric, showing no vestige of the fear he had felt earlier towards Hywel, was strengthened by the sight of the friar in such disarray. 'She's not involved, magister. I happened to see her in the garth just now and asked her to accompany me – a request to which she kindly agreed.'

'Why? Because you're frightened of me?'

Alaric ignored that. Instead he announced, 'I have here the book of Al-Gerber, or a copy at least. Would you care to take a look?'

As if fearing it was some kind of jest Hywel

reached out for it. His hands were shaking. Reverently he held it up to the light. The glow that entered his expression beatified him. Time was distilled into that one moment. Then the glow slowly faded. He jerked a glance towards the silent group. 'Do you have anything to tell me?'

The boys eyed each other and shook their heads. 'What should we have to tell you, magister?' Alaric looked puzzled. There was no doubting that his response was genuine. His fine, fair face could conceal nothing.

'This?' Hywel held the book up so they could all see it. He had not opened it. 'Who has had it in their possession since you took it from the ship, Alaric?'

Alaric remained mute.

'Is this how it was when you found it?'

'Exactly so, magister.'

Hywel threw it down onto his work bench. 'Let it be sold on without my meagre contribution. May the purchaser not rue the day.'

He began to laugh in a choking sort of way,

half-way between a snarl and a cry, and he leaned forward with both hands over his face as if to conceal the extent of his grief. There was no other word for it. He was grief-stricken. His shoulders heaved. 'Get out!' he muttered, 'Go! Get out! Leave me! And take this with you!'

When nobody took him at his word he got up, pushing the book into Alaric's grasp, then lunged towards them all, lashing out until, not wishing to strike a master, they bent their heads under his fists and scrambled to get through the door. Lucie ran out after them shouting, 'What's wrong? What's happened? I don't understand!'

Hildegard took hold of Hywel by the arm and dragged him back. 'Stop this! Isn't that what you wanted? Alaric is acting in good faith. What on earth is the matter with you?'

He swung on her, ferocious, his eyes flaming, and then the strength left him. He turned with a strangled cry and flung himself down into the chair and put his head in his hands with his shoulders shaking. 'It is all lost,' he sobbed. 'Everything.

Gone. Finished. I may as well throw myself into the waters where that book should be.'

'You seem to me,' Hildegard began in a pacifying tone, 'to give way to extremes of emotion sometimes, often to little purpose. Let's look at this. Alaric brought you the book when he need not have bothered. And all you do is berate him! Whatever has disappointed you is not his fault. I would have thought you would be better than this, Hywel.'

His head jerked up as if she had slapped him. 'Don't you understand? It is gone!'

'What is it?'

'The Stone! Why else would I want the book? It was to have been the means to smuggle the Stone into the country. Right under the nose of the king's enemies!' He raised his face to the ceiling and closed his eyes to get a better grip on himself. 'Why do you imagine Prince Owain was here?'

'Tell me.'

'He has left Arundel's service as his personal body-guard. After the last bloody parliament he could not go on! When he fought in Scotland it was as part of King Richard's army. He had no idea that Arundel would turn against the king. When he understood his intentions he eschewed his fealty. Owain knows me of old. He knows my interests and the extent of my contacts in a certain area of hermetic study. He asked me if I could obtain the Stone he'd heard about. "Let's get some gold into Richard's coffers, buy him an army, and at the same time buy our own freedom from England!" That was his high purpose. It became mine too.'

'Is that why he came here to Netley?'

'Instead of riding straight back to Wales and safety, yes! When those militia men of Arundel's arrived he couldn't risk the probability that they had tracked him down with orders to assassinate him...the way Gaunt had Owain Lawgoch assassinated in France by that paid killer John Lamb. I told him I would receive the Stone when the cargo was unloaded and send it to him at Sycharth. It was to have reached me as part of a jeweled book cover, looking like nothing but another ordinary semi-precious stone. Master John would have been paid for the safe delivery of an innocuous import. The abbot would have got his book, and his sacristan would have been happy. Prince Owain – well, now you know about him. No losers! Instead – the hand of God they're calling it in the garth - that bolt of lightning setting fire to the ship and the monk sent by the abbot to make sure the book was saved, poisoned – and finally, the Stone, gone!'

'Did Abbot Philip know about it?'

He shook his head. 'It's heresy even to think it.'

'Who else on board might have…?'

They both looked at each other with simultaneous astonishment.

'She…?' His eyes narrowed.

'How would she know what it was…?'

'She couldn't…A bright jewel…Some bauble to adorn her gown?'

'Or, if as valuable as she believed, something

that might change her life forever?' said Hildegard slowly.

He became himself. Hildegard witnessed the change. He pulled his garments together with an apology for his appearance and began to move hurriedly about the workshop. 'She's here. She came back. Why would she do that if she knew what she possessed? Did she find a buyer in Hound? Quick, we must hurry. We must coax the truth from her by any means we can. Hurry, Hildegard, you re as deeply involved in this as ever.'

As Hywel strode across the garth with Hildegard beside him the three who had been ejected from his workshop, seeing the expression on Hywel's face and that they were now out of his line of fire, took up the rear. When they reached the women's guest quarters Hildegard took over.

'Wait here!' She raised her eyebrows at Lucie but, reluctant to face her mistress yet, she shook her head.

Decisively Hildegard ran up the stairs to the second floor dortoir and seeing the door half open, stepped through.

Save for Delith herself it was empty. She wasn't sleeping. Instead she was rummaging through her bag, tossing clothing onto the floor then replacing one or two things until she heard someone behind her. She turned.

'Oh, it's you, lady. Are you looking for someone?' Her tone was belligerent and without any sign of deference.

Hildegard went up to her. 'In fact, I was looking for you.'

'Now you've found me. Fortune shines on you. The pilgrim ship is leaving soon. I'm joining it and just repacking my belongings to take down there as that useless maid of mine has failed in her duty.'

'Would you like her to come and help you?'

Hildegard's glance had alighted on a small object wrapped in one of the veils Delith often wore. Delith reached for it and was about to put it in the bag. Then for some reason she changed her mind and with a sly smile placed it on the bed. She shook out a blue gown then refolded it. It was not in the sort of condition anyone would want to take on pilgrimage, despite its colour, as it was torn and crumpled. Hildegard was surprised that someone with as much love for clothes as Delith would bother with it.

'What? This?' She had caught sight of Hildegard's expression. Pushing a lock of black hair from her face she smiled. 'I'll let Lucie have it. She should be grateful. She can always mend it if a little tear offends her.' She threw it to one side. Rummaging around she came up with another one. 'She can have this too. I don't want it. Cheap, nasty stuff.' A garment of a different hue was thrown aside as well. 'My lady, happy though I am to have you watch me prepare to leave did you have any reason for searching me out?'

'Yes, it's this. On the night of – ' But she got no further. A tremendous shout followed by screams rose up from outside and then they heard a crowd shouting and clamouring like people under attack. Believing it was something to do with the armed gang employed to protect the abbey Hildegard ran to the window. Delith followed. They both peered down. It was difficult to make out what was going on.

'I'm going down!' Hildegard ran to the door expecting Delith to follow but when she looked back she was simply standing staring down as if too shocked to move.

Without wanting to waste time Hildegard ran for the stairs and descended at a rapid clip to reach the yard just as a crowd came swarming round something in the garth.

It was set down on the baked earth but too many people were clustering round for her to see what it was.

Spotting Egbert in the crowd she wove round the onlookers towards him. 'I thought the abbey was being attacked. What is it?'

'It's the body. They've managed to get him out at last.' He crossed himself.

'Do they know who it is?'

'He's in a horrible state.'

'Yes, but – '

'It's that fellow who arrived on the night of the storm. The one in the yellow cotte.'

'Oh.' She stared at him as everything shifted into place.

When he muttered, 'They're blaming the mercenaries. That captain was heard having words over a dice game and they think it's him. A group have gone to look for him to call him to account.'

'Oh no! They have the wrong man! Where are they now?'

'Up near the corner where they used to dice.'

When Hildegard raised her head she saw a group of lay-brothers approaching the corner. They were disappointed to find no sign of any of the mercenaries and instead came running back towards the group guarding the body. 'Anybody seen them today?'

'Not since that wagon rolled in.'

'They'll be in the sacristy getting the cargo out

to take back to Arundel,' someone suggested.

Murmurs of agreement gave him the authority to march across the garth with a small army of followers.

Hildegard watched them go then went over to the crowd hanging round the body.

'Lionel, he was called Lionel,' she said as she looked down at him.

But for the yellow cotte, now soaked and discoloured by its hours in the culvert, it would have been difficult to recognize him as the fellow who had walked into the abbey that night of the fire. His face was swollen with water and the rigor still held him. His whole body was clenched and it was no wonder it had been difficult to prise him from his death trap.

Hywel appeared beside her. 'Let's take a look before anyone else gets here.' He bent down with Hildegard beside him. The man was lying on his side and Hywel ran his hand over his head. 'Ah, look here, look at the back of his head.'

'What is it?'

He guided her hand and she felt a lump beneath her fingers. 'A blow to the head?'

'A cudgel? A stone?'

'Or was it sustained in his fall?'

'Some heavy object is more likely,' she suggested. 'The stream winds through grassy banks there. Nothing to harm anyone should they slip.'

'Or were pushed.'

'You think he was hit and then pushed?' she whispered. People were pressing in close to try to hear what they were saying but not wishing to set off alarms or a man-hunt driven by rumour, she glanced at Hywel for confirmation. He gave a slight nod.

'Where are you fellows taking him?' He sat back on his heels.

'To the mortuary, magister.'

'Yes, best get him out of this heat.'

A few burly lay-brothers, with no qualms about touching a dead body, lifted him between them and with their escort of excited followers started for the mortuary attached to the north wall of the church.

Before they got far Hildegard caught up with them. 'Hold it. I just want to…' She had seen something in the dead man's hand. It was scarcely visible. A shaft of sunlight had momentarily picked it out.

Mystified, the men stopped and laid their burden down.

'It's just this.' She began to winkle a finger inside the tight fist holding the last thing Lionel had grasped as he fell into the water. It was impossible to force open his fingers.

'If it's something he's got in his hand you'll have to wait until the rigor leaves him. A few hours, no more.'

While this was going on the guard at the door of the sacristy was discussing matters with a mob who thought it their duty to bring justice to the abbey. His tone was reasonable but firm.

'Look at it like this,' he was heard to say. 'You've judged and condemned these men without hearing their side of the story. Instead of acting like a lot of savages and dragging them out to summary justice wouldn't it be more reasonable to give the matter a few moment's thought and, if you have any evidence, to put the matter before Abbot Philip? Summary justice is not our way.'

One or two brawny lay-brothers joined him and stood shoulder to shoulder with folded arms staring back at the mob. It was clear the latter were not going to get their way without a few broken heads. Muttering, they began to disperse.

Hywel, although curious about what the dead man might have been holding in his hand, was far more interested in retrieving the Stone from Delith, if she had it.

'If she had it, or has it,' he panted as he ran alongside Hildegard with the other three following at their heels. 'And if she has not sold it to somebody in Hound. If, in fact, she has ever had it, come to that. Or if she would be willing to sell it to me. Or I could get a message to Prince Owain to let him know we have it, that's if she has it still, or if not – '

'Hywel, why don't you save your breath until we find out if she's even here or not? We have to find her first, then you can ask your questions.'

When they ran out onto the top of the bank they saw that a crowd of pilgrims had settled on the strand with their luggage. Some had evidently been there since the rumour had spread that Master John had acquired a ship for them. Now food was being eaten and flasks emptied.

Easy to spot among them was Delith.

She was still wearing the russet gown but had adorned her black hair with a cheap-looking crispinette from which one of her veils floated.

Hywel was the first to crunch over the shingle towards her. She was collecting shells, arranging them in patterns in her lap as she sat waiting on her luggage waiting for the ship.

As he approached she looked up with a brazen smile. 'Oh it's you. Are you coming with us too, magister? We can always use a friar to brighten our voyage. Perhaps you'll be good enough to read the signs to tell us what sort of sea trip we're likely to encounter?'

'You'll need a necromancer for that, lady. Now may I ask you something?' Without asking her permission he sat down beside her. 'Let me say at once, there'll be no harm to you if the answer is yes and I will pay you for what I want.'

'That is the usual way, friar – as I'm sure you know.'

Hildegard heard this and wondered if Hywel would explode with rage but he spoke as softly as to a child. 'It's simply this. A little trinket was unloosed from the cover of a book that was sent to me by a friend from Outremer. It quite spoils the look of the thing to have one worthless little stone missing and I believe you saw the book on board the St Marie and, perhaps thinking how pretty the stone was – although there are prettier ones – thought to take it as something to remember that terrible night by…'

Delith did not answer straight away. When she did so it was to laugh in Hywel's face. 'You think me so sinful, magister…to think that I would steal!'

'In the heat of the moment I'm sure it wouldn't have felt like stealing.'

'Perhaps not.' She looked thoughtfully out across the water. 'What makes you think I have it?'

'I hope and pray you have it.'

'Because it means much to you?'

'Indeed.'

'Was this friend in Outremer your lover?'

His lips tightened. 'No, he was a colleague working on a study of rocks and their qualities. Nothing you would find interesting or relevant to your life here.'

'And you think me not only sinful but stupid as well, that I would admit to possessing something like that?'

'You have no reason for suggesting I think ill of you and there is nothing stupid about admitting to the truth.'

'This little stone, then, if it's so empty of worth, why not substitute another?'

'That one was sent to me particularly.'

'Your friend will never know you've put another in its place.'

'That is not the point. It means something – in the language of stones,' he added. 'Much like the language of flowers where a red rose means I plight my troth…'

'So this worthless little stone was a sign that someone had plighted their troth to you?'

'No, that was just an example of…'

'I'm not sure I believe a word you say. I believe it has more worth than you're admitting.' She levelled her blue, calculating gaze on him.

'I am so desirous of it I will pay whatever you ask, as I've already said.'

'But have I told you I have it?'

He eyed her narrowly. 'You have not told me you have it not.'

A movement and a rising murmur from around them made them look up. Hildegard, listening carefully to Hywel and Delith from where she stood on the bank, raised her head to see what everyone was looking it.

From out of the murmur a shout arose. 'The ship! This must be her!'

A smallish cog with a big square sail, well set, was turning in from the deep mid-channel to approach the channel nearer the shore. A shout on board had the sail dropping with a thud and the whole ship shuddered as an anchor chain rattled over the stern and hit bottom, and then she was caught and turned her bows in a drifting, slow gyration until she again faced towards the sea.

'Good timing, it's right on slack water. That's as close as she's able to get. Come on everybody, to the boats!'

A general movement of bustling excitement took over as everyone began to pack away their food and pick up their bags and started jostling towards the water-line where a row of small boats were laid up.

Delith rose to her feet. 'How much?' She looked directly at Hywel and waited, tapping her fingers on the strap of her bag.

Hywel rose to his feet as well. He knew, as,

probably, did Delith, that he had no means of making payment on him. 'I will bring money…'

'I want it now or never. I'm about to leave.'

'I can have you stopped from going on board – '

'Try it!'

'On suspicion of theft. Do you know what will happen to you when the stone is found in your possession?'

'You'll have to find it first, friar. Do you intend to search me…personally?' Her eyes gleamed with challenge. 'Do so. Come now, everyone!' she shouted. 'This friar wishes to get his hands on me. Do you want to witness this?' She turned back to Hywel as, stopped in their tracks, a dozen pilgrims turned to watch. 'Your move, my dear man. Take your time. I'm ready and waiting.'

She arranged herself in a provocative pose.

Convinced it was a bluff, that the stone was somewhere on her, Hywel nevertheless hesitated.

'Perhaps your maid and I might search your clothes while the friar looks inside your bag?'

Hildegard stepped forward. Lucie followed.

By now the small boats ready to take the pilgrims on board had emptied again as everyone began to realise that something interesting was happening further up the beach.

One or two men standing close enough to hear what had been said, urged the friar on. 'Do as you're told, magister. You heard the lady!'

'I'll give you a hand!' another called.

'Aye, and so will I!'

Smiling, Delith called, 'Go ahead, boys. This won't cost you a penny.'

Hywel was white-faced with rage. He knew he was bested and he squirmed in humiliation.

Then Gregory and Egbert who had merely followed in puzzlement when they saw the others running from the abbey stepped forward. Gregory said, 'If there is a dispute over abbey property I'm sure we can expect the abbot to give a fair judgement when the matter is put before him.'

The smile left Delith's face. 'I haven't time for that! The ship is about to leave. Do you think I'm going to let it go without me after waiting here all this time?'

She bent to pick up her bag but Egbert took it from her grasp. 'If you will, mistress, remain here on the beach. I shall personally go and fetch the abbot or one of his representatives to settle this matter before the ship sails. It is not our intention to thwart your plans to go on pilgrimage. Far from it.'

With a glance at Gregory to hold the fort until he returned he strode off up the bank.

The other pilgrims, even the ones who had offered to help Hywel make a personal search, turned sheepishly towards the boats with their belongings.

'They will take up all the best places on deck,' Delith wailed, with a weighing glance at Gregory. Thinking she might sway him she added, 'I've so looked forward to visiting the shrine of our dear Saint James at Compostela. You wouldn't have me miss my chance to absolve my sins, would you, brother, and to pray for my dear departed husband?'

'Indeed not, mistress. And I can guarantee you will be on that ship as soon as this matter is sorted out to everyone's satisfaction.' He turned to Hywel. 'I'm sure you know an accusation of theft is a serious matter?'

Hywel gave him a dark look.

Almost before they had seen him out of sight, Egbert reappeared at the top of the bank. He was accompanied by a group of lay-brothers. He beckoned to Hildegard to come up.

'Where's the abbot?' she asked.

'The sacristan's coming down instead. He's just locking up. But these fellows have something for you.'

One of them held out his hand. 'Is this what you were trying to make him give up, domina?'

Into her palm he dropped a small piece of torn fabric. It was blue.

Scarcely giving herself time to thank him she ran down the bank to the beach. 'Have you checked her luggage?' she demanded. It seemed nobody had moved since she had gone up to speak to Egbert.

'Search all you like, domina.' A sneer curled Delith's upper lip. 'You'll find no stone of any kind in there. Go ahead!'

Remembering that Delith had taken out the blue gown to give to Lucie she hesitated. 'Lucie, you know your mistress's garments, their colours and fabric, do you recognize this?' She held out the scrap for Lucie to take. She fingered it for only a moment before saying, 'It looks like a piece torn from one of mistress's gowns.'

'Was it torn last time you saw it?'

'Not that I remember. I would have repaired it if I'd known about it.'

'But you did not know about this, did you?'

The girl shook her fuzz of blonde hair.

'You did not know about it because after it happened your mistress hid the garment at the bottom of her bag.' She swiveled to hurry back up the bank. There was only one way to confirm her suspicions and link Delith to the death of Lionel and that was to find the gown and see if the pieces matched. In her heart she knew there was no doubt but it was only fair to Delith to demonstrate the truth of what she suspected.

At the top of the bank she turned to look back.

The group on the beach had not moved but the rest of the pilgrims were already being taken across in a flotilla of little boats. In the time since the replacement vessel had arrived the light had changed as the sun began to slide behind the bank on the other side of the water, drawing down with it all the shades of red in a crimson fluorescence shot through with gold and silver flecks and a softer hue like the pink on the wings of seraphim. A lurid glow at the heart of this effulgent outpouring tinged everything turned towards it with the colour of blood.

The tide held everything in suspension at the moment of its turning. After flooding unstoppably upstream the change was undetectable, water particles gathered and gained in volume and, at the point of fullness, like the moon with its own waxing gathered into itself, they would start out on their next phase, a waning in the case of the moon, a torrent of water from the rivers and inland lakes, from the marshes and streams and reed-beds, in the case of the ebbing tide as it flowed back to the sea.

Without waiting to observe the moment, feeling part of it, Hildegard hastened back inside the abbey precinct. It was exceptionally quiet. Vespers sent the singing of the choir spinning in harmony into the empyrean. Unhindered by the need for explanations she ran up the back stairs onto the upper floor and along the corridor to the women's guest chamber. Everything was as they had left it.

In moments she had snatched up the blue gown from where it still lay on the floor and held it up. The piece of torn fabric fitted the tear in the neckline exactly.

By the time she returned to the bank top… everything on the beach had changed.

CHAPTER FIFTEEN

The sun was now resting on the horizon in its final blood-red descent into night. The St Marie, black against its radiance, was straining at her anchor chain which was pulled taut by the increasing power of the ebb.

In this unearthly light the first person she noticed on the beach was Gregory. White-robed and elongated he was reaching out as if to restrain someone. Hywel was kneeling on the shingle nearby staring fixedly towards the water. Egbert was standing further up the bank with a couple of lay-brothers with a restraining hand on each of them. Jankin and Alaric, a little lower down, were simply staring at something at the water's edge. No-one moved.

Then she saw what held them in thrall.

It was Delith. She was backing into the shallows with Lucie. They were both already up to their knees in water. The hems of their gowns were dark and streamed away from them, carried by its force. Delith held her maid's arms by her sides with one arm wrapped around her.

In her free hand she held a knife to Lucie's throat.

As Hildegard moved down the bank as unobtrusively as she could she heard Delith shout something. No-one moved.

Noticing Hildegard, she gave a scream of warning.

'Nun! I'm warning you! Come any closer and she'll die!'

The knife glittered in the crimson light. With one arm hooked round Lucie's body, she pinned her helplessly as she began to back towards the last remaining boat lying half in the water. Her intention to climb on board was clear. What she then hoped to do was not. Again no-one moved.

Hildegard called. 'Release your maid. What harm has she done to you?'

'Back off! I mean what I say! Don't try me!'

With agonizing slowness Delith felt behind her

for the boat with one foot and forced Lucie inside without taking the knife from her throat.

Jankin let out a roar of rage but was helpless to do anything for fear of the blade so close to his beloved's white and slender neck.

Wondering how she was going to get the boat into the water Hildegard saw the same question occur to Delith. Enraged she swore at the people on the bank then gave a massive push backwards, leaping over the side as it trundled into the tide and the waves took it. She fell on top of Lucie, the knife visibly in place, as the ebb, gripping in its pent force the boat, began to drift it down-stream, away from the beach and away into the nearside channel.

At the same moment, as Lucie was momentarily released from Delith's stranglehold, she hit her in the face, stood up, then recklessly flung herself over the side into the water.

Delith screamed in fury. Grabbing the paddle, she yelled, 'Get back into this boat!'

In response Lucie began to swim for the shore

but did not get far before she began to flounder in her long skirts. Delith dug the paddle into the flood and turned the bows towards her, intent on pursuit.

With a feral howl that twisted the heart, Jankin could wait no longer but shouting Lucie's name, lunged down the beach straight into the water. He was up to his knees then to his waist before he hesitated with sudden indecision but throwing fear aside, he launched himself towards his love with outstretched arms, her name ripped from his throat again and again.

A voice shouted, 'He can't swim!' and someone ran down the beach and threw themselves bodily into the water and, before Hildegard could see who it was, began to swim with powerful strokes towards him.

Hildegard noticed that Lucie went under then came back to the surface, spluttering and gasping for air, and Jankin, desperately trying to reach her, vanished then reappeared, and was carried closer by the ebb. Their fingers touched then both of them went under.

The swimmer who had gone in was Hywel. He swam under the water in an effort to find the drowning couple but rose to the surface without them. Delith swung the boat towards him then lifted the paddle like a weapon. Before she could bring it down Jankin spluttered to the surface and Hywel, ignoring the paddle, swam towards him, grabbing him by the arm and forcing him into a life-saving hold before beginning to swim back towards the shore.

Lucie had disappeared completely. Delith was probing the water with her paddle and Alaric, quicker than Hildegard in ridding himself of his garments, had already plunged into the water and was almost at the place where Lucie had last been seen before Delith noticed him. She stood poised to strike as he neared the boat but Alaric, hearing the warning shouts from those by now scrambling into the water, dived under and he, too, disappeared from sight.

He was gone.

The surface of the water was covered by a sheen like crimson silk as the tide gathered its force and smoothed flat its rippling waves.

'Oh heaven's! Both of them!' Hildegard's heart was clenched with fear as she ripped at her habit and tried to disentangle herself from its enveloping folds. Egbert came running down from half-way up the bank ready to dive into the water. But then something amazing happened.

Alaric's head broke the surface a little way downstream where the current had carried him. Although he appeared to be trapped by something submerged underneath when he began to swim towards them they saw that he was pulling something after him. It was Lucie. He was dragging her by her gown but she was splashing, hindering him somewhat until he spoke to her, and then they drifted together, away from the threat posed by Delith, to where they eventually reached the shallows further down.

They lay in the shallows for a moment but many helpers ran to bring them ashore and one strapping lay-brother lifted up the girl in his arms and carried her onto the bank. Alaric, regaining his breath and as lithe as ever, loped after them, escorted by a posse of youths, and flopped down on the beach when he reached the rest of the group.

'Is Jankin safe?' he asked Hildegard as she came up.

The apprentice was lying face down on the grass. Hywel was pumping water from his lungs with an assured skill. After a few moments Jankin lifted his head and groaned and then he was suddenly sitting up and looking wildly round. 'How did I get here?...Where's Lucie?' And when he was reassured by the sight of her sitting on the grass he rose shakily to his feet and stumbled towards her to clutch her in his arms as if he would never let her go.

Meanwhile, Delith, trying to control the boat in the increasing rush of the outgoing tide, held it off-shore long enough for them to hear her jeer. 'Take her then! I shall buy twelve maids when I'm a lady in France. And I have your stone, friar! Do you still want it?'

She pulled at her bodice and took something from it. 'Why don't you swim out and get it? Come on, friar. Here it is! Look!'

She held it up. 'Do you want it? How much are you offering?' She began to laugh. 'Fools, all of you! You'll never catch me!'

Hildegard went to the water's edge and shouted across. 'Delith, did you kill Lionel?'

'You know as well I do, nun. You have the evidence there in your hand. He was evil. He needed to die. I'm glad I killed him. It was easy. One blow with a stone on his thick skull and down he went! Just my luck the stream was diverted into the kitchen sluice. I nearly got away with it, didn't I? He got what he deserved. And now I'm going to get what I deserve!' Her laughter rang with triumph.

Hildegard put a restraining hand on Egbert's sleeve as he made as if to go after her. 'Let her go,' she murmured, 'give her a chance.'

Turning the bows of the boat towards the opposite shore Delith began to paddle against the tide for Deep Dale purlieu.

They all watched as the boat headed into the setting sun until it was no more than a speck on the crimson expanse of Southampton Water. Soon they noticed that instead of maintaining its heading towards the purlieu where she might live outside the king's writ, the boat turned, was caught by the tide, like a leaf on the ebb, and was borne away towards the place where three waters meet. Soon they could see her no more.

The light faded.

A single star, Venus, Hildegard supposed, became a bright point in the darkness, and then the moon appeared in full and effulgent glory from behind the trees.

Making their way back to the abbey they came to the gatehouse and had to stand aside as the wagon belonging to the earl came scraping underneath the arch. The waggoner and his lad sat at the front and the canvas cover was tied neatly down behind them. Only when it drew level were voices heard within, accompanied by the dull clanking of something like steel, swords, maybe, rattling in their scabbards.

The night porter was the only one to wave it off. He turned to Egbert as they rattled off down the lane. 'I hinted that you were only waiting for reinforcements. A remark about militant monks impressed them. I doubt they'll be back.'

Egbert grinned. 'It's not a bad idea. I'll put it to the abbot himself.'

'And by the way, brother, you can keep that key for a while if you like. Your own swords are still safe within and available should you need them.'

'That's unlikely now they've gone.' Egbert slapped the fellow on the back. 'Peace and quiet for a while, eh?'

Soon, wearing dry clothes and supplied lavishly with food and drink, everyone remained in the warming room until long after compline, going over what had happened and celebrating the dangers that, in different ways, had been overcome.

Jankin and Lucie sat holding hands looking dazed. Hywel was white-faced and mostly silent. The two monks were content with flagons in their hands. And again, Alaric was the hero of the hour.

'You must teach me to swim like that, Alaric,' Hildegard heard Jankin ask.

'As well as somersaults? With pleasure. It's scant reward for teaching me to read.'

He shot a guilty glance at Hywel who merely smiled, though still tight-lipped. 'I'll teach you more than he can. You might as well start on some Latin as well. Then get yourself thrown out of the abbey. Set up as a magician in the weekly markets. You'll soon become a rich man.'

'I don't think Alaric would want...' began Lucie but Jankin tapped her hand and shook his head.

'I'd be feeding fishes now if it wasn't for you, magister,' he said. 'I concede your Welsh superiority in the matter of swimming.' He grinned.

For once Hywel did not come back with a retort. His sight was turned inwards to his own dark griefs.

Hildegard could see how much it was costing him to acknowledge the loss of the Stone. What trouble these ambitions cause men, she was thinking, when her thoughts were interrupted as a messenger entered.

'It's Mistress Beata. She's with a priest now and would like you all to attend her if you will.'

Alaric was first on his feet. 'Has she taken a turn for the worst?' he demanded, his gentle voice tinged with concern.

'It looks like it,' replied the lad with the message. 'Are you coming?'

Alaric almost ran from the room and more slowly the others followed. 'She wants us all?' asked Gregory of the lad.

'I think she wants an audience. She has something to say. Remember this bidding war she's started for some old book?'

Beata was propped up and when they entered the infirmary Alaric was already plumping up her pillows and tidying some oddments on the little shelf beside her bed. A priest sat on the ledge of the partition that separated her cubicle from the empty one next to it.

Master John had arrived before them and found a chair for himself. When he saw Hildegard enter he got up. 'Domina, pray take my seat…'

She thanked him but shook her head. 'You are more involved in this than I.'

Her attention had been drawn to another figure sitting next to the bed. Her heart gave a lurch. Hubert smiled up at her and waved a hand towards his bandaged leg. It was held in a casing of plaster to keep it in position. 'Forgive me, I cannot get up.'

'Of course you can't. Don't even think it.' A stool was found and she sat next to him. 'Are you meant to be doing this?'

He reached for her wrist inside her sleeve and made an amulet round it with his fingers. 'Hywel tells me so.'

The others arranged themselves, overflowing the cubicle and fetching chairs from elsewhere, then they waited to hear what Beata had to say.

'Welcome, my friends…' she began but was straightaway interrupted by the arrival of the two sisters. They looked flushed and harried.

'Has she - ?' began Mistress Sweet before glancing at the bed. Observing Beata's cool smile and the fact that she was still very much alive she fell silent and bowed her head in embarrassment.

Mistress Sour went to the bedside. 'We came as soon as the boy found us. I trust you have news for us, mistress?'

'Indeed I have. My decision is made. It took some time because my sympathies lie with you, Friar Hywel. I know you cannot offer me a proper price and I cannot wait until you find someone who wants the book enough to pay for it. The cash is important to me and you will understand there is some urgency to the matter.'

She turned to the two sisters. 'You need not wait. I will not sell to you. Here, take it back.' She reached for the trinket Ceci had offered her. 'You are best off buying and selling in the market place where you started. I wish you well.'

With a somewhat ill grace Ceci picked up the trinket and it was noticeable that she avoided the glare her sister gave her.

'We'll stay and see who comes off best if you don't mind, mistress.' Genista sounded chastened and Beata nodded her agreement.

'I won't keep you in suspense. I have decided to offer the book to Master John, not because he's my husband, but because he offered the highest price and I even have his gold here as proof of his interest.'

She indicated a leather bag and, poking it with one yellowed finger nail, made it clink with the sound of coin. 'Dear John. I am grateful, as ever. And as I am on my death bed and want to say what I have never said before, and certainly not in front of others, I will say this. I have had a good life with you. I would not have had it otherwise. We argued and had our ups and downs but in the end we got along, didn't we?'

John leaned forward and took both her hands in his. 'My sins never went unnoticed by you. I have you to thank for making my life relatively blameless. But you are not finished yet. I know you, Beata. You will fight your corner and never give in.' He kissed her hands. 'My old sweetheart, the best of them all. I salute you.' He raised his head. 'But now, where is the book?'

Beata turned her head. 'Alaric, my dear, fetch it if you will.'

'Where is this hiding place?' Hywel asked Hildegard. She shook her head. 'Since he took it out of the sluice I have no idea.'

They all watched as Alaric eyed one of the wooden roof beams above their heads. He took a spring upwards to grasp it by both hands. With an acrobat's lithe skill he swung himself onto it and stood upright, balancing for a moment, in all his glorious youth and strength, then he ran nimbly along it to the place where it abutted the wall.

His long fingers stroked the white-washed surface until he found what he was looking for. Edging a stone from its position he revealed a cavity, took out a small parcel in a waterproof bag, and held it up.

'I would never have thought of looking there.' John said with chagrin.

Alaric swung down, feather-light, from the beam and handed the parcel to Beata with a flourish.

It was difficult not to applaud and Jankin and Lucie did so.

'What will happen to it now?' asked Mistress Sour.

Master John answered her. 'I will hand it over to Abbot Philip, who will pay me for it, and he in his turn will hand it on to this knight who has been causing him so much trouble, and he will pay for it. What the knight will do with it is to sell it on to the earl. At each exchange someone will make a profit.' He smiled at her. 'That's how it's done, mistress – '

'As I now so well understand.'

'And what will you do with your profit, my dear Beata?' John reached for her hand again. Maybe he expected her to hand back the leather bag when she lifted it off the shelf and held it on her lap.

'You're right to ask, why would someone at death's door need money? I do not need it for myself. My husband, with my help, has always kept me well, and I have enough for my present small needs. But there is someone here who can put it to good use. It will enable him to buy the future he deserves.'

Turning to Alaric she held out the bag of coins. 'Take it my dear boy, and buy your place as a novice with the Cistercians. One day you will be abbot, either here or elsewhere, and you will do much good. My blessings on you for all your kindness.'

'Well,' said Hywel. He made no further

comment.

Hildegard helped Hubert hobble back to his own cubicle where the two monks joined them. As he passed on his way out Hywel stopped by the bed for a moment but did no more than give a stark, black glance at Hildegard as he asked Hubert if there was anything more he could do for him.

'You've got me on my feet, brother, that's the main thing. I shall be ever in your debt.'

Hywel raised a hand in farewell.

Hubert beamed happily at his three Cistercians. 'Have I news!' He looked round at them, teasing them into a state of suspense until Gregory threatened to break his other leg.

'C'mon, Hubert,' Egbert agreed. 'What news can you have, lying here day after day? We're the ones out and about having adventures.'

'Well, it's this,' Hubert relented. 'I have arranged with Master John to book passage for us on a boat leaving from Lymington within the next week. It will take us all the way back to the East

Riding on its usual route after delivering ale from the brewery at Meaux. What do you think? Can you tear yourselves away from here in time?'

On her way to her chamber after saying goodnight to Hubert and his monks, Hildegard, troubled by Hywel's palpable grief, decided to call in to say goodnight.

Now she had been sitting with him a little while and although he greeted her well enough and had offered some apple elixir, his mood was dark and it stopped her from being able to put into words what she wanted to say. She found herself telling him about their departure and how it had come about.

'You see, Hywel, the abbey at Meaux sends its ale down to its house in Lymington and they send back what we need in imports from France and other places. One trading cog. Always busy between the two places. Beaulieu monks are often seen about the abbey at Meaux just as monks from Meaux are seen in Lymington.'

'I see.' He looked thoughtful but did not put

into words what was on his mind. All he asked was, 'When do you leave?' When she told him he replied, 'I may not see you again, in fact, I doubt whether I'll have time to see you go. I may have too much work to do.' He refused to look at her but then, with a speaking flash of his eyes, he asked, 'Would you like to take some tinctures back with you?...Come to my store. Let's see what we can find.'

Leaving his little workshop they walked in the light cast by the moon to the drying shed. The gardens lay in peaceful silence with the scent of night-flowering herbs filling the air with sweetness.

Suddenly Hywel thrust out a hand to pull her back. 'I don't think we should…'

He was staring into the darkness under the vines.

When he made no move she followed his glance. In the patterned shadows cast by the moon she could just make out a shape on the ground. Jankin and Lucie were curled up together on a blanket. They were sound asleep.

'Like two little mice in a nest,' whispered Hywel. 'Leave them be. I'll get your cures in the morning before you leave.'

He took her by the hand and lifted it to point at something. The flightless blackbird was roosting above them like a guardian angel as they slept.

Before she said good night she wanted to ask what he would do next but the same stillness, a guard of some kind, fenced him in. They returned to the workshop but she stood uncertainly with her hand on the latch just inside the doorway.

The air was thick with unspoken thoughts. Eventually he murmured, 'I know…You don't need to say anything.' He reached for her hand. 'It would never have worked.'

'Your magnum opus or the alchemical marriage?'

'Both. I have not reached the necessary level of perfection…but…all the rest?...other times, other places…maybe better fortune?'

'At Netley?'

He shook his head. 'I came here at the behest of my prince. He would not come into England without allies of his own.'

'You mean to say you're…'

'Of course…I assumed you knew.'

So Abbot Philip had been right. There was a spy in his abbey.

'What will you do next?'

He gave her his sudden sweet, sad smile and his dark eyes kindled for a moment. 'I may return to Wales if Prince Owain intends to lead us against you. He'll need prophets and poets…and alchemists and their elixirs to repair broken limbs.' He held out his hand. Hildegard accepted it and felt its pulsing warmth match her own.

When he opened the door for her, moonlight flooded over Cloister Garth. It was as bright as day but its shine had a cold light. It made everything unreal in the chasms of night hidden beneath its silvered veil.

She set off to cross the garth. When she was half way she turned to look back. Hywel was standing in his doorway, silently watching her leave

Climbing the back stairs up to her chamber she heard quite a lot of noise in the usually hushed corridor and when she went to have a look she saw a group of lay-brothers lugging more baggage down the main stairs.

Lissa emerged from the dortoir dressed in a green pelouse for travelling in. She came straight to Hildegard, saying. 'I'm so glad I've caught you. At last we're ready to leave! You've no idea how much luggage we have. I hope they've saved room for us. I think we must be the last to go on board.'

Her abundant red hair was tightly plaited and almost entirely hidden under a snood.

'Have a safe journey, mistress. I hope Simon finds a saint to bless him with long life and happiness.'

A man's voice was heard below in the entrance. 'Farewell, domina. Safe journey.'

'There he is, my dear old owl!' exclaimed Lissa. 'After today's excitement we're really hoping for a peaceful and pleasant crossing into France.' With a final glance round she hesitated. 'There's only one person I haven't managed to see…Master John.' She pursed her lips. 'I'm sure he'll forgive me for leaving without saying farewell. I hear he's being kept busy now that his wife is rallying again.' She turned to the stair with a little tightening of her lips. 'Coming my sweet owl, wait for me!'

She grasped Hildegard by the hand. 'Safe journey home to Meaux, dear Hildegard.'

Next morning when Hildegard went into Prime she stood at the back with a congregation made up almost entirely of lay-brothers. Even the two sisters had left after making an arrangement with the cellarer to buy their cheese.

It was strange to think that the people she had come to know over the last few days had gone from her life forever. The abbey looked desolate without its guests. Friar Hywel and his apprentice were nowhere to be seen.

Afterwards she went for a walk outside the precinct. The wide waters looked strange without the two ships lying at anchor off the beach. The St Marie had been taken up river and her replacement had finally sailed in the early hours before the tide changed, bound for France at last.

Finding herself standing alone above the pool Alaric had shown her and, as there was no-one around, she scrambled down and after a quick look round saw how well it was screened from the path by the bushes. Lured by the sight of the water, she quickly stripped off her outer garments and, clad in only a knee-length muslin shift, stepped into the shallows.

She gasped. It was like ice but fresh and clean and she swam about for a little while, getting used to it, until, being carried further up-stream that she wanted, she began to beat her way back.

It was then she noticed a pile of clothes crammed under the roots of a tree overlooking the water.

She swam over to take a closer look. There was no-one around and it seemed peculiar to find a set of clothes lying there. They were damp to her touch. She climbed onto the bank and had a proper look.

They were old style, woven from fustian - a knee length shirt for someone of middle height, a woolen tunic, breeches in the same rough cloth, no boots, she noticed, and no belt.

Worried that someone had come for a swim and got into difficulties she looked about but could see no sign of anyone. Unsure what to do she decided to leave the clothes where they were hidden and mention them to someone she could trust when she returned indoors.

As it happened she found Alaric scrubbing the tiled floor of the kitchens when she poked her head in. On hands and knees he glanced up when she greeted him.

'Alaric,' she began, 'This is a most strange thing.' The kitchen was empty but even so she lowered her voice. 'When I was at the pool you showed me, guess what, I found a pile of clothes, neatly folded but wet, as if someone had been swimming in them. I'm worried that someone might have –'

He scrambled to his feet in alarm. 'You found them?' He came to her and whispered, 'They were supposed to be hidden.'

'They were but - ?'

He took her to one side. 'Listen, I can let you into the secret because I know you won't pass it on.' He glanced round. 'They belong to one of the pilgrims. In fact, he is just the opposite of a pilgrim. He doesn't believe in the saints nor in the Eucharist nor in any of that - '

'What? You mean he's a - '

'He asked me to take a bag on board the ship for him and to make sure his name was on the list of passengers. But he did not sail.'

She lowered her voice. 'Is this connected to that conversation we had a few days ago about Wyclif and his fellow Lollards?'

Alaric nodded. 'He had to lure everyone into thinking he has fled into exile. It's safer for him. They'd have dragged him back and thrown him into prison if they'd found him.'

'But what about his clothes?'

'He swam back from the ship before she sailed. I left dry ones for him to change into. He'll be miles away by now.'

'Oh, Alaric! Tell me, was he that quiet fellow who was always reading?'

He nodded again. 'A very learned and kindly man. He told me he fell foul of his bishop in open debate and was forced to flee for his life.'

'Then it will remain our secret.'

'I'll go and fetch his clothes when I've finished here. Then, my news...!' His eyes sparkled. 'I have bought my place! Next week I shall be joining those novices in the cloister and shall take part in their lessons without having to skulk around behind the pillars!'

She could not restrain herself from hugging him. 'Remember one thing, my dear Alaric, remember my warning about being too open in your speech…?'

'I remember. But I believe I can do more from within the church than from outside.'

It was quite an event when they finally came to leave two weeks later. Everyone turned out to see the Abbot of Meaux emerge from his incarceration in the infirmary with his leg encased in plaster. He insisted on trying to manage on his own, of course, but eventually he was coaxed into a chair already brought out by some muscular lay-brothers and they hoisted it onto their shoulders with the abbot in it to a great cheer from a crowd of well-wishers.

Headed by the Abbot of Netley himself, the procession made its way over the garth and out beneath the gatehouse. With only a short stop for Egbert to hand over a key to the porter in exchange for a couple of swords, it progressed slowly and with much acclaim down the tricky incline to the beach.

A sturdy looking boat had been commissioned from Master John to take them down as far as Calshot where they would board a trading cog bound for the north of England.

'This time we're for home, finally, and without hindrance!' Hubert looked up at the walls of Netley Abbey as the boatman cast off and flung out his arms as if to embrace everyone in it. 'Farewell, Netley!'

Egbert patted his newly retrieved sword and made himself comfortable. 'Those French pirates had better keep their distance now? Eh, Gregory?'

'Until we get bored,' he suggested. 'Then we'll welcome a friendly encounter or two. It's going to be a joy to be home again after seven long years.' He began to sing a sailor's lament with an ironic intonation that gave an ambiguous twist to his words. Hildegard could not imagine either of the monks settling down in the peace and quiet of Meaux for long.

When she looked back the crowd of abbey people who had escorted them to the water side they were still waving in farewell. Abbot Philip in his gleaming robes stood out from the rest but as the distance between the boat and the shore widened it was still possible to make out the prior, the sub-prior, the sacristan, the cellarer, even Brother Heribert, as well as the rest of the lay-brothers they had come to know.

Alaric ran into the water and pretended to swim after them. Then he did a handstand and a couple of somersaults and Jankin made a passable attempt at a cartwheel while Lucie jumped up and down with excitement.

Their boat was piled with gifts. It looked as if everybody had turned out to see them off. All except one. Hildegard felt for the promised cures inside her bag.

She watched the shore recede until without warning a lone figure came out at the top of the bank and began to walk along it. In the grey robes of a Franciscan friar it could only be one man.

Hywel.

He came to a stop, looking down-river as the sweep of the current carried them with increasing speed towards the sea.

Hubert, noticing him, turned to Hildegard. 'Are you sorry to leave?' He took her hand.

'Somewhat…But I'm looking forward to going home again.'

'Me too.'

He glanced back towards the shore with the lone figure standing on the bank. 'I think you broke his heart…' With a cautious smile he murmured, 'I wonder if you're going to break mine?'

THE END